Anne Baker

LOVE IS BLIND

headline

First published in 2012
by HEADLINE PUBLISHING GROUP

1

Cataloguing in Publication Data is available from the British Library

ISBN 978 0 7553 7835 7

Typeset in Baskerville by Avon DataSet Ltd,
Bidford-on-Avon, Warwickshire

Printed and bound in Great Britain by
Clays Ltd, St Ives plc

Headline's policy is to use papers that are natural, renewable and
recyclable products and made from wood grown in sustainable forests.
The logging and manufacturing processes are expected to conform
to the environmental regulations of the country of origin.

HEADLINE PUBLISHING GROUP
An Hachette UK Company
338 Euston Road
London NW1 3BH

www.headline.co.uk
www.hachette.co.uk

This book is for my friend and neighbour
Sue Tillotson, to thank her for the many patient
hours she has spent trying to teach me
twenty-first century computing.

CHAPTER ONE

Early June 1938

'WHERE CAN YOUR FATHER be?' Beatrice Rushton was peering up and down the road from the bay window in her sitting room. 'It's gone seven o'clock.'

Her eighteen-year-old daughter Patsy had been asking herself that for the last hour. 'Perhaps he's forgotten the time.' Dad was usually as regular as clockwork in all he did.

'Surely he can't still be fishing?' There was irritation in Beatrice's voice. 'This isn't like him.'

'It's only salad tonight, Mum.' Patsy had already made it and set the table. 'Couldn't we have ours now? I'm hungry.'

In the mirror over the fireplace, Patsy could see herself curled up in the corner of the green velvet sofa, with her long straight hair held back with an Alice band. Dad said she looked like her mother, but she couldn't see much resemblance. Both had fair hair, but Patsy's was honey-coloured and shiny, while Mum's looked faded because it was turning grey.

Beatrice was frowning in indecision. It made her look older than her forty-four years; she was large-boned but gauntly thin and angular, while Patsy was petite and pink-cheeked.

'I suppose we might as well have ours. I'll need to keep some for Barney anyway. I don't know what the men in this family are coming to; they must think I'm running a hotel.'

Barney was Patsy's 20-year-old brother. 'You make a pot of tea, Patsy, and I'll cut some bread.'

Mum had been pretty when she was young, with features that were regular and finely chiselled. In old photographs she looked quite beautiful. Patsy studied her own face and was less pleased, she thought her mouth too big and her chin too determined. They both had deep blue eyes, but Patsy knew hers were inclined to stare too inquisitively at everything. Mum was a lot taller than she was, taller than Dad, come to that.

'You haven't finished growing yet,' both parents assured her. But Patsy thought she had. She would be quite happy to stay small and dainty.

Mum was set in her ways. There had to be a clean tablecloth for Sunday tea and a few flowers on the table if flowers could be got from the garden. Today they had pink roses, the first of the summer.

It had been an ordinary Sunday until now, a day bright with sunshine but with a cool breeze. Dad liked them to go to church together for the ten o'clock service and until a couple of years ago, they'd always gone to St James's as a family, but then Barney had dug his heels in and refused to go.

'Church means nothing to me,' he'd said from beneath his eiderdown. 'I need a lie-in on Sunday mornings.'

'You shouldn't stay out so late on Saturday nights,' Dad had retorted. 'Get up now and get yourself ready for church.'

Mum was indulgent to Barney, while Dad laid down the law and expected obedience, but he was no longer getting it. Since then, only Patsy had accompanied her parents to church on Sundays.

Dad was devout; he believed in peace on earth and wanted to help everybody. Patsy went because she always had and didn't want to upset Dad. She thought her mother went to show her smart new hats and high heels to the ladies of the parish.

This morning, before going, Patsy had helped Mum set a shoulder of lamb to roast on a low light, together with thyme and parsley stuffing, roast potatoes and new season's cabbage. It had made an excellent lunch which they'd all enjoyed. Barney had followed that with a double helping of apple pie and custard. It had been his breakfast too as he'd had nothing but the cup of tea Mum had taken upstairs to him.

Barney had gone out on his motorbike after lunch. He'd said he was meeting a friend. Patsy understood that to mean he was meeting Madge Worthington, his girlfriend.

Often Dad took Mum out for a little run in the car on Sunday afternoons. They drove round the pretty Wirral villages, or went to New Brighton to stroll along the promenade. They always took a flask of tea and often some cake too, to picnic in the car. But today, Dad had wanted to go fishing and Mum had said she'd prefer to rest on the bed and then perhaps sit in the garden if it was still sunny.

Mum was very proud of her garden. She'd only achieved a garden when they'd moved from the flat over the workshop in the north end and rented this very pleasant newly built semi-detached in Forest Road. It had a number on the gate but Beatrice had wanted that changed to a small plaque that named it as Fern Bank because it sounded classier. They all felt they were going up in the world and that Dad was building up his business, a workshop making inexpensive women's clothing.

Birkenhead had many small clothing workshops. They'd heard that another new one was being set up to make sportswear with the Fred Perry emblem on it. Rumour had it that it was owned by the great British tennis champion himself.

Patsy often spent her Sunday afternoons with her friend Sheila Worthington, but today she'd not made a definite

3

arrangement to do that. 'Can I go fishing with you, Dad?' she'd asked.

Usually he liked taking her. Last night, they'd both gone to New Brighton to dig up sand worms for bait while the tide was out.

'Well . . .' he said frowning heavily, which told her straight away he wanted to be alone. 'Things aren't going well in the business. I can't get enough work to keep the girls busy, I need to give this some thought and I don't have time at work. You'd be bored, Patsy. Some other time, eh?'

So she'd watched Dad's squarely built figure walk to his Morris Eight and drive away. Then she'd got out her bike and gone round to see what Sheila was doing. The Worthingtons lived close by in Shrewsbury Road in a much larger and older house. They had no car but there was a garage and the doors were open. Patsy could see her friend with her brother John who was helping her mend a puncture. Her bike was standing upside down on its seat and handlebars.

'I'm glad you've come.' Sheila beamed at her. 'I was about to come round to your place to see what you were doing.' There were four Worthington children in the family. They were all good-looking with dark lustrous hair and fair, clear skin.

'You were going to show me the new dress your mother's made for you,' Patsy said. 'I'm dying to see it.'

'Not now.' Her brother swung Sheila's bike back on to its wheels. He smiled at Patsy. 'Dad doesn't like us taking friends in on Sunday afternoons.'

'He and Mum have a rest on the bed after Sunday lunch.' Sheila giggled.

'We're forbidden to disturb them,' John added. 'Sheila, why don't you go out on your bike now I've mended it?'

Patsy understood that discipline was much stricter than in her own home. She knew the family quite well; Sheila was the youngest, Barney had started walking out with Madge her older sister and Mum was on speaking terms with their mother.

Mrs Worthington had roped in Mum as one of her helpers. She was setting up a local branch of the Women's Voluntary Service which was being formed to provide welfare services in the event of war. She'd been a schoolteacher before she married and Patsy thought her a formidable woman. Mr Worthington was even more so; even Mum was in awe of him. He was an accountant working for the council.

'Let's go for a bike ride then,' Patsy suggested. 'What about a trip to West Kirby?'

It had been a glorious afternoon with crowds out on the shore as well as on the promenade. They'd bought ice creams and watched the dinghy races on the Marine Lake. Patsy had come home feeling contented and full of fresh air.

But now Mum was growing anxious, she was pushing the food round her plate and eating little. When they both heard a car outside, Mum leapt to her feet and rushed to the front room to see if it was Dad. She came back slowly.

'It's visitors arriving next door. D'you think Dad could have had an accident? You know what he thinks of weekend drivers, a danger to everybody else.'

'He'd have phoned.' Patsy could see from her mother's face that she was afraid he could have been too badly hurt for that. 'Somebody would have let us know, wouldn't they?'

'Perhaps.'

They finished their meal and covered the remains of the cold meat and salad. After they'd washed up the few plates they'd used and there was still no sign of Hubert Rushton, Patsy said, 'I'm going out to look for him.'

'I'll come with you.' Beatrice was screwing her face with worry.

'No, Mum, better if you stay here. What if he comes home and there's no one here? I'll go on my bike.'

'Do you know where he's gone?'

Patsy hadn't asked where he planned to fish and in Birkenhead they were surrounded by water. Dad sometimes took her for walks round the docks, to the East Float in particular. Most of the dock facilities were lying idle in the depression and, to Patsy, the dock wall had seemed an ideal place to fish from.

Dad had smiled at her suggestion. 'The Mersey estuary is not the best place for fish and the docks take their water from there. You see, some kinds of fish live in salt water and other kinds live in fresh water. With big tides funnelling into the Mersey twice a day, the salt content of the water is ever changing and suits neither. Very few species of fish can cope with that.'

Patsy could see her mother's hands trembling. 'I think he probably went to New Brighton promenade,' she said. But she knew he couldn't still be fishing there at this time of the evening, the tide would be too far out now.

Her mother's anxiety was infectious. Patsy shivered as she got her bike out from the back of the garage and set off. The sun had gone and the wind was cold. She was horribly afraid that something must have happened to Dad; he'd never stayed out like this before.

Patsy knew the way well. As children, she and Barney had been brought here often in the summer. A donkey ride along the beach had been a special treat. They'd thought it great to have a seaside resort on the doorstep and made full use of it.

The old promenade stretched for three miles along the

Mersey from Seacomb Ferry and in recent years it had been extended several more miles along the King's Parade which fronted the Irish Sea. On it had been built the largest open-air swimming pool in England.

Patsy rode through the streets of New Brighton. The pubs and cafés were still open and brightly lit. There were holiday-makers to be seen enjoying themselves. Patsy freewheeled down the hill and round the corner on to the new part of the promenade which led away from the town.

She knew this was a popular place for fishermen. The sea wall was thirty to forty feet above the sand and with a high spring tide like they'd have had this afternoon, it would have been possible to fish from the promenade.

Patsy loved coming here when there was a high spring tide. The waves hurled themselves against the wall again and again, only to crash back in wild frenzy to fill the air with the scent of the sea. It turned the sea water white with ever-moving spume and sent a fine spray into the air with droplets sparkling like diamonds in the sun. Sometimes the waves came right over the promenade wall to swamp the pavement and even the road.

The night was quiet and dark, though there were lights on in the distant buildings and she could see two ships blazing with lights heading for the mouth of the Mersey. Here, a short distance along the prom, there were few people about, apart from a rare courting couple.

During any summer afternoon there would be lots of cars parked along the pavement, but she'd ridden almost a mile before she saw the dark mass of a solitary car parked neatly against the kerb. Another few yards and she could see it was her father's.

Her heart turned over and began to thump. She didn't

know what she'd expected but it wasn't this. Its lights were not switched on. She thought perhaps Dad had fallen asleep in the driving seat, but no, the car was empty.

Her mouth was dry as she dismounted and propped the pedal against the pavement. She went to the car; it wasn't locked, but otherwise everything was as she'd expect it to be. But where was Dad?

The strength was ebbing from her knees, she was really frightened now. She crossed the pavement to the sea wall. The tide had receded, and it was a long way out now and lapping gently on the wet sand. It was too dark for her to see anything down there.

'Dad,' she shouted. 'Dad, where are you?' She shivered in the chill wind. It was as though he'd disappeared off the face of the earth.

She walked a little further along the prom. Every so often, there were small alcoves in the wall from which stone steps descended down the side of the prom wall to the sand. These provided an ideal place from which to fish, out of the way of pedestrians and sheltered from the wind.

Dad had said she must use the beach in town near the pier rather than this part because here the tide could sweep in rapidly through wide gullies in the sand and sometimes cut people off from the steps.

'Oh my God!' Patsy jerked to a standstill. She could see her father's fishing box protruding from the next alcove. His metal bait bucket, decorated with pictures of Mickey Mouse, was balanced on top. As a child it had belonged to her, she'd built sandcastles with it.

'Dad?' Her voice was snatched away by the wind. She was breathless when she reached the spot. 'Dad?' she screamed over and over. 'Dad? Dad? Where are you?'

She could see he wasn't here, but the folding camp chair he'd brought to sit on was, and so were his two fishing rods and basket.

'Dad?' She felt sick as she looked down the stone steps. It was too dark to see the bottom ones but she knew they were covered by the tide twice a day and were slippery and green with seaweed. Dad wouldn't go down there, he'd warned her not to. The promenade wall cast a black shadow on the beach below, it was too dark to see anything on the sand.

Patsy was shaking and very frightened now. She didn't know what to do next. She was some distance out of town. If Dad had wanted to buy something, he'd surely have got back in his car and driven. Tears were prickling her eyes. Perhaps he'd failed to start it? Perhaps he'd walked back into town looking for a garage? But it was Sunday night and getting late now, would there be a garage open at this time? Perhaps he'd gone home on the bus? She knew she was clutching at straws.

She felt desperate. What should she do? Something must have happened to Dad, but what? He might be in need of help. She ran further along the prom but there was no sign of him that she could see. She'd have to go home and tell Mum.

First, she collapsed his camping chair and carried that and his other belongings back to his car. It took her several trips to get everything into the boot. She was surprised his stuff hadn't been stolen. She lifted the lid on his basket and saw he'd caught two plump whiting. Dabs and whiting were what Dad usually brought home though he said he'd heard sometimes sea bass and codling were caught here. Probably he'd caught others that were too small and thrown them back. He must have been here for some time. The fish would make his car smell, so she transferred them to the basket on the handlebars of her bike. She would have liked to lock his car up, but without his keys she couldn't.

Full of dread, Patsy climbed on her bike and pedalled as hard as she could for home, though she could hardly see where she was going for the tears glazing her eyes. She was relieved to reach Forest Road without further difficulty where she found all the lights were on in Fern Bank. She went straight round the back, let her bike fall on the grass and rushed in through the back door, shouting, 'Has Dad come home?'

Her mother was slumped on the sofa in the sitting room looking grey with worry. She knew immediately that he hadn't. Patsy threw herself down beside her.

CHAPTER TWO

'MUM, I FOUND DAD's car but no sign of him!' The tears were running down her face as she tried to tell her what she had found. She knew she was hardly coherent. 'You must ring the police,' she said, 'tell them that he's disappeared.' Patsy knew she was giving way to panic.

Her mother pushed her away. 'No sign of an accident you say? I don't understand why he hasn't come home. Daddy shouldn't stay out like this without telling me, he must know I'd be worried.'

'Mum, if Dad could come home I'm sure he would. I'm afraid something has happened to him.'

Beatrice was shaking her head. 'But what?'

Patsy got slowly to her feet, she knew she had to pull herself together and do something. She snatched up the phone in the hall and asked the operator to put her through to the local police station. She was able to tell her story more clearly this time. She learned that they would class him as a missing person.

'We would like you to come down to this police station either now or first thing in the morning and bring a recent photograph of him,' she was told. 'In the meantime, we'll contact the New Brighton force and ask that an officer check the area.'

Her mother had the bureau open immediately and was

searching through the drawers for photographs. 'How about this one?'

She held up a lovely picture of father and daughter taken in the back garden at Easter. To see Dad with his arm round her shoulder pulling her closer made Patsy catch her breath. 'Will they want one of him alone?' Another was held up. 'Yes, I'll take it now,' she choked.

'Do you think you should? It's after midnight.' Beatrice sounded in a flat spin. 'Would it be safe? Where is Barney? He should be home by now.'

At that moment, Patsy heard the put-put of his motorbike coming up the road. She knew he usually switched the engine off before getting this close, but he would have seen the lights were still on.

Beatrice had heard him too and went rushing out. Patsy followed more slowly. Mum threw herself in Barney's arms and sobbed out that Dad was missing. Patsy turned back and put the kettle on to make some tea. Her mother and Barney were both on the sofa in the sitting room when she took the tray in. Barney had always been able to comfort Mum better than she could.

Dad said Barney had been on the front row when good looks were being handed out. He was built like a sportsman, tall, lean, broad-shouldered and exuding strength. It gave a wrong impression. In reality he despised all sport and was a thorough layabout. He had wavy hair the colour of ripening wheat and had recently grown a pencil moustache that made him as handsome as a film star. Patsy's friends said he looked like Ronald Colman.

Patsy's hair was paler in colour and she thought he made her look washed out when they stood side by side. Also she envied him his waves, she thought her hair was too plain and straight. His eyes were wide-set and tawny in colour, his chin firm and his nose straight. He was very handsome and knew it. His smile was infectious and he was always looking for a good time. Patsy often saw girls eyeing him up.

Mum adored him and said he was the spitting image of Arnold, her much loved brother, who had been killed in the trenches in the Great War. Barney's birth had been long anticipated and he'd been named Barnaby Rowland Arnold John.

Patsy had arrived four years later and been given the names Patricia Beatrice with very little fuss. Good looks, Patsy thought, made Barney popular, everybody loved him and wanted to be his friend. Dad said that Mum was inclined to spoil him.

For years, Barney had been allowed to stay out until midnight whenever he wanted to, while Patsy needed special permission to stay out until ten o'clock if she wanted to go to the pictures with Sheila Worthington.

'Barney, you'll go to the police station, won't you?' Beatrice implored. Now the police were involved she understood Dad's disappearance was serious, but Barney seemed hardly concerned.

'Do I have to, Mum? They won't be able to do anything until daylight tomorrow. I'm tired, I want to go to bed, and anyway, I don't know where Dad went.'

'Aren't you worried about him?' Patsy flared.

Even Mum spoke firmly to back her up for once. 'The sooner the police have the photograph and all the details about him, the sooner they may find him.'

'If you take me there,' Patsy said, 'I'll tell them what they need to know.'

Barney pulled a face, but a few minutes later Patsy was

astride his motorbike, clinging on to him, with the wind blowing through her hair. She loved riding pillion, though Barney seldom took her. At one in the morning there was nothing on the road as they went into town. Patsy found the police station scary and was glad to have Barney striding in ahead of her full of confidence, with his head held high.

A constable received them politely and helped them fill in a form giving Dad's particulars and details of his appearance. While they were there a call came through from the New Brighton police force to say an officer had been along the promenade to see if there was any sign of their father. He'd found his car but nothing else.

'We'd advise you, sir, to lock it up or move it away as soon as possible, or you may find some or all of your father's belongings have been stolen.'

'Tomorrow,' Barney said. The officer pursed his lips. 'Early, as soon as I can use public transport to get there. I came here on my motorbike, but I'm the only other driver in the family.'

'We're very worried about Dad,' Patsy said and started to recount how shocked she'd been to find his belongings and realise he was missing.

'Quite so. The New Brighton force has promised to make a more detailed search as soon as there's enough light to see.'

Barney took her home. As they passed her bicycle, Patsy remembered the whiting she'd brought home and took them inside to put in the larder.

Mum was waiting up for them, her face now ravaged with tears. It took a long time to calm her down.

'I'll make more tea,' Patsy said. 'We can all take a cup up to bed.'

'I need more than tea,' Barney complained. 'I'm starving.'

'I saved you some salad.' His mother was wringing her hands. 'It's still on the table in the dining room.'

'I don't like salad. I could do with something hot. What about those fish you brought in, Patsy? Did Dad catch them?'

'Now?' Beatrice asked. 'You're not going to start cooking now?'

'Yes,' Barney insisted. Patsy got out the frying pan and cleaned the fish while Barney took Mum up to her bed with a cup of tea.

As soon as he'd finished eating, Barney went straight up to bed, taking his cup of tea with him. Patsy wrapped the fish bits in old newspaper and put them out in the bin, and propped the back door open for ten minutes while she got ready for bed. Mum hated the smell of fish hanging about her kitchen. It was very late indeed when she put out her light that night.

It was nine thirty when Patsy woke up the next morning feeling sleep-fuddled. Had they all overslept? The house was completely silent. Her spirits sank as she remembered the events of the day before. Then it hit her that she should have been at work since eight o'clock. She'd been apprenticed to Wetherall's in Bold Street in Liverpool for the last three years to learn women's tailoring.

She leapt out of bed and charged to the big back bedroom where her brother was still fast asleep. She hauled his bedclothes off him and tossed them over the bottom bed rail. 'Get up, Barney, for goodness sake.'

'Leave me alone, Patsy,' he grunted. 'I don't want to get up yet.'

'Come on, you've got to get Dad's car back.'

Before rushing downstairs to the phone she peeped through

the half-open door of the front bedroom, where Mum seemed to be still asleep. Patsy needed to explain her absence to Mrs Denning, her boss.

'I'm so sorry. My father's been missing all night.' She was breathless. 'I found his car abandoned in New Brighton and we're desperately worried about him. We've all overslept. Would you mind if I didn't come in today?'

Mrs Denning was sympathetic. She took a great interest in the personal affairs of her staff and always wanted to know every detail, so Patsy talked to her at length and told her all her fears and forebodings.

'Take a day or two off,' her boss told her. 'Until you know what's happening, you won't be able to concentrate on work, will you? Keep in touch with me.'

Barney was coming downstairs as she put the receiver down. 'You could just have told her you were sick,' he said. 'It would have saved all that.'

'No point in telling lies, Mrs Denning is very kind.' Patsy put the kettle on to boil.

'Is there any bacon?'

'You're not going to start cooking again?' she asked sharply. 'Why can't you just go? It'll only take you half an hour or so. You can have breakfast when you come back.'

'I can't go anywhere until we find Dad's spare car keys. Do you know where he keeps them?'

'No, you'll have to ask Mum.'

'She's asleep.'

'She'll want to be woken up for that.' Patsy ran up to her mother's room and found she was just stirring. She asked about the spare car keys.

'I don't know where Dad keeps them,' she muttered. 'Try in there.' She pointed to his bedside cabinet.

'We'll have to find them,' Patsy said and started systematically lifting out the contents of the drawers. Barney came up with a cup of tea for his mother.

'What are you doing?'

Patsy thought he looked shocked, his mouth opened and closed. She lifted out a bunch of keys. 'Could these be for the car? What d'you think, Barney?' He was gazing at the large bulging manila envelope that had covered them and seemed transfixed.

'Let me see,' his mother said. 'Yes, they're for the car.'

Patsy held them out to her brother. Slowly his hand came out to take them, and she could have sworn it was shaking.

'Those are they,' he said and slid them in his pocket.

Her mother lay back on her pillows. 'I feel absolutely useless,' she said. 'Without Hubert we won't be able to cope. He knows that, he shouldn't leave us like this. He knows I need his help. So do you, Barney. What will become of us without Hubert?'

Barney sat on the side of his mother's bed, holding her hand and trying to comfort her. She fondled his hair. Barney and Mum had always had this sort of relationship. He was still Mummy's little boy.

'I'd get going if I were you,' Patsy told him firmly. 'At this rate the car will be stolen before you get there.'

'You're becoming a real bossy boots,' he complained, but he got up and followed her down to the kitchen.

'I'm sorry, Barney, but I feel desperate about Dad. What could have happened to him?'

'Perhaps he decided to have a night on the town. Perhaps he had a skinful and went to sleep on one of those benches. If so, he'll be shocked to find his car has gone.'

'Don't be silly, Dad would never do that. How can you

make childish jokes now? Aren't you worried about him?'

'I expect he'll turn up again soon.' Barney poured himself a glass of milk, cut a slice of bread, spread it thickly with butter and went like a homing pigeon to the two cold sausages in the larder that Mum had told Patsy she could put in a sandwich to take for her lunch today. He folded his bread round them. 'OK, I'm on my way.'

Barney set off for the bus stop munching on his sandwich and was just in time to see a bus pulling away. Just his luck! Now he'd have twenty minutes to wait, so he might just as well have had his breakfast first.

He leaned back against the wall and took Dad's spare car keys out of his pocket. He'd almost panicked when he'd seen Patsy scratching about in Dad's bedside cabinet and pulling out that bulging envelope. It had made the years spin back to when he was a child.

He'd had mumps when he was nine years old and been kept off school. He hadn't felt that ill, it had been rather nice to get into Mum's bed after Dad had gone to work and Patsy to school. Mum wanted him to stay in bed until she'd lit the fire and it was burning up. She'd come back to bed for an hour after she'd seen the others off, but eventually he was left alone because she had to get up to tidy the house and go out to buy food.

One morning, he'd seen the drawer in Dad's bedside cabinet had been left slightly ajar and pulled it open. That big manila envelope had been there then. He didn't know why he took it out. It looked old and had been torn open. He could see it was stuffed with important-looking documents.

It was plain curiosity that led him to look through Dad's belongings – something to pass the time. The envelope contained the family's birth certificates, marriage certificate and insurance policies.

Barney looked for his own birth certificate and spread it out on the sheet in front of him. '*Barnaby Rowland Arnold John Tavenham-Strong*,' he read and recoiled in shocked disbelief.

After a moment, with hammering heart, he examined the document more carefully. It gave his birthday as 6 December 1917 which was right, so it must be his. His father's name was given as Rowland Charles Arnold George Tavenham-Strong, his profession as army officer.

Barney was still struggling to get his breath when he looked for Patsy's birth certificate. She was Patricia Beatrice Rushton, so no shocks there. He searched on and found his mother's marriage certificate. She had been Beatrice Rosanna Tavenham-Strong, widow, and she hadn't married Hubert Rushton until 1919. So the man Barney knew as his father was no relation.

That left him shaking and he wished now he'd not pried into the contents of that envelope. It must be a secret because Mum and Dad kept it hidden and neither talked about it. He wasn't part of the family. He wasn't who he'd thought he was. Hubert Rushton wasn't his father though they pretended he was.

Barney began having nightmares about what he'd seen. For weeks, he said nothing to anybody about it. He was afraid he would be scolded for searching through his parents' private drawers. But one night, he'd woken from that nightmare in a storm of terrified tears to find his mother in his bedroom trying to comfort him.

'Whatever is the matter, Barney? Has something frightened you?' With her arms round him he'd told her about his nightmares and what he'd seen, admitting that he'd searched through their personal possessions and private documents. He'd expected her to be cross with him but instead she seemed frightened. Then she'd burst into tears.

'Don't worry about it, Barney,' she'd choked. 'Put it out of your mind and go back to sleep. It's of no importance.' She'd tucked him up vigorously, snapped the light off and left him to it.

Barney lay there shivering. Clearly it was of great importance. Mum couldn't even bring herself to talk about it. That he'd mentioned it at all had upset her. It had brought real fear to her face and that scared him. He knew nothing at all about his real father and Mum wouldn't talk about him.

Hardly a day passed when he didn't think about it and worry about it. Hubert Rushton still sat at the head of the table. Barney still called him Dad because his family expected it of him, but it changed the way he thought about him. Now he could see that Hubert, short and plump, looked nothing like him. He knew deep down that he tried to be a father to him, but the fact that he wasn't his biological father made Barney hold back. Guilt consumed him. He loved his mother and hated to hurt her.

Barney lit a cigarette and looked at his watch. Where was this bus? Nothing he tried to do ever turned out as it should. He was fated to have everything go wrong on him. It always did.

He knew his mother and Patsy were desperately worried about what might have happened to Hubert, but it was hardly touching him because he had a far greater worry of his own. This time he really had done it. His parents would be furious with him when they found out.

They never stopped harping on at him, saying that it was high time he learned to hold down a job. It wasn't as though that was his fault. Barney's troubles had multiplied when he'd left school and told his parents he didn't want to work in the family business.

'In the current depression, it's hard to find any other opening for you,' his mother said. Dad thought he should be grateful to be given a job at all.

'I'll teach you all you need to know to run this business,' he told him. 'All my life it has provided me with a reasonable living. With average luck it'll do the same for you.'

Goodness knows he'd tried very hard to make himself useful there, but making women's clothes was just not Barney's idea of a career. His friends had laughed at him. 'We're hoping to get into Laird's shipyard, that's man's work,' they'd said, though he knew they'd failed to find any employment.

Barney had done his best to explain to Dad that he wanted a man's job, but once he told him he wanted to leave, things between them had never been the same, even though he'd found himself a job he thought he'd like better.

'You're a bigger fool than I thought you were,' Dad had told him, 'if you think delivering bread is a better job than learning to run the family firm.'

That had rankled, especially when he discovered Dad was right. Working for a bakery, delivering supplies to local grocery shops using a horse and cart had turned out to be pure slavery.

Love is said to be blind, but Dad saw his every fault and nagged at him to change his ways. 'It's no good relying on us for everything,' he told him.

His parents were always asking him if there was anything that really interested him, anything he'd like to do to earn his living. Barney spent a day watching the ships, freighters and liners entering and leaving the Mersey and thought he might like to go to sea. But when he tried it, he knew he'd made another mistake. Once again it hadn't worked out.

Barney believed he'd done his best. There were lots of people out of work. It wasn't as though he was the only one and jobs were hard to get when everybody was after them. Goodness knows, he'd tried, but the jobs always went to someone else. It was hardly worth trying, it only frustrated him when he knew he could do the work if only they'd give him a chance.

Barney could see Dad's disappearance was tearing Mum and Patsy to bits, but he hadn't the energy to worry about what might have happened to him. He had been living with his own worry for weeks. He was already worn down, and in some ways Dad's absence was a relief. Hubert would be absolutely furious with him, and it was only a question of time before the storm broke over his head. He could think of no way to avoid it.

CHAPTER THREE

Patsy had made tea and toast by the time her mother came downstairs. Beatrice looked round-shouldered and lethargic and slumped at the kitchen table with her head in her hands. 'What am I going to do, Patsy?'

She knew Mum had always leaned heavily on Dad. Without him she would need support from herself and Barney. 'When we've had breakfast we'll ring the police and ask if they have any news of Dad,' she said.

She was about to do that when the front doorbell rang. Mum was crowding behind her when she went to answer it. There was a policeman on the doorstep.

He introduced himself as Constable Freeman and asked if he might come in. Patsy led the way into the sitting room. 'Please sit down.'

'You have news of my husband?' Beatrice's voice wavered.

'Mrs Rushton, the New Brighton force has been searching the beach and prom since first light. I'm afraid they've found no sign of him, apart from his car which is parked on the promenade.'

Patsy's heart sank. Her mother said, 'Oh dear! How are we to manage without him?'

'I do urge you to make arrangements to move his car before it is stolen. It isn't locked.'

'My brother has already gone to fetch it home,' Patsy said. 'We're more worried about my father.'

'Yes, of course.' The officer got out his notebook. 'We'd like a little more information. May I ask, Mrs Rushton, if your husband had any problems?'

'What sort of problems?' Beatrice demanded, very much on edge.

Constable Freeman cleared his throat. 'Does he have problems at home, family problems, that sort of thing? I suppose I'm asking about his state of mind.'

'No,' Beatrice said sharply.

'Nothing new,' Patsy added. 'My brother has no job—'

'He's looking for work,' Beatrice interrupted. 'He tries very hard.' She was wringing her hands. 'It's the depression.'

'Your husband has his own business, a small factory making clothes, I understand.'

'Yes.'

'Does he have worries there?'

'In this depression, almost every business has problems.' Beatrice was indignant.

'Does your son work in the business too, Mrs Rushton?'

'Not really. Well, he helps a little from time to time. He makes local deliveries occasionally.'

'He started working for Dad when he left school,' Patsy tried to explain. 'But it didn't suit him; didn't suit either of them really.'

'Barney found himself another job,' Beatrice added defensively.

'But he hasn't a job now, you said.'

'Barney's had a succession of jobs,' Patsy said into the silence. 'Right now he's unemployed except for the odd deliveries he does for Dad.'

'I see, so that must be a worry for your father.'

'There are lots of people out of work at the moment,' Beatrice said sharply.

'Yes, of course there are, and work is hard to find.'

Patsy was frowning. 'Work is hard to find for a business too. Dad has to keep his staff working to make a profit. I think he was worried about that,' she said. 'I wanted to go fishing with him but he said he wanted to go alone, that he needed time to think.'

'Was his fishing trip planned, or taken on the spur of the moment?'

'It was planned,' Patsy said. 'I went with him on Saturday evening to collect worms for bait.'

'He often went fishing?'

'No, just occasionally.'

There was a long pause as the officer chewed at his pencil. 'He didn't leave a letter?'

'Why would he leave a letter?' Beatrice asked irritably. 'He was coming home for tea.'

'I see.' He paused. 'He gave you no reason to think he might take his life?'

Patsy gasped and heard her mother's throat gurgle with distress. A scarlet flush ran up Beatrice's cheeks. 'No,' she wailed. 'He'd never do such a thing.'

'He'd never leave Mum,' Patsy confirmed. 'Never leave any of us.' He knew they couldn't manage without him. Mum was sobbing openly at the suggestion.

'What about his social life? Does he have friends you don't share?'

'No.'

'Does he often go out alone?'

'Never.'

'Mrs Rushton, he went fishing on his own – unless he was planning to meet someone.'

'No. No, I'm quite certain he wasn't. No.'

'I'm sorry to distress you, Mrs Rushton, but these are questions I have to ask. We do need to know.'

Beatrice sniffed and mopped at her eyes.

'So he left here at about two o'clock yesterday afternoon, and nobody has seen him since?'

Patsy swallowed hard and nodded.

'And he'd be able to fish from the promenade for how long after that?'

'I think it depends on the height of the tide,' Patsy faltered.

'High tide at New Brighton was at three twenty-five yesterday. For how long after that would he be able to fish from the prom?'

Patsy shook her head. 'I have no idea.'

The officer was looking at her mother again. 'Was your husband well?'

'Yes,' Beatrice sobbed. 'He ate a good lunch.'

Patsy was suddenly conscious of the sound of Dad's car on the drive. Beatrice rushed to the window.

'It's only Barney,' she said, biting her lip.

A key scraped in the lock and he was with them an instant later, bringing a draught of cold air with him.

'Oh,' Barney said when he caught sight of the police officer. 'I wondered who that bike belonged to.'

'I'm Constable Freeman. I'm here to get more details to add to the information you gave us last night.'

'You haven't found him then?'

'Not yet. Well, that seems to be all for the moment, Mrs Rushton. I'll be in touch if there's any more news. Let us know if he returns, or if you hear any more.'

Beatrice showed him out and came back to sit with them in silence. Patsy listened to the ticking of the mantel clock with a sinking feeling in her stomach. The suggestion that Dad might have committed suicide had shocked them all. Mum's tears were drying on her cheeks but an occasional sob still shook her gaunt frame. They were all scared and on edge, but Barney seemed paralysed; he looked absolutely terrified.

Beatrice sat up straighter. 'Barney, please put the car in the garage. Your father never liked it left out on the drive.'

'I'll be going out again. I wonder if I might use it? Until Dad comes back, that is.'

Patsy felt her muscles tense. She could see Mum was shocked at that suggestion.

'Daddy wouldn't want you to use his car.'

'But just while—'

'Mum, Barney,' Patsy said, 'don't you think we should go down to the workshop and look at the books? Dad did tell me he needed to think about things. He was worried about the business.'

'This is all too much.' Beatrice wiped her forehead. 'I really don't feel up to it.'

'Tim will be wondering why Dad hasn't turned up, won't he? And we should make sure all is well down there. Mum, it's our livelihood.'

'Yes, Mum,' Barney said. 'If Patsy thinks Dad has problems, we should try to find out what they are.'

'I know nothing about what's happening down there,' his mother said. 'He hasn't talked to me about the workshop for years. He talked to you, Patsy, because you're going to help him run the business in another year or two. You and Barney go.'

The telephone bell rang in the hall. 'Could that be Daddy?'

Beatrice's mouth was a thin white line of anguish. As nobody else moved, Patsy went to answer it.

'Hello, is that you, Patsy?' The voice was hesitant, she recognised it immediately. It was Tim Stansfield, her father's assistant. 'Erm . . . Mr Rushton hasn't come in yet. I was wondering whether he was sick and if he'll be coming in later.'

'Oh Tim! We're all worried stiff. Dad's disappeared, something must have happened to him. We're just on our way in to see you. Is everything all right there?'

'Well . . . yes. It's just that normally he's as regular as clockwork.'

'We'll see you shortly and tell you what's happened then.' Patsy went slowly back to her family. She knew Tim quite well, because she was used to visiting the workroom. Dad wanted her to learn how to run it.

'Patsy's right, Mum.' Barney got to his feet. 'We ought to find out exactly what is going on. Let's all go now.'

Mum was shaking her head. 'I don't want anything to do with it. Daddy didn't need my help, he was happy to do everything himself. You go, you know more about it than I do.'

Patsy turned on her impatiently. 'Mum, you need to take an interest in it. It's our only means of income.'

Beatrice looked ill. 'I've got a terrible headache. I don't feel up to it.'

'Shall I find you some aspirin?'

'Only lying down in a dark room would help.'

'We none of us feel like going,' Barney said. 'I certainly don't.'

Patsy got to her feet. 'The business won't run itself. If Dad isn't there, one of us will have to keep an eye on things.'

'There'll be cash in the accounts which we're going to need,' Barney added. 'We don't want to lose money, do we?'

'Daddy could be back tomorrow, and we won't need to do anything.'

'I hope he is.' Patsy was sucking on her lip. Without Dad running the place, it would be like a ship without a rudder. 'We should all sit down, look over the books and talk to Tim. We need to make decisions. Somebody will have to see to the day-to-day running of the place.'

'Can't Tim keep an eye on it for a day or two?' Beatrice asked.

'No,' Barney said.

Patsy knew he didn't like Tim. They'd been in the same class at school. He'd told her that Tim had been a swot and the teacher's pet. When Barney had walked out, Dad had advertised for a lad to take his place and chosen Tim from those who'd applied. Dad said he was bright and hard-working. After that Barney liked him even less.

'Come on, Mum.'

It took Beatrice time to get herself ready, but at last they persuaded her into the passenger seat and set off. Patsy sat behind them, trying not to give way to panic. She felt that her family was unlike most others, it was split down the middle, with Mum and Barney on one side and her and Dad on the other. It was not a harmonious family.

Dad was a gentle person, kind and generous, and though he tried to provide Mum with everything she asked for, there had been no sharing of work between them. Poor Mum was not a strong person, she looked after the house and did the cooking, but Dad did everything else. He made all the decisions for the family. Patsy loved him dearly and they were all going to miss his energy and drive.

Barney pulled up outside the workshop. It was a smoke-blackened three-storey building quite close to Birkenhead North Station. The business had been started by Patsy's grandfather at the turn of the century and her father had worked in it all his life without losing his enthusiasm for the garment industry.

There was a two-bedroom flat on the top floor and the family had lived there until they'd moved to Forest Road. Patsy knew her mother had agitated to get away from the flat. They needed three bedrooms to live decently, she'd said, and she'd longed for a garden for years. Forest Road was in a good residential area, the workshop was not.

Barney seemed full of confidence behind the wheel of Dad's car, but when the time came to go into the workshop, he and Mum hung back. Patsy led the way, she knew the place well. It had long been her ambition to work here and help her father run the business.

It had been Dad's idea that she should start a seven-year apprenticeship at Wetherall's when she'd left school at fourteen. 'Stay long enough to learn all you can about high-class tailoring,' he'd told her. 'Be able to recognise an expensive garment, take an interest in the fashion scene, learn to cut out and use a sewing machine, and after four or five years, you'll know enough to be a great help to me.'

Patsy was working five and a half days a week at Wetherall's and loved it. On many Saturday afternoons she came straight here to learn more from Dad. The train from Liverpool put her down almost at the workshop door. He'd bring sandwiches from home for their lunch and they'd make cups of tea in the old-fashioned kitchen of the flat. The seamstresses had all gone home by the time she got here but sometimes Tim stayed on.

Today, although it was sunny outside, all the electric lights were on in the workroom. Two rows of sewing machines, fourteen in all, were powered by an overhead belt-driven system. The machines whirred and buzzed but the girls chatted all the time, they had no trouble making themselves heard.

Patsy knew most of them by name and usually when she came in they'd call their greetings. Today, their heads were bent silently over their sewing; she guessed the news about her father had made them fear for their jobs.

Tim Stansfield, looking very concerned, came hurrying to meet them. He was a tall and well set up young man with a mop of unruly light-brown hair. He was thoughtful and serious, but when he smiled, his face lit up with friendliness. He was always amiable and was popular with the rest of the staff.

'Hello,' he said. 'I'm very sorry to hear about Mr Rushton. What a terrible thing to happen.'

Barney was short with him. 'Shall we go to the office?' He looked down on Tim. Even Mum did, because he'd been brought up in Dock Cottages which had been notorious for being the worst slum in Birkenhead. They were not cottages at all but large blocks of tenements, three hundred and fifty in all, built in 1844, and since 1937 they were being pulled down, one block at a time.

The office was a cramped and dusty place but, like the whole building, it smelled of new cloth. Tim busied himself finding chairs for them all, while Patsy started to fill him in about what had happened to her father.

Barney interrupted to quiz him about the business. 'Is there something wrong here, something that would worry Dad? The police are asking.'

'There's the perennial problem of getting orders. As you know, things have been slow for the past few years. We've had trouble finding enough work to keep the girls busy. Your dad was worried about that, but it's slow everywhere, nobody has much money to buy clothes these days. We talked about it,' he looked at Patsy, 'the other Saturday when you came in.'

'The machines are all running.' Beatrice was shaking her head as though she didn't believe him. 'You seem busy enough to me.'

'Yes, well,' Tim said, 'Patsy suggested we get the girls to make aprons, oven gloves, stuffed toys, that sort of thing, out of the cut-offs. The leftover scraps of material, you know? We have lots of it. We thought that was a good idea and Mr Rushton is selling them to a stallholder in the market. It keeps the girls busy.'

'Does it pay?' Barney demanded in officious tones.

'Every little helps,' Tim said. 'It keeps the workshop ticking over.'

'Ticking over isn't good enough,' Barney said. 'There are bills that have to be paid. If there's not enough work, some of the women will have to be laid off.'

'We are two down since the beginning of the year,' Tim tried to explain. 'Rita Johnson retired and Colleen Smith got married and went to live on the other side of Liverpool. It was too far for her to come from there.'

'More will have to go,' Barney said firmly. 'We can't afford to keep them on if there's no work coming in. It's paying wages for nothing.'

'Many have worked here for years,' Tim said. 'Mr Rushton was reluctant to lay them off.'

'You must have known about this, Patsy,' Barney said. 'I thought you already had one foot in the business.'

'Yes, as Tim told you, we have talked it over. It's nothing new, we all knew about that, didn't we, Mum?' They went on to argue for the next half hour about what could be done about it.

After poring over the books, Barney said in disgusted tones, 'It looks as though the business is earning next to nothing.'

'I know Daddy was doing his very best.' Beatrice was indignant. 'I said I could cut back, economise on the housekeeping. We must do that now.'

Patsy felt sick. 'The rent for our house is our biggest expense,' she said seriously. 'But Dad owns this workshop outright. We could give notice and move back to this flat.'

'I'm not going to live here again,' Beatrice exploded. 'Down in the depths of the north end? Daddy knew how much it meant to me to get out of it. He'd never ask me to come back. I couldn't.'

Patsy dared say no more. For her, it was a comfort to know that if things got really bad, they would at least have a roof over their heads. There was Dad's car too, they could sell that, though Barney wanted it and would fight tooth and nail to keep it.

'Let's take the account books home,' Patsy said. 'It'll be easier to concentrate there. We need to take a close look at them and find out exactly how things stand.'

'We'll do that.' Barney was already gathering the ledgers up.

Patsy had seen enough of the accounts to feel hurt that Dad hadn't pointed out more strongly just how bad things had become. Now she thought about it, he'd been reluctant to talk about the accounts for the last six months. Perhaps he didn't want her to worry. She should have probed more.

She was afraid there was a real possibility that the business

33

could go bankrupt. Dad had had a problem, a big problem; he must have been at his wits' end. And the worst thing about that was it gave him a real reason to take his own life; it made it more likely he had committed suicide and that didn't bear thinking about.

CHAPTER FOUR

'SLOW DOWN, BARNEY,' HIS mother told him on the
journey home. 'You're driving much too fast.'

Patsy knew they were all· emotionally fraught. The
atmosphere was doom-laden and the future seemed bleak.
Once back at home the family sat at the dining-room table
with the open ledgers in front of them. Patsy saw immediately
that the business had earned much less this year than last.
That sent a shiver down her spine.

'Dad hasn't had a decent order in for the last three months.'
Barney was shocked.

'Couldn't you get some orders, Barney?' Beatrice pleaded
with him. 'You're good at talking to people. And there's no
reason why you can't go in every day until Dad comes back.'

'Me?' he said plaintively. 'No, I wouldn't know where to
start. What do I know about the rag trade? Patsy knows more
about women's clothes than I do. Dad had big ideas about
what she could do for the business.' That struck fear into
Patsy's heart.

Barney fixed his handsome eyes on her face. 'He thought
that with you he could cut out the middleman,' he sneered.
'You could design the clothes and they could be run up in the
workshop and sold directly to the shops instead of waiting for
orders.'

'We can't do that now,' she pointed out. 'It would take

35

money up front to work that way. Anyway, I'd need Dad's expertise.'

'You had big ideas about it too, you were all for it.'

'Yes I was, but now . . . Please, Barney, you haven't got a job so it wouldn't be hard for you. Both of us ought to work in the business, give it our best and do our utmost to keep it going. Without Dad, everything will be different; our best chance of sorting this out is to stick together.'

Barney snorted with contempt. 'So the big ideas were all pie in the sky?'

'It's the depression,' Beatrice said helplessly.

He turned on her. 'Dad has let things sink too far.' The women stared silently at him. It's too late to do anything now. The best thing is to sack all the staff and close the place down while there's still something to salvage.'

'No,' Patsy wailed. 'Some of them have worked for Dad for over twenty years. They need their jobs and we need to earn our living too. We have to keep it going.'

'Well, that's up to you.' Barney was getting cross. 'If you think you can turn the whole thing round, you go in and do it.'

'Patsy's serving an apprenticeship.' Beatrice was shocked. 'She mustn't break that off. Eventually it will give her a trade, a means of earning a living.'

'It was always Dad's intention to take her into the business,' Barney pointed out. 'He didn't expect her to complete seven years. He said she'd learn all she needed in half that time. Now's the time to throw it over. Why not? She's earning next to nothing at Wetherall's anyway.'

Again the silence dragged on. 'You can't expect me to handle this,' Barney told them. 'Patsy, the business was always going to be your baby. You'll have to decide what can be done with it.'

Patsy could feel herself shaking. If only Dad were here . . . Barney wasn't going to be any help, and she didn't think he knew enough about the business anyway. He'd never been interested in it. Dare she do it on her own? What if Dad never did come back, would she be able to manage? The prospect terrified her.

All day they argued the same facts over and over. Patsy lost her patience, Barney lost his temper and Beatrice wept. Stress levels were high, and overhanging all that was the black worry of what could possibly have happened to Dad.

Patsy felt they were all paralysed. They were doing nothing but sitting about waiting and wondering and arguing. She was glad to go to the shops to buy food and take over the preparation of meals.

In the evening, Barney drove off in his father's car without asking his mother if he might.

'That's very naughty of him.' She wept again. 'He knows Daddy doesn't like him using it, he's afraid he'll damage it. We must stop him.'

Patsy had a little weep when she got into bed that night. She felt overwhelmed by what was happening, and she did not sleep well.

The next morning, Barney had been awake for some time before he got up. He could hear his mother and sister talking as they ate breakfast, but he was too far away to hear what they said. It would be about Dad or about the business, it was all they could think about and he couldn't stand any more of that.

When he heard Patsy go out, he swung his feet out of bed. He'd go down and get some breakfast. It was on his mind that he should tell Mum that he, too, had a problem, give her some warning of what was coming, but she'd switched the wireless on.

He could clearly hear every word that was being said about preparing for another world war. All England was worried stiff that war was imminent. Barney sighed; he and his family had worries that were much closer to home. It tended to keep their minds away from general problems like war.

As soon as she saw him, Mum started again wondering what had happened to Dad. That really depressed him. Barney was afraid he'd got himself into one hell of a fix. For weeks now, Madge Worthington, his girlfriend, had been telling him she was pregnant and that he was the father. She was probably right about that but the worst thing was, she was pressing him to marry her.

There was no denying Madge felt desperate. She was almost out of her mind, but without a job there was no way he could do it. He couldn't pay his own way, let alone support a wife and kid.

Why did it have to be Madge? The Worthingtons were well in with his family. Madge's mother and Mum knew each other and both would be mad at him. Patsy would be at his throat and want to hear every last detail because she was as thick as thieves with Madge's little sister. Sheila Worthington was her friend and always hanging about their house. He'd been half afraid that Sheila might already suspect and tell Patsy, but it seemed she hadn't yet. Now the problem with Dad had put everything else out of Patsy's mind.

Mum fried him bacon and egg, but twittered on about Dad, giving him no chance to tell her about Madge. This problem was going to bring down a can of worms on his head. Between one thing and another, he'd have to get away from here.

He'd promised to meet Madge at two o'clock this afternoon. She was partway through her training to become a primary school teacher, and in order to earn some pocket money she'd taken a holiday job in the café at the end of the pier in New Brighton.

She worked during the busy periods at lunchtime and in the early evening. They gave her a couple of hours off in the afternoon which didn't give her enough time to get home and back on the bus, so she wanted his company. On a fine day they could lie together on the sands but wet days could be difficult.

The pubs would be opening so Barney decided to go down to the Golden Lion and have a pint first. He really needed something to cheer him up. He drove off in Dad's car before Mum got round to forbidding it.

There was a jolly crowd of holidaymakers in the pub and it was half two before he left. He sucked one of the peppermints he kept in his pocket so that Madge wouldn't smell beer on his breath. Really, he didn't want to see her, she was no fun any more and she'd only nag him about getting married.

He dragged his feet somewhat as he walked along the pier, though he thought it a magnificent structure and usually enjoyed coming here. On the main deck was a tower sixty feet high and beyond that he could see the ferry from Liverpool disgorging more day trippers on to the landing stage. There was a large building known as the Pavilion at this end of the pier. Inside was a theatre where daily performances were given as well as the café where Madge was working.

The door pinged as he went in. Many of the tables were empty now, but Madge was still working behind the counter, serving a customer. She saw him and waved. Barney watched her speak to the manageress and then come towards him.

She didn't look well, her face was white and there were deep mauve shadows beneath her eyes. She'd certainly lost her bloom. His eyes went to her belly to assess how much longer they might be able to keep her condition a secret. It was noticeably more rounded than it used to be.

'I thought you weren't coming,' she said, taking his arm and hurrying him outside.

'I'm sorry, Madge. With Dad gone missing, everything is at sixes and sevens at home. I came as soon as I could.'

'Barney, we absolutely have to get married. You said we'd go to the register office in Birkenhead to see if we could set a date for it. Ask if there was anything we needed to do before we could.'

'I went there on my own,' Barney lied. 'Neither of us is twenty-one yet. We both need permission from our parents before we can be married.'

'Then let's face them together tonight and get it settled.'

Barney's heart turned over at the thought. 'My mother's in a terrible state at the moment.'

'If her mind is elsewhere, that would surely make it a good time. She'll have less to say to us.'

'She's going out tonight.' Barney wanted to put all that off for as long as he could.

'Then come to our house.'

Barney was trying desperately not to agree.

'You did say you loved me.' Madge was growing agitated.

'Of course I love you,' he assured her, but he was no longer sure. This trouble was changing everything.

'My dad will kill me when he finds out.' Her face was twisting with anxiety. 'We've got to get married. My family isn't going to like this even if we do.'

Barney felt trapped. 'What are we going to do for money? You know I haven't any.'

'I've saved a bit but I don't care about the money. We'll manage somehow.'

He felt sick, he didn't want to marry her. That had never been his intention. To leave home, get right away from all these troubles seemed the only course left to him.

By the time Madge had to go back to work, Barney's mind was made up. The time had come for him to bail out. If it was all right for Dad to do that when things were difficult, then it was all right for him. He drove the car home and then rode his motorbike down to the garage he'd always used.

He'd bought his bike from old Tommy Vance who was a fat and fierce-looking man of about sixty, and his bike shop was always open. Barney had decided he'd try and sell it back to him to get funds for his trip. He'd thought it was worth twenty-five pounds but Tommy offered only fifteen. 'Take it or leave it,' he said.

Barney thought he was being done, but he had to take it. He had to have money if he was going away. Since Dad had not taken his car, he might as well do so, as he was the only other family member who could drive it. That afternoon while Patsy was in the workshop and his mother down in the kitchen preparing their evening meal, he crept into her bedroom and hunted through the drawers in Hubert's bedside cabinet for the car ownership and insurance papers. He would need those. He hated having to do this, there was a malevolence about that stuffed manila envelope, it scared him. But he gritted his teeth and shook out the contents to remove the documents he wanted.

The next day, he filled the car up with petrol, packed this clothes and belongings carefully, and when Mum's back was turned loaded his possessions into the boot and locked it. He was ready now. He set his alarm clock for five thirty and put it under his pillow so nobody else would be disturbed by it.

The next morning he crept downstairs, made himself some corned-beef sandwiches and took a full packet of biscuits from the cupboard. After all, he didn't have all that much money and he wanted to start by having a couple of days' holiday. Every year when he'd been small, Dad had taken them away for a week in a boarding house in Conway and they'd all enjoyed that. It would do him good now and he'd see how he got on there. Perhaps he could get a summer job in a hotel. That would suit him well enough.

Patsy got up on Thursday feeling she had the cares of the world on her shoulders. Both Mum and Barney were expecting her to make big decisions about the family's future.

As the youngest member of the family, they'd treated her and her ideas with little respect up to now. She ached with self-doubt about what she should do. Mum was still tearful and Barney had distanced himself from their troubles. He was doing his own thing as usual.

Patsy decided she'd cycle down to the workshop and take the account books back to Tim. He needed to write the figures in daily to keep them up to date. As soon as she went inside she felt a change in the atmosphere: everybody was more cheerful.

'We've got an order.' Tim was beaming and quite excited. 'And it's big enough to keep us going for three weeks.'

'Where from?'

'That agent your dad went to see last week. I told you about him, didn't I? It's to make children's clothes for British Home Stores. Right up our street.'

'That's good.' Patsy piled the ledgers on Tim's desk and flopped down in her father's chair. 'A help, but it won't solve the problem. We'll need a lot more work than that.'

She was feeling low and was soon pouring out all her anguish about her father's disappearance and her family's expectations of her. 'If only Dad were here,' she said, tears in her eyes. 'He'd know what to do for the best.'

Tim's hand rested on her arm for a moment. 'I miss him too. He was a good boss, he taught me a lot; encouraged me to try all sorts of things. He helped me grow.'

'Me too, but where do I go from here?' Patsy asked. 'Barney reckons it's too late to do anything. What would you do if you were me?'

Tim pulled a face. 'I know what I'd like you to do, but that isn't the same thing, is it?'

Patsy sighed. 'You want me to come in every day and try to pick up the reins from where Dad dropped them? Tim, I'm not sure I'm capable of that.'

'You're more capable than your mother or brother.'

'It would mean walking away from my apprenticeship.'

'That's a big step, but your dad said that was always your intention.'

'Yes, but everything hinges on whether we can get enough work for the business to survive.' Patsy frowned. 'If things don't go right, it wouldn't be so easy for me to get another job. I won't be time served.'

'No, I see it's a big risk for you, but I believe it's what your father would want you to do. He was teaching you all he could about the trade.'

Tim's face was thoughtful and serious; Patsy felt she had more support from him than from her family. 'You're right. I know you're right, but . . .'

'Give it all you've got, Patsy. That's what I want you to do and I'll do everything I can to help. We all will. The thought of this business closing down scares me rigid. Your family would lose its livelihood and we'd all lose our jobs.' He was gnawing at his lip. 'Perhaps I shouldn't encourage you to do it. What if it all goes wrong? I wouldn't want you to feel I talked you into it. I'd blame myself.'

'No,' she said thoughtfully. 'There's no blame attached to trying.'

'It's been a happy place to work, everybody is friendly and we all knew where we stood with the boss.'

Patsy rubbed her face with both hands and took a deep breath. 'I'll do it. I can't just walk away. This business has provided my family's living for over fifty years. Dad spent his life managing it.'

Tim's face lit up in a beaming smile. 'I'm delighted, it's the best thing for all of us, I know it is.'

'You've helped me make up my mind,' Patsy said, and then the phone rang. She leaned forward and as soon as she picked it up, she could hear someone crying softly. 'Mum, is that you?'

'Yes, Patsy, you must come home. I don't know what to do.'

She'd thought her mother had been calmer and better able to cope this morning. 'Have you had more news?'

'Yes, the police have come round again. They say a body has been washed up on the Welsh coast and they think it could be Daddy. It's been brought to Birkenhead. They want somebody to identify it.' She was in floods of tears.

Patsy swallowed hard, there was a lump the size of a golf ball in her throat. It sounded as though Dad must have drowned. It was the worst possible scenario. Did that mean he'd killed himself?

'Patsy, are you there?'

'Yes, Mum.'

'The policeman is here. He wants to take me but I can't do it.'

'What about Barney? He'll do that for you.'

'He's gone out, Patsy, I'm here by myself. Anyway, I don't believe Daddy can be dead.'

Patsy was curling up in horror. She felt sick. Why couldn't Barney be there when he was needed?

'You'll have to come home,' Beatrice sobbed.

'All right, Mum. I'll be there in ten or fifteen minutes.'

'Do hurry, dear.'

Patsy put the phone down and was almost in tears herself. She told Tim what had happened as she put her jacket on. 'Barney's no help at all. You'd think he'd want to support Mum at a time like this, but he's off out enjoying himself again.'

'I doubt he'll be enjoying himself.' Tim was serious. 'When he came here the other day, he seemed very intense, sort of stricken. I'd say he was a worried man.'

'Then I wish he'd worry about Dad,' she said sharply, 'and about the business, instead of leaving everything to me.'

'Patsy,' Tim said quietly, 'I could identify your father. I've shared his office, worked alongside him every day for almost four years.'

She was biting her lips. 'I've never seen a dead person. But if it is Dad, I want to see him. I could be sure then about what had happened, couldn't I?' She turned to him. 'Will you come with me?'

Tim's dark eyes were full of sympathy. 'Of course I will. Good job I came on my bike this morning.'

'Thanks, Tim. I feel I need somebody to lean on right now.'

45

This time the police officer had come by car and he took them to the small Victorian mortuary that still served the town. They entered it across a cobbled yard and were shown to a tiny office, where they'd been sitting for the last fifteen minutes talking to a man who seemed to be in charge. Patsy felt she wasn't taking in all she should. She was clinging to Tim's arm, feeling that the world as she knew it was coming to an end.

She'd been asked twice whether she wanted Tim to identify the body on his own and she'd told them she did not. To accept that it really was Dad, she wanted to see him. She had to see him.

There were white tiles everywhere, and they were crowding in on her. She felt as though there was a block of ice inside her, it was all very frightening. Tim pushed his fingers into hers, interlocking them; she could feel his shoulder held firm against hers.

A man in a shapeless green gown and white Wellingtons led them towards a table with a sheet-covered body lying on top. 'Are you ready?' he asked. Patsy closed her eyes, tightened her fingers round Tim's and prayed she was going to see a complete stranger. She couldn't bear to think of Dad being in a place like this.

Tim was gripping her arm with his other hand and she heard him whisper, 'Yes, it's him. No doubt whatsoever.'

'Tell us who he is please,' the officer said. 'Give us his name.'

'Hubert Rushton, my boss.'

Patsy opened her eyes then. So it was her father! 'Yes, yes,' she agreed but in truth she hardly recognised him. His body was swollen, his face looked blue and red and there were bad grazes all over him. Poor Dad was dead and never could come back to them! She could feel the tears rolling down her cheeks as they hurried her out of that fearsome place.

Once outside on the pavement back in the normal world, Patsy took great gulps of air. It seemed sparkling fresh now they were away from that cloying smell of disinfectant, although the town air was heavy with smuts that could blacken the bottom of white petticoats.

'Are you all right?' Tim was offering her his handkerchief.

'Yes.' She mopped her face and blew her nose. 'As right as I'll ever be now.' She could feel anger growing inside her. 'Why has Dad done this to us? He must know how much we need him.'

'Come on, we'll catch a bus. I'll see you home. I expect your mother is on tenterhooks waiting to hear.'

'How could he kill himself?' Patsy burst out. 'I know things are bad in the business, but you'd think he'd want to stay and help, not leave us to get on with it.'

She felt Tim's arm go round her shoulders. 'We don't know that yet. Nobody does. Didn't they say they were going to do an autopsy and they'd let you know the result?'

Patsy had to agree that was what she'd been told. She could see their bus coming and blew her nose again.

Once they'd found seats, Tim said, 'I don't believe he did kill himself, he wasn't the sort of man to do that. Anyway, he was always talking about the future. He was looking forward to the time when you'd be working with him.'

'But he was washed up by the sea on the Welsh coast.' Patsy stared out of the window. 'There's no way that could happen if he hadn't intended to drown himself, is there?'

Tim shook his head. 'As yet, we have no answer to that. We'll have to wait to hear the coroner's verdict.'

When they reached Fern Bank, their bikes were still

propped up against the garage wall. Tim turned his round.

'Won't you come in and help me tell Mum?' Patsy implored.

'Better not,' he said awkwardly. 'Your brother has probably come back and he doesn't like me. He'd resent me at a time like this.'

Patsy nodded numbly; he was right about that. 'Thanks for your help, Tim.'

'If there's anything else – you know where I am.'

CHAPTER FIVE

PATSY WENT INDOORS AND found her mother alone in the silent sitting room. She turned an anguished face towards her. 'Well, was it Daddy?'

Patsy hesitated, not wanting to say 'yes' baldly to that. She knew what a shock it was going to be.

'Was it Daddy?' Beatrice demanded more heatedly. 'I can see it must be.'

'Yes. I'm sorry.'

Her mother's face crumbled, tears ran down her cheeks. 'Oh my God!'

Patsy went to sit beside her on the sofa and put her arms round her.

'What are we going to do?'

'I'll give my notice in at Wetherall's and see what can be done with the business.'

'But if Daddy couldn't make it pay, how can you?'

'We'll manage, Mum. Somehow we'll manage.'

'I can't stand it. Now they say there's no avoiding another war. It's been on the news and it's in the newspaper. I haven't forgotten what the last one was like. You wouldn't believe what life was like in the trenches.'

Patsy knew that, to her mother, the horror of the last war had never gone away. The thought of another was too intense to bear. She roused herself. 'Where's Barney gone?'

'I don't know. I thought he was still asleep until that policeman came. I went to wake him up and found he'd gone out. He must have got up early for once.'

'A fat lot of help he is,' Patsy burst out. 'He's useless.'

She went upstairs to the bathroom, but on the way opened Barney's bedroom door. It was not like him to get up early. The bed was a mess as usual but his bedside table lacked its normal clutter. There was only his ashtray full of cigarette ends. Somehow the room seemed different. She opened his wardrobe door and saw a lot of empty hangers; the clothes remaining were old ones he no longer wore.

'My goodness!' she said aloud. 'Mum, he's gone!' She turned to his tallboy and yanked some of the drawers open and that confirmed it. 'Mum!' She went flying back down the stairs. 'Mum, Barney's gone, gone for good. He's cleared out, taken all his clothes.'

'He can't have, dear.' Beatrice met her in the hall. 'He'll be back, I told him I'd get steak for his dinner.'

'He won't, and I bet he's taken Dad's car.' Patsy shot out to the garage and came back slowly. 'That has gone too, would you believe it?'

'Barney wouldn't do such a thing.' Her mother was indignant. 'He knows the car belongs to Daddy.'

'He's gone all right, and guess what? So has his motorbike!'

'He can't drive both, don't be silly.'

'He'll need money to go off on his own. I bet he's sold his motorbike. It looks as though he's gone for good.'

'No, I can't believe that!' Beatrice rushed out to see for herself and returned to collapse on the sofa in tears again. 'Surely he'd have said something if he meant to stay away? This is a nightmare. The second in the family to disappear!

Could Barney be thinking of drowning himself too?'

'No, not him,' Patsy said. 'He wouldn't take Dad's car if he meant to do that.'

Her mother looked up, her face agonised. 'If he's gone for good, surely he'll have left us a note?'

'Possibly.' Barney would know what a worry this would be to Mum. Especially now, when they'd just found out Dad had died in terrible circumstances. Except Barney didn't know that, he hadn't been sufficiently concerned about Dad to wait to find out.

Patsy went back to his bedroom to have another look but no, there was no note. Perhaps he'd left it downstairs. But after a good look round, she was unable to find one.

'I can't understand why he's gone,' Beatrice sobbed. 'Deserting us when we really need him. I mean, where could he go? Who is going to look after him?'

'Look after him! Mother, he's abandoned what he feels is a sinking ship. He wants to get away from us. He thinks he'll do better on his own. You know if there are any problems, he never wants to get involved. He's a coward.'

'You don't understand just how nervous he is.' Beatrice was wringing her hands. 'What are we going to do now?'

'We need to eat,' Patsy said. 'What is there for lunch?'

'I couldn't eat a thing,' her mother wailed.

'It's half past one and we'll both feel better if we eat.' Patsy was already in the kitchen looking through the larder. There wasn't much there except cheese. She turned to the tins in the cupboard. 'Beans on toast, that'll do. I'll go to Wetherall's this afternoon and tell Mrs Denning I want to leave. I wonder if she'll want me to give notice. I need to start at the workshop as soon as possible.'

* * *

Tim was blinking hard trying to keep the tears back as he got on his bike and cycled slowly back to the workshop. He felt torn in two. He hadn't wanted to leave Patsy, not when she needed his help and seemed to be asking for it. But he'd never been inside her home before, and he didn't think Mrs Rushton would welcome him. She was a distant and haughty woman and the thought of dealing with Barney's aggression had made him say no.

How he'd ached to put his arms round Patsy and offer her real comfort. To see her father's body after it had been in the water for so long had given Tim the shivers. Patsy had been close to her father, what must she have felt? It filled him with pity for her. It wasn't fair to thrust so much responsibility on to such a young girl.

She must like him because she'd turned to him for help in her hour of need, though goodness knows, she had no one else to turn to.

He felt he'd known Patsy for years. How often had he stayed at work on a Saturday afternoon in order to see her? He'd enjoyed her company, she was outgoing and friendly; if she'd been one of the seamstresses, he'd have asked her to go to the pictures with him long ago. He'd not found any other girl so easy to get on with, and it hadn't taken him long to accept that he fancied her. But how could he dream of having her as his girlfriend when she was the boss's daughter and he was the office help? He was proud to have been able to help her today.

Tim, like the rest of the workforce, was shocked by Hubert Rushton's sudden and terrible death. He'd been a kind and considerate boss and they'd been fond of him. At lunchtime they couldn't stop talking about the likely outcome. It frightened them all. Could the business carry on without him, when work was so hard to come by?

'Barney will take over,' one suggested. 'He's the only son.'

But they knew Barney too well. He'd walked away from this business and had carried on walking away from a dozen other jobs. Now, to earn pocket money, his father sometimes allowed him to drive the van, delivering finished work. But they all knew he wasn't capable of running the business even if he was prepared to try. They kept telling each other that he'd never be able to make it pay.

Tim shuddered when he thought of Barney taking charge. When they'd been in the same class at school, Barney had ignored him, but now when they came face to face at work, he was openly nasty.

One day, Mr Rushton chanced to see how Barney treated him and when he stalked off, Tim said apologetically, 'I don't know what I've done to upset him.'

The boss pursed his lips. 'Take no notice, he's jealous.'

That surprised Tim. 'Of me?'

'You're doing the job I wanted him to do,' he said. 'He failed and walked out but you're making a success of it. You're showing him up, aren't you?'

'Am I?' Tim had never thought of it like that. 'Poor Barney.'

'Save your sympathy,' his boss said wryly. 'He might do better if he tried harder.'

Mr Rushton didn't mention it on that occasion, but Tim had heard him say Patsy was twice as capable as Barney. He often talked about her and what he hoped she could achieve. Tim had built up his impressions of the family not only from the sewing-room gossip, but by hearing his boss speak of them. He had been very close to his daughter.

Tim couldn't remember the boss ever talking about his wife, and he'd hardly seen her until now. He thought her a handsome lady but rather haughty. She was far too grand a person to come into the workroom and do a day's work. With Barney being unhelpful, there was nobody to do it but Patsy.

She was very young, very pretty and popular with the women. They alternately mothered her and teased her. She gossiped and laughed with them but they didn't hold out much hope that she could run the business. 'She's just a kid,' they told each other. They all knew how Mr Rushton had been struggling to keep it afloat and that there couldn't be a worse time for Patsy to take over.

Tim knew what it was to lose a father. He'd lost his own only eighteen months ago and it had left him grieving and feeling his responsibilities. Now he was head of the family he needed to look after his mother, but his father had died in bed after a long illness. How much worse it must be for Patsy; she was younger and had far greater responsibilities. As far as Tim was concerned, there was nothing he wouldn't do for her.

It was a lovely early summer morning and now he'd escaped, Barney started to sing. He felt as free as a bird. The hedgerows were lush with new leaves, long grass and wild flowers. He loved driving Dad's car and he took the coast road into Wales. The sky was blue and cloudless and before long the sun came up and now it was sparkling on the sea.

He'd just gone through Prestatyn when a girl with a haversack on her back thumbed a lift from him. After one glimpse of her white-blond curls, he pulled up with a jerk and leaned over to open the passenger door. She had a round face, a pert upturned nose and wore a lot of lipstick. 'Any chance of a lift into Rhyl?' she asked.

'Every chance. Hop in.'

She heaved her haversack on to the back seat and settled

beside him. Her legs were long, shapely and bare, she was just the sort of girl he admired.

'Going there on holiday?' he asked as he put the car in gear and moved off.

'No, I live there. My holiday is over.' Barney immediately wondered if this girl would make it worthwhile staying in Rhyl for a few days. He could always go on to Conway later. She had 'come hither' green eyes and a wide smile.

'What's your name?'

'Jeanie. Jeanie Wilson.'

Barney turned on the charm and gave her an edited version of his circumstances. He found out she'd spent most of the winter in Liverpool, staying with her Aunt Lil and working in a big department store; she said she'd had a marvellous time.

'My mum wanted me to come home. Rhyl's a great place in the summer. For the last few years I've had a summer job in an ice-cream factory. I wrote and asked them if they'd have me back and they said yes.'

'Do you think there's a chance of me finding a job there?'

'What sort of a job would you want?'

'Anything. I could drive an ice-cream van, couldn't I?'

'You look the sort who'd want an office job, or perhaps in something in theatricals. There's always lots of shows on the pier as well.'

Barney knew he couldn't afford to hang about waiting for the special job to come up that he'd really enjoy, not now he'd left home. 'I just want something to tide me over for the summer. So I can stay at the seaside and have a good time.'

'Well, this ice-cream factory always takes on extra staff for the summer, temporary and part-time. You won't have any trouble if that's all you want. I could show you where to apply.'

Barney was delighted. 'That would be fine. I don't want to

work all hours. We all need a bit of fun, don't we?' He glanced at her to find her green eyes were watching him eagerly.

'I couldn't agree more.' She had the sort of smile that seemed to linger on her lips, it came and went and came again. 'I could show you all the best places to go.'

This was what Barney wanted to hear. It was a bit of luck meeting Jeanie like this. He knew now he'd done the right thing to get away from home, he should have done it ages ago and ditched Madge Worthington and all that trouble. If Dad could do it, there was no reason why he shouldn't too.

Patsy was upstairs getting ready to go to Liverpool when she heard the front doorbell ring. Mum hadn't been able to stop crying, and Patsy knew she wouldn't want to go to the door in tears, so she ran down to see who it was.

When she saw it was Sheila's mother Mrs Worthington, she opened the door wider, thinking she'd come round to offer sympathy. She was a large woman, tall as well as stout, and she had a strong personality to match. Where she led, she expected Mum to follow.

'Is your mother in?' she demanded.

'Yes, do come in. Mum's upset, of course, but she'll be glad of your company.'

'No she won't, not when she hears what I've got to say.'

Patsy was taken aback by Mrs Worthington's bristling aggression. Until now she'd thought her a polite and friendly woman; Patsy had always been welcomed when she went round to call on Sheila.

It was only then that Patsy saw she had her elder daughter Madge with her. Mrs Worthington swept into their sitting room, almost dragging Madge with her.

Beatrice stood up to greet her. 'Rosemary, how nice . . .'

Then she saw Madge and stopped. The girl had obviously been crying, her face was blotchy, her whole stance was hangdog.

'Is Barney in?' Rosemary Worthington demanded.

'No, I'm afraid not,' Patsy answered. 'What's the matter?'

'Tell them, Madge,' she ordered. 'It doesn't look as though anybody knows about this.'

Madge burst into tears and could say nothing.

'He's got her pregnant, that's what.'

'Oh my God!' Beatrice collapsed back on to the sofa, her face paper white.

'Five and a half months gone she is, and none of us knew. Barney had better marry her quickly. Make an honest woman of her before her father finds out. When will Barney be back?'

Patsy was struggling to get her breath; she was shocked to the core. This must be why Barney had gone! What a rotten thing to do, to leave Madge to face this alone.

There was a heavy silence. 'We don't know,' Patsy said at last. 'He's disappeared.'

'What?'

'We've just found out. He's packed his clothes and taken Dad's car.'

Madge wailed like an animal in pain. 'He agreed we'd be married,' she sobbed. 'He said he'd meet me from work yesterday and come home with me to tell Dad.'

'But he didn't show up,' her mother said.

Madge mopped at her face with a damp handkerchief. 'After that we were going to come here together to tell you and get the wedding arrangements started.' She looked from one to the other in despair, realising she could expect no help from Barney. 'My dad'll kill me when he finds out,' she sobbed. 'He'll throw me out.'

'Come and sit down.' Patsy took Madge's arm and led her to an armchair. Madge looked pregnant; it was hard to understand how everyone had failed to notice until now. She felt sorry for her, she looked really downcast. What a cad Barney was to disappear like this! Even from him, she'd have expected some loyalty.

'I think your son is a scoundrel.' Rosemary Worthington was angry. 'He's a swine to do this, get a girl in trouble and then clear out and leave her to face it on her own.'

'He hasn't got any money. No job either. He can't afford to keep a wife and family.' Beatrice was making excuses for him.

'Then he should have thought of that before he got our Madge in this condition. He's ruined her. She can't go back to college and train to be a teacher now. What sort of a career is she going to have after this? And who does he think is going to pay for this baby? She won't be able to go on working in that café for much longer.'

'I will,' Madge said. 'I'm all right.'

'Such a disgrace for the family.' Rosemary Worthington pulled herself up to her full height. 'Her father works for the council and she has a brother training to be a priest. This reflects on us all.'

Patsy cringed. It reflected on them too. Barney had no doubt told Madge he loved her and promised marriage. And this was how he'd let her find out that he was rejecting her. He hadn't even had the nerve to tell her to her face! For Madge, it was a very public rejection of the worst sort.

'We've got our own problems.' Beatrice was crying softly. 'We've heard this morning that Hubert's body was washed up on the Welsh coast. Patsy had to go and identify him.'

'I'm sorry. We had heard he was missing,' but Mrs Worthington wasn't going to let them off the hook. 'We all need to discuss this with Barney and work out what is to be done. Could you arrange a time for this as soon as possible?'

'If he comes back, we certainly will,' Patsy said.

'If he comes back?' Rosemary Worthington stormed. 'Surely he'll have to if he has no job?'

Patsy didn't believe he would, not if he could possibly avoid it. 'We'll help you, Madge, all we can,' she managed. There was nothing else she could say, no further comfort she could offer. This was the ultimate disgrace for any girl. It was the message drummed into them all.

Beatrice went on crying all day and they could talk of nothing else. 'I can't believe this of Barney,' she said. 'We brought him up properly to know right from wrong. Daddy and I took him to church every Sunday.'

Patsy didn't go over to Liverpool to see Mrs Denning at Wetherall's as she'd planned, she felt she had to stay with her mother and try to comfort her.

'We could offer Barney's bedroom to Madge if she has nowhere else to go,' she suggested.

Mum was wringing her hands. 'I don't know, she'll have no money. We can't afford another dependent now.'

'We'll see what her family does.' The thought of being in Madge's position made Patsy shiver. 'If her father really does throw her out and none of her relatives take her in, then I feel we'll have to.'

The next morning brought a postcard, a lovely view of the mountain railway on top of Snowdon. Patsy handed it to her mother. 'I think it's from Barney.'

'I can't read it, dear, not without my glasses.' Mum often said that but now her eyes were glassy with tears and red-rimmed.

Patsy read out the message he'd scrawled on the back.

Dearest Mummy,

I've had to go away because I'm too much of a burden to you and Patsy. You'll be better off without me. With all this talk of a coming war, they're asking for volunteers for the forces. I feel my best plan is to join up and serve my country. I don't want you to worry about me. I'll be all right.

Love to you both from Barney.

'Not a word about Madge.' Patsy was shocked. 'Doesn't he have a conscience?'

'I do hope he hasn't joined the army.' Beatrice was aghast. 'That would be quite the wrong thing for him.'

'He's probably done nothing yet,' Patsy said. 'He's probably climbing Snowdon and enjoying a little holiday. Surely he won't rush into anything like that.'

'He won't like being in the forces. It's not his sort of thing.'

'One thing is certain,' Patsy said. 'If he does, he won't be able to get out when he's had enough.'

CHAPTER SIX

BARNEY HAD REALLY TAKEN to Jeanie, they were getting on like a house on fire. He reckoned he'd fallen on his feet. They had a drink in a smart pub and then he bought her a posh lunch with a bottle of wine at one of the big hotels on the seafront.

It was a warm sunny day and after that he drove along the front until they'd left the crowds behind. On a quiet part of the beach he spread Dad's car rug out on the sand and drifted off to sleep, lulled by the calling of the seagulls and the lapping of the waves. Jeanie slept too.

In the late afternoon, she said, 'Come on, I'll take you home. If Mum likes you, she'll probably ask you to eat with us tonight.'

She directed him to the outskirts of town and got him to park in front of a small stone-built terraced cottage dating from the last century. He carried her haversack and followed her inside. The front door opened off the pavement straight into their living room.

'This is my mum,' she said by way of introduction and gave her a potted version of all Barney had told her about himself. Wanda Wilson was an older, plumper version of Jeanie, with the same flyaway pale hair, the come-hither eyes, a low-cut blouse and lots of make-up. She made a fuss of them; there was a meal of boiled ham and chips to welcome Jeanie home and Barney was invited to join them. Jeanie told her mother they'd known each other for some time.

'Barney was in Rhyl last summer. He worked in the ice-cream factory with me. Then we met in Liverpool by chance at the beginning of my holiday.'

Barney smiled at Wanda. 'It was lovely seeing Jeanie again and I decided to come back with her and spend another summer here.'

'What did you do during the winter?' Wanda wanted to know.

'I worked for my dad. He has his own business, a small workshop making women's clothes. But he's not so busy in the summer.'

Barney had resigned himself to sleeping in the back of the car that night because he wanted to keep his cash to have a good time with Jeanie, but she asked her mother if he might use their spare room. Wanda did not seem over-keen, but then he understood that she worked a night shift as an orderly at the local cottage hospital.

'I'm looking for lodgings,' Barney told her, 'for the rest of the summer. I'd like to have somewhere homely, where I can live as family. I can pay the going rate.'

'I can't let you stay here with Jeanie. I'm out at work six nights a week, it wouldn't be right.'

'Oh Mum, you know I'm nervous at night on my own in this house. Just to know there was somebody else here would make me feel safe. You can trust me, can't you?'

'Yes, but what about your friend?'

'I'm very trustworthy,' Barney said. 'We're all grown-up, aren't we?'

When it turned out Wanda was running late for her shift, Barney offered to run her to the hospital and that seemed to settle it. She named a modest weekly sum and he was in. Jeanie came with them to the hospital for the ride.

'Now don't forget, Barney,' Wanda said as he dropped her off at the hospital gates. 'I trust you to behave yourself while you're in my house. Any trouble and you'll have to go.'

'I promise you there'll be no trouble,' he told her. As he drove off, Jeanie was giggling.

'What time does your mother come home?' he wanted to know.

'She works till seven in the morning and gets home about half past.'

'Excellent,' Barney said. 'Shall we stop off for a drink before going back? It's a bit early for bed.'

'No, I'm tired. I feel like an early night.'

'Jolly good, so do I.'

When Jeanie let him into the cottage, he followed her up the steep stairs. 'Mum and I sleep on this floor,' she told him. 'Our spare room is up another flight.' This was even narrower and steeper.

'This is marvellous.' Barney was pleased when he saw the room. 'Couldn't be better.' It was an attic room with a ceiling so low he couldn't stand up near the outside walls, but it was the biggest room in the cottage, covering the whole floor space on the second storey. It had two tiny windows, one looking over the street in front and one looking over the back yard to the hills behind.

Jeanie ran down to get some clean sheets and a duster, and they made up the double bed together. 'Room for both of us in here,' Barney suggested hopefully.

'Why not?' Jeanie giggled.

Barney was delighted with the way things were turning out. While he unpacked one of his suitcases, Jeanie removed the worst of the dust. Then she took him down to see her bedroom. He watched her ruffle up the bedclothes.

'So Mum will think I've slept here.' She smiled. 'We'll be more comfortable in the double bed, won't we?'

Barney was dazzled. Jeanie was an amazing girl, no coyness or pretence about her. He'd really fallen on his feet. 'Tomorrow,' he said, 'I'll get some French letters.' He wasn't going to make the same mistake twice.

'That's a good idea, but you'll need one tonight.' Jeanie was fishing one out of her handbag.

'You're a girl in a million,' he told her and gave her a hug and a kiss. He'd had to work a lot harder on Madge to get this sort of thing.

The next day, he drove Jeanie into work and she took him to the boss's office and said, 'This is Barney Rushton, Mr Duggan. He's a friend of mine and he'd like a summer job with you.'

The boss looked up from his paperwork. He had very little mouse-brown hair left, his scalp was shining through it and he was very much overweight. 'Right, Jeanie, leave him here with me for five minutes. Come and sit down. Barney, is it?'

'Yes, Barney Rushton, sir.' He smiled and set about being as charming as he could. This was a job he badly wanted. If he landed it, he could have a superb summer here with Jeanie and Wanda.

'I'm looking for temporary sales staff. Tell me about yourself. Have you sold ice cream before?'

'Not ice cream but I've sold bread and cakes. I've done lots of other things too. I've worked in a bar and a restaurant and I've worked for my dad in a clothing factory. I'm very adaptable.'

'Good. Can you ride a bike?'

'Er . . . yes. I had a motorbike until recently.'

Mr Duggan smiled. 'This will be a pushbike incorporating an ice-cream freezer unit, A "stop me and buy one", you know what I mean?'

'Yes.' Barney felt a searing disappointment. He hesitated. 'I was hoping, sir, to be selling from an ice-cream van. I've had a driving licence for over three years.'

'I do have a couple of vans, but it's the "stop me and buy one" salesmen I need now. Are you interested?'

Barney felt he had no choice. 'Yes, sir, I'm very interested.'

'Good. You understand this is a temporary position? It might last until the end of the summer or it might not, depending on the weather and the trade. You'll be paid on results, a percentage of the sales you make. Fill up this form for me with your name and address, age, etc.'

While Barney was doing that, Mr Duggan went on talking. 'I'm glad you've come in this morning because we're running a training session. Can you start now? Good, we have two other men starting. I'll take you along to our Mr Morris who will acquaint you with our stock and demonstrate our machine and how you must look after both. There's some elementary bookkeeping to learn too.'

By the afternoon, Barney was out on the promenade pedalling a very heavy machine, but the sun was shining and the girls came clustering round to buy his ices. He was more than happy to be able to pay his way and settle in with Jeanie for the summer.

Patsy was not sleeping well. She'd meant to go over and see Mrs Denning, it was on her conscience that she'd put it off for so long. Then the problem of how to keep the girls in the workshop busy and make the business profitable was preying on her mind. It had worried Dad so she knew it wouldn't be easy.

She knew he'd had plans that would make the workshop more profitable in the long run. Instead of waiting for orders from some middleman, they would design garments to be run up in the workshop and sold direct to the retail trade. But that meant she would need to buy the cloth first and pay the seamstresses to make the garments up. It would take longer for the business to be paid for the work done and cash flow would be even slower than it was at present. She couldn't stop thinking about it. It was better than thinking about what might have happened to her father.

She decided to cycle down to the workshop and talk to Tim. She wanted to ask his opinion on what would be easier to sell to the retail trade, women's blouses or children's dresses? She'd drawn up a blouse pattern with the fashionable sweetheart neckline, but children grew out of their clothes quickly, and many mothers would buy for them rather than for themselves.

Patsy had in mind to try a child's dress on similar lines to those worn by Shirley Temple in her films. She'd buy good quality cotton material that would wash well and not fade.

She was getting out her bike when a policeman came cycling up. She recognised Constable Freeman and felt her heart turn over. He'd said he'd return to let them know the result of the autopsy and she was afraid it would be more bad news about Dad.

'Is your mother in, Miss Rushton?' he said. 'I've come to have another word with you both.'

'Yes, come in.'

Her mother was pulling herself to her feet as Patsy led him through the kitchen to the sitting room. Her face paled.

'Do sit down, Constable,' she said, her manner stiffly formal. 'You have news for us?'

'Yes. Dr Paulson, our pathologist, carried out an autopsy on Mr Hubert Rushton yesterday afternoon.'

Patsy was clenching her hands; her mouth felt dry. She heard her mother's voice croak with anguish, 'He drowned?'

'No, there was little water in his lungs. He was found to have suffered a massive stroke. Dr Paulson thinks he must have stood up and felt dizzy, and then fallen down the steps of the promenade into the sea.'

Patsy felt woolly with shock but it was better news than she'd been expecting. 'Then he didn't commit suicide?'

'No.'

'He must have been in awful pain.' Beatrice was visibly quaking. 'Poor Hubert, to die alone like that.'

'Dr Paulson thinks he died quickly. If he'd been alive when he fell into the sea, there would have been more water in his lungs.'

'It's good news, Mum.'

'Yes. I am to tell you that the inquest will be held tomorrow morning at ten o'clock and that you can put any questions you have to Dr Paulson then.'

When he'd gone, Patsy threw herself down on the sofa and mourned the fact that Dad hadn't died here with his family around him. To have it happen where it did must have been terrifying for him. She would have liked to tell him how much she loved him, but at the same time she was full of relief. Dad hadn't killed himself.

The next morning she could feel her mother shaking when she took her arm to walk to the bus stop. The inquest was being held in a room reserved for the coroner next to the police station and morgue.

Patsy was surprised to find it was a court of law. Dr Paulson introduced himself and some of his colleagues to them. Later she heard him tell the court that he had performed an autopsy on Mr Hubert Rushton and found that he had had an arterial blockage in his brain; in other words, a massive stroke. He found him to be suffering from atheroma of the cranial arteries, serious heart disease with an enlarged heart and scarring of the muscle caused by several previous smaller strokes.

Dr Paulson went on to say, 'This case has been complicated by the fact that Mr Rushton was alone, and at the time and date he was on the sea wall in New Brighton, a spring tide would have been reaching its maximum height. Undoubtedly he would have had a few moments of acute pain and felt dizzy. Either he fell, or was washed off the steps by a large wave.'

Patsy had been holding her breath, and she let it out slowly as she heard the court find that Hubert Rushton had died from natural causes. The family were informed that his body would be released for burial.

'Thank God for that,' her mother murmured, and dissolved into tears again. 'If he'd been at home, there was nothing anyone could have done for him.'

When they were on the bus home, Patsy said, 'Mum, do you know how to go about arranging for Dad to be buried?' One glance at her mother's face and she knew that she didn't. 'We'll ring the vicar when we get home,' she said. 'He'll help us.'

The vicar came round in the early afternoon and arrangements were set in motion. He sat on the sofa next to Mum and encouraged her to choose the order of service and the hymns she'd like to have. A date and time six days later was chosen. It was the vicar who suggested they look for a will and explained what they'd have to do about probate.

As soon as he'd gone, Patsy took her upstairs to see if they could find a will. They came across it almost immediately, together with a note telling them this was a copy and the original was with his solicitor. Patsy only glanced at it; as she'd expected, Dad had left everything to her mother.

'You'd better handle this, Mum,' she said. 'Just telephone the solicitor. Tell him of Dad's death and ask him to apply for probate. He'll tell you if there's anything else you need to do.'

'I can't believe how much there is to do when somebody dies,' Beatrice complained although she had done little up to now.

'We should be glad the vicar could tell us what to do.'

Later that afternoon Patsy rode her bike down to the workshop to see Tim, because she knew he'd lost his father quite recently. He was a great help. He recommended an undertaker and said he'd ask his mother to help her with the funeral tea.

'We should close the workroom that morning as a mark of respect,' he said. 'I'm sure most of the girls will want to go to the service at the church. We were all fond of him.'

'We'll do that,' Patsy agreed. 'Thanks for thinking of it. I'll go in and tell the girls now.'

Patsy wanted Tim's mother, who had worked in catering for some years, to organise the funeral refreshments for them, as otherwise the job would fall on her, but she needed to get her mother's agreement. She was cycling home up Forest Road when she saw Sheila Worthington cycling towards her.

'Patsy,' she was calling. 'I was just coming to see you.' They both dismounted and Patsy could see her friend was upset.

'We've had some dingdong rows at home. Dad's furious with our Madge. He's giving her hell and telling her she's got to get out. Mum's going spare, she's trying to persuade him to let Madge stay because she's nowhere else to go. But he said no, not now when everyone can see the disgrace she's bringing on the family. Our Gordon is training to be a priest, you know, and that makes it even harder for Dad to accept. She can come back later, but she's got to have the baby adopted, he'll not have her bastard living in his house.'

'Oh my goodness!' Owing to her own problems, Patsy had given little thought to Madge's. 'Let's go to my place and talk to Mum.'

Sheila gulped, her eyes were full of misery. 'Dad's forbidden me to have anything more to do with you, but I told him I'll not have that.'

'Heavens! This is not your fault or mine, but since Barney is my brother, I feel we should help Madge if we can. I'll ask Mum if she can use Barney's bedroom for the time being.'

'That would be a great help. Mum has been trying to find Madge somewhere to go. She's fixed up for her to go to a mother and baby home, but they only want her there for six weeks before the birth and six weeks after.'

'Poor Madge.'

'Yes, she never stops crying.'

'Come on then, let's see if Mum will agree to her moving in with us.'

Patsy knew her mother didn't want Madge in her house, she was anything but welcoming. Patsy's cheeks burned with embarrassment, as Sheila couldn't help but see it.

'Our Madge is desperate,' Sheila said. 'She's at her wits' end.'

'It's only for a couple of months, Mum. Barney doesn't want to use his room. It's only fair that we offer it to Madge.'

Mum didn't have the strength to refuse to allow Madge to

come. Patsy took Sheila upstairs and got her to help put clean sheets on the bed and Hoover the carpet.

'Tell Madge everything is ready for her now and she can come as soon as she likes.'

'I'll bring her round,' Sheila said. 'Thank you. You're a real friend to do this for us.'

'I'm ashamed of my brother. To disappear like this is cowardly and uncaring. He's gone without even knowing what happened to Dad, he doesn't care about him either. He wouldn't have made a good husband or a good father. Tell Madge she's better off without him.'

'But your mother . . .'

'She can't believe it of him. She's always thought the sun shone out of Barney.'

That evening, Patsy was washing up after she and Mum had eaten the scratch supper she'd made, when the front doorbell rang. Madge was on their doorstep, accompanied by Sheila and also her brother John who was carrying her suitcase. Patsy took them all straight upstairs to the room Madge was going to use.

'I'm sorry to force myself on you like this,' Madge said to Beatrice who followed them up.

'Don't you worry about that,' Patsy said. 'You're welcome to stay with us, isn't she, Mum?' Beatrice had to agree. Patsy really felt for Madge. She'd changed from being a very pretty girl to one who looked exhausted and downright ill.

'Why don't we all go to the pictures tonight?' Patsy suggested. She and Sheila usually went once a week and she thought it would take Madge's mind off her troubles.

Mum was horrified. 'We can't possibly go,' she objected. 'Not when Daddy's just died. It wouldn't be right.'

Patsy felt overwhelmed with problems. 'Mum, it would do us all good. Dad wouldn't mind, I'm sure. He'd understand.'

'It's Bette Davis in *Jezebel*,' Sheila said. 'It's said to be very good.'

'I'd like to see it.' Patsy was determined to take Madge. A film was one thing she could still enjoy. She'd be bound to feel uncomfortable on her first night with them if they stayed at home. 'Come with us, Mum. Forget your troubles for once, you'll feel better if you do.'

'No, I'd rather not. I don't think *Jezebel* is the sort of film I'd want to see anyway. You youngsters go if you must.'

They did. John paid for them all and bought them ice creams in the interval. Patsy had a relaxing night out and enjoyed it. Madge was more in control of her tears by the time they returned home. Patsy packed her off to bed with a hot milky drink.

The next morning, she had to take Mum shopping for mourning clothes and she had great trouble convincing her that she did not want to buy black clothes for herself.

'We haven't much money, Mum, and I've already got a grey two-piece that would do nicely. I'd rather wear that.'

Beatrice's lips were pressed into a stiff straight line. She felt Patsy wasn't showing Daddy enough respect. As a child, Patsy had worn clothes made in their sewing room. With careful cutting out it had often been possible to get an extra garment out of the material. Beatrice, too, had occasionally worn dresses made there, and Gladys still occasionally acted as her dressmaker to give her what she thought of as more upmarket styles. But for mourning clothes, Beatrice wanted only the best. It took her a long time to decide on which black hat, coat and dress she wanted.

When they got back, Madge had made a thick farmhouse

soup from the vegetables she'd found in the garden. 'I want to make myself useful while I'm with you,' she told them. 'I'm very grateful for what you're doing for me. I don't want to be a burden. I know you have troubles of your own.'

CHAPTER SEVEN

PATSY HAD BEEN DREADING the funeral. She was glad when Tim said his mother wanted to discuss what refreshments they had in mind for the mourners.

'I'll bring my mother to the workshop to talk to her,' Patsy said. 'She'll want to be involved in that. Let's fix a time for tomorrow.' But she found her mother was reluctant to come and had to be persuaded. They were late arriving.

Mrs Stansfield was of matronly build and seemed to know exactly what would be needed. 'How many people do you want to cater for, Mrs Rushton?' she asked.

'I don't know. What d'you think, Patsy?'

'It'll be mostly people from the workroom, and men working nearby who knew him.'

'That's what I think,' Tim said. 'I suggest you put on a small buffet of sandwiches and finger food in the flat upstairs. Do you agree, Mrs Rushton?'

'It's not been lived in for years,' she protested. 'It'll be filthy.'

'No, it isn't,' Patsy said. 'That's a good idea. Dad always had his lunch in the living room and he used the kitchen to make tea.'

'I'd like to give Daddy a good send-off,' Beatrice sobbed. 'The workshop seems . . . you know, a bit downmarket. I don't want it to be a cut-price funeral.'

'The alternative is to hold it in your own home,' Tim's mother suggested.

'Have all those sewing women there?' Beatrice was indignant. 'They wouldn't know when to leave.'

Patsy was afraid her mother sounded a terrible snob and was ashamed to hear her say that in front of Tim and his mother. She said, 'The church hall then? The vicar did say it was available.'

'You'd have to pay for the church hall, Mrs Rushton, if you had it there,' Mrs Stansfield said, 'and it isn't any better. I think the flat over the workshop would be ideal. You and your family can talk to the mourners but leave when you want to.'

'The girls won't want to lose pay,' Tim added. 'We can close the workroom for the morning. They can go to church for the funeral at eleven o'clock, and then it'll be lunchtime when it's over. It'll be handy for them, they can come back to the flat for refreshments and they'll be on the spot to work the afternoon session.'

'Aren't we going to close it for the whole day?' Beatrice's indignation flashed again. 'As a sign of respect for Daddy?'

'Yes, we can if that's what you want, Mum. But we'll have to pay the staff.'

'Good gracious! But you've no work for them to do anyway.'

'Patsy's keeping them occupied using up the scraps for aprons and peg bags,' Tim reminded her.

'We'll do it,' Patsy decided. 'Close for the day. How many do we need to cater for, Tim?'

'Thirty to forty at the most.'

'That sounds a lot,' Beatrice objected. 'We don't want food to go to waste.'

'Mum, if there's any food left over the girls will take it home for their children.' The seamstresses were mostly of middle age, but Dad had always referred to them as girls.

'The most economical way is for you to buy the food, Patsy,' Mrs Stansfield told her. 'Our Tim will help you. I'll work out how many loaves it'll take, and what I'll need by way of fillings. Eggs and lettuce, some boiled ham, that sort of thing. And you can order a few sausage rolls and meat pies from Pride's Bakery. They always go down well.'

'I'm very grateful,' Patsy said, 'to have you organising it for me.'

'I'll make the sandwiches in the morning and set it all out, and be there to make the tea and hand things round,' she said. 'You'll have plenty of cups and plates in your canteen that can be used.'

'And how much are you going to charge for your services?' Beatrice demanded.

'Nothing.' Mrs Stansfield's plump face broke into a smile. 'Mr Rushton has been right good to our Tim. We counted him a friend.'

When she'd gone, Beatrice said, 'I want the flowers to come from our garden. Daddy worked-hard out there, helping me grow them. He loved flowers too.'

They'd never had a better display of flowers in the garden. The roses were in their first flush of the season and all were in full bloom at once. Madge had spent one summer holiday working in a florist's shop and was good at arranging them. She took Beatrice out to help her pick them the evening before the funeral.

'We'll pick a lot, impossible to have too many,' Beatrice said. She chose a white floribunda called Iceberg and mixed them with a white hybrid tea rose called Evening Star.

They picked yellow Moonshine, pink columbine and multi-coloured anemones and sweet peas.

Later, when Patsy came home from work she took her into the dining room to see what they'd done. The room was filled with a heavenly scent. The white roses were in a great glamorous sheath tied with purple ribbon. The card read, '*To Hubert, sadly missed. From your loving wife, Beatrice.*'

There was also a bunch of sweet peas and scabious with a card Beatrice had written saying they were from Barney. Patsy went out to the garden and picked another great bunch of deep bronze and cream roses and wrote a card saying, '*To my beloved father, I'll never forget you.*'

The morning of the funeral was very dark and wet. Patsy felt it suited her mood. She'd never been to a funeral before and didn't know what to expect. The church felt cold but there were more mourners than she had expected. She recognised some of the agents Dad had dealt with, and many were owners of the small businesses near their own.

Beatrice was dressed from head to foot in black and hardly raised her eyes from the ground. Tears were streaming down her face. Madge insisted on coming too and because Beatrice thought a hat essential wear for church, she'd loaned her one. It didn't suit her.

Patsy wore her grey suit and matching tam, but because it was raining she needed to wear her mackintosh on top. The only one she had was blue and Mum thought it most unsuitable and was cross with her. Patsy forgave her as she knew they were all very tense at this terrible time. She hung on to her mother's arm and pulled her close, she could feel her quaking. Bereavement had come with savage suddenness.

For Patsy, the worst part was seeing the plain oak coffin standing on its bier at the front of the church and knowing that her father was inside. The top was covered with flowers. Tim and his mother had sent a wreath and the girls in the workshop had had a collection and bought another.

It was still raining when the time came to follow the coffin to the churchyard. A forest of black umbrellas sprang up and escorted them to the graveside. Beatrice was crying openly. Her heels were sinking into the rain-soaked earth and she was worried about the effect on her new hat. The floral tributes were removed from the coffin and laid out along the side of the path.

As prayers were said, the coffin was lowered into the deep hole, and at the words '*earth to earth, ashes to ashes, dust to dust*', Beatrice used the small brass shovel to cast some of the soggy soil turned up by the gravediggers on to the descending coffin.

When the service ended, the mourners lost little time in getting out of the rain. Patsy stood looking down on the coffin far below and thinking what a terrible end it was for her father. She plucked one long-stemmed bronze rose from the bunch on the path and cast it down on the coffin to say her last goodbye to him. Her mother was waiting impatiently for her at the church gate. Patsy took her arm and the mourners filed past and offered their condolences. Patsy had to introduce one or two to her mother.

'You remember Mr Bentley, don't you, Mum?'

'No, I don't believe . . .'

'We went to his flat for tea last Boxing Day,' Patsy prompted.

'I was very fond of Hubert,' Mr Bentley said gently.

Patsy knew Bill Bentley quite well. He had a similar small garment factory within a short walking distance of their own and as a child Dad used to take her by the hand and they'd stroll up to see him. The men would have a smoke and a cup of tea, and the girls in his sewing room would make a fuss of her. When she had a birthday, Bill Bentley would give her a penny for every year she'd lived. Dad counted him a friend.

He looked old and very much overweight. 'I'm so sorry, Patsy,' he said, patting her on the shoulder. 'Such a terrible way for your dad to go. I'm going to miss the chats we used to have over a pot of tea.' A podgy hand shook her mother's and she invited him to take refreshments in their old flat.

As Mrs Stansfield poured cups of tea for the guests, Patsy could see her mother was acutely uncomfortable. She was barely in control of her tears and when a second person asked where Barney was, she broke down. 'Take me home,' she said to Patsy. 'This is a party; it's no place for me. I want peace to remember Hubert.'

Patsy hadn't even finished her first cup of tea and felt it was too soon for them both to go. She considered walking her mother home and coming back.

Bill Bentley came to her rescue. 'Mrs Rushton,' he put down his half eaten sandwich. 'Let me run you home in my car. This is too much for you today.'

'I'll be home soon,' Patsy told her. 'I'll not stay very long. Thank you, Bill, we'll both be grateful. You will come back?'

Patsy was glad to have the funeral behind her. The next morning she rode her bike down to the workroom and told Tim she was going over to Liverpool to see Mrs Denning in Wetherall's workroom. It was nearer to do that and walk across the road to catch the train from Birkenhead North Station than walk from home through the park to Birkenhead Park Station.

Last night she'd had another little weep in bed and her mind teemed with lists of things she had to do. One of the most important was to end her apprenticeship and take control of the workshop now that she knew Dad definitely wouldn't be coming back. She got off the train in Liverpool and from there it was a short walk to Wetherall's.

She'd been doing it twice a day and hardly looking at her surroundings, but today, when she was passing a large second-hand car showroom, she couldn't help but notice that there was a Morris Eight offered for sale. It looked exactly the same as Dad's and, like his, it was a 1936 model. She paused to look at the price card. One hundred and twenty pounds! By rights it was Mum's car now, Barney never should have taken it, and the way things were looking, Mum might well be grateful for a sum like that.

Patsy thought it would help to see the people she used to work with and the familiar workroom, but it brought a lump to her throat. She'd been happy both here and at home over the last three years. The people she'd worked with had heard of her trouble and several gave her a sympathetic hug.

'There was a piece in the *Echo* about your father's disappearance,' she was told. 'An awful thing to happen.'

By the time she saw Mrs Denning, it was all Patsy could do to hold back her tears. Mrs Denning ushered her into her office and sat her down. 'You poor child, you must be at the end of your tether.' She was a motherly woman with a lot of frizzy grey hair. 'You can't be thinking of coming back to work?'

Patsy sniffed and shook her head. 'No. You know my father had his own business, a small garments factory making women's clothes? I'll have to run it now. I came to ask a favour. Could I leave without working out my notice so I can get on with it?'

She found her boss very understanding. Patsy went on to tell her about being asked to identify a body that had been washed up on the Welsh coast, and how it had turned out to be her father.

A cup of tea appeared in front of her. She sipped it and went on to recount the horror of believing he must have killed himself because of having insufficient work to keep his workshop running.

'I really need to find more orders to keep our business going.'

The tears were rolling down her face by this time but she went on to tell Mrs Denning that her mother was overcome by grief and loss and was unable to help her. And that her brother Barney had disappeared after getting her friend's sister pregnant. 'There seems to be no end to our trouble, and I don't know where to start.'

'Of course you can leave straight away,' Mrs Denning told Patsy. 'And there's one thing I can help you with. Come and see what we're working on now.'

Patsy followed her to the cutting-out room. There were rolls of superfine khaki cloth piled everywhere. 'The thought of another war is terrifying,' Mrs Denning said, 'but it's bringing us big orders. We're making dress uniforms for army officers.'

It took Patsy a few moments to realise what that could mean for her business. 'We couldn't do fine tailoring like you do here.'

'No, but the government is gearing up for war. Uniforms of every sort will be needed, for the Civil Defence and for the women's services. I'm told that for some uniforms, the material will be cut out by machine and will only need sewing up. There's a whole new market opening up. I'm sure you'll be able to get orders from there.'

'It's a market we hadn't thought of, but I certainly will

now.' Patsy was pumping her hand. 'Thank you, thank you, you must be right. I'll be forever grateful if I can get orders for uniforms. It could be our salvation.'

That banished her feeling of gloom. She went back on the train with the name, address and telephone number of the person who had handled the order Wetherall's had received. She kept opening her handbag to re-read what Mrs Denning had written: Mr Rupert Alderman. She couldn't wait to tell Tim and find out if they could get a work order.

That afternoon, Patsy sat at her father's desk staring at the phone. She was scared of ringing the number, too much hung on it. She thought of asking Tim to do it, but no, Dad would have done it himself, and if she was going to take his place she would have to do it. Holding her breath and full of trepidation, she made herself lift the receiver and heard the phone ringing in some distant office.

When she got through to Mr Alderman, he seemed pleased to hear that she was seeking work orders. He explained that he was a local civilian agent acting on behalf of the War Office and that he would need to visit her premises and see that the standard of work being turned out would meet their require-ments. He made an appointment to come three days hence.

Tim waltzed her round the office when she told him. 'You've done it, Patsy. This could save your business. Your dad would be proud of you. We're all proud of you.'

They went to the sewing room to tell the girls and ask them to do their best work because it was going to be inspected. Patsy felt she could see a way out of their problems after all.

Patsy felt her life had turned a corner. Madge Worthington had taken Barney's place in the house and was making herself useful in a way he never had. Beatrice had seemed to resent her at first, but Madge had kept her part-time job and insisted on paying for her keep. In her time off, she took Beatrice shopping for food and for little walks in nearby Birkenhead Park. She made meals and helped tidy up.

'If I keep busy, it helps to take my mind off my troubles,' she told them. They both knew she was worried stiff about what the future would bring.

Beatrice took to Madge and was soon reconciled to her presence in the house. 'Have you got your layette ready?' she asked her. 'I could be knitting bootees and a bonnet for you.'

'It's not up to me to provide clothes for it,' she told them defensively. 'I'm having it adopted.'

'Are you sure that's what you want?' Beatrice asked her.

Madge choked out, 'I don't have much choice in the matter. I can't work and look after a baby. Dad said I could come home but I wasn't even to ask if I could bring a bastard child.'

'You'll go back home afterwards?' Patsy asked.

She shook her head. 'I don't want to. Dad'll never let me forget this. Perhaps I'll join up. If I could find a job and somewhere to live as well, I'd jump at it. It would get me away from him, wouldn't it?'

'It would give you a very different life, probably a good thing for you.'

As the weeks went on, the café where Madge had found her summer job was slowly reducing staff and would close completely at the end of September. The owner was keeping her on to the end because she knew of her difficulties and that Madge was in need of the money.

On the day Madge came home from work for the last time she ran straight upstairs and hid herself in her bedroom. Patsy was in the kitchen with her mother helping her get their evening meal ready. They both knew that was unusual behaviour for Madge.

'Can you hear her crying?' Patsy asked in dismay. 'What can we do? She must be feeling terrible.'

'Go up to her,' Beatrice said. 'You can comfort her better than I can.'

Patsy ran up and knocked on her door. 'Madge, I know you're upset, I want to come in.'

When Patsy went in, Madge lifted her face from her pillow. Her eyes were red and her cheeks wet. 'I didn't want you to see me like this,' she sobbed. 'When you're doing so much for me, it makes me seem ungrateful.'

'No it doesn't. Come here.' Patsy sat on the bed and pulled Madge nearer so she could put her arms round her. 'I know you must be feeling low right now.'

'I feel so fat and ugly,' she wailed. 'Nobody wants anything to do with me.'

'I do and even Mum's come round, she likes having you here.'

'But Barney's cast me off and so has my family.'

'Not all your family,' Patsy reminded her. 'Sheila and John are still coming round to take you out, and your mother isn't happy about what your father's done. Once you've had this baby you'll be able to put it all behind you.'

'I don't think I ever will.' She hid her face on Patsy's shoulder in a storm of tears.

Patsy patted her back as though she was a child. 'We'll help all we can, Madge. You mustn't worry.'

'You and your mother have been marvellous about it,' she choked.

'Your baby is related to us. We feel very much involved. I'll be an aunt and Mum a grandmother. We're so sorry Barney's treated you like this. To disappear and leave you to fend for yourself is despicable.'

'Your mother – I think she forgives him. She makes excuses for him.'

'Perhaps, but we both want to do all we can to help you.'

Madge looked up, her dark eyes swimming with tears, her voice thick with emotion. 'I loved Barney. I trusted him,' she said. 'I never thought for one moment he'd do this to me. He promised to look after me, promised to marry me.'

Patsy shuddered, she'd always been wary of relying on Barney to do anything, but even so . . .

'Don't ever let a boyfriend do this to you.' Madge's lips set into a hard line. 'Get the wedding ring on your finger first. The shame and disgrace makes me feel awful. Believe me, any pleasure you get is short-lived and it's never worth the agony of not knowing what's going to happen or how you're going to cope.'

It took Madge a long time to control her tears. 'There's a saying: marriage is the price decent men pay to have sex and sex is the price women have to pay to get a husband.'

Patsy smiled. 'That's a bit cynical. If you'd married Barney, I think you might have paid an even greater price. You'd probably have had to look after him for the rest of your life.'

Madge managed a watery smile.

'Come on, wash your face and let's go downstairs. Mum's making dinner, it'll all be ready now.'

'There you are,' Beatrice said as they went down. 'I was just about to give you a call.' She started dishing up the meal.

'Sorry if I've kept you waiting,' Madge said. 'Patsy's been trying to straighten me out.'

'I'm glad she's succeeded.'

'She hasn't, but she's consoled me by reminding me I have friends.' Madge helped carry the steaming plates to the dining room and they all sat down.

'What I've done can't be straightened out that easily,' she said quietly. 'I'm bringing another person into the world. His father doesn't want him and I can't keep him because I can't both work and look after him. No child deserves to be an unwanted child, does it? He'll be up for adoption. I've agreed to give him away to strangers.'

'I knew that would bother you.' Beatrice had stopped eating. 'It's been bothering me.'

'He'll go to somebody who wants him,' Patsy said.

'But I'll not see him again.' Madge choked back a sob. 'I'll know nothing about him. To me, he'll always be on my conscience, a baby starting life at a disadvantage, a baby who should never have been born.'

'Don't say that!' Patsy was aghast. 'He could have a very happy childhood.'

'We all need love, Patsy.' Madge put down her knife and fork. 'Every child does to grow up well-balanced and happy. He'll know his parents didn't want him.'

'I want him,' Beatrice broke in suddenly. 'I'm his grandmother. There's no need to give him away to strangers. I'll bring him up.'

Madge's jaw dropped open and there was a moment's dead silence.

Patsy recovered first. 'It would be a big undertaking, Mum, to bring up another child,' she said gently. She had a thousand reservations. 'D'you feel you'd be up to it?'

Beatrice was stiff with determination. 'Of course I'm up to it. I'm only forty-five. Lots of women of my age are bringing up children.' She turned to Madge, 'What do you say? There's no reason why I shouldn't have him, is there? Would you want me to bring your baby up?'

Patsy could see bewilderment, relief, indecision and confusion fleeting across Madge's face. 'I've told them at the mother and baby home that I want to have it adopted.'

'But you can change your mind, can't you? You haven't signed any papers?'

'No.'

'You could come here and see him as often as you want, hold him, push him out in his pram. He'd grow up knowing his mother and be brought up as part of his own family.'

Patsy said, 'But you would have all the work of feeding him, caring for him.'

'That's what I want to do. Look after him, bring him up. He would give me a reason to . . .'

Understanding was dawning on Patsy. 'Mum is missing Barney dreadfully,' she explained. 'A new baby would help fill the gap in her life. He's our flesh and blood, after all. Think it over, Madge.'

'Yes, think it over. I'd love to have Barney's baby. I've felt bereft since he disappeared. I do hope it's a boy.' Beatrice sounded hopeful. 'I can't bear the thought of him going to strangers.'

'I don't know whether I'll be able to pay anything towards his keep,' Madge stammered. 'I'll try but . . .'

Patsy smiled. 'You won't need to. Our business is picking up. The baby will have a ready-made family here, so it won't cost the earth. You'll be able to stay in touch and see your baby grow up.'

'I'll be happy to adopt him legally if that's what you want, if that would bring you peace of mind.' Beatrice's eyes were shining, her cheeks were scarlet. 'You could even decide against going to the mother and baby home. You could stay here with us and have the baby in the local maternity hospital.'

'No, I can't batten on you like that. You've already done so much for me, you've been so kind.'

'You must think this over carefully, Madge, before you say anything. Take your time. Let us know when you've made up your mind.'

Patsy knew her mother wanted to do her best for Madge, and also do what Barney should have done, but most of all she really wanted to take care of this baby. It had to be the best thing for everybody. Except possibly for herself. Patsy knew her mother too well. Was she wrong to be afraid that Mum would find it too much? She'd be taking on a big responsibility.

The next morning, Beatrice went into town and bought four ounces of white baby wool to make a matinee coat and bonnet.

Days passed and every evening Beatrice got out her knitting and the matinee coat began to grow. Patsy knew her impatience to have an answer was increasing too. At the same time, she could see Madge growing more stressed.

On Sunday, the three of them spent the evening together listening to a play on the wireless to the accompanying click of Beatrice's needles.

When the programme finished and a string quartet began to play, Madge said, 'I'm sorry, Mrs Rushton, I know you're waiting for an answer from me. I know the baby would be better off with you than with strangers but the more I think about it, the more mixed up I feel. I've been trying to make up my mind but I just can't. I don't feel in control of my life any more. Things are happening to me that I don't want, and I can't stop them.'

Patsy could see the tears welling in her eyes and wanted to comfort her. 'Don't worry, Madge . . .'

'If anything, I feel I should keep the baby myself though I know that will be impossible. I feel I should make decisions and plan for the future but I don't know what it will hold. I can't think . . . I know I'll eventually give birth, but it's as though there's a brick wall beyond that and I can't see over it. I can't even imagine . . .'

'We're asking too much,' Patsy said.

Madge nodded and blew her nose. 'I'll have to leave things as they are for the moment. Perhaps when I've had the baby, I'll be more myself and know what is best for us all.'

'We shouldn't have tried to press you,' Beatrice said haltingly. 'I got carried away by the thought of bringing up my grandchild but it's very sensible of you to wait and see how you feel when you have the child in your arms.'

Patsy got up and gave Madge a hug. 'You go up to bed,' she told her. 'I'm going to make the cocoa. I'll bring some up to you.'

'Goodnight, Madge,' Beatrice said. 'I know things are difficult for you.'

Patsy had now settled in to working full time in the workshop. She'd been nervous to start with about whether the seamstresses would accept her taking over her father's duties. They were mostly of a much older generation and they'd known her as a child.

In the office she let her worries out to Tim. 'I must seem a slip of a girl to them, will they do what I ask of them?'

Tim laughed. 'That bothered me when I started, but your

dad led me into the sewing room and announced that I was to be his assistant and they must take note of all I said and carry out my instructions.'

'I'm sure he'd do that for me too if he was still here.' Patsy pulled a face.

'It didn't stop them arguing that they knew an easier way to work or insisting they should do it their way.'

'That's mutiny! What did you do then?'

'I said Mr Rushton wouldn't put up with all this messing about and I'm not going to either. You are to do the job exactly as I've just told you. I got out as fast as I could after that and hid in the office. I needn't have worried, the work was always done as I'd directed.'

'Thanks, I must remember that.'

'It didn't stop them shouting out ribald comments, of course, but I didn't mind that. There's no malice in them.'

'Perhaps they'll be kinder to me,' Patsy said hopefully.

She felt things were settling down. In countless ways she still missed her father, and so it seemed did many of the staff. They spoke of him often with genuine affection.

Patsy prepared for Rupert Alderman's visit, priming the girls and laying out samples of the recent work they'd done. On the morning he was expected, she could feel the tension in the air, they all knew how important it was to be given this contract. To Patsy, it meant the business could survive and she'd earn an income to support herself and her mother. For the staff it meant continued employment. They were all on edge; Patsy was up and down from her desk, unable to concentrate on anything.

'You're like a cat on hot bricks,' Tim told her. She was watching from the window and saw the agent arrive.

Tim ran down to meet him. He showed him into their office and then went out, shutting the door quietly behind him. Patsy had expected an older man. Mr Alderman came towards her with his hand outstretched. He seemed to be in his mid to late twenties.

Patsy shook it. 'Please sit down, Mr Alderman,' she said. His dark eyes levelled with hers and held her gaze; confidence shone out of them. He was very good-looking with tightly curling dark hair cut short, with little curls hanging over his forehead. He was tall and held himself well; his expensive suit looked as though it had been tailored for him. He had a wide smile, perfect teeth and an unusual cleft in his chin.

She found herself talking too fast, saying much more than she'd intended. She told him about her father's death and that she'd felt catapulted into running his business.

'Mrs Denning told me.' He smiled and suddenly he seemed friendlier. 'She said you wished to tender for a government contract to make uniforms for the forces.'

'Yes. I'm afraid I don't know how to go about it.'

'Don't worry about that, I'll help you.' Again he smiled.

Patsy told him about the sort of work they did. About what she'd hoped to do, design and make up garments ready to sell straight to shops so she could cut out the middlemen.

'Would you like to come and see our set-up and what we're making at the moment?'

She felt more relaxed once she got him into the sewing room. The overhead belt-driven power system buzzed. Every sewing-machine needle danced up and down, every head was bent over its work.

'You seem busy,' he said.

'Yes, we're working on a largish order from British Home Stores at the moment.' She took him to examine the garments they'd finished and pointed out the high standard of the work.

'Yes, very well-finished,' he agreed and held up a child's blue gingham dress. 'Not tailoring, I see.'

'No, we don't do much of that, though we did make a few blazers for children in the spring.'

'You specialise in children's wear?'

'No, it's mostly for women. We do shirts for men occasionally, and curtains, but it's whatever work we can get.'

'Good, I can get you plenty of work.'

Patsy warmed to him. 'Shall we go back to the office? It's difficult to talk above the noise here. What about a cup of tea?'

'Thank you,' he said.

Patsy thought things were going well. Once back at her desk, he took some forms from his briefcase and pushed them in front of her.

'I can't help you cut out the middlemen, but I can find you all the work you can handle. It will be military uniforms of one sort or another. Garments will have to be made exactly to the pattern, no variations of any sort are allowed.'

'I understand the need for that.'

'Good. We have the cloth dyed and made up to order, and these days we are having some of our garments, like shirts, cut out in multiples by machine. Would you be happy to receive garments cut out and ready to seam up?'

'Yes, I don't see why not.'

'Each comes with buttons that you'll have to stitch on and a size tag to fix centre neck. We supply the thread too. Do you have a machine for sewing buttons on?'

'Yes we have. What would I earn for making up each shirt?'

Rupert Alderman pushed one of the forms in front of her. The prices were laid out clearly and were surprisingly generous. 'As you can see, we price them by the hundred.'

He was filling up another form on her behalf and telling her he thought it would suit her staff to start on shirts and underwear, as that was closer to the work they were already turning out.

'How would it be if I sent you three hundred shirts to see how you get on?' He pushed that form towards her. 'Sign on the bottom,' he said. 'The work has to be of a good standard.'

That didn't faze Patsy. Dad had never allowed sub-standard work to go out.

'The girls will get quicker as they get used to running up the same garment,' he said. 'The country is going to need a lot of military uniforms.'

'Yes, I heard on the wireless this morning that it seems conscription is coming.'

'I hope not yet.' He laughed and his gaze held hers again. 'We need time to get organised, we don't want too many soldiers until we've got uniforms for them.'

Patsy was delighted with the outcome. 'Thank you, Mr Alderman.'

'You must call me Rupert. I feel we're going to get along well together.'

'Patsy,' she said faintly.

He was repacking his briefcase. 'I'm hungry,' he said. 'How about coming out for a spot of lunch to celebrate your first contract?'

'Thank you, that's very kind, but—'

'Do you know of somewhere nice to go?'

'No . . .' Patsy was at a loss. 'There are no restaurants round here, nothing fancy. There's a fish and chip shop, that's all. Mostly we bring sandwiches to have with a bowl of soup made here in the canteen. There'll be plenty of soup and you can share my sandwiches. Come on, I've got cheese and lettuce today.'

'I can't possibly eat your sandwiches.' She could see she'd embarrassed him. 'You'll be hungry all afternoon.'

'Of course you can, we keep biscuits here. Sometimes as a treat we send out for cakes or . . . Shall I ask somebody to run out for a couple of pork pies? That'll more than fill us.'

'All right,' he said, 'provided you let me pay.'

She ran down to the workshop and spoke to Tim. He said, 'I'll ask Vera to go.'

Patsy took Rupert upstairs to the flat, where she put on the kettle and set her sandwiches on a plate on the living-room table. Vera brought the pies. Martha Dixon brought up two bowls of soup and made them a pot of tea. Recently, Patsy had been eating lunch up here with Tim, but today he stayed out of the way.

'Nice to have space and privacy like this,' Rupert said.

Patsy told him her family had lived here for many years. Rupert said he lived in a bachelor flat that was smaller than this over in Blundellsands on the outskirts of Liverpool. He talked of the beach and restaurants within easy walk. All the time, his eyes were playing with hers. She thought he was attracted to her and it was sending little thrills of excitement down her spine.

After an enjoyable hour in his company, he said he had another appointment to keep. When she went down to see him out, she had a closer look at the two-seater car she'd seen pull in outside their front door. It proved to be the latest model Jaguar. It had been Barney's ambition to own an open two-seater like this, but even he had thought of it as pie in the sky.

'Your first consignment of work should be here next week,' he told her. 'I'll come and see you again a few days after that.

Next time I'll take you out to lunch. There'll be restaurants in Birkenhead.'

Patsy raced back up to the flat, wanting to be alone. She was fizzing inside, boiling over with joy that it seemed with one stroke the business would be turned round. They'd all been so worried that there wasn't enough work available. If only Dad were here to witness this!

But it wasn't just that. Rupert Alderman had set her emotions on fire, and left her reeling from the impact. She was in no doubt as to the cause. She liked him, was attracted to him and she thought he felt the same about her. She'd never really had a boyfriend before, not really. She'd gone to dances with Sheila and her brother John, who was keen on ballroom dancing and said she was good at it too. He'd even taken her to the pictures by herself, but he'd never lit any flames within her as Rupert had.

Tim, too, had singled her out at some church outing. They'd had a good time that day but Tim was just a friend. Rupert touched her senses, something about him promised much more. Everything in her life had taken a positive turn, she could hardly believe it. Now the future was suddenly brighter, she was going to push the agony of the last few months behind her.

CHAPTER EIGHT

THE NEXT MORNING PATSY went to work with a spring in her step, knowing that to make a real success of Dad's business was now within her grasp. Dad had often told her she'd be able to manage it. He'd been trying to build her confidence, of course, but thinking about her father brought her memories alive. She knew there was one thing he would want her to do, so she pulled on her coat, got out her bike again and rode up to see Bill Bentley.

She found the lights switched off in his sewing room and all the machines idle. He was at his desk in his cramped office and looked the picture of misery.

'How are you, Mr Bentley?' she asked. He was older than Dad, overweight and now looked stiff and defeated.

'These are very difficult days.' He sighed. 'Life isn't easy, it's almost impossible to find enough work to keep going. I've had to put my girls on a three-day week. I don't suppose you're doing any better.'

'Yes I am, I'm doing wonderfully well.' She smiled and told him how she'd found all the work she wanted making military uniforms. 'Enough work to keep us all busy,' she said. 'The country's gearing up for war.'

She told him about Rupert, his opinions and some of the facts she'd learned from him. She'd brought along an official letter she'd received from him giving the address of his main office, together with their telephone number. 'Ring them,' she urged. 'They'll be glad to give you work too.'

'Really?'

'Yes, conscription is coming and the government has to have uniforms ready.'

He leapt up and crushed Patsy to him in a great bear hug, a huge smile lighting up his podgy face.

'Aren't you a one? If this works out I shall be undyingly grateful and so will my staff. Unlimited work, you say? It's right kind of you to think of me.'

'My dad was fond of you,' she told him. 'He told me you used to help him.'

'We helped each other where we could. We used to watch each other's backs. Now his little girl is helping me, he'd be right proud of you.'

Ten days later, Patsy and Tim were eating their lunch when Gladys showed Bill Bentley up to the flat. He looked very much better, he had colour in his face and his step was lighter.

'I've come to thank you,' he told Patsy. 'It's all happening so quickly for me. We had our first visit from the Ministry of Defence agent on the following Tuesday.'

'Yes,' Patsy said. 'Rupert came here that evening.'

'Rupert Alderman is our agent too,' Tim explained. 'I think he comes more often than the business requires. He's been paying court to Patsy since he first set eyes on her.'

'He seems a nice lad, you could do worse, Patsy.'

She let that pass. She felt it was too soon to talk about Rupert being her boyfriend; he had taken her out to lunch and they were just getting to know each other.

'Mr Alderman came to my place to make sure we were capable of doing the work he wanted and he drew up my contract. But on Friday he brought another man to see me called George Miller. He's going to be my agent.'

'Odd that you should have a different agent when our workshops are so close,' Patsy said.

Bill beamed at her. 'He's about my age. I don't think you'd want him paying court, Patsy. In fact he mentioned he has three sons he's afraid will be called up if war should come. Anyway, I've signed my contract and we've taken our first delivery of sailor's shirts to seam up. Couldn't be easier work, the girls like it.'

'We've all fallen on our feet.' Patsy smiled. 'Have a cup of tea with us?'

'No thanks, I need to get back, I'm busy at last. I'll be grateful to you for ever, Patsy.'

'You were Dad's friend,' she said. 'He'd have been cross with me if I hadn't spread the news to you.'

When he'd gone, Tim pulled a face and said, 'Looks as though Rupert Alderman was so struck with you, he couldn't bear to hand you over to this other fellow.'

Patsy hoped he was right.

Preparations for war were gathering speed. Patsy heard that Rosemary Worthington had telephoned Beatrice and invited her to attend the WVS meetings and help the war effort. But Beatrice had taken against Madge's mother. She thought she should never have agreed to Madge being put out of her home. She told Mrs Worthington she already had too much to do to take on any more, though she knew she could have found time.

Madge was due to move into the mother and baby home soon and Patsy could see she was growing more anxious about it.

On her last day with them, Madge said, 'You've both been very good to me. Thanks for everything.'

'Having you here has been good for us,' Patsy said. 'We've got over a bad patch together. Having you here cheered us up.'

That evening, Sheila came round and they all went to see Margaret Lockwood and Michael Redgrave in Hitchcock's *The Lady Vanishes*. They had cocoa and cake when they returned home, and Sheila stayed for it. It was quite a jolly little party.

The next morning, Madge packed her suitcase, stripped her bed and took the bus to the mother and baby home on her own. She said that was what she wanted to do.

Over the following weeks, Patsy was thrilled at the way things were going in the workshop. They had as much work as they could cope with. Tim brought the account books to her desk to show her the profit they were beginning to make.

'This situation will go on,' he said. 'Since Hitler's forces streamed across the Austrian border and seized control of that country in March, everybody says it's only a matter of time before this country is at war. Uniforms are going to be needed in ever growing numbers. You should think of expanding this business,' he said. 'Not only is that in your own interests, but in the interests of our country too.'

Patsy thought about it. 'I've taken on two more girls to make up for those that left, but our power system will take three more sewing machines. I'm going to order them now, and we'll advertise for three more girls.'

'You've made the business profitable.' Tim grinned at her. 'Congratulations. Your dad would be proud of you.'

'He could have done it too,' she said. 'This war is going to change everything.'

'Will three more machines be enough?'

'Three more is all we'll be able to fit in the workroom.' Patsy said. 'We'd have space in the cutting-out room for more, but for the time being I'll leave it at three. It feels great to be in this position.'

It also felt marvellous that she'd met Rupert Alderman in this way and he'd helped her do it. He was coming to see her again tomorrow and he'd invited her out to lunch.

'This time we'll push the boat out,' he'd said. Patsy could think of nothing else. She'd wash her hair tonight as she wanted to look her best, but what should she wear?

She went to work the next morning wearing her best blue dress. Tim complimented her on her smart appearance. 'Is it today Rupert Alderman is coming?' he asked.

She smiled. 'He's taking me out to lunch.'

She could see Tim didn't want them to become too friendly. She'd sensed he was holding back when Rupert had been in the office last time.

Rupert arrived smartly dressed in his grey business suit, smiling broadly over the big bunch of flowers he'd brought for her. He had the confident manner of one who knows exactly what to do in any situation. He chatted to Tim while she put the flowers in water and brought the vase back to her desk.

Rupert's gaze met and held hers, making her heart turn over. 'I've booked a table at the Queen's Hotel,' he said. 'I'm told it's quite good. Have you been before?'

'No.' Her family hardly ever ate out, and even if they did, it would be tea and cakes in a café to celebrate a birthday.

'Let's go straight away,' he said. 'We can talk over lunch. I can check the work you've done when I bring you back, though I know I hardly need to.'

He escorted her down to his car and opened the passenger door for her. As she got in, his hand brushed hers and she felt a thrill run up her arm.

She was fascinated by the formality of lunch at the Queen's. She had a glass of wine and found the food delicious. It felt like high living. Words were spilling out of her. She told him she was eighteen and he seemed surprised.

'You look young,' he said, 'but you seem too efficient at the job and too sophisticated away from it to be eighteen. I thought you were older.'

That pleased her.

The time went by in a flash though Patsy was aware their lunch had taken the best part of two hours. The girls would have gone back to their machines ages ago. It made her feel guilty that she'd been enjoying herself.

On the return journey, she sat back in the small bucket seat and watched Rupert drive, saw how he concentrated on the road. She knew he must have been conscious of her gaze because he turned briefly and gave her a fleeting smile.

'I have a few forms to fill in for the Ministry,' he told her. 'About checking the standard of work you turn out.'

'You did that last time, didn't you?'

'I did, and it was excellent.' He laughed. 'But I have to do it every time I visit. I'm an agent for the Ministry of Defence. Everything has to be done by the book.'

Patsy took him to the sewing room and introduced him to old Arthur Moffat who was pressing the finished garments and packing them in boxes. 'Arthur trained as a tailor. He's been in charge of the cutting room for years, but now with your work . . .'

'You're doing me out of a job, mister,' he told Rupert.

'And this is Gladys, she specialised in cutting out too.'

'You're not thinking of laying me off, are you, Patsy? I've been right scared that you might. Arthur has too.'

'No, Gladys, certainly not. You're a good seamstress too. Anyway, both you and Arthur know how to turn your hands to everything. Somebody has to do the pressing and packing and oversee things generally.'

Patsy moved on down the line of sewing machines. All the time, Rupert was picking up completed garments and examining them. Now he paused behind Ida who was expertly guiding the foot of her machine along a seam. He patted her on the shoulder. 'You're the fastest worker in Birkenhead. Your stitching is top notch too.' He turned to Patsy. 'Right, I've seen all I need down here. Can we go back to your office?'

Once the door was shut Rupert slid his briefcase on to her desk and walked towards her. Patsy saw the look of longing in his eyes and suddenly he swept her into his arms to kiss her full on the mouth. Patsy clung to him, feeling she was in heaven.

'I've wanted to do that since I first saw you,' he murmured and went on showering butterfly kisses all over her face.

Patsy's heart raced. Rupert was a lovely person, really lovely.

'But I'll have to go,' he told her. 'I have an appointment in Liverpool. I should have been there fifteen minutes ago.'

'I thought you had forms that had to be filled in,' she said.

He smiled. 'Tonight will be soon enough. I've got better things to do when I'm with you.' He dropped a final kiss on the end of her nose.

'Thank you for the lunch, I did enjoy it,' she said.

'So did I, especially the company. Bye bye.'

It took a long time for Patsy's heart rate to slow down, and she couldn't concentrate all afternoon. Rupert filled her mind. She daydreamed about him for the rest of the afternoon and knew she was falling in love. He was exactly the sort of man of whom her mother would approve.

The future had become golden, both as regards the business and on a personal level. Patsy had never felt happier, her life seemed to have taken wings.

Tim felt hot with anger and stayed out in the yard checking in the delivery of work that Rupert had organised. He'd seen Patsy with him in the sewing room, smiling up at him, her eyes dancing. His anger made no sense, he'd been delighted at what Rupert was doing for the business and everybody working in it.

He couldn't admit he didn't want Patsy to feel such shining happiness. He didn't want to deny her anything; rather, he wanted to give her the world. Rupert was the problem, he couldn't compete with him. Rupert was handsome enough to turn any girl's head. He had a good job, a smart car and plenty of money. Rupert was sophisticated, he knew how to treat a girl, take her to restaurants and theatres.

Patsy usually told Tim where they went and what they did, and he wanted to know but it went through him all the same because he knew he couldn't entertain her like that. Tim felt he had nothing to offer a girl like Patsy; she employed him. He put himself out to do his very best for her, but it was work. Why should she look to him for anything more?

Whenever Tim saw Rupert, heard his pleasant middle-class voice, it made this monster grow inside him. How could he admit to feeling such jealousy? He wanted to be everything to Patsy, he wanted her to love him. He couldn't remember a time when he hadn't been in love with her.

CHAPTER NINE

PATSY WAS TRYING TO work at her office desk but there was more noise from the sewing room than usual. The girls squabbled like magpies and were always heckling each other. No, most of the noise was coming from the canteen as the mid-morning cup of tea was being served. Dad had allowed an official fifteen-minute break morning and afternoon and provided cups of tea and told them to leave their machines. The last thing he needed was food and drink spilled on the garments they were making.

Dad had felt he had to keep his workers happy. 'They'll do twice the work if they think you're meeting them halfway,' he'd told Patsy. 'Also, the human body needs a break every so often.' He paid them for that daily half hour as though they were working.

'They need refuelling too,' Dad had believed and had instructed Martha Dixon who was in charge of the canteen to make soup to serve in the dinner hour. Dad had bought a fish kettle that straddled two burners on the stove, ordered bones and meat scraps from a local butcher and vegetables from the market to be delivered regularly and charged his girls halfpenny a bowl for it.

'They appreciate it if they have to pay,' he told Patsy. 'It's no good giving it to them for nothing.' Even so, she'd couldn't help but hear the meat referred to as dog meat and the vegetables as over-ripe rubbish thrown away by the market stalls. Dad had smiled when she told him that. 'It's just their way. It doesn't mean they don't appreciate what I offer. Our girls are sometimes the only member of the family in work, and yet they go hungry themselves, preferring to feed their children and husbands. As far as I'm concerned, it's not a kindness,' Dad had gone on gruffly. 'It's good business practice, I get more out of them if they're fed.'

Patsy could pick out the nasal tones of Martha Dixon trying to curb their impatience, but Vera Cliffe had a more strident voice that could cover any other. Patsy sighed, she was holding forth on some grievance. Dad's attitude had been paternalistic, but that was not something she could adopt. They treated her and Tim as though they were just out of napkins.

Tim said, 'Your dad told me I had to be strong with them, and you must be even stronger. They'll expect you to know how to manage everything, and I wouldn't change anything your dad started unless it's absolutely vital. They thought the sun shone out of him.'

She went to have a word with them and the heckling argument stopped as soon as they saw her.

Gladys told her afterwards that Mrs Dixon had put more soup in some bowls than in others and some had felt short-changed. 'Just a storm in a teacup.' She laughed. 'And Mrs Dixon has got the message.'

As the weeks passed, Patsy saw more and more of Rupert. He would often drive from Blundellsands when there was no need to check on the work she was doing. 'I just want to see you,' he told her. He was inviting her out for meals and to cinemas and theatres. The kisses he gave her afterwards set her on fire. His touch made her catch her breath and to be held close against him was pure delight. She told her mother about him and Beatrice suggested inviting him to Sunday tea so that they could meet.

'Thank you, I'll look forward to it,' he told Patsy. 'I feel I'm making progress now I'm invited to meet your family.'

Beatrice got out her embroidered tea cloth, her best china and made special cakes for the occasion. Rupert chatted in his easy fashion about how thrilled he was with his present job. He told them that he'd attended a well-known independent school, that his home was in Yorkshire and that his father was a professor at Sheffield University, teaching maths.

'When I got this job I decided to leave home and find a pad of my own,' he told her. 'Yorkshire is the heart of the woollen industry, and I have contracts with many firms there to manufacture cloth for uniforms. I decided to come to Lancashire because it's here that cotton is manufactured and cotton is needed for uniforms too.'

Beatrice thoroughly approved of him. 'He's a real gentleman,' she told her daughter afterwards. 'You're lucky to meet a man like him through your work. He'll be able to provide well for a wife. There aren't many like him round here.'

Patsy felt very lucky. Rupert made her feel special. She wanted to be with him all the time and when she wasn't, she thought about him. Soon Rupert admitted he preferred the privacy of the flat over the workroom to watching a film or a theatre show. 'I'd rather stay there with you than go out,' he said.

Patsy did too, but she pulled a face. 'It's all very shabby.'

'If that bothers you, it wouldn't take much to smarten it up,' he said, looking round. 'A coat of paint on the walls, new curtains, that sort of thing would make a world of difference.'

She mentioned it to Tim the following day. 'A good idea,' he said. 'It would be a shame to let the flat deteriorate. The lino under these carpet squares is in good condition. It's a very comfortable place to have lunch and we can talk over business problems in complete privacy.'

She knew he was right. Dad had done nothing to the place since they'd moved to Forest Road. Rupert worked out a colour scheme for her and she went out with Tim to buy paint and paper to redecorate. Gladys's husband Tom was an interior decorator. He had a full-time job but was always looking for work in the evenings and at weekends to earn a little extra. Patsy had heard the sad tale of how their daughter Esther had died of tuberculosis and they'd had to bring up their two grandchildren.

'Tom will be delighted to have the job as long as you aren't in too much of a hurry,' Gladys told her.

'There's no particular hurry,' Patsy said. 'What I want is a clean-up job and all this brown woodwork painted white to make the place seem lighter.'

Tom started work, and sometimes Gladys and her granddaughter came to help him.

'This is our Flo,' Gladys said. 'You know about my second family, don't you?'

'Yes. Hello, Flo, but I didn't realise you were now a grown-up young lady. My dad spoke of you as a child.'

'Our Flo is fifteen now and working. They all grow up eventually, thank goodness. Not that it brings any end to the problems.'

Flo looked pale and undersized to be fifteen years old.

'What sort of work do you do?' Patsy asked.

'She's been taken on as an apprentice at Headley's and she doesn't like it.'

'Oh dear,' Patsy said. 'Why not?'

'They aren't nice to me.'

'So you plan to be a tailor?'

'I did, but they say I'm too slow.'

'Slow at sewing?'

'Yes, they're always harrying me to get things finished.'

'Well, nobody can expect you to be as quick as your gran. She's been doing it for forty years or so and you're just starting.'

'They're on piecework at Headley's, you see,' Tom explained. 'The faster you work, the more you earn. Nobody has enough time for anything there.'

'I don't suppose,' Gladys was eyeing Patsy warily, 'you'd give her a job here? She isn't slow; she's a good kid really.'

The girl's large frightened eyes settled on Patsy's face. Patsy hardly knew what to say; Dad had seen Gladys as a bulwark of his business and would have given her almost anything.

'Well,' she said, 'we don't have an apprenticeship scheme, we're too small and we aren't specialised enough, so you'd be throwing away the year you've already served.'

'I know.' Gladys's chin wobbled. 'But she's very unhappy there. Here everybody is friendly, and puts themselves out to help each other. I'm sure the girls would show her what's what. Anyway, she can sew straight seams and generally make herself useful.'

'I'm sure you can, Flo.' She looked a poor helpless kid, but Patsy reminded herself that Flo was only two or three years younger than she was herself.

Gladys sighed. 'You'll bear our Flo in mind if you need another beginner?'

'Of course. Make yourselves some tea when you feel like it,' Patsy told her. 'You'll find tea and sugar in the kitchen, but there's only enough milk left for one cup each.'

'Thanks. Flo can pop home for more if we need it.'

* * *

A couple of weeks later, Patsy buttonholed Gladys. 'How is Flo? Is she still unhappy at Headley's?'

'Yes, very, but I make her stay because it's not easy to get jobs these days.'

'We're doing better here, Gladys, as I'm sure you've noticed, and perhaps we could do with another pair of hands. If Flo would like to come, I'd be able to offer her a job now.'

'Really? She'll jump at it.'

'Many would say she's better off where she is. Make sure she understands that it isn't an apprenticeship.'

'She knows the score all right, don't worry about that.'

'All right, bring her in to see me first thing on Monday morning.'

'Thanks, I will.'

'I hope she'll turn out like you and stay for years.'

The following Monday Gladys brought Flo to the office. Tim was at his desk just settling down to work. Flo's hair was still being cut by Gladys. Today it was held back by multiple Kirby grips, and she didn't look old enough to be at work.

'How long have you been working at Headley's?' Patsy asked her.

'Fifteen months,' Gladys answered for her. 'She'll have to give a week's notice before she can come.'

'That's all right.'

'She's not slow, I'd say she was quicker on the uptake than most, but she won't be able to make up a complete garment. Set in sleeves and all that.'

'I know, Gladys. I'm going to ask one of the girls to take you under her wing, Flo, and teach you to be a good seamstress.'

'Thank you, miss,' she whispered.

'I can do that,' Gladys said eagerly. 'I'll look after her.'

'No, I've decided it will be Vera Cliffe.'

'Not Vera . . .'

'Yes, better if it's not a relative.'

'But Vera can be a bit rough.'

Tim had recommended that Vera do it. 'She always stands up for the underdog,' he'd said. 'She's always sympathetic to those in trouble, though she doesn't get on with Gladys. Perhaps it'll improve their relationship.'

Patsy smiled from Gladys to Flo. 'Vera will decide which part of the garment you make up and will finish it off. We expect our garments made up to a very high standard, Flo, and if you know the work you've done is not exactly as it should be, if you make a mistake, you must unpick your work and do it over.'

'Our Flo doesn't make mistakes like that.' Gladys was indignant.

'We all make mistakes,' Tim put in gently, 'especially when we're doing something new.'

'I certainly did,' Patsy agreed. 'And there's nothing to be ashamed of, Flo, if you find you have, but you mustn't leave it and hope Vera won't notice.'

'No, miss.'

'If you're in any doubt, Vera will decide if it's good enough. And you must finish off seams securely and snip off all bits of thread.'

'I do, miss.'

'But what we really need here is someone to run our errands, help here, there and everywhere. We'd like you to help with the pressing and packing of work done, that sort of thing.'

'That's what I do at Headley's.'

'Yes, well, in other words we're looking for a general factotum.'

The girl's face was screwing up. 'I don't know what that means.'

'To start with, Flo, you're going to be at everyone's beck and call. We want a person who willingly turns her hand to anything.'

'Oh yes, I'll do that.'

'What about her wages?' Gladys put in.

'What are they paying you at Headley's?' Tim asked Flo.

Patsy had discussed this with him, and he'd told her she should have asked this before telling Gladys to bring the girl in. Fortunately it was a little less than their starting wage.

'We can offer you a little more,' Patsy said, quoting the figure, 'because this isn't a recognised apprenticeship, but we'll do our best to turn you into a good seamstress. I'm sure your gran will keep us to that.'

Soon the ceilings in the flat were all whiter than white again, and the old wallpaper replaced with what Rupert had helped Patsy to choose.

'You've rejuvenated the place,' Tim said one lunchtime as they moved from the dining table to the comfort of the three-piece suite to drink their tea. 'It's beginning to look quite smart.'

'I'm going to replace some of these furnishings too,' Patsy said. 'They're faded and shabby-looking.'

On his next visit, Rupert approved wholeheartedly of what had been done. 'You spend a lot of time here; you want it to look nice. You're lucky to have a place like this where you can entertain your friends in private. Anyway, you can afford it.' He smiled at her. 'You're earning good money.'

'The curtains look a little tired, don't they?'

'Limp and dreary,' he agreed.

'I'll find some nice material, something we both like and get Ida Jones to run them up for me. She's one of our most experienced seamstresses.'

Patsy began to dream of marriage. She found herself staring into the windows of jewellery shops to eye the displays of engagement rings. Rupert would be bound to want to buy her one, he was very generous. Should she choose a diamond? Some of the coloured stones were very pretty. A sapphire perhaps?

She had in mind to suggest to Rupert that they should make their first home in the flat after they were married. She thought he could work just as easily from Birkenhead as from Blundellsands. Not that he'd asked her yet, but he told her often now that he was in love with her and love and marriage went together, didn't they? Besides, they were spending more and more of the time they were together in each other's arms. He often let his fingers run through her pale gold hair.

'It's lovely, Patsy,' he told her, 'and it reaches halfway down your back, but wearing it loose like this makes you look more like a schoolgirl than the owner of a thriving business.' He wound a handful round her head. 'You'd look fantastic if you put it up.'

Patsy tried it that night when she was going to bed. She could see that it would suit her, but there was so much of it that the only way she could get it up would be to plait it first, and plaits twisted round her head was not the look Rupert had in mind. She would need to cut three inches or so off it to get it up in a sophisticated style.

When she told Tim she needed an hour off work to get her hair cut, he said, 'What do you want to cut it for? You have beautiful hair, it looks very nice as it is.'

But she wanted to please Rupert and when he said he

would come the following week and take her out to lunch, she made an appointment for that morning at the hairdresser's and decided she'd have it washed, cut and styled up in a bun on top of her head. When Rupert saw her, he said, 'You look marvellous, a real glamour girl. I love it.'

After they'd had lunch, they saw a carpet square in a shop window that they liked and he persuaded her to buy two identical ones to cover the lino in the living room. 'It's only the sofa and chairs that look shabby now,' he said.

Patsy laughed. 'I'm not going to replace them, it would cost far too much.'

'No need to,' he agreed. 'The springs are all in good condition. Loose covers would be all you need. I know of a firm quite close to here that would make them. I've put business their way.'

He walked her round to see samples of their work and they offered her a discount. Patsy decided she'd have it done. 'The flat will look fresh and clean and completely different.'

When she returned to work, Tim twirled her round and said he liked it too. 'It makes you look a very sophisticated young lady.'

The next morning, when she tried to get her hair back up into its bun, she found she hadn't the skill of the hairdresser. It took her a long time and it didn't look as good. Half of the bun fell down while she was having breakfast and, losing patience with it, she dashed back to her bedroom, took out all the pins and decided to wear it loose as she always had. That didn't look right either, it wasn't lying smoothly down her back.

She had to wet it in the bathroom and comb it through again. She was late getting to work that morning. Tim smiled when she told him why.

'You've got beautiful hair,' he told her. 'I like it better this way.'

'You didn't like it up in a big bun?'

'Yes, it suited you but it made you look older. Why make yourself look thirty when you're only twenty?'

Patsy laughed. 'Perhaps I'll be able to cope with a style like that when I am older.'

CHAPTER TEN

A T THE END OF the summer Barney had known, as had everybody else employed at the ice-cream factory, that his job would end. He'd tried hard to get another but with the end of the holiday season, half the population of Rhyl was looking for work.

Jeanie had shrugged her shoulders. 'This happens every year.'

'So what do you do?' He'd had a good time with Jeanie and Wanda, taken them out to pubs and to the seaside entertainments. He hadn't saved much.

'I stay here until Mum kicks me out; then I go to Liverpool. It's easier to get work there.'

'It's not that easy,' he told her. 'I've struggled for years to find a decent job on Merseyside but I never did manage it.'

'Something will turn up.' She smiled. 'It always does. We'll be all right here for another week or so. After all, Mum likes you and you've been treating her well all summer.'

'I'm her lodger.' Barney was afraid she'd treat him differently if he couldn't meet his weekly payment.

'You're my boyfriend too,' Jeanie said. 'That makes you almost one of the family. Couldn't we go to stay with your mum for a week or two? I'd like to meet your relatives.'

'No,' Barney said, thinking of the problems that could have been building up there since he'd left.

'Won't your mum be pleased to see you again after all this time?'

'I'd rather not,' he said shortly. He didn't want Jeanie to hear about Madge. Living there, they might come face to face with her and what could be more embarrassing than that? No, he couldn't risk taking Jeanie there. Mum and Patsy would pounce on her anyway, and give them both a rough time. He didn't want to face Mum and Patsy on his own either; they'd give him hell.

Now that Patsy was spending more time with Rupert, she was seeing less of Sheila but they still went to the pictures once a week and she kept her up to date with news about Madge.

She wasn't happy in the mother and baby home; it seemed none of the girls were. Only close family members were allowed to visit and the time was strictly limited to two hours on Sunday afternoons. Madge was keeping well but dreading the birth itself. Patsy knew she'd been given 13 October as the due date and that afternoon she rang the home and asked if Madge had had her baby. It seemed she had not.

Sheila told her a few days later that all was well. Madge had had a baby girl weighing seven pounds two ounces and both were well. The following day Patsy received a letter from Madge giving her the same news and saying she was going to call her Katrina. *Since I've held her in my arms I've decided I couldn't possibly part with her*, she wrote. *She's mine and I intend to keep her, come what may..*

'I rather expected this after what Madge said that Sunday night,' her mother said. 'I shall write and tell her that when she's discharged, if she has nowhere else to go, she's welcome to bring the baby here until she can get back on her feet.'

It took only a few days for Beatrice to receive a reply.

I'm very grateful for all you and Patsy have done for me. On Sunday, my mother brought Great-Aunt Grace to see me and Katrina. She is eighty-three and not in good health. She's reached the stage when she isn't able to get out much on her own, and says she needs someone to live with her to provide company and give her a hand with the household chores. She's asked me if I would like to do it and I jumped at the chance. She has a nice house in Bebington so I won't be all that far away. I feel very lucky because I'll be able to look after Katrina myself. I'll bring her to see you when I'm settled there.

Barney had begun to dither about the mess he'd left at home. He knew he'd treated Madge very badly, leaving her to face pregnancy on her own. During October he felt really churned up, his stomach was upset and he wasn't sleeping well. The date the baby was due was imprinted on his mind and as 13 October crept closer and closer, he agonised about Madge, wondering how she was coping.

What made it worse for Barney was that he had to keep it all to himself. The last thing he wanted was for Jeanie to find out. He gave her to understand he had a stomach bug.

He toyed with the idea of phoning Madge, but he didn't know whether she was still at home. She'd been afraid her father might kick her out when she could no longer hide her pregnancy, and by now that would have happened. The thought of speaking directly to her father or mother appalled him. Anyway, it was not the sort of thing he could apologise to Madge for and expect to be forgiven.

On the day the baby was due he'd been unable to think of anything else. He'd vomited twice and felt ready to die. He would have liked to know whether it was a girl or a boy and if mother and child were well.

He knew now he should never have turned tail and run, that had been most unwise. Barney was afraid he'd made a big mistake and bitterly regretted leaving home. Patsy must have been furious at being left to run the business. She was just his kid sister, he should have stayed and done that, but of course Dad could be back by now. He was curious about what could have happened to him, and wondered if he should ring his mother.

He didn't dare tell Jeanie any of this, and she was less than sympathetic about his upset stomach.

'If you run really short of money, you could always sell your car,' she suggested. 'That's as good as money in the bank, isn't it?'

'It isn't,' he protested. It was registered in his father's name; that would complicate matters if he tried to sell it.

'Why not?' Jeanie wanted to know.

'We both like the car, I want to keep it.' If Dad was at home, he'd be livid that he'd taken it. No way could he go home without it.

'Well, with this war coming, you can always join up. There are posters on every hoarding urging men like you to volunteer.'

'Perhaps I will,' he said. Hadn't he thought of that himself at the beginning of the summer? It would be a good way to escape all these problems.

November came and they were still hanging on at Wanda's place. Barney was finding it difficult. Not only was Wanda dropping hints about being short of money and how much he owed her for his lodgings, but the weather had turned wet and windy and all the fun places he used to take Jeanie had closed down for the winter. Now they had all day to amuse themselves but without much cash, things were not so much fun.

'We've got to get the hell out of here,' he said to Jeanie. 'Your mother's making me feel uncomfortable.'

'I'll take you to my Aunt Lil's house in Liverpool where I spent last winter,' she said. 'We'll both have to job-hunt in earnest and try to earn a bit, but there's much more to do there and lots of lovely shops.'

'Your Aunt Lil is unlikely to welcome me as well.' Barney was unhappy at the thought.

'We'll be all right there for a while. If things turn sour, I've got Aunt Cissie in Chester, we could move on.'

Barney was glad to get away from Wanda, he knew he'd outstayed his welcome in her house. He was glad to get away from Rhyl too, now the weather had turned cold and the visitors had gone. Liverpool, with its neon signs lighting up the dark nights, was more to his taste. Aunt Lil opened up her home to them and seemed pleasant enough to start with. Jeanie soon found a job in one of the big department stores in Liverpool and loved it.

Barney thought he had a job too when he was taken on as a labourer at Cammell Laird's. He was put into a gang of men building a ship but they took little notice of him. The interior of the vessel was a vast empty space as the decks were not yet in. The sound of riveting made his head ring and Barney didn't feel safe because it was all scaffolding and ladders on the inside. Also he felt useless because he didn't know what they expected of him.

He was relieved when at last his first day there was coming to an end. He was given the job of returning a heavy bag of tools to the stores, but felt unable to climb down the ladder with such a cumbersome heavy bag, so instead he tossed it over the side. It made a terrible clatter as it crashed to the ground and his overseer was furious. He was sacked on the spot for doing that and they told him if anybody had happened to be below at that moment, he could have killed them. Barney was unable to find another job and Aunt Lil clearly disapproved of him.

'We'll move to Aunt Cissie's in Chester,' Jeanie said. 'You can try your luck there.' But while she slid effortlessly into a job as a barmaid at the Eagle and Child, Barney couldn't find anything to suit him.

Neither of Jeanie's aunts seemed to like him, and it wasn't only because he was another mouth to feed. Aunt Cissie was grey-haired, stern and disapproving. She was Wanda's sister, but twelve years older than her. After their mother died, she had had to bring her and Lil up. Barney thought her an interfering old busybody.

On their first morning with her, she'd stood over them at breakfast with her arms folded and said, 'Jeanie, see sense, can't you? You're just like your mother, she did this sort of thing too. How else do you think she got you to bring up on her own? You're going to find yourself in the same boat, young lady, mark my words, you will.'

'She never will,' Barney assured Cissie. After what had happened to Madge, he'd got that organised. 'I love her. I'll always look after her.' Jeanie squeezed his hand under the table and smiled with pleasure.

He thought Cissie was doing her best to separate them. 'You ought to marry her,' she told him when she caught him on his own. 'Not just share Jeanie's bed with all the advantages of marriage and none of the responsibilities.'

Barney blanched when he heard marriage suggested again.

Jeanie was working only the evening shift so they had little cash to spend. In the evenings he went to the pub with her because he didn't want to stay at home with Aunt Cissie.

Several times when they were together, she had burst out to Jeanie, 'He's no good to you, and he's just hanging on so you have to support him. You'd be better off without a fellow like that. He's got a handsome face and a posh manner but you'll soon get fed up with that. He's a lazy sod, he won't even bring in the coals for me.'

'I would,' Barney protested, 'if you would just tell me that's what you want.'

'You're half blind, are you? You can't see what needs doing about the house? It's not right for you to live on Jeanie,' she went on sternly. 'You're an able-bodied man, why can't you stand on your own feet? Show some backbone, join the army. And as for you, Jeanie, go back to your mother before it's too late.'

Barney felt things were becoming fraught between him and Jeanie as a result.

He did his best and kept applying for jobs although he was becoming disheartened. One he really fancied was at Chester Racecourse, but though he was called for interview, the job went to someone else. If there was one thing Barney really hated, it was being short of money, and at the same time being dependent on Jeanie and her aunt for handouts.

Things came to a head a few days later. It blew up in moments from what he thought was just another minor tiff about money.

'You could get us some more if you wanted to,' Jeanie said. 'You could sell your car; that would put us in funds. We'd be able to have a little holiday somewhere exciting, London perhaps.'

'But we enjoy the car. We can get out and about in it.'

'We haven't recently. There's no point in keeping it because we have no money for petrol. All my spare cash has to go on beer for you.'

Barney's toes curled with embarrassment. That wasn't true. He knew Jeanie brought him free pints when the boss wasn't looking, and to be honest he didn't enjoy watching the fellows at the Eagle and Child chat her up. He couldn't help noticing that one of the barmen was always laughing and joking with her. When he'd asked Jeanie about him, she'd said Vince was the licensee's son and worked in a bank, and that he helped his dad out on busy nights. Barney liked him even less after that. He was tired of Jeanie joining in all the fun and ignoring him.

When he'd complained about that, she'd said she was there to work, and hadn't time to talk to him when he was there.

'We could move to your mother's place and spend a few weeks there,' Jeanie suggested.

'You know I don't want—'

'That's another thing,' Jeanie flared up, her face crimson. 'It's always what you want. Aren't I good enough for your mother? You won't take me home to meet your family, Barney, and you're no fun any more. I'm fed up. We can't go on like this. Aunt Cissie's right, I'll be better off on my own. I'm going back home.'

That really scared him. If Jeanie left him he'd have nobody. Better a hundred times if he'd stayed at home with Mum and Patsy and helped Madge where he could, but what was he to do now?

Jeanie handed in her notice at the Eagle and Child. The licensee told Barney that evening that he was sorry to hear she wanted to leave. 'She's good for business,' he said. 'She's good at chatting up the young men. She brings them in, that one.'

He was right too. Who could resist her rosy cheeks and shining green eyes? And everybody commented on Jeanie's smiles. They came and went across her face like sunshine and showers. She had a way of reaching out to touch him when she laughed, but it was not just him, she did it to everybody she talked to. Of course she brought the young men in.

Though right now with him, Jeanie was straight-lipped and determined to go. And Cissie was horrible; the way she treated him was destroying what little confidence he had. He was on edge and trying not to show it. He'd always been scared of being found wanting, scared of being measured against Patsy.

He'd always known his sister was cleverer than he was. Dad had known too. Only Mum had understood how nervous he was and had tried to help him. But would she forgive him for going off and staying away for months, not knowing what had happened to Dad?

Fear had always twisted his gut and made him feel ill, and it was doing that now. Even beer made him vomit. His upset stomach was back with a vengeance.

There was no way he could stay on alone at Aunt Cissie's. For a start, she wouldn't have him. Barney was faced with the choice of going home to Mum or joining up.

CHAPTER ELEVEN

PATSY WAS AWARE THAT she and Rupert were growing closer. These days he would often call in the workshop just before they closed at five thirty. She would take him up to the flat and make a tray of tea. Rupert would bring chocolate biscuits or sometimes cakes to make it a real treat.

Always, she'd end up in his arms on the sofa. They were becoming more intimate. Rupert's hands were inclined to stray under her jumper. To have him stroke her bare skin sent shivers of delight up and down her spine. She loved the sensation but she knocked his hands away. She knew where this could lead and she feared it. Madge's agony was too fresh in her mind to risk anything like that happening to her.

Rupert cuddled her closer and said he was sorry. 'I can't help myself, I love you so much. I can't keep my hands off you.'

The following week, when she felt Rupert was going too far again, she told him exactly what had happened to Barney and Madge. 'Her father threw her out of the house and she had nowhere to go. It's ruined all her plans for a career in teaching.'

'What about your brother?'

'He disappeared, he couldn't face it. It's the woman who suffers when that happens.' Patsy was convinced of that. 'The man can go swanning off somewhere else and go on enjoying life.'

'I wouldn't let that happen to you.' Rupert seemed indignant she would even think he might. 'Good Lord, no. In this day and age contraception is possible, and if the unthinkable happened, which it wouldn't, nothing would tear me away from you.'

'I know all that,' she said. 'I heard it all from Madge but I have my own way of making sure it doesn't happen to me.'

Barney kept on thinking about joining the army. To start with it had seemed a romantic adventure. He thought he was the sociable sort and would enjoy living with a lot of men of his own age. Volunteers were highly thought of in the present climate of approaching war.

When they'd first come to Chester, Jeanie had known the city better than he had, and had taken him on many sightseeing trips. He'd walked the city walls, visited the military museum in the castle and learned all about it being a Roman fortress and, in addition, that Chester was now the Army Headquarters of Western Command.

Barney had seen a recruitment office there and without giving it any thought he'd swaggered inside and told the recruiting sergeant that he wanted to join the army. 'I want to do my bit for the country. I'm afraid war is inevitable,' he'd told him.

'Maybe, maybe not. We don't really know yet, do we?' He was invited to sit down. The sergeant seemed friendly. 'The army will give you a good career, if you are found to be suitable. You'll have to pass a medical exam and during your preliminary training you'll have an IQ test and a general assessment to find the best place to fit you in.'

The sergeant went on talking as he handed Barney a booklet of information about the army and a collection of forms he would need to fill in. 'Any trouble with the police?' he asked.

'I've had the odd speeding ticket,' he admitted. 'Nothing else.'

'You have a car?'

'Yes, a Morris Eight.'

The sergeant was interested in cars and discussed the Morris Eight at length. 'Not that you'll have much use for it when you join up,' he said. 'Everything you need is provided for you inside the barracks and you'll not be allowed out for the first few weeks.'

'Not allowed out?' Barney was shocked.

'That's to help you settle down to army life. You'll not lose out; we have a cinema here and a NAAFI where you can buy beer and cigarettes. And also anything you want, tea, cakes, that sort of thing. You'll be undergoing basic training.'

'What does that consist of?'

'Drill, physical exercise of every sort and weapons training. We aim to keep you pretty busy. You probably won't want to go out.'

Barney didn't think he was right about that. He couldn't imagine not wanting to go out.

'As a volunteer,' the sergeant went on, 'you will be required to sign on for a period of twelve years, five on active service and seven on the reserve.'

That horrified Barney. Sign on for twelve years! It put him right off. He'd never stayed in any job for even twelve months; he couldn't see twelve years ahead. He got outside as quickly as he could. But after he'd seen Jeanie on to the Crosville bus to North Wales, he had thought about it again. What else could he do?

He'd walked round the city walls and viewed the castle

from every possible viewpoint several times already, and now he went again, eyeing the sentries standing guard at the gates. It looked a very well-maintained place, with neatly clipped grass and the Union Jack flying on the buildings inside.

In order to stay away from Aunt Cissie, he bought himself a pork pie for his supper and went back to the King's Head where he made a pint of beer last all evening. At ten thirty he used the key Cissie had given Jeanie to get inside her house and tiptoed up to bed. He felt lost there on his own. The next morning there was no avoiding Aunt Cissie who said pointedly, 'I take it you'll be leaving today?'

When he said yes, she offered him tea and toast before sending him back upstairs to pack up his belongings. Her front door closed behind him with a firm click. He hadn't eaten well yesterday and soon felt hungry. The thought of joining up and being provided with bed and board on a permanent basis now seemed very tempting.

Barney walked aimlessly round the shops although he had few coins to jangle in his pocket. He bought some sweets to appease his hunger then went back to the recruiting office and told the sergeant that he'd thought it over carefully and that he was sure army life would suit him very well. Being entitled to three meals a day as well as sleeping quarters made it impossible to resist.

'Let's see if you'll suit us then,' the sergeant said. 'The doctor is here. You can wait your turn and have your medical now.'

Barney was pleased to find there would not be a long delay over the preliminaries. The sooner he could settle in, the better he would like it. There was only one man waiting ahead of him. He chatted, and said his name was Alec. Barney had no worries about his health and was found to be medically fit, category A1.

On the way out, he asked the recruiting sergeant how soon he could start. He was running out of money and had nowhere to sleep tonight.

'We have an intake joining tomorrow,' he was told. Barney was relieved. He could manage to hold out that long. He was given some forms to sign and found the lad he'd chatted to while waiting to see the doctor was doing the same. 'Return tomorrow at midday,' they were told.

Barney suggested they have a beer and gave Alec a lift to the pub where Jeanie had worked.

'Gosh,' he said. 'You've got a lovely car and you can drive.' He was impressed. Opposite the pub was a café, and when Alec saw it he said, 'I'm hungry, how about something to eat first?'

Barney was glad to agree. They each had a plate of stew, dumplings and cabbage, followed by jam roly-poly and custard. He felt better after that but he didn't want to be on his own and was reluctant to say goodbye to Alec. He drove him home to the suburb of Littleton to a house not unlike Fern Bank, but he was not invited in.

He remembered then that he had nowhere to leave his father's car, and wished he'd asked Aunt Cissie if he could park it outside her house and have her keep an eye on it. Now it seemed his only course would be to sell it. He drove to a big garage where he'd seen cars for sale, but they wanted to show it on their forecourt and take a commission when they managed to get a buyer.

Barney wanted the money in his pocket before he joined up. It took him all afternoon to find a garage that would pay cash. They agreed a price of a hundred pounds but when he was told the banks had now closed and he couldn't have his cash until tomorrow morning, he said he would keep the car overnight and return tomorrow at ten o'clock.

He'd given his name as Hubert Rushton to the garage owner to tie in with the ownership papers.

'I'd like to hold on to them,' the garage owner said when Barney put out his hand for them. 'Usually I show them to the police to make sure the vehicle hasn't been stolen before I hand over any money.'

Barney was nervous about doing that. He didn't think his mother would have reported it as stolen to the police, but it wasn't really his. However, he felt he had no choice if he was going to sell it by tomorrow. He smiled and brazened it out.

It was getting dark by that time; he found a quiet spot in a suburban road and parked his car well away from a street lamp. Then he walked back towards the city and bought himself fish and chips for his supper. On the way he'd passed a pub. He found it again and spent the last money he had on a pint of beer and made it last until closing time. Then he went back to the car, pulled his mother's car rug over himself, curled up on the back seat and went to sleep.

The next morning, he exchanged the car for the hundred pounds; went to a bank and opened an account in his name and paid most of the money in. He felt he was doing the sensible thing.

Barney found he'd joined the Cheshire Yeomanry as an infantryman and within a few days he was afraid he'd made another bad choice. They made him look a sight by cutting off most of his hair. The fact that all the new recruits were shorn almost to the scalp did not ease his hurt. He'd taken pride in having his hair cut exactly to his taste so that it enhanced his looks.

He was allotted a bed in a barrack hut that he shared with

twenty-nine other new recruits. His bed was a long way from the central stove and the weather was turning cold.

The corporal in charge of his hut seemed to have it in for him right from the start. He found fault with almost everything he did and required him to do it over again. He shouted at him as though he was an idiot, and if he failed to follow the strict and complicated rules, he held him up to ridicule in front of the others.

They were woken up each morning by a trumpeter blowing reveille at the door of their hut. It was still dark at that time and to Barney it felt like the middle of the night. They were all expected to be on their feet within seconds and running for the ablution block. There weren't enough sinks for them all and the water was cold. Shaving was hell.

After throwing on his clothes, Barney was expected to strip his bed. Making it was not enough, all the blankets had to be taken off and folded and the sheets wrapped round them box fashion, and all his kit had to be laid out on his bed in an exact pattern. Each bed had to look identical. Barney had no aptitude for such neatness, and after breakfast came barrack room inspection.

In addition, there were parades and he had to clean and polish his boots until he could see his face in them. His mother had made his bed for him and washed his clothes, and his father had cleaned the whole family's shoes on Sunday morning before they went to church. He'd still cleaned Barney's even after he refused to go.

Barney hated his boots, they were heavy and uncomfortable and always failed to pass inspection. Alec, the lad he'd befriended during the joining-up process, showed him how to spit on them and rub the boot blacking in hard. He'd polished them for hours and they were still said to need more effort.

He loathed doing drill, marching up and down on the parade ground while the sergeant screamed at him. Even worse was the physical activity designed to improve his fitness and strength; the long-distance runs left him exhausted. He was scared of the guns. They were evil things and the last thing he wanted to do was to learn how to fire them. He felt full of foreboding when he learned that six battalions of the Cheshire Regiment were trained as machine-gun specialists and their main training centre was here at Chester Castle.

As for the other men he was being trained with, most were a rough lot and they sniggered at his efforts. He had little in common with them and felt consumed by anxiety and fear. He'd never felt more alone in his life.

In his agony he wrote to Jeanie, a real outpouring of his hatred of army life. He told her how much he was missing her and said he was sorry they'd quarrelled and he wanted to make it up. He waited two weeks and when Jeanie didn't reply, he wrote to her again, begging her to drop him a line but she didn't.

He wasn't getting enough sleep, he had no time to relax and there was no privacy to be had anywhere. Some nights when he got into his hard narrow bed, he had a little weep. He was exhausted physically and mentally, to the point where he could no longer think straight. Army life seemed very alien.

On 6 December he would come of age. He felt he was facing a miserable birthday. There would be nothing to mark it out as a special day for him, he would have no cards or gifts. He'd told nobody he would soon turn twenty-one, the lads would think him pathetic if he had no post and nothing arranged. He wished he'd gone home instead of joining up. Mum would have made it a day of celebration.

* * *

Patsy had been really worried about her mother in the summer when they'd had all their troubles. She knew it had taken her some time to get over Dad's death, but recently she'd thought Mum was improving. Having Madge in the house had helped her and she'd missed her when she went.

Last Sunday, Madge had come with Sheila and brought the baby to show her off. Katrina was very pretty and Mum could hardly bear to put her down in her pram. Patsy had held her and her round blue eyes had stared up into her face.

'She's adorable,' she told Madge. 'I can see why you couldn't let somebody else have her.'

'I feel very lucky to be able to share Aunt Grace's home,' Madge said. 'She loves Katrina and wants to nurse her for hours.'

But since then, Beatrice had become tearful and seemed sunk in gloom again. They were in the kitchen washing up after their supper. 'What's the matter, Mum?' Patsy asked. 'Is it too quiet for you now there's just you and me?'

'It's everything.' Beatrice blew her nose hard.

'No, it isn't.' The business is making money. We have enough to live on and can stay in this comfortable house.' Patsy was afraid she'd been spending too much time with Rupert and her mother was feeling neglected.

'I feel dreadful. It's Barney, I suppose.'

'Let's go and sit down.' She took her into the living room and they sat down together on the sofa.

'I can't help worrying about him. He's not like you, he can't manage by himself, he's very anxious – nervous, you know.'

'He never struck me as being nervous.'

'He's needed a lot of help. I do hope he's all right. I wish I knew where he was so we could get in touch.'

'He knows where we are, Mum. If he wanted help I'm sure he'd come home. He knows you'll always give it.'

Her mother burst into tears. 'It's his birthday tomorrow. He'll be twenty-one and come of age.'

'Come of age!' Patsy had to laugh, though really she was cross with him. 'Barney hasn't grown up yet. If he ever gives us a thought, he'd know you must be worried sick about him.' He could write and send an address, but to say that now would only distress Mum more.

'There are things I want to give him,' Beatrice sobbed. 'Things he should have. His daddy's gold cufflinks.'

'I never saw Dad wear cufflinks,' Patsy said. 'That wasn't his style.'

That only made Mum sob more loudly. 'You don't understand.'

She was right. Patsy didn't understand why her mother was so distressed. Surely it couldn't just be Barney's birthday?

'Try me, Mum,' she said. 'If you explain, I'll understand.'

Beatrice blew her nose again. 'I had a letter from the solicitor this morning about Daddy's will. He's obtained probate and he wants me to make an appointment to see him. He suggests I bring you too, he wants to see us together.'

'Why?' Patsy had left dealing with the solicitor to her mother. She was mopping at her eyes, and Patsy could see she was trying to pull herself together.

'I might as well tell you now. You're a good girl.' She sighed. 'Your father has left everything to me for my lifetime but he wrote the will so that the business is entailed. It will be yours when I die.'

'Oh! I didn't expect . . . What about Barney?'

'Hubert wasn't Barney's father. I'd been married before.'

Patsy gasped. 'I didn't know! Why didn't you tell us? Gosh, I can't believe it.' Her eyes were searching her mother's face, but Beatrice wouldn't meet her gaze. 'D'you know, I've always had the feeling that our family was in two parts, with you and Barney on one side and me and Dad on the other. Tell me about Barney's father. What happened to him?'

'I was eighteen when we were married.' Beatrice paused and wiped her eyes again. 'When the war came, Rowley was made an officer, a second lieutenant.'

'He was killed in the trenches?'

'No, but at the start of the war he was sent to Ypres.' She gave a little choking sob and stopped. Her cheeks were crimson and Patsy could see the perspiration standing out on her forehead.

'But why hide that? Weren't you proud that he was fighting for his country?'

'Yes, yes of course I was, but . . .' She broke off and was silent for such a long time, Patsy was afraid she would say no more.

'Go on,' she urged.

'I wanted us to be an ordinary normal family. I wanted you and Barney to grow up together as brother and sister.'

'But we did, I believed we were. It must have been awful for you to lose your husband when you had a baby.'

'He hadn't been born, Patsy. I was still carrying him when Rowley died.'

'A real tragedy for you both and a terrible loss, but I still can't see why you'd want to hide it. Lots of women lost their husbands in the last war.'

Beatrice nodded and sniffed into her handkerchief. Patsy straightened up on the sofa and felt for her mother's hand.

'Barney thinks Dad – my father – is his too?'

'No, he found his birth certificate years ago. Barney knows his father was Rowland Tavenham-Strong.'

'Does he?' Patsy was doubtful. 'He's never so much as breathed a word of that to me. I've never heard it mentioned. Why did Barney keep it quiet?'

She sat stock still, knowing now that something dreadful must have happened. She could see tears welling in her mother's eyes.

'I was having Barney and I couldn't cope with Rowley. Everything suddenly unravelled and went horribly wrong.'

Patsy could see stark fear in her eyes. 'What went wrong?'

'I can't.' Her mother was racked with anguish and in floods of tears now.

'How did he die?'

Her mother was hardly able to get the words out. 'In a terrible way, I can hardly bear to think about it even now.'

Patsy put an arm round her shoulders and pulled her closer. 'Poor Mum,' she murmured. 'Widowed twice and both husbands died in a terrible way. You have to put it all behind you, shut it out of your mind.'

The following week her mother made an appointment with the solicitor. Patsy could see Beatrice becoming more stressed as the day approached. They were received with gentle kindness by Hubert's solicitor and the situation was exactly as Patsy had been told, so there were no surprises for her mother there.

When they returned home, Patsy made some tea and said, 'There, it's over now. You can forget about it.'

'No, it isn't over,' she said. 'I ought to tell you about Barney and his father. You should know or you'll never understand.'

It was only then that Patsy realised it wasn't Hubert's will that was upsetting her mother. 'Go on then, Mum. Tell me about Barney and his father. I would like to know.'

She drank most of her tea before she started. 'When Rowley was killed I had to go home to have our baby. I felt numb for a long time. My father had died and Mother had very little money. I knew I'd have to get a job as soon as I could, but everybody had heard of Rowley's death and the awful circumstances surrounding it. Employers didn't want to know when I told them my name.'

'Tavenham-Strong?'

'Yes.'

'That's a nice name.'

'It's not the sort of name people forget. Many didn't want to know me.'

'Why not? But you did find work, didn't you?'

'Yes, your father took me on.'

'What? But I thought you were a shorthand typist.'

'I was.' Beatrice nodded, her eyes dark with misery. 'I was to do the office work for him.'

For as long as Patsy could remember, Dad and Tim had taken care of that. She pulled her mother closer. 'Mum, I had no idea that you'd ever worked in the business. You never told us that.'

'I thought I'd gone up in the world when I married Rowley. His family were wealthy and they didn't want their wives to work, and of course officers' wives didn't work either. While marriage to Rowley was a step up socially for me, a couple of steps really, marriage to Hubert was a social step down for an officer's widow.'

Patsy was shocked. 'Mum! Dad was lovely.'

'Yes, I know. Don't get me wrong, I was glad to marry him. We had a good marriage, he loved me.'

'He always treated you as though you were a grand lady,' Patsy said. It made her wonder if Rowley Tavenham-Strong had been the love of her life and poor Dad second-best. 'But you must have been grateful for Dad's dependability and kindness. He always seemed a strong person with both feet on the ground.'

'He was, but Barney isn't like him. That is why I worry about him. You don't see it, but I know he's a very sensitive person; he's emotionally insecure, always anxious and nerve-racked, and he looks so very like Rowley. He needs support in all sorts of ways. I'm afraid Barney won't be able to manage on his own. Some people can't stand stress. Rowley was like that too. His was a divided family. I do wish I knew what Barney was doing.'

'On that postcard he sent, he said he was thinking of joining up.' It was still on the mantelpiece propped up against a vase of spills. Patsy saw her mother's gaze go to it.

'That frightens me too: I'm certain the army would be the very worst place for him. When I think what it did to his father.'

Patsy sighed. 'I didn't realise you'd had such a hard life, Mum.'

She nodded and dissolved into tears again. 'When Hubert died, I felt I'd lost my lifeline. You're strong like he was. You're a real chip off the old block.'

'Yes,' she said. But she didn't feel this heart-to-heart talk with her mother was helping her to understand. She still had no idea how Barney's father had died, and why his name was so abhorrent. But she knew it was no good trying to carry on talking to Mum when she was as upset as this. She would try again in another day or so when she'd calmed down.

CHAPTER TWELVE

B ARNEY SAW THE CHRISTMAS fare on sale in the NAAFI, the decorations going up and heard the carols on the wireless. He couldn't ignore it and each day it crept closer. It drove his spirits even lower to find the other lads looking forward to it and talking of the possibility of getting leave over the holiday.

Everybody cheered when it was announced that they would all be granted a seventy-two-hour pass over the Christmas holiday. 'Smashing,' they chorused. 'We've got three full days, Christmas Eve, Christmas Day and Boxing Day.'

Barney understood that he didn't have to go away. He could stay here in the barrack room if he wished. There would still be plenty of military personnel around and Christmas dinner and other celebrations would be provided, but to be alone in the barrack room over the holiday would be awful, and the others would think him pathetic.

To spend Christmas in a hotel without the company of family or friends would be no picnic either. Barney had another weep in his bed that night; his only other alternative was to go home, but after all this time he dreaded doing that.

The recruits were allowed out of barracks now and as Barney had money from selling the car, he asked at a hotel in Chester if they had a vacant room over Christmas, but was told they were fully booked. He decided there was nowhere he could go but home, but he couldn't walk in on them without warning. Not after all this time.

He bought a Christmas card to post to his mother and wrote in it that he had joined the army and was stationed in Chester. He told her that he had a seventy-two-hour pass over the holiday and would like to come and spend it with her. Deliberately he withheld his address, fearing Patsy might write back telling him not to bother, that they didn't want to see him after what he'd done.

He was dreading coming face to face with Patsy and having to ask what had happened to Dad. He might well be there, probably was by now, and he'd certainly be angry with him because he'd taken his car without permission and then sold it. Worse still was the thought of coming face to face with Madge.

It all scared him rigid. He decided to draw out seventy-five pounds from his bank account and give it to Dad in lieu of his car. He'd have to try and placate him in some way. Barney would have liked to go in his civvies and forget all about the army over Christmas, but if he wore his uniform that would be proof he really had joined up and was doing his duty for his country. He hoped that way to make a good impression and they'd let him stay over the holiday.

As Christmas drew closer, his fellow soldiers became more excited at the prospect. Barney felt tense with dread and full of gloom. Most of his fellows left the evening before, but he elected to spend another night in barracks. He tossed and turned all night, and worried himself sick about facing his family.

On the morning of Christmas Eve he got up too late to have breakfast and went into Chester to have egg and bacon in a café. He joined the last-minute shoppers and bought a bottle of sherry for his mother and some chocolates for Patsy. As he was passing the entrance to a cinema, he felt a gust of warm air and on the spur of the moment he put off coming face to face with Patsy by going inside to see *Tarzan's Revenge*.

He slept through most of it and it was dark when he came out. He couldn't put off catching the train to Birkenhead any longer. His chest felt tight with trepidation on the journey and seemed worse as he walked the familiar route across Birkenhead Park. The night was very dark here and hoarfrost was settling on the asphalt. He could hear the distant roar of traffic and see the glow of town lights in the sky all round him.

His steps slowed as he trudged up Forest Road. The windows of Fern Bank were all lit up and he could see into the sitting room. A good fire glowed in the grate and a decorated Christmas tree had pride of place in the corner. It all looked bright and welcoming.

He shut the gate quietly, crept up the drive and made himself ring the front doorbell even though he had a key. He heard footsteps running up the hall and the door was thrown open. His mother, her face bright with smiles, threw her arms round him in a hug of joy.

'Barney dearest!' She kissed him. 'I've been so worried about you. Where have you been? Thank goodness you've come back.'

Barney found himself sweating with relief as he was drawn into the warmth and the door closed behind him. It looked as though they'd accept him back. 'It's lovely to be home, Mother.'

He looked up to find Patsy surveying him from the kitchen doorway. 'Happy Christmas, Barney,' she said. 'Welcome home.'

He was giving her a hug when his mother said, 'I thought you might come home now you've got a daughter.'

'What?'

'You just had to come and see her, didn't you?'

Barney could feel the strength ebbing from his knees, he felt light-headed. 'You mean she's here?'

'No.' Patsy laughed. 'But she's not far away. Madge is living in Bebington now with a great-aunt. She couldn't bear the thought of putting the baby up for adoption, she's keeping her.'

Barney had seen Madge's pregnancy as a blip on the horizon that would soon cease to worry either of them. But now it seemed the problem would be with him for ever.

'Katrina's a beautiful baby,' Beatrice assured him, 'absolutely beautiful. Madge chose her name, of course; do you like it? I wanted to bring her up; after all, I am her grandmother. We none of us wanted her to go to a stranger.'

Barney felt sick. He could feel bile rising in his throat. Never in a month of Sundays would he have believed this was possible. He found it hard to accept he had a daughter. He couldn't think, his head was full of fog. He'd given no thought at all to what Madge might do about the baby. All he'd wanted was to get right away and have nothing to do with it.

'She weighed seven pounds two ounces at birth,' Patsy went on, 'and she's gaining weight rapidly now. The great-aunt nurses her on and off all day. Madge seems happy with the arrangement.'

'I am glad,' he muttered. His voice sounded flat and insincere to his own ears. 'Excuse me, I must go,' He made it to the bathroom and locked himself in, then stood retching over the lavatory, trying not to make any noise. Then he splashed cold water on his face and sank down on the edge of the bath, feeling as sick as a dog. He could hear them downstairs and knew he had to join them as soon as he could or they'd see how badly this news had thrown him.

Patsy was poking up the sitting-room fire, shovelling more coal on, when he rejoined them.

'How are things in the business?' he asked her. He wanted to change the subject, talk about anything as long as it wasn't that baby.

'Great, everything's going surprisingly well, we've turned the corner.'

'You've got more work?' That didn't please him. He'd been imagining Patsy struggling in vain to make ends meet.

'Yes. The country's gearing up for war. Suddenly we're all busy making uniforms for the forces. We've all the work we can cope with.'

'Marvellous,' he said, trying to sound more pleased than he felt.

'I see you really have joined up. Are you enjoying life in the army?'

'It's great.' He forced a smile. If Patsy had bettered things at home, he wasn't going to admit he'd made things worse for himself.

'Barney?' His mother's voice was shrill. She was looking at his uniform. 'You're an ordinary soldier? I'd have thought they'd make you an officer.'

'No, Mum.' He had difficulty getting his breath. 'I'm just a private.'

'You're officer class! The army should have realised.' She was radiating dismay.

'Some of us have to start at the bottom,' he blustered.

She patted his arm. 'I expect you'll rise through the ranks quite quickly.'

Barney had no such expectations. To hide his embarrassment he dug into his kitbag of overnight things and brought out the presents.

'Put them under the tree, darling. We can't have them until tomorrow. Isn't it exciting, having you back for Christmas?'

'I'd better take my things upstairs.' He slung his kitbag over his shoulder and set off.

'We've had to change things round a bit,' Beatrice called.

Barney ignored that and opened the door to his bedroom. It seemed different.

Patsy had followed him up. 'That's my bedroom now,' she told him. 'We've made up the bed in my old room for you.'

'Oh,' he said before he could stop himself, 'I was looking forward to sleeping in my old bed.'

Patsy smiled at him. 'I thought once Madge left I might as well move in here. It's a much bigger room than mine.'

'Madge moved in here?' Barney was horrified. Again he felt he couldn't breathe.

'Her father threw her out when he found out about the baby. The Worthingtons always said he was very strict.'

'She had nowhere to live.' His mother had come up too and for the first time he saw censure on her face. 'We thought it was the least we could do for her. You were naughty, Barney, going off like that.'

'More than naughty.' Patsy was more severe. 'It was a terrible thing to do, Madge was very upset.'

Barney wished they'd stop talking about the baby, he couldn't stand much more. He swallowed hard and answered as calmly as he could, 'Yes, I'm sorry. What happened? She's living in Bebington, you said?'

'You should have kept in touch,' his mother murmured. 'The baby is well and she's managing. You ought to go and see them while you're this close.'

Barney felt as though the floor was coming up to hit him. He couldn't cope with this.

'I'll give you Madge's address and phone number,' Beatrice went on.

'She had a difficult time on her own,' Patsy added. 'Surely you realised she would? She couldn't go home because her dad said he wouldn't have her bastard under his roof. It was her mother who arranged for her to live with her Aunt Grace; she thought it would suit them both. You ruined her career, Barney. She had to leave her teacher training college halfway through the course. Ruined her life, really.'

'I didn't mean . . .' Barney bent double trying to gulp oxygen into his lungs. He was always struggling for breath these days. There must be something wrong with him.

'You should have been here to help her. Surely you felt you owed her that? Madge found it very hard to get over the birth but I think she's on her feet again now. Sheila thinks she's besotted with her baby. She says her Aunt Grace has thrown her a lifeline.'

'You could still marry her,' his mother suggested. 'Probably that's the best thing for all of you. Madge is a lovely girl, she's got plenty of guts. You'd be all right with her.'

Barney's mouth was dry. This was worse than he'd expected, a hundred times worse. He tossed his kitbag on the bed in the small bedroom and sat down beside it. 'I've a lot of catching up to do. What about Dad?'

His mother sank down beside him. He could feel the blood pounding in his head when he saw the tears running down her cheeks. Slowly she recounted what had happened to Hubert.

'I'm sorry, Mum.' He took her hand in his. 'I feel awful about leaving you and Patsy to cope.'

'And Madge.'

'I wish now I'd stayed. Please forgive me.'

'I'm glad you've come back.' She gave him a wavering

smile. 'I'll not worry now I've seen you're all right.'

The next time he looked up, Patsy was leaning against the doorpost. 'Have you brought Dad's car back?'

He felt full of resentment at Patsy and wished she'd leave him alone. 'No, once I joined up I had nowhere to keep it. I thought it better to sell it.'

'Sell it?' she echoed. 'You might have phoned to ask if we wanted it. I've started taking driving lessons.'

'Why?'

'Why not, Barney? I thought it would be nice to take Mum out for a little drive once in a while. That was what Dad used to do. And there's the delivery van, I thought it would help if I could manage that although we hardly use it these days. The government delivers and collects the work we do.'

Barney felt urgently in his kitbag again. 'I've brought the money for you, Mum. The car would be yours now, wouldn't it?'

'I suppose you thought by doing this it would make everything right again.' Patsy was still eyeing him from the doorway, and sounded angry. 'How much did you get for it?'

That made him cringe because he'd already made up his mind to lie. 'Seventy-five pounds,' he said.

'You were done,' she railed at him. 'You know the garage where Dad used to get his car serviced? The owner told me and Mum straight off he'd give us a hundred. Fancy you letting it go for less than it was worth. I thought you knew a lot about cars.'

Barney was full of hate for Patsy. Trust her to put him on the wrong foot again. She'd always managed to be one step ahead. She made him feel useless. His heart rate was rocketing upwards, he shouldn't have come.

But Patsy gave him a smile. 'Come on, it's Christmas. Let's

go downstairs and forget all this. It's only what we expected anyway.'

Trust his sister to get a jab in at him where she could.

'Mum's cooking steak and kidney pie to welcome you home,' she told him, still smiling. 'It should be nearly ready.'

They kept on asking him questions but Barney could no longer think clearly. He gave them an edited version of what he'd been doing since the spring. He knew he shouldn't mention Jeanie, Mum and Patsy wouldn't approve of him finding another girlfriend so soon after getting Madge into trouble. He had to be careful about what he said about army life too. He'd made out he was quite enjoying it.

But everything felt different; Barney was no longer at ease with his family. He went to bed that night in Patsy's very inferior room and was filled with envy for what his little sister had achieved. It was as though they'd changed positions in the family. She had now become the senior sibling and had even had the cheek to point out where his duty lay with regard to Madge. He felt suffused with guilt, embarrassed by his failure to look after her, and by the fact that his mother had taken her in. They were doing their best to provide a happy Christmas and that made him feel even worse. He felt too emotionally charged to enjoy anything. He was on edge the whole time.

He had another surprise when he heard Patsy had a boyfriend and that he was invited for supper on Boxing Night, and even more surprised when Rupert turned up. He was the sort who would look at ease in any situation. He came forward to shake his hand, saying he was delighted to meet Patsy's brother. His accent was plummy, just like his commanding officer's. Nobody would doubt that Rupert was officer class. He brought flowers for Beatrice and perfume for Patsy, and he couldn't drag his eyes away from her. Barney didn't doubt they were in love and felt envious. Lots of girls had attached themselves to him, but he'd never managed to find one he could truly love. He'd never have believed little Patsy could attract a man like Rupert. She'd really fallen on her feet.

Rupert kept them entertained all evening, drawing Barney and his mother into the conversation. He knew exactly when to help carry dishes in from their kitchen and when to sit back.

He offered to carve the duck Patsy had cooked. 'If you don't mind, Barney? If it's usually your job, I don't want to push myself in.'

'No, I don't mind.' Barney wouldn't have known where to begin, Mum usually carved their joints.

Rupert did it expertly.

As the evening went on, Barney began to feel restive. He had to be back in barracks before midnight and was afraid few buses would be running on Boxing night. As it was, he'd have to walk to Park Station to get a train. He had his biggest surprise of all when Rupert said, 'I'll run you back to your barracks. I'm driving to Sheffield to stay with my parents for a few days, so it's no problem.'

Barney brought his kitbag down while Rupert thanked Beatrice for her hospitality. Patsy came outside to see them off and he kissed her with no sign of the embarrassment Barney would have felt doing it in front of the family.

Rupert's Jaguar two-seater took his breath away. It was the car he'd hankered after since his teens, his dream car. He'd really missed having his dad's Morris Eight since he'd sold it.

Barney was billeted in Napier House which had been built in 1830 as barrack accommodation for Chester Castle. Rupert could get no nearer than the wide front gate, which was very grand and through which the classical lines of other fine buildings could be seen across the barrack square. Barney was pleased to see his barrack-room corporal talking to two of his roommates on their way in. They looked twice at Rupert's fine car and heard his fancy voice wish him goodnight and a Happy New Year. Barney reached for his kitbag, tossed it over his shoulder and offered seasonal greetings to those he knew.

The barrack room was miserably cold and comfortless because the stove had gone out. One or two of the men were already in bed but most were still out savouring the last hour of their freedom. By the time Barney got into his hard, narrow bed, he was really cross with the way things had turned out for him. His dad had gone for good, but Mum and Patsy would have news about Madge and the baby every time he went near the place. There'd be no getting away from that.

He was glad he'd been accepted back into the family fold, but he now realised he'd made the biggest mistake of his life when he'd left. He should not have let Patsy push him out. As soon as he'd gone, everything had come up smelling of roses for her.

He found it hard to believe she was actually making money from the business, a lot of money, more than Dad had earned in recent years, while here was he earning pence for volunteering to fight for his country. And he was being given a terrible time for his trouble. It wasn't fair. What really angered him was that he'd have been earning that money had he stayed in the business.

Now the country was gearing up for war, they were all making money, the depression was over. It stood to reason that if Patsy could do it, he'd have had no trouble. He could have lived at home in comfort all these months and be thinking of buying himself a decent car now.

Then there was Patsy's posh boyfriend who clearly earned a considerable amount. If he married her she'd spend the rest of her life in luxury, while he had nothing. Barney had liked Jeanie, but her family had less money than his own, nobody could call her posh. In fact, his mother would be sure to say she was common, but anyway, she'd ditched him.

Unable to keep his tears back, he pulled his blankets over his head. The lads were coming back in ones and twos, it wouldn't do to let them hear him; they'd make fun of him. He wiped his eyes on his sheet and he knew he had to stop before he made his eyes red and puffy. He'd tried so hard to make a decent life for himself but nothing turned out right for him. The gods favoured Patsy. There was no doubt about that.

Chapter Thirteen

For Barney, the days after Christmas were miserable. He couldn't get over the embarrassment he'd suffered when he'd faced his family. Patsy had been particularly sharp with him. He writhed inside every time he thought about what she'd said; it made him feel guilty too and a real cad.

Patsy didn't realise how lucky she'd been to have the business handed to her on a plate just when the economic tide was turning. Yes of course he was envious, who wouldn't be? Just to think about it made him angry and frustrated.

Everybody was telling Patsy how clever she was. She was getting rich and having a good time, while he had very little money to spend and life in the army was hell.

He was sitting on his bed reading a newspaper that had been left lying around in the canteen, when Alec came in with a letter for him. After lunch, when they could collect their mail, the other lads would go to see if there was anything for them, but Barney never bothered because he didn't receive any. He recognised Jeanie's scrawl immediately and was pleased that she'd come round sufficiently to write to him.

His pleasure was short-lived. The three-page letter was a cry of woe.

I'm scared stiff and I don't know what to do. I can hardly believe it but I'm pregnant. There's no doubt about it, Barney, I've hung on just to be absolutely sure. I haven't dared tell anybody yet but I've let it be known that I don't like my job at the Co-op and I've given in my notice. I've written to Aunt Cissie asking if I can come and stay with her and I'll be there next week. We've got to get married and do it quickly.

He sat up, feeling quite shaky. Oh God, not again! Barney was sure he'd been very careful. Could she be having him on? No, probably not; it was his usual rotten luck. He felt angry and couldn't think straight about what he should do for the best.

That evening, Alec and some of the lads were going out for a drink and asked if he wanted to go with them. It was a half-mile march to the pub they favoured so he rarely went, but now it was what he needed. Once there, they talked football while he slowly calmed down and let the problem turn round and round in his mind. How could he possibly face Mum and Patsy with the same problem over again? And so soon! They'd talked on and on about Madge and her baby.

He'd really missed Jeanie and it had upset him when she'd wanted to go home on her own. He'd felt bereft without her. Jeanie was OK, they got along really well. He could marry her, why not? He'd turned twenty-one now and in the army that meant he'd be entitled to a marriage allowance. It would mean he'd be earning more money for the same amount of hours and that would make him feel better. When he got posted from here, he might even be allotted a house, an army quarter they called it, and whatever happened he might be able to live with Jeanie off the base. That would be a vast improvement for them both.

The next day he sought out his sergeant and asked if he might have his advice on an urgent matter. He told him he'd got his girlfriend in the family way and needed to get married immediately. 'What is the best way for me to go about getting a marriage allowance?'

He was told how to apply. He did that and then wrote a quick note to Jeanie telling her that the marriage was on.

The next day he tore that note up and wrote a flowery proposal of marriage. He told her he loved her, had missed her and couldn't wait to get married. He finished, *Come back to Aunt Cissie's place and we'll arrange it as soon as possible.*

Jeanie arrived and he knew he was doing the right thing as soon as he saw her happy smiling face. He took her to a pub where they weren't known and sat in a corner talking about the coming baby.

'It gave me the shock of my life to find out I was preggers,' she told him.

'It did the same for me when I read your letter,' he said. Barney had been horrified at the thought of being a father for the second time and asked, 'Do you want this baby?' He understood women were supposed to want babies, but he knew Jeanie well enough to think she might not.

'I tried to get rid of it by sitting in a hot bath and drinking gin, but all that did was get me drunk. I'd like to have it taken away, but I don't know anyone who would do it and there are terrible tales in the papers about what can happen to girls who go to back-street abortionists. I've had a terrible few weeks worrying about this, but then I decided if we got married, I could just have it and settle down.'

Some days later, Barney was told he was entitled to a marriage allowance and it would be paid from the date on his marriage certificate when that was presented. Jeanie arranged to have the ceremony on a Saturday morning in the register office at Chester, as Barney was now entitled to a forty-eight-hour pass on alternate weekends.

This brought him face to face with another problem. After the embarrassment he'd suffered at Christmas when he'd gone home, he knew that to tell his family he was about to marry Jeanie would bring him a lot of hassle. If he went ahead without telling them, it could cause more trouble. If, or when, they found out, they might never let him back into the family fold.

He had to think about Jeanie too. She was curious about his family and thought they were richer than hers and good for a handout from time to time. She wanted to meet them; it would be better to bite the bullet, so to speak, and invite them to the wedding.

Mum had made a real fuss of Madge's baby, no doubt she would of Jeanie's once she got used to the idea. All the same, he had to screw up his nerve to ring his mother.

'I'm going to get married,' he told her, 'in two and a half weeks' time.' She thought at first he meant he was going to marry Madge and was full of joy.

'No,' he had to say. 'No, to somebody else. I want you and Patsy to meet my bride.'

He was left in no doubt that he'd dropped a bombshell. 'Married in two and a half weeks' time, don't be absurd, Barney, that won't be possible. Who is this girl? What's the hurry?' she kept asking. 'Now you're in the army you can't set up a home for this girl. What are you rushing into marriage for when you won't be able to live together? What is she going to do? After all, she'll want to be reasonably near Chester so she can see something of you when you have time off.'

'Jeanie has an aunt in Chester and so to start with she's going to board with her.'

'I don't think you've thought this through, Barney dear. You shouldn't rush into it. You need time to save up and to get to know this girl.'

He didn't tell her why, he couldn't. 'We've made up our minds, Mother,' he said with as much firmness as he could put into his voice. 'I already know Jeanie well. We worked for the same company all last summer.'

'I still don't think you understand, Barney. It takes time to organise a wedding. If you put it off until the better weather in the spring, I will—'

'It's already organised, Mother. I'm of age'

'I know but you shouldn't . . . We really ought to know your fiancée. You must bring her to meet us. If you marry—'

'Mum, we're going to.'

'Once you're married she must come and stay with us for a while so that we can get to know each other properly.'

She kept him talking in the public phone box until he ran out of change.

Beatrice put the phone down and felt ready to collapse. She took two aspirins, closed her eyes and went to lie down on the sofa. She was still there inert when Patsy came home from work.

'Don't you feel well, Mum?' she asked.

'I feel terrible.' Beatrice levered herself up into a sitting position. 'Barney is getting married but not to Madge. I'm horrified.' She relayed the details, repeating to Patsy almost word for word all she'd said to Barney.

'I'm totally shocked,' she went on. 'I don't think Barney knows what he's doing. Where did he get this girl from? And poor Madge! If he's ready to get married, why isn't it to her?'

'I don't know,' Patsy said. 'This Jeanie must be really special to make him decide to marry her so quickly – unless he's got her pregnant too.'

'Don't be facetious, Patsy.'

* * *

Jeanie was looking forward to seeing Barney's home and meeting his family. She made a big effort to look her best and was determined to be friendly. She wanted them to like her. Barney was like a cat on hot bricks. She guessed he'd never have taken her near his mother if he hadn't been about to marry her.

His little sister let them in; she was very pretty, but then with a brother like Barney she was bound to be. But she also had an air of bustling efficiency about her, while he was less alert and took less interest in what was going on around him.

As her coat was hung on the hallstand, Jeanie caught a glimpse of the table set formally for tea in the dining room. Then she was led into the sitting room to meet his mother. Beatrice greeted her but remained seated. Jeanie sat too and made an effort to keep a smile on her face and look more relaxed than she felt.

His mother was not welcoming, there was a haughty look on her face. She said, 'You live in Rhyl, I understand, and took Barney in as a lodger.'

'Yes, it's nice there in the summer.'

'Tell us about your family, we need to get to know you.'

Jeanie wasn't sure what Barney had told them and didn't want to contradict him. 'Mum helps in the local hospital,' she said cautiously.

'I do wish I had the stamina to do that sort of thing,' Beatrice said. 'She's a volunteer?'

'No, she's an orderly. They pay her for it. I don't think she'd choose to do it if they didn't.'

She saw Beatrice's nose wrinkle ever so slightly. 'She has to go out to work then?'

'Yes, if she wants to eat. Like we all do.'

'What about your father? What does he do?'

'I think he was a sailor, but I don't really know. I never knew him. Mum doesn't talk about him.'

'Oh, she must find it quite difficult having no family to help her.'

'Mum manages fine. She has two sisters, they're very close. I stay with them quite a lot. My Aunt Cissie brought up both my mum and my Aunt Lil because their mother died young.'

'They must have had a hard life.' There was the slightest touch of disdain in Beatrice's voice.

'I think they have quite a good time in their own way.' Jeanie was not taking to her. She knew from the moment Beatrice had set eyes on her that she thought she wasn't good enough for her son. Her mother-in law was a stuck-up bitch.

Barney watched this taking place. Jeanie was looking her best, her white-blond hair was newly washed and in fluffy curls like lamb's wool. Smiles kept coming and going on her plump face, her cheeks were rosy and her green eyes shining.

Barney knew his mother wouldn't approve of the outfit she'd borrowed from Wanda for the occasion. She'd think her heels too high and her skirt too short. Her pregnancy did not show, in fact she looked quite sexy in the leaf-green hat and coat, but Mum wouldn't like that either. Barney was quite shocked to find his mother a little weepy. She sat back and took no further interest in them. That brought home to him how much this was upsetting her.

It was Patsy who took charge, made a pot of tea and shepherded them all to the dining room. It was Patsy who kept the conversation going, telling him how Beatrice had made the cakes they were cating, about the flowers in the garden and how the family business was faring.

Jeanie felt a touch of frost in Barney's manner to Patsy and knew he was jealous of how she was keeping things going.

Two weeks later, they were married with very little fuss. It had been agreed by Jeanie's family that they should all go back to Aunt Cissie's house after the ceremony and she'd lay out a buffet wedding breakfast on her dining table. Aunt Lil made two bowls of trifle and bought a chocolate cake from the Co-op because Jeanie had praised it. Jeanie bought two tins of pink salmon and Wanda went out that morning to buy some salad ingredients to go with it.

Barney couldn't sleep there the night before because Cissie needed the space for her two sisters. On the morning of his wedding he took the bus there wearing his uniform. The three sisters were all dressed up to the nines. Jeanie had chosen a pale mauve wedding outfit, an edge to edge coat over a matching dress. It was the height of fashion and Barney told her she looked very smart.

She had organised a taxi to take them all to the register office where his mother, Patsy and Rupert were waiting. Beatrice introduced Rupert to Jeanie's relatives. He told them he'd only be able to stay for the ceremony as he was working and couldn't take more time off.

Jeanie whispered that Patsy looked very classy in a suit of pearl-grey set off by a scarlet hat with veiling. She'd brought her box Brownie camera and took photographs of them all.

Beatrice felt tired and out of sorts by the time she and Patsy were on the train going home. Her new shoes were crippling her and she'd have loved to slip her feet out of them.

'What d'you think of Jeanie?' she asked Patsy. 'I'm afraid she's not the sort of wife I'd have chosen for Barney.'

'Mum, you can't expect to choose his wife.'

'Well, you know what I mean.'

'I think she'll suit him well enough. She's all smiles. She looks very happy.'

'She looks a tart. And so does her mother.'

Patsy laughed. 'You say Barney makes up his mind in too much of a hurry, but so do you. You'll probably like Jeanie when you get to know her.'

'Madge is a much nicer girl. I can't understand why he was in such a hurry to marry this one when he'd refused to marry Madge when she was pregnant. Now he's married this girl, he'll never come back to live with us. I feel I've lost him.'

'Mum, you must put that out of your mind.' Patsy wanted to be sympathetic but she didn't feel that way about Barney. 'When he was growing up, you sacrificed everything for him. You've run round after him like a nanny for years, cooked and washed and cared for him in every way. He left home of his own accord, you didn't throw him out. Now he's of age, an adult, grown up, you must untie him from your apron strings and let him do things in his own way.'

'He's very unsure of himself, you know. Makes important decisions on the spur of the moment and then changes his mind ten minutes later. He's full of enthusiasm for a job at one moment and can't stand it the next. I don't know whether he's got it in him to manage anything.'

'He's managed to get himself a wife, Mum. Let her take your place now.'

Beatrice sighed and shook her head. 'I'm much happier about you and Rupert. You know where you're going and I'm sure you'll cope, but Barney . . .'

'If there's anything Barney wants,' Patsy retorted, 'he'll be sure to ask for it, he always has. It's time you started thinking of yourself.'

* * *

Barney and Jeanie agreed the wedding went off very well, but no sooner were they on the train to their honeymoon hotel in Southport than Jeanie complained of feeling unwell. 'I've got backache and cramps in my belly. I feel a bit sick too.'

'You must have eaten too much of that trifle.'

Jeanie had booked them into a small family-run hotel.

'I'm pleased with this,' Barney said, but Jeanie was taking no interest in her surroundings.

'I feel worse,' she said and for once couldn't stand him holding her. 'I've got to lie down, just leave me in peace for a bit.' She lay down on the bed and closed her eyes so he tucked the eiderdown round her.

Barney began to worry, this was not like Jeanie. He was about to go down to reception to ask where he could find a doctor to attend her, when she began to cry out in pain. He ran down and asked advice from the owner, who sent for an ambulance.

Barney went with her to the hospital and had a panic attack in the ambulance. He was given oxygen and made to lie down until his breathing returned to normal. Jeanie suffered a miscarriage an hour after reaching hospital. Barney was sent away and spent his wedding night alone, feeling lonely, sorry for himself and somewhat confused. His honeymoon was ruined. He was worried about Jeanie, but mighty glad about her miscarriage.

The next morning he went back to the hospital to see how she was, hoping she'd be able to join him in the hotel for lunch. The ward sister was sympathetic because they were on their honeymoon but told him Jeanie would need a D&C before she'd be able to come out. She was on tomorrow morning's operating list.

159

Barney was allowed to spend ten minutes with her but was told to return in the official visiting hours of between two and four o'clock. Jeanie said she felt all right but she looked subdued. By the afternoon she was smiling again although she knew he'd have to report back to the barracks before midnight.

'Don't say anything about me having a miscarriage,' she said to him. 'I don't want Mum or Aunt Cissie to know. I told nobody but you I was pregnant. Better if it stays that way.'

Barney couldn't agree more. 'But wasn't Aunt Cissie expecting you back tonight?'

'Yes, but I can ring her from the phone box downstairs and tell her I've changed my mind, that I'm going home to Rhyl for a few days.'

'But you told Mum and Patsy you'd go to see them next weekend while I have to stay in barracks.'

'It was only an invite to Sunday tea. I'll see how I feel by then. Either I'll go or I'll cancel that too.' Jeanie sighed. 'If they let me out of here by Thursday I might go home to see Mum. I told her I'd come soon to pick up more of my clothes. Bring me in three postcards of Southport so I can let them know what I'm doing. We won't spell out about the miscarriage to anybody. Nobody needs to know I'm in hospital.'

'You'll come back to Chester, won't you? I can get out for a few hours almost every evening now.'

'Yes, of course. Aunt Cissie has agreed to have me as a lodger so I can be near you when you have time off. I'll be back in time for your next weekend pass. She'll be happy to let you share my bed now we're married.' Her face was wreathed with smiles. 'You aren't sorry, are you?'

'No, I feel I've been let off the hook.'

She giggled and her whole face screwed up with fun. 'I meant sorry about getting married.'

'Of course not,' he said. 'I do love you, Jeanie.'

'As far as the baby's concerned, I feel I've been let off the hook too.'

But on the way back to barracks Barney wished Jeanie's miscarriage could have happened a week earlier. He told himself that of course he wasn't sorry he'd married her, but it would have been nice not to feel pushed into it.

CHAPTER FOURTEEN

J EANIE LAY ON HER hospital bed with her eyes closed. She didn't feel ill, but she needed to think about her changed circumstances and what she should do now. She was euphoric that she'd lost the baby. Pregnancy had been a crisis she'd had to resolve, but as things turned out it had resolved itself. She needn't have done anything. She'd wanted to marry Barney because he was the father, and marriage would appease her relatives.

Jeanie was very fond of him; he was great in bed, a good-looking fellow. Her relatives thought him posh, but he had no common sense, no money sense and no drive. There was no point in wondering whether she'd have married him, he'd never have got round to asking her if it hadn't been for the pregnancy scare. But now the knot was tied.

Once Jeanie knew she was likely to be discharged from hospital on Thursday morning, she sent off her postcards. One to her mother announcing that she was coming to collect more of her clothes and would spend the weekend with her, one to Aunt Cissie telling her she was going home to Rhyl, and one to her mother-in-law cancelling her Sunday afternoon visit. She wrote a letter to Barney telling him what she was doing.

After the anxiety, rush and panic of the last few weeks, she was glad to be able to relax at home. Mum was pleased to see her and told her she'd done well for herself marrying into the

Rushton family. She agreed, and when she returned to Aunt Cissie's house in Chester, they spent their first evening together sitting one each side the fire drinking tea and discussing her in-laws.

'The Rushtons are a rich family,' Jeanie told her aunt. 'They've owned their own business for over seventy years. Beatrice says they're doing well and I reckon this coming war will ensure they continue to earn even more money.'

'Even though that slip of a girl is said to be running it?'

'I suppose her mother's really in charge.'

'But why isn't Barney working in their business? What did he join up for?'

'He says he wanted to fight for his country,' Jeanie said.

'The fool! He needs to grow up and find out what life is really like. Why did he spend all last summer selling ice cream in Rhyl?'

'He wanted to be with me.'

'It was romance? He was falling in love with you?' Aunt Cissie laughed.

'Something like that. We had a good time last summer.'

'Couldn't he see you'd both have a good time for the rest of your lives if he'd stayed and worked in the family business? He'd have been able to earn enough money so that after a few years you'd be able to live in a nice house, have a fine car and do whatever you wanted. I don't think he knows which side his bread is buttered.'

'Things weren't so clear,' Jeanie said. 'His father was still alive and running the business.'

'His mother dotes on Barney. She'd let him do anything. He should never have joined up and left everything open for his little sister. You'll have to point things out to him, Jeanie. See that he gets his share or he'll be pushed out altogether.

There'll be plenty earned by that business for all of you to live reasonably well. Barney will get posted away and his sister will forget about him being due for anything. If I were you, I'd stay close to that mother and daughter and make friends of them. The trouble with Barney is that all his life he's had everything handed to him on a plate. He's never had to look out for himself. He's not like us, having to slave and save for everything we have.'

Jeanie listened carefully and took it all to heart. In her family, Aunt Cissie had the reputation of having financial acumen. She was the only one of the sisters who had accumulated any savings; Aunt Lil and her own mother lived hand to mouth.

A few days after the wedding, Patsy set off to work on her bike but made a small detour to the chemist shop where she'd put in three rolls of film to be developed. Rupert had given her the roll from his Leica camera to put in at the same time. He'd laughed at her Box Brownie and said she could afford a better camera now. She didn't want to stop and look at her pictures in the street and found Tim was already working at his desk when she got there.

'I've got the wedding photos back,' she said as she opened the packets on her desk. Her Box Brownie had only eight postcard-sized pictures on the roll but she was delighted with them. 'They're good. I'm thrilled with them. I think Jeanie will be too.'

Tim came over to have a look. 'They're excellent, your brother looks like a film star.'

Patsy laughed. 'Don't tell him that or he'll be off to Hollywood.'

'You Rushtons are a handsome family. I'd say you look

smarter and prettier than the bride, and she's not bad either.'

'Rupert's taken many more photos than I did. His are absolutely first class, aren't they?' She was passing them over to him one by one.

'It's because he has a more expensive camera. Was this taken at your home?' He held one up.

'Yes, on Boxing Day.'

'Oh!' Tim paused. 'It's serious then, you and Rupert?'

Tim had never been invited to her home and something in his voice told Patsy he was envious that Rupert had. His dark eyes were staring into hers. She could feel his emotion and knew this was important to him. She felt she had to be honest. 'Yes. Mum invited him to meet Barney.'

'Oh!' He was embarrassed now and wouldn't look at her. It took him a few moments to recover. 'I've brought something to show you. Yesterday, we were talking about expanding the premises, so on the way home I called in at the estate agent selling the building next door and got the details.'

'Oh good, let's have a look.' He passed the brochure over and Patsy studied it. 'This used to be a typing school. Two separate rooms downstairs – between the two, we'd have room for eight sewing machines.'

'I've measured it up, it would take ten.'

She laughed. 'Thanks, Tim. I can rely on you to do a thorough job. Would it be better to buy the next-door building or extend out into the yard behind here?'

'Or make the flat into another sewing room?'

'Mum suggested that when I tried to talk to her about it.'

'It makes sense, Patsy. It would be the cheapest way to get more space.'

Patsy was very much against it. 'I've just spruced the flat up. I've spent money on it.' The flat was part of her dream world. She hoped one day she'd marry Rupert and it would be their home.

She frowned. 'It would make more sense to buy the building next door if it was semi-detached to the workshop, but it isn't.'

'I see more advantages this way. Once you own it, you could take the fence down in between and be able to drive straight through to the yard at the back. It would be more convenient to load and unload there instead of through the front and you'd have more parking space.'

'So we would. That's a good idea, Tim.' Patsy stretched backwards in her chair. 'Dad used to talk of building on the back. That's what he dreamed of doing if the business improved.'

Tim smiled at her. 'You're bound to be influenced by your dad's ideas, but things are changing all the time. The house next door was not up for sale when he was alive so that wasn't something he could consider.'

'And suddenly there is so much work for everybody, the situation has changed completely.'

'Yes, if you want to take full advantage of that you'll need a larger workforce. If you still think you'd be better off putting up a single-storey building at the back, you need to think of the time it would take as well as the cost.'

'The time it would take to build?'

'Not only that, you'd be waiting around for months for planning permission. It would be quicker to buy next door. I understand it isn't difficult to change the use of business premises.'

'Tim, you do talk sense. What would I do without you to sort me out? I'll ring the estate agent and ask for the key.'

Before the end of the afternoon, the key was delivered to

Patsy. 'Come on,' she said. 'Let's go and see if it would suit. This is quite exciting, isn't it?'

Tim had to throw his weight against the front door to open it. 'The wood has swollen with all the recent rain,' he said. 'It'll be all right when it dries out.'

Patsy looked up the narrow hall with a flight of steep stairs at the end leading to the upper floor. The place felt cold and smelled of damp, and her first feeling was of disappointment. 'It's very shabby.'

'You'll get it cheaper because of that,' Tim pointed out. 'You'll need structural work done here and that will ruin any decorations, good or bad. My dad was in the building trade, he used to talk to me about it sometimes.'

'What do you think we'd need done?'

Tim gazed round. 'You'll want one big room in here, so knock down the walls that aren't weight-bearing. That window at the back is wide enough to change it to a double door by knocking out the brickwork below it. That would make it easier to get the cloth in and the finished garments out. Then the whole place will have to be rewired to get enough power for the sewing machines. There's quite a big kitchen, better to leave that so the girls can make tea there. Would there be room for a table and a couple of forms for them to sit down and eat at lunchtime?'

'Tim! You make me see the possibilities.'

'There's an outside lavatory – just the thing for the men.'

'And a bathroom upstairs.' Patsy ran up the stairs to see it. 'Quite a modern bathroom, it's better than ours in the flat.'

'It's been put in quite recently,' Tim pointed out. 'The girls would love it.'

In a state of indecision, Patsy asked, 'So you think it would be a good idea to buy it?'

He got out his tape measure and said, 'With the walls out, there'd be room for at least a dozen machines here. I think it's feasible, but you could get another opinion before you decide.'

'I wish Dad was here. He'd know the best thing to do.'

'That's the really hard part.' Tim looked at her with a wry smile. 'Managing on your own.'

Back in the workshop, the girls were putting on their coats and getting ready to go home.

'Before I do anything else,' Patsy said, 'I'm going to take the account books up to the flat and make sure there's enough business to warrant expansion on this scale. After all, we have already taken on five more seamstresses and bought three new machines and squeezed them in where we could.'

In their office, Tim took the books out of the drawers in his desk and put them under his arm to take upstairs.

'You don't have to stay,' she said. 'You've already worked a full day.'

'So have you. I'd like to stay, you've got me interested.'

'Thanks, Tim. You're a good friend. Come on up, I'll make a cup of tea first.'

They set about adding up the earnings for the last six months. 'Better than my wildest hopes,' Patsy said when they had a figure. 'I knew the amount was going up every month but I can hardly believe this. Dad would think it marvellous. I do wish he'd lived long enough to see it.'

'I'm delighted for you, Patsy,' Tim said. 'These figures mean you won't need to borrow money to expand the business and it makes sense to do it now.'

'I know – my head's in a whirl. I must think about it.'

'Why don't you ask Bill Bentley to look at it and get his opinion?'

'That's a good idea.'

When she rang him the next morning, Bill's voice was hale and hearty. He said, 'Do you a favour? You know I'm more than glad to have the chance of that.'

He walked down within the hour and agreed with Tim that the building next door could be a sound proposition.

'You need the opinion of a good builder before you decide. One who will not charge over the odds and will see any difficulties next door before he starts knocking the place down.'

'I don't know any builders.' Patsy frowned.

'I know one you could trust. He did some work for me a couple of years ago – urgent repair work, not a big job like this. He lives near me and I know he's looking for work. Shall I ask him to come round?'

'Yes please,' Patsy said. 'I'll keep the key to next door until he's seen the place.'

'You're doing the right thing by expanding now.' Bill looked approvingly at Patsy. 'A right chip off the old block,' he said to Tim.

Ten days later Patsy received from the builder a detailed list of the work needed to convert next door to another sewing room and told the estate agent she wanted to buy it.

Because she was under twenty-one, she had to explain it all to her mother and take her to see the building, as she needed her signature on the documents. Beatrice was quite nervous about signing for it. 'It's such a lot of money,' she said. 'Can you afford it?'

For Barney, having Jeanie nearby meant he had a companion for his time off and they had money to spend on having a good time. Jeanie found herself another job in the local Co-op which gave them a little more.

With his basic training now finished, Barney began to hope

his working life would improve. But he discovered that he, together with all his intake of recruits, had been assessed as having the right aptitude and would now be given specialist machine-gun training here at the castle.

Barney was afraid he wouldn't be able to do it. Guns of all sorts scared him but he found the machine gun particularly menacing. It could kill swathes of men in one sweep. He knew he had to do something and forced himself to approach the warrant officer who was running the course. Very politely, he said, 'Sir, I understood that as a volunteer I'd be given a choice of trades for which I would be trained.'

'You've all volunteered for the army,' he was told, 'and what we need are men capable of handling a machine gun. Look upon it as part of your basic training. Perhaps you'll be able to go on to something else later.'

'Yes, sir.'

'What training do you have in mind? What trade?'

'I'd like to be a despatch rider, sir,' Barney said. 'I already have a civilian licence to drive both cars and motorbikes. It's something I enjoy. I know I'd be good at it.'

'Well, possibly, but we need to find out how good you are with a machine gun first,' he was told.

Barney put it down to his usual ill luck; he rarely found himself doing work he found congenial. 'I don't like guns,' he said, forcing the words out.

His unit was told they'd be taught about the different parts of the mechanism, how the gun worked and how to maintain it in tiptop condition. Later they'd be taken to the shooting range. Barney found his fellow recruits were looking forward to that part but it scared him to death, though he knew that to start with they would not be using live ammunition.

That night Barney had a nightmare: the warrant officer

had given each one of them a gun, and the whole unit had turned them on him and threatened to fire. He heard someone screaming but didn't realise it was him until he'd woken up half those in his barrack room. That made them aggressive towards him which seemed to make the dream a reality. From then on, he felt as though something was lurking in the background ready to pounce on him.

The next day his unit had their first lesson. Real machine guns were given to them to handle. Barney couldn't drag his eyes away from his. He hated it from the moment he set eyes on it and didn't want to touch it.

They were shown how to strip the gun down to its various parts, clean them and put them back together. Barney felt all thumbs and could see his hands shaking. He took a deep breath and paused. All round him he could hear little clicks as others pushed the pieces together as they'd been shown. He peeped to see how the man next to him was managing. He had the gun almost reassembled. His confident hand felt for the last part and clicked it home.

Barney grabbed two of the parts in front of him and pressed them together, but nothing happened. He pressed with all his might. He heard no click but felt a searing pain shoot through his little finger on his left hand.

He screamed and everybody turned to look at him. He was in agony and saw blood beginning to seep out. He panicked and another scream ripped through his throat though he tried to silence it. He sensed the warrant officer close beside him. 'I've hurt . . . I've hurt my finger.'

'You've caught it in the mechanism.' His voice sounded a long way away. 'How did you manage that? You'd better go to sickbay and get it bandaged.'

Barney's head was swimming but he tried to move towards

the door. 'Watch what you're doing, Private Rushton, or you'll get blood on your uniform.'

Everything was swirling round him and going black, he was swaying and knew he was going to pass out before he reached the door. Moments later he could hear distant voices all shouting at once. Then a voice he recognised, the warrant officer's, said, 'He's only fainted, he'll be all right in a few moments.'

Barney lay on the floor in excruciating pain, trying to lift his hand to see the cause. The next moment, with a man on each side of him, he was jerked to his feet and marched off to the sickbay. The pain was killing him, he couldn't breathe. He'd never known such agony.

The nurse was sympathetic. 'I'll get you something for the pain. You've crushed your little finger.'

The pain felt almost as bad an hour later. A doctor came to see him. 'I'm sending you to the hospital, you've broken the bone in your finger and the first joint isn't bending as it should.'

Barney came round from the anaesthetic to find he'd had his left little finger amputated just below the first joint.

'The bone had splintered and the joint damaged beyond repair,' the surgeon told him. 'But it needn't stop you doing things. You'll be left with a neat stump instead of a little finger.'

Barney's face was wet with tears, he was afraid it wouldn't be as simple as that. He felt a pall of dread at the thought of handling a machine gun again. He told the surgeon as clearly as he could that he'd never bring himself to fire one, not after what had happened. The thought of going into battle armed with one made him feel desperate.

He was kept in the military hospital for four days; the pain didn't go away but it eased somewhat. He felt terrible and couldn't sleep in the ward, there was too much light and noise.

He was taken to see a psychiatrist in his clinic and was questioned about guns. He was asked if the loss of his finger was really an accident or whether he had intended to harm himself.

'It was an accident,' Barney said. 'Truly it was. Why would I ever want to hurt myself?'

Jeanie came to see him and brought him cigarettes which he was allowed to smoke in the day room. When he was discharged he was given a week's convalescent leave. Jeanie took him back to Aunt Cissie's. 'Now we're married she's happy to have you there,' she said.

But Barney was still uncomfortable in her house. He couldn't forget her previous lack of welcome. He'd already rung his mother to tell her of the accident and when he rang her again, she invited him to bring Jeanie to spend his week's convalescence with her.

'Do come,' she said. 'We'll get you well again and it's high time we got to know Jeanie.'

Jeanie was keen to see more of Barney's childhood home and the business that supported his family. Fern Bank sounded quite grand and when she'd first seen that it was a modern semi-detached house she'd been disappointed. Nevertheless, it was larger and more comfortable than her old home and she was impressed with its neatness and cleanliness and the trouble Beatrice went to when serving meals. Jeanie was ready to relax and enjoy being treated as a guest in their house. She was expecting to have her first taste of luxury.

Barney was complaining that his hand was painful and he was not feeling well. Jeanie knew things had been difficult for Barney's mother and sister while he had been in Rhyl with her last summer. She'd already sensed his feelings of guilt about

that and also his envy that Patsy had managed very well
without him. He spoke of Patsy having taken advantage of his
absence to better her own position and that now she had a
greater say in how the family finances were managed.

It seemed the family always ate their main meal in the
evening when the day's work was over and they could sit
round the dining-room table. On the first evening she was
there, Jeanie was impressed to find the table beautifully set
with an immaculate white damask cloth and a silver bowl filled
with pink rosebuds.

She wanted to find out all she could about Barney's family
because he'd rarely spoken of them. She politely asked
questions of them but when she felt the conversation was
beginning to sound like a grilling, she began talking about her
own childhood in Rhyl to keep them interested.

Jeanie was complimenting Beatrice on her cottage pie when
she noticed she'd dropped a little of it on to her dress and tried
to wipe it off on her handkerchief.

'If you would use the table napkin I put out for you, you
would have saved that,' Beatrice told her in ladylike tones.
'That's what they're for.'

Jeanie was embarrassed to find the other three had all used
theirs and her napkin was the only one still folded beside her
place. She was even more embarrassed when the dinner plates
were collected and she found she'd left a smudge of gravy on
the tablecloth too. Her mother-in-law was regarding it icily.

'I'm sorry,' Jeanie said. 'I'll wash it off for you afterwards.'

'There's no need, dear,' Beatrice said in her haughty
manner. 'I prefer to have my tablecloths lightly starched by
the laundry.'

That made Jeanie feel knee-high; it seemed Beatrice judged
her to be unable to eat in a civilised manner. Barney kept

muttering that it didn't matter, but she could see it had embarrassed him too.

Patsy brought in the apple pie and custard that was to follow, and while they were eating that, Barney asked, 'Is it all right if I bring Jeanie down tomorrow to see the business?'

'Yes, of course,' Patsy said. 'You can show her round yourself.'

'Thank you,' Jeanie said. 'I've heard so much about it, I'm looking forward to seeing it.'

'We'll come after lunch,' Barney said. 'And I've been wondering about the old delivery van. I'd like to borrow it to drive Jeanie round to see places of interest while we're here.'

'Will you be able to drive?' his mother asked anxiously. 'You have a big bandage on your finger and you said it was still painful.'

'I'll take care not to bang it,' he said. 'Is that all right with you, Patsy?'

'No,' she said. 'No, I'm not keen on that idea.'

'Why ever not?' Barney was trying to laugh it off. 'It would do the old van good.'

Jeanie watched Patsy's blue eyes bore into Barney's face. 'I'm afraid you'll drive it back to Chester and I'll never see it again. After all, you did that with Dad's car.'

'Would it matter?' Barney blustered. 'It's just standing there, isn't it? You said you no longer have to deliver the work you complete.'

'That's mostly true.' Patsy looked round the table and gave Jeanie a wry smile. 'Though we still get work from a few of our old customers and they want things done the old way. But it isn't exactly standing still, Barney. I'm learning to drive. Do you remember Bill Bentley, Dad's old friend?'

Barney shook his head.

'He takes me out in the van to practise. I've arranged for him to take me tomorrow afternoon after work. So you definitely can't have it. I'll be sitting my test next month and need all the practice I can get.'

'Barney can take you out to practise,' Jeanie said. 'I'll be happy to sit quietly in the back and see Birkenhead that way.'

'So he could,' Patsy said. 'But Mr Bentley's quite keen to teach me. His wife died not so long ago and he said he was getting a bit depressed, and that he needs different things to fill his life and more to do. So thank you but my way suits us better.'

It turned out to be a very uncomfortable evening for Jeanie. She decided that she didn't like her in-laws, and she was never going to take to them. Beatrice was horribly toffee-nosed and looked down on her. She was amazed at Patsy's decisiveness, but it didn't please her. While she kept her grip of iron on the business, Barney was never going to get his fair share of the family money.

CHAPTER FIFTEEN

PATSY SIGHED AS SHE got ready for bed. Barney had lost no time trying to take over the company van, but she'd half expected him to do that.

She had moved back to her little bedroom so Jeanie and Barney could use the larger one, and was quite happy about that. She'd chosen everything in here and it was comfortingly familiar.

The next day, Barney brought Jeanie down to the workshop at about half past three and they spent the best part of the first hour walking round the premises talking to the staff. When they came up to the office, Patsy introduced Jeanie to Tim.

Barney ignored him and said, 'My goodness, Patsy, the place has really grown, I wouldn't have believed it.'

Patsy smiled. 'I told you we were expanding to take advantage of all the work flooding in.'

'Yes, but you've done it so quickly.'

'No point in letting the grass grow under our feet,' Tim said.

'We're buying the building next door to expand further,' Patsy told them. 'It seemed the best way to get the work space we need.'

'Gosh, buying another building?' Jeanie's plump and pretty face was never still. Patsy could see amazement on it now. Usually it was wreathed with smiles that came and went, making her seem always happy and good-humoured. Patsy found her likeable.

'What about a cup of tea?' Barney suggested to Patsy.

'Of course,' Patsy said. 'I'll make one upstairs in the flat. You and Jeanie might as well see what I've done up there too. Bill usually has a cup with me before he takes me driving. What about you, Tim? Are you coming up for a cup of tea?'

'Not tonight, Patsy, I'd like to get on home.' Usually he stayed but she knew he and Barney didn't get on. Barney was already leading the way up to the flat.

'Ooh, it's gorgeous,' Jeanie cooed as soon as she saw the living room. 'It's so bright and big. You've made it lovely.'

'You've done all these improvement up here too?' Even Barney was impressed. 'It used to be quite dark and shabby.'

'It didn't take much,' she said, 'just a coat of paint and some new carpets and curtains. Dad wasn't interested, he rarely came up here except to eat his lunch, but space is more important now.' She took them to the kitchen while she put the kettle on.

'There's everything here,' Jeanie marvelled, looking round at the larder, the cooker and the Belfast sink.

'A bit old-fashioned,' Patsy said, 'but it all functions and it suits the style here, doesn't it?'

Jeanie was off to see the rest of the place. 'Quite a big bathroom too,' she called.

As Patsy got out the cups and saucers, she heard Barney say, 'We all lived here when we were small but there are only two bedrooms so we had to move. We needed three once Patsy was growing up.'

She knew they'd moved on to inspect the bedrooms. Jeanie had dropped her voice but the whisper drifted back, 'It would be an ideal place for us to set up home.' For the first time Patsy wondered if she'd been wise to bring them here. 'All we'd need would be a bed and some mats in here. The curtains are lovely.'

Patsy froze. She didn't want to lose her flat. She heard Jeanie urge, 'Ask her if we can.'

'Not now,' Barney hissed.

'The place is hardly used.'

Patsy went to the kitchen door and strained her ears to hear more. She heard Barney say, 'She's using the bedrooms as storerooms, isn't she? This one is full of work waiting to be done and the other is finished work waiting for collection.'

'We could easily move that somewhere else,' Jeanie answered. 'It can't be a convenient place for storerooms, can it? Not up all these stairs? I'd love to live here.'

Patsy felt her cheeks flame with anger. Barney believed everything owned by the family could be his. She wasn't going to let him take the flat, it was more important to her than the van. She felt thrills run up her spine every time she thought of Rupert, and was sure he was on the point of proposing. That was why she'd done it up with such care. When they were married it would be their home.

Hadn't Rupert helped her choose the colour scheme and the two carpet squares in the living room? It was done up to their taste. It was their flat. Patsy decided there and then that Barney was not going to collar it for himself and Jeanie.

She heard the doorbell ring. Gritting her teeth she hid her anger and ran down to let Bill Bentley in. 'Come and have a cup of tea first,' she said. 'My brother and his wife are here. Barney can't get over how much we've expanded recently.'

She provided chocolate biscuits and Bill's favourite short-bread with the tea and they sat round the dining table to chat as they had it. Fifteen minutes later, with the teacups empty,

Patsy got to her feet. 'Time to go,' she said. 'Can't keep Bill hanging about when he's come to give me driving practice.'

'I'll wash the cups up first,' Jeanie said.

'They can wait till morning,' Patsy assured her, rattling her keys. She wanted Jeanie and Barney outside. 'I need to lock up for the night now. Everybody's gone home.'

'All right,' Barney said. Patsy could see he didn't like being pushed out. 'Are you going anywhere near our house? You could give us a lift home, save us having to walk.'

Bill caught her eye. 'I think having passengers would put Patsy off,' he said. 'Probably better if you let us get on now.'

'Thank you,' Patsy whispered as she got in beside him and started the engine. But she was still very much put out and couldn't concentrate on her driving. She was making a lot of mistakes. Bill laughed when she told him why she was cross, and suggested they give up, put the car back in her yard and he'd take her to the nearby New Dock Hotel for a drink to calm her down.

Her mother had told her it used to be known as the Blood Tub because fights regularly broke out amongst their clientele, but in the early part of the evening it was quiet. Bill took her into the lounge and bought her a glass of orange squash. She told him how Barney had taken Dad's car and then sold it, and that now he was angling for the flat.

'They can't move in there unless you give them the keys,' he said. 'Just say no.'

Later, over a special supper of Mum's steak and kidney pie, Jeanie began telling Beatrice how fascinating she'd found her tour round the business.

'I can't believe how much Patsy's managed to expand it.'

Barney smiled first at her and then at their mother.

'And do up the flat on top as well,' Jeanie added.

'Have you seen it, Mum, since it's been done up? It's really lovely now.'

'Yes, Patsy took me to see it, but I never liked it.'

'A shame it isn't used much.' Barney shook his head.

'We're quite short of storage space in the workshop,' Patsy said. 'I need it for that.'

'Not a nice place to live really, down in the industrial area,' Beatrice said. 'They're pulling down those blocks of tenements nearby and making such a racket. I'm sure the place must be full of dust.'

'They're all down now, Mum, the site has been cleared.'

'I'd love it,' Jeanie said, her face wreathed with smiles.

Barney said, as though he'd just thought of it, 'It would make a first home for me and Jeanie. Now I'm married I could do with a home of my own.'

Beatrice slowly put down her knife and fork. 'I can see that you might want a base . . .'

'But Barney,' Patsy interrupted, 'you've joined the army. They will decide where you live and it could be the other side of the country.'

'But I have to think of Jeanie.'

'Of course you do.' Patsy was aware of Jeanie's smiles coming and going. 'But if you get posted to Catterick or some other home station, Jeanie will want to go with you and find lodgings, won't you, Jeanie?'

Jeanie couldn't bring herself to deny that. She stared at her silently.

'You'd find that much easier to do if you didn't already have a home here. I think you'd be wise to delay that for a bit and see what the army requires of Barney. He might just as easily be posted to some war zone on the other side of the world.' Patsy saw him flinch at that. 'We'd love to have you live with us, Jeanie,' she said. 'We have plenty of room here and I'm sure you'd find it comfortable.'

'Patsy's right,' Beatrice said. 'You need to stay flexible at the moment, Barney. Wait and see where they're going to send you.'

Jeanie had to hide the resentment she felt for Patsy. She knew she must not make an enemy of her at this early stage. Patsy had been very high-handed about not allowing Barney to use the van and now she had flatly refused to let them move into that flat. His mother could have been persuaded, but Patsy had deliberately turned her off. Jeanie felt very put out.

Later on that evening when they'd all gone to bed, Jeanie snuggled up to Barney and whispered, 'You've got to stand up to Patsy. You let her walk all over you.'

'I don't.' He was indignant.

'You do. You're as entitled to use the things the family wealth has bought as she is. We're married now and need a home of our own. You let her talk you out of moving into that flat though I'd love to live there. It's barely used and she's your little sister. Why should she decide what you can do?'

'Well,' Barney tried to justify himself, 'she's done it up.'

'So what? Where else would she get the money but from the family business? I'd have loved to do it.'

'Yes.' Barney pondered for a moment. 'But Mum was married twice, I have a different father. The garment business came from Patsy's dad.'

'Good Lord!' Surprise made Jeanie pull herself free from his arms. 'I didn't know that, why didn't you tell me?'

'Nobody told me about it. My father was never mentioned when I was growing up. I found out by accident when I was nine years old.'

'Did that upset you?' She came snuggling up to him again, eager to hear all about it.

'Yes, of course it did. I wasn't who I thought I was.'

'Tell me about your father.'

'I don't know much about him,' Barney admitted. 'Mum doesn't want to talk about him. I only found out because I came across my birth certificate and found my name was different.'

'What was your name?'

'Tavenham something.'

'What?'

'Tavenham-Strong, that's it. My father's name was Rowland Tavenham-Strong.'

'Double-barrelled? That's posh. Why do you call yourself Barney Rushton then?'

'I think that must have been Mum's idea. She wanted us all to be one family.'

'But does that mean I'm really Mrs Tavenham-Strong?'

Barney sounded irritable. 'I don't know, do I?'

'You should have asked. Why didn't you?'

'Oh, I don't know. Mum was all uptight, I just wanted to push it into the background and forget I'd ever seen that birth certificate.'

'You could have asked her a day or two later.'

Barney sniffed and sighed heavily.

'Did your dad work in the garment industry too?'

'No. He was an army officer.'

'Goodness!' Jeanie was surprised again, even a little excited. 'Perhaps he had more money than Patsy's father.'

'No, Mum talked of being hard up – back in the years of the depression.'

'But his family might have, probably did have. Haven't you ever wondered about them?'

'No, I was just a kid.'

'Unless your mother changed your name by deed poll, I think you are still legally Barney Tavenham-Strong. You can't just change your surname because you fancy something different, not in this day and age. You should find out more about your father.'

Barney complained irritably, 'How am I going to do that?'

'You could start by asking your mother.'

'It would only upset her. Cause more trouble.'

'Why should it? His family might welcome a grown-up grandchild into their midst. They might be as rich as Croesus.'

Barney yawned. 'I'm tired. I want to go to sleep, Jeanie.'

He turned over and she knew by his breathing that he fell asleep straight away. But she was intrigued by what he'd told her. She tossed and turned for ages, her imagination running riot. Did Barney have another richer and more exciting family than the Rushtons?

The next morning, Patsy had barely sat down at her desk when she heard an agitated rapping on the office door. Tim was taking off his coat and opened the door. A very distressed Martha Dixon came in waving the petty cash book. 'It's all gone,' she said. 'I don't understand it. Somebody must have taken it.'

Tim took the book from her hand. 'Come and sit down, Mrs Dixon. What has gone? The petty cash?'

'Yes, like I said. It's all gone. The cash box is empty but there should be £4.17s.5d. here.'

'Don't worry,' Patsy said. 'It's not the end of the world . . .'

'But I do worry. It's theft.'

'You've just discovered this?'

'Yes, I went to pay the milkman. He's here waiting.' She looked at Tim. 'You gave me five pounds only yesterday morning. I know I haven't spent it all.'

'I'd better go and pay the milkman,' Tim said and disappeared.

'The cash box was locked up in the cupboard. It was only when I looked inside . . . I don't understand it.'

'What did you buy yesterday?' Patsy got up to pick up the petty cash book from Tim's desk. 'A pound of tea,' she read out. 'Four pounds of sugar and a pound of ginger biscuits.'

'That's right.'

'So you opened the cash box to get money out for those?'

'No, I bought them on the way to work. I took the money out in the morning, the same time I put the five pounds in. Mr Stansfield was with me.'

'And you didn't open it again until now?'

'Yes, I sent out for Vim and some soap.'

'At what time?'

'In the afternoon. The money was there then.'

'Come and show me where you keep the cash box,' Patsy said and followed her back to the kitchen. Tim was there with the empty box.

'I locked it up in here with the shopping before I went home last night. But I think I left the cash box on top for a while yesterday afternoon,' she admitted, wringing her hands. 'We should tell the police.'

'No,' Patsy decided. 'Carry on keeping the cash box locked in the cupboard where you hang your aprons.'

'It's never happened before and I didn't do anything different.'

'Don't worry about it, Mrs Dixon,' Tim said. 'I'll start you off with another five pound float.'

When she'd gone, Tim said, 'It is worrying all the same. We've never had any trouble with money disappearing here. It would be hopeless asking her who had been in her kitchen yesterday because people are in and out all the time. At break times they're all milling around.'

'I know. Barney was here yesterday afternoon.'

'But he wouldn't steal, Patsy.' There was disbelief in his voice. 'Would he?'

Patsy's lips were straight and stiff. 'I'm afraid he might. He wouldn't see it as theft, you know. Just taking back a little of the business which he'd see as a fraction of his rightful share.'

'Oh God! For less than five pounds? Surely Barney wouldn't dirty his fingers for that sort of sum?'

'He would.' Patsy knew small sums had gone missing in the past from the housekeeping purse. 'They don't pay a soldier like him very much. I didn't dare ask him but it's probably a shilling a day.'

The following evening, when supper was over and cleared away, Barney and his mother had gone to sit by the fire in the sitting room. Patsy had washed up while Jeanie had dried. They were in the kitchen putting the last of the cutlery away when the front doorbell rang.

'I'll get it, Mum,' Patsy called as she went up the hall.

From the sitting-room door Jeanie heard a girlish voice ask brightly, 'Patsy, how are you? Is your mum in? She asked me to bring Katrina round to see her next time I came home.'

Jeanie could see a pram being manoeuvred into the porch and a baby being lifted out.

Patsy's cheeks had flushed bright pink and she seemed to have difficulty getting her words out. 'This is my friend Sheila Worthington,' she choked out in Jeanie's direction, 'and her sister Madge and baby Katrina.'

Patsy stepped back, overcome by embarrassment, and seemed almost paralysed. The visitors were sweeping towards the sitting room. With desperation in her voice, she managed, 'This is Jeanie.'

Jeanie was all smiles. 'Barney's wife,' she added, wanting to appear friendly.

There was a dead silence, nobody moved a muscle. Then Patsy tried desperately to right the situation. 'You'd better come up to my bedroom,' she said. 'We'll have a chat up there.'

Madge's mouth had dropped open. 'Barney's wife?' She tightened her grip on the baby who was alert and looking round.

Beatrice came into the hall. Jeanie saw Barney half hiding behind her, his face puce as his gaze latched on to that of the baby. Katrina opened her mouth and let out a wail of protest. Jeanie felt the whole house flooding with the most acute embarrassment, but she wasn't sure why.

Barney leapt to life, elbowed his way past the visitors without looking at them, snatched his mac from the hallstand and without a word dashed out of the front door, slamming it behind him.

'Come in. Come to the fire, Madge.' Beatrice looked painfully uncomfortable.

Madge was in tears, she lifted wet blue eyes to meet Jeanie's gaze. 'You're Barney's wife?'

'Yes,' she said. Her mouth felt dry.

'How is Katrina?' Beatrice asked in her social voice. 'She certainly seems to have gained weight.'

'She's fine. I don't think I'll stay, Mrs Rushton.' Madge took the baby out to her pram and began tucking her in.

'We shouldn't have burst in on you like this,' Sheila said, looking at Patsy. 'I didn't realise Barney would be here, or his wife.' Jeanie felt Sheila's gaze assessing her. 'Everything's changed, hasn't it? I did tell Madge that Barney was married. She found it hurtful, of course she's upset.' Madge was pushing the pram to the gate.

'That baby?' Jeanie caught at Patsy's arm. 'Is it . . . ?'

'Yes, it's Barney's,' she said coldly. 'That's why he went off to Rhyl last summer.'

CHAPTER SIXTEEN

J EANIE BURST INTO TEARS as the front door closed behind the visitors. 'I find it hard to believe Barney fathered that child,' she wept. After all, he'd married her when she'd been pregnant, so why not Madge? She felt she'd been given a kick in the stomach. Madge was pretty and seemed on good terms with the family. 'He didn't tell me,' she wailed.

Patsy put an arm round her shoulders and drew her to the sofa. 'He wouldn't,' she said. 'That's Barney's way.'

Beatrice pushed a small glass into her hand. 'You've had a shock,' she said. 'I haven't any brandy, I hope port will help.'

Jeanie tossed it back. 'It's going to take more than this.' She felt vengeful. She meant to make Barney pay for his secrecy, but Beatrice took it that she wanted more port and refilled her glass.

'He's not playing fair, he should have told me before we were married,' Jeanie ranted.

'That's typical of Barney,' Patsy said sympathetically. 'He can't face up to what he does. He never could.'

It was an hour or so later that they heard Barney let himself in with his key. Jeanie shot into the hall to find him taking off his mackintosh and carefully hanging it up. When he turned round, she could see he felt contrite. 'I'm sorry, Jeanie.' His eyes were red as though he'd been crying. 'Sorry, Patsy, I embarrassed your friends.'

'You embarrassed everybody. Did you have to shoot off like that?'

'I'm sorry. Goodnight, Mum, I'm going up to bed.' He headed for the stairs.

'It's only half past eight!'

It was only when Jeanie heard the bedroom door click shut behind him that she ran after him. Barney was lying on top of the eiderdown, he hadn't even taken off his shoes. Tears were streaming down his face.

'You've had a baby with another girl,' she accused.

'I should have told you, Jeanie,' he wailed.

She flopped down beside him. 'You certainly should.'

'I was afraid you wouldn't marry me if you knew.'

'Barney, you'd got me pregnant too, I needed a husband. You knew that.'

'But then you lost the baby. After that you wouldn't have.'

'Don't be daft. We were already married by then.'

'But would you have if . . .'

'Give over, for God's sake. What's done is done, no point in worrying about that now. Why didn't you marry this other girl?'

'I don't know,' he cried. 'I met you.' His brown eyes were pleading for forgiveness.

'Don't try to butter me up.' Jeanie pulled a face. Barney was the sort of man she despised. Why, she wondered, had she ever imagined she was in love with him? 'Is there anything else I should know about? Anything you haven't told me?'

'No,' he was emphatic. 'No.'

'There are to be no more secrets between us. I don't want any more shocks like this.'

'Of course not.' He was contrite. 'There won't be. I need another handkerchief. I can't find one in that case.'

'For heaven's sake, Barney,' Jeanie let her irritation show, 'don't expect me to wait on you.' She opened the case and tossed one to him.

'Thanks.' He blew his nose. 'My finger hurts, I don't feel very well.'

'Oh God! I can't stand you playing the wounded soldier. You should have been more careful where you put your finger. Do stop moaning about it or I'll go back to Rhyl for the summer.'

'No, Jeanie, don't leave me. I need you.'

'Then stop being a pain in the neck and show a bit more backbone. If you want me to stay, have another go at Patsy about letting us have that flat. If I had a home of my own, I'd stay.'

'I'm not happy about the flat either. I reckon she's planning to keep it for herself and nothing I say will change that.'

'You've got to try. Patsy's doing you down, it's important that we have a home. I want you to do something about that.'

Barney sat up and started to get undressed.

'It's a bit early to go to bed, isn't it?' Jeanie asked pointedly. 'It would be better if you came downstairs and had another word with Patsy now. Let's try to get this flat sorted. Surely you can see it will be just as hard to face them in the morning, harder perhaps.'

'I'm past doing anything more tonight. I'm too tired.' He was mopping at his eyes again. 'I told you my finger hurts. It's throbbing and I've got a terrible headache.'

'Barney, do you expect me to feel sorry for you? What a yellow-bellied fool you are. I'm going downstairs to talk to Patsy, she'll be making cocoa soon.'

'Will you bring me a cup up here?'

'No,' she said shortly. 'If you want cocoa, come down and get it.'

'I can't, tell them I'm not well.'

Jeanie felt her eyes had been opened. As a husband, Barney was no great catch. He was never going to set the world on fire. In fact, if she wanted anything done, either she would have to motivate him or be prepared to do it herself. Perhaps it was as well to know where she stood with Barney.

That night she couldn't find the energy to re-open discussion with Patsy about the flat. Perhaps she should have done. Patsy and her mother were being sympathetic and fussing round her. But to know she wasn't the first girl Barney had got pregnant had knocked the wind out of her.

Barney had had enough, and Jeanie wasn't keen on staying on either, so at breakfast he told his mother that they would return to Chester and spend the last night of his convalescence in Aunt Cissie's house.

On their last evening, they were all listening to the nine o'clock news on the wireless when it was announced that conscription was coming into force immediately.

'I hope they've built up a large enough stock of military uniforms,' Patsy said. 'They're going to need them now.'

Barney looked up and sighed. 'I deliberated for ages about joining up,' he said. 'But if I hadn't, I'd be forced to now, wouldn't I? So in the long run, it's made no difference. I'd have ended up exactly where I am, in the army.'

He saw Patsy looking at him in amazement. 'No,' she said. 'You would not. If you'd stayed to work in the business you'd be in a reserved occupation.'

'What?'

'Didn't you listen to the announcement? There's a long list

of reserved occupations. Producing military uniforms is bound to be on it. Tim is the only one it's likely to affect. There's Arthur of course, but he'll be too old to serve in the forces.'

Barney knew Jeanie was watching him. She knew he already regretted taking off for Rhyl instead of staying to get rich in the business. Now he had another reason to lament his choice.

'Barney dear,' his mother tried to soothe, 'you're in the army because you chose to be. I did wonder whether it was a wise choice for you at the time, but you've settled in and you do say you like it.'

He couldn't sleep that night; every time he thought of how Patsy had poured scorn on him, Barney cringed. She'd made him feel totally humiliated. Mother trying to soothe him had only made him feel worse. Everybody thought he was stupid, and he was beginning to think so himself. Everything went wrong for him. It always had. He kicked himself for opening his mouth about conscription. Patsy had only just smothered a laugh about that.

This visit had soured things between him and Jeanie. As soon as she'd got him on his own, she said, 'What a bloody fool you are, Barney. Whatever made you volunteer for the army? You could have stayed here and be raking in the cash through the business.'

They went back to Chester on the bus and Aunt Cissie made a fuss of him. She'd got some beer in and had made his favourite steak and kidney pie.

When he reported back to work, he found his fellow recruits were spending the day out on the firing range with their machine guns. Barney was relieved to be told that as he'd missed the earlier instruction sessions he would not be allowed to rejoin them at this point. Instead he was sent to work temporarily in their transport section and given the job of polishing up the already spotless and shining staff cars.

The sergeant in charge spoke of his being posted to the Royal Army Service Corps where he'd be taught a motor trade. Barney saw that as the first stroke of luck he'd had in years, he wouldn't have to cope with machine guns after all. It seemed like a reprieve. He relaxed and told the sergeant that he already had civilian licences to drive both cars and motorbikes, and he was asked to produce them for inspection.

After that, he was occasionally given the task of chauffeuring a senior officer. He thoroughly enjoyed being out and about driving a large and powerful car. Barney cheered up, his working life had improved. Perhaps the army wasn't going to be too bad after all. He was looking forward to a permanent posting well away from Chester.

Jeanie was glad to escape from Fern Bank. What had happened there had lowered her expectations of what marriage to Barney would bring. It was habit and the need to forget her disappointment in her husband that kept her smiling.

She was more at home in Aunt Cissie's house. On the first evening they spent alone they sat by the fire drinking tea; and Cissie fired questions at her about how she'd got on with her in-laws. Jeanie felt raw about what had happened and didn't want to talk about that. Instead she told her that Barney's name was not Rushton but Tavenham-Strong, and built the story up into a romantic mystery that even Barney didn't understand.

Aunt Cissie found it intriguing and was quite excited. 'Rowland Tavenham-Strong.' She let the name roll off her tongue. 'He sounds an important man.' Her face screwed with concentration. 'I think I've heard that name somewhere before but I can't remember. What regiment was he in?'

Jeanie shook her head. 'I know nothing else about him, neither does Barney, just that he was an officer.'

'You'd think he'd want to find out everything he could about his own father.'

'Yes.' Cissie's enthusiasm was firing up Jeanie's imagination. 'I do wonder if Barney might have another richer and more exciting family than the Rushtons.'

'Why don't you try to find out?'

'I'd love to but I wouldn't know where to start.'

'The army keeps records of everything and everybody. There's a military museum in the castle. I expect the people there would be able to help you.'

'Would they? Come with me tomorrow and let's ask. Wouldn't it be great if I could trace Barney's other family?'

'He'd be amazed, wouldn't he?'

'Especially if they're rich, and what if they're all old and dying off and have nobody to leave their money to?'

Cissie laughed. 'I wouldn't bank on anything like that. If they were rich you can bet Beatrice would have stayed close to them.'

'Still, no harm in finding out.'

'You'll need his full name, and the years he served in the army. Do you know his date of birth?"

Jeanie was excited. 'I took the precaution of writing down his name when Barney told me about him. I didn't want to forget it.' She ran up to her bedroom to fish a piece of paper out of her handbag. 'Here it is, Rowland Charles Arnold George Tavenham-Strong, and his profession was army officer. That's all I know. Will it be enough?'

'How would I know? But there won't be many with a name like that. We can try.'

The next morning they got up early and went to the museum. Jeanie surveyed the exhibits and within ten minutes whispered to Cissie, 'This isn't going to be any help. This is the history of the Cheshire Regiment going back to when they fought with bows and arrows. We don't even know if Barney's father was in this regiment.'

'We'd better ask.' Cissie took her arm and led her back to the foyer at the entrance where they'd seen several attendants.

Jeanie pulled her to a halt in front of one and brought out her slip of paper. 'I wonder if you could help me,' she said. 'I understand the army has always kept full records of the officers who serve in it.'

'Yes, they keep records of everybody who serves, men and officers.'

'Is it possible for us to see records like that? We're trying to find out more about a relative.'

'Yes, but they aren't kept here. You'll find them in the Public Records Office.'

'I'm trying to find out more about my father-in-law, where he served and all that,' she said.

He smiled, 'The historical records we keep here may be of interest to you.'

Jeanie held out her slip of paper and said, 'His name was Rowland Charles Arnold George Tavenham-Strong. I think he served in the last war.'

She saw the attendant's expression change. He was gazing at her intently. 'You know the name?' she asked. He was silent and she got the impression that he didn't want to admit he did.

'I've heard of him,' he said at last. 'Lieutenant Tavenham-Strong.'

'Was this his regiment?' Cissie asked.

'I'm not sure, it could have been. We have nothing about

him here. It's not the sort of thing we put in our museum.'

'Where would we be likely to find out more?'

'Well, you could ask in the reference library. Or the newspaper offices keep back numbers. The papers used to publish a lot of information about major battles and there were always lists of soldiers who'd been killed. If I were you, I'd try to look through the newspapers of the time.'

'We don't know what time that would be.'

'The last war was nineteen fourteen to eighteen.'

'Of course.'

To Jeanie that sounded like a lot of newspapers to look through.

Cissie hurried her away. 'We'll try the reference library first.'

Patsy had been looking forward to the summer, but it was blighted by the fear of war. It seemed to be growing ever closer. Beatrice started to stockpile sugar, tea and tinned foods. She was growing ever more edgy.

'We nearly starved last time,' she said. 'By the last years of the war the shops were empty. Nobody doubts now that war will come, the only question is when.'

The next morning at work, Patsy found a whole load of leaflets had landed on her desk about the steps businesses should be taking to prepare for hostilities.

'Gosh,' she said to Tim, 'we are advised to arrange air-raid shelters large enough for all our employees, unless there is a nearby public shelter they can use.'

'Well, I can tell you quite definitely there isn't going to be a public shelter near here.'

'Are you sure?'

'Yes. Patsy, I've decided to join the Civil Defence Service.

I went to my first meeting last night and heard all about public shelters.'

She stared at him for a moment. 'What does that entail? You're not leaving me? I need you here.'

'I know you do and I've no intention of leaving. Although making uniforms is classed as essential work, I want to do something more to help the war effort. I'm being trained to help in air raids. It'll be in my own time, unless we get raids during the day.'

'Gosh, Tim, you're going to be busy. You could find yourself working day and night.'

'I can see people looking at me and wondering why I'm still a civilian. They used to hand out white feathers in the last war to men like me. But before I came to work for your dad I tried to join up as a boy soldier. The army wouldn't have me, I failed my medical.'

'Why? You look fit.'

'I had TB when I was a child. I was in hospital for two years. They reckon I'm under par.'

'You're never ill, never off work.'

'I'm all right, perfectly all right. But it has apparently left scars on my lungs.'

Patsy smiled. 'It's like you not to make a fuss. So what is the best thing to do about providing an air-raid shelter for the staff?'

Tim frowned. 'I'm not sure. Why don't you ask Bill Bentley what he's going to do?'

'Good idea, I'll ring him now,' she said but before she could pick up the phone, he rang her, wanting to talk about it.

'I got a whole load of bumf yesterday,' Bill said, 'about preparing for war. I'm going to use my cellar as the staff air-raid shelter. You've got cellars too, haven't you?'

'Ours smell horribly dank,' Patsy said. 'I hate going down there.'

'They are said to be the safest place in an air raid. Mine are being swept out as we speak and I'll put some seating down there. That should be all that's needed.'

'Right, I'll do the same.'

'Have you had the letter saying we must prepare for an immediate blackout if war is declared and that we'll be fined if we show any light?'

'Yes, what are you doing about that?'

'Once winter comes, none of us will be able to work unless we can put the lights on. I've just had a word with George Miller about it and I ordered my blackout cloth straight away. It's Ministry of Defence material, dense enough to show no light through it. Ask your boyfriend about it, Patsy.'

'Thanks, Bill, I will.'

When she related the news to Tim, he said, 'Well, we have Arthur who is used to measuring up for things like that. Shall I ask him to do it?'

'Yes, get him to measure up for every window, including those in the flat.'

'Don't forget Fern Bank,' he said. 'You'll have to have blackout there as well.'

'This is going to be a big job.' Patsy sighed.

Ten days later, Rupert had arranged for the cloth to be delivered and Arthur had cut the curtains out. Patsy helped him carry the bundles to each of her sewing rooms.

She announced to the girls, 'We're going to stop work on uniforms to sew blackout curtains. We don't need a fancy job on these. Don't bother making side seams where there is a selvedge edge, we'll be throwing them away as soon as this war is over.'

Many came over to finger the material. 'It's made to the government standard,' Patsy went on, 'and the trade price to me is a shilling a yard. If any of you want to make blackout curtains for your homes, Tim will put in another order for you at the same price. And as I know you don't all have a sewing machine at home, you can stay on and use the machines here if you want to.' Most of them accepted the offer.

'Don't forget you'll need an air-raid shelter at home,' Tim said to Patsy. 'Have you decided what to do about that?'

'No, I'll have to talk to Mum about it.'

Patsy was more concerned about running her business, and for her the weeks of summer were both busy and exciting. Not only were all her sewing machines working at full tilt, but her plans for the building next door were taking shape. The workmen were in and she and Tim were trying to decide how best to use the extra space.

Bill Bentley's workshop was also working at full stretch and he was very interested in their plans to expand the business. Patsy and Tim walked him round their new premises and talked about their future plans.

'You've got years of experience,' she said to Bill. 'Just like Dad, he'd know without thinking what was the best thing to do. Tim and I are still a bit wet behind the ears for a major overhaul like this.'

'You're fitting everything in very neatly, not an inch of space wasted,' he told Patsy. 'Your dad would be proud of you. But keep in mind that this avalanche of work can't last for ever. The time will come when you need to go back to the old way of working. Don't get rid of your cutting-out tables.'

'No I won't.' Patsy was seeing quite a lot of Bill Bentley, he was coming down at least once a week to eat his lunch in the flat with them and he was taking her out to practise her driving regularly. She had a date to sit her test and was getting nervous about it, but he reassured her, saying he thought her driving was competent and he was sure she'd pass. He invited her and Tim up to see his workshop to see how best he could push more sewing machines in.

'He's like a father to you.' Tim smiled. 'But he needs you too. You bring something other than work into his life.'

'I'm grateful for his help,' she said.

The day of the driving test arrived, and Patsy was dreading it. Bill had arranged to take her on a fifteen-minute driving practice beforehand to relax her. He timed it so they ended up at the test centre on time. She was tense as they walked into the building but felt fine once she was behind the wheel again, even though the examiner was beside her now. She pretended he was benign Bill, and when at last she was told to return to the test centre and park, she knew she'd avoided making any bad mistakes.

To be told she'd passed put Patsy in a euphoric mood and for the rest of the day she couldn't settle down to work. She couldn't stop laughing and talking to Tim so she didn't allow him to work either.

'I'm very envious.' Tim laughed with her. 'I'd love to learn to drive.'

'Why don't you save up and take lessons then?'

'For me that wouldn't be possible,' he said. 'Well, not now. I told you my mum fell and broke her leg, didn't I?'

'Yes, how is she?'

'She's out of hospital but still in plaster. Not managing all that well really. My married sister Eileen comes down from Preston quite a lot to help. We're coping, but now mine is the only wage coming in and it won't run to driving lessons. Not at the moment.'

Patsy felt guilty. She'd taken flowers to his mother when she'd been in hospital. It had been a bad break and had meant an operation and a lengthy stay there. She'd inquired after Mrs Stansfield from time to time, but she'd not considered how her problems must affect Tim. She hadn't given enough thought to that.

'You've been very good coming to work every day,' she told him. 'And you work overtime too, sometimes.'

'Patsy, I'm glad to have the job. I enjoy working here.'

'I'm afraid I thought your domestic problems were over once they started pulling Dock Cottages down and you'd moved to a different house.'

'The problems have changed a bit, that's all,' he said.

CHAPTER SEVENTEEN

PATSY WAS SO THRILLED at passing her driving test she couldn't calm down, she couldn't wait to tell Rupert her good news. When he came at half five, he gave her a congratulatory hug and went back to his car to get the bottle of champagne he'd brought.

'Lovely.' Patsy laughed. 'It's the first time anybody's bought champagne for me.'

But she tried to stop him opening it. 'You and I can't drink all that on our own, not now. We'd both get drunk and then how would you drive home? We'll have our usual tea.'

He pulled a face which made her feel she hadn't pleased him.

'Nonsense,' he said, pulling her into his arms. 'I've brought champagne so we can celebrate and we're going to have it now.' The bottle was encased in a black wrapper. 'I got the shop to cool it and I've brought us two champagne glasses.'

'I'm not used to luxury like this.'

Her family occasionally drank sherry before Sunday lunch and might possibly have port too at Christmas, but wine was considered a luxury. Champagne was beyond their purse.

'I've never tasted champagne before.'

Rupert laughed. 'And you'd have put it off now if I'd let you. You aren't one for the high life, Patsy.' The cork came out with a jubilant swoosh.

'It sounds romantic, doesn't it?' She smiled. 'Gosh, champagne.' She took a sip and the bubbles went up her nose. 'It's lovely, thank you, Rupert.'

'Here's to your success. You said you were going to buy a car if you passed, Have you decided what make to get?'

'Everybody is full of advice about that.' She giggled.

'I reckon an MG Midget would suit you.'

'Barney said exactly the same about the SS Jaguar.'

'So what are you going to get?'

'A Morris Eight, the same as Dad had. I've already called round to Spencer's, the local garage, to look at this year's model.' Tim had gone with her. He was very interested in cars.

'You don't want to buy it there. I could probably get a discount for you in Liverpool.'

'I've already ordered it, Rupert. I rang Mr Spencer as soon as I got back from taking the test.'

'You're in too much of a hurry.'

'My dad bought cars from him. He said it was handy having him round the corner when things went wrong and that he was always very helpful.'

'Oh Patsy! You're a real sober-sides thinking of what might go wrong. You'd have looked a real picture driving an open car. Don't you want to feel the wind in your hair? You ought to relax and have more fun.'

'I do have fun,' she protested. Tim had been as excited as she was about the Morris Eight. Mum had been too. 'I'm having fun now drinking champagne with you.' He had refilled her glass and she was beginning to feel a little tipsy.

'Why don't you give a proper party to celebrate,' Rupert suggested. 'You could have it here at the flat. It's a smashing place to hold a party. You say you don't use it enough.'

'That's a good idea, but I do use the flat. I have lunch here with Tim every day. Bill Bentley drops in to eat with us sometimes and that develops into quite a party though he brings his own sandwiches and we drink only tea.' She laughed again. 'Honestly, I wouldn't know who else to ask.'

'Me, for instance, and your mother.'

'Yes of course. Hang on, yes. It's Bill Bentley's birthday next week. He'll be sixty-one and he's been very good about taking me out to practise my driving. Yes, we'll have a party. Bill needs cheering up.'

'Good, I'll bring some nice food and drink.'

'Not champagne, that's far too extravagant, especially at lunchtime.' Patsy was frowning now. 'My friend Sheila works in Liverpool and probably wouldn't be able to get here for a lunch party.'

'Evening would be better. We can all finish work for the day, let our hair down.'

'No, it wouldn't. Tim has to get home to his mother. She's broken her leg and he's looking after her. She isn't well.'

Rupert's smile had faded. 'That isn't the sort of party I had in mind,' he said. 'It doesn't sound as though it's going to be a barrel of fun.'

Patsy felt uneasy. Recently she felt they weren't always seeing eye to eye. She was disappointed that Rupert hadn't invited her to meet his parents or see his home in Blundellsands. She took a deep, steadying breath. 'Lunch is probably the best time for most of us,' she told him. 'You'll come, won't you, Rupert? I want everybody to get to know you.'

'Of course,' he said, refilling her glass again.

Before long, Patsy felt his arms tighten round her and his mouth come down on hers and when after a while she felt his hand on her bare skin feeling her breast, she edged herself away from him. She was upset. Had he tried to get her tipsy on champagne so she wouldn't object to his hands going up her jumper?

'You disappoint me, Patsy,' he said, looking at her with sorrowful eyes.

That evening at home, Patsy lifted the phone when it rang to find it was Barney. He was keeping in touch with Mum now and ringing her regularly. She invited him and Jeanie to her party.

'I won't be able to get away,' he told her, 'but Jeanie might be able to.'

She then rang Sheila to invite her. 'Sorry, I won't be able to come,' Sheila told her. 'I'll be at work and it would be an awful rush in my dinner break.' Patsy was afraid they were drifting apart since Madge had had Barney's baby. They were not seeing much of each other any more.

'How are Madge and Katrina?'

'They're both fine. Katrina's walking now,' she said. 'With all this talk of war I'm thinking of joining the WRNS. I feel I need a change.'

Patsy wished her all the luck in the world.

'You too,' Sheila said. 'But it looks as though you're having the luck anyway.'

The following day, which was Friday 1 September, German troops marched into Poland in the early hours of the morning. On the following Sunday morning, Patsy listened with her mother to Neville Chamberlain speaking on the wireless.

He told the nation that Britain and France had issued an ultimatum to Hitler to withdraw from Poland or face war and as there had been no response, he declared that Britain must consider itself to be at war with Germany.

Beatrice was in tears and seemed absolutely terrified. 'I dread to think of what Barney will have to face,' she sobbed. 'What we'll all have to face.'

Patsy understood that the First World War was still in the forefront of her memory and did her best to comfort her, but her mother's fear communicated itself to her, and she shuddered all day at what was in store for them.

On Monday she went to work but everybody was in a black mood. Many had memories of the shortages they'd suffered in the last war and of the relatives they'd lost. Nobody was in a party mood now, it was the last thing Patsy felt like, but the guests had been invited and everything was arranged for Tuesday, the following day, because it was Bill Bentley's birthday.

Early on Tuesday morning Rupert telephoned to say he had an urgent job to do and wouldn't be able to spend time at her party, but he'd drop off the hamper he'd ordered.

'Oh no! I so much wanted you to be here.'

'I'm sorry, Patsy. I'm disappointed that I have to miss it.'

She said to Tim, 'We're going to forget the war and all our troubles today. We're going to enjoy ourselves.'

Patsy wore her best blue dress for work that morning, and brought with her the birthday cake she'd baked for Bill, which her mother had iced and decorated. She also brought the two bunches of flowers to decorate the flat that Mum had picked in her garden last night. There was a large bowl of pink roses and a tall vase of scabious and baby's breath. The posy of sweet peas for the table was scenting the whole room.

She'd asked Flo to dust round for her and help her set out the contents of Rupert's hamper on the dining table. It was a magnificent buffet of luxury food that Patsy had never tasted before she'd met Rupert; there was smoked salmon and Dee shrimps, several salads and a fancy trifle. The flat was looking its best on this bright and sunny late-summer morning.

At lunchtime, Patsy went down to the workroom and sent her senior employees up to the flat. She took Tim up with her and poured drinks for them all. She'd invited Tim's mother too, but he said that, with her bad leg, she wouldn't be able to manage the stairs up to the flat.

Bill Bentley arrived and was overcome to see all the trouble they'd gone to. He thought it was to celebrate his birthday. Patsy told him it was a shared celebration because at last she had a driving licence.

Beatrice and Jeanie arrived at the same moment. Jeanie was very smartly dressed in a close-fitting red satin dress and very high heels. With her crinkly white-blond hair fluffed up, her big green eyes and smiling lips moving all the time, she looked glamorous.

Patsy got them all up to the table, pushed plates into their hands and told them to help themselves. This was the time of the staff dinner break and she knew they must be hungry, but nobody seemed at ease.

She'd felt sorry for Jeanie since that toe-curling scene when Madge had come to see them. If she loved Barney as much as Patsy loved Rupert, that must have come as a terrible shock to her and how could she trust him after that? It couldn't bode well for the future. Patsy had liked Jeanie, she'd always been ready to give a hand with any job they were doing and was giggly and full of fun.

But the party wasn't going with a swing. Jeanie and Mum were standing side by side but looked as though they had no more to say to each other. Patsy went over to try and get them chatting again.

* * *

Jeanie did not intend to mention to the Rushtons that she was trying to find out more about Barney's father. She'd decided that first she would tackle them again about letting her and Barney live in the flat. Patsy had fobbed her off last time by saying it was too soon for them to settle down when Barney could be sent to the other side of the country, but everything had moved on since then.

It was no good waiting for Barney to do anything. He was like a limp lettuce when it came to asking for this flat. Jeanie had already sounded Beatrice out and she didn't seem to be against letting them have it. Now she needed to tell Patsy that Barney had been given his new posting and how much the flat would suit them.

Jeanie gulped down her first glass of sherry because a little alcohol was said to give one confidence. She played with the smoked salmon she'd put on her plate, not sure that she liked it. When she saw Patsy coming over to them, she knew this was the chance she'd been hoping for.

'How is Barney?' Patsy asked.

'I'm worried about him,' Jeanie said. 'I do wish he hadn't joined up. I mean, now that we're at war he'll be in mortal danger.'

'He may never be sent near any fighting.' Patsy was trying to console her.

'I'm hoping that too.' Jeanie gave her one of her big smiles. 'He's got his posting, it's to be Liverpool.'

'I'm pleased,' Beatrice said, 'because you'll be so much nearer.'

'Barney's whole battalion is about to be moved out of the castle to the Dale Barracks, but he is to be posted to a Royal Army Service Corps unit in Liverpool. He's very pleased.'

'When will he be moving?' Patsy asked.

'Soon.'

'And this will be a permanent posting?'

'He hopes it will be but who's to say now war has been declared? Everything is so uncertain.' Jeanie was biting her lip. 'I wish I knew what was going to happen.'

'We none of us know . . .'

'Barney needs the security of a home. If we had some sort of a base it wouldn't be so bad. We feel as though we're living out of suitcases.' Jeanie smiled again and looked her sister-in-law in the eye. 'Patsy, we'd really love to live in this flat.' She was aware that Patsy was trying to stop her and also that the guests nearby couldn't fail to hear what she was asking for. 'It would make the perfect starter home for us and we'd be willing to pay rent.' She hoped if she asked in front of everybody, Patsy would be too embarrassed to say no.

Patsy was taken aback and looked as though she was struggling to make a decision. 'It's a bit difficult because there isn't a private entrance. There's no way to shut it off from the business.'

'That wouldn't bother us.' Jeanie was in her stride now.

'What I mean is, there'd be no security for our stock. We couldn't lock the place up when we leave at night.'

'I'd be glad to act as caretaker. I'll be your security guard.'

'I'm sure you would, but . . . To be honest, Jeanie, I did the place up for my own use.'

It was Jeanie's turn to be taken aback. Patsy had not mentioned this before.

'It's too early for me and Rupert to talk about our plans, but I'm hoping that in time I might need it as my first home.'

'Oh!' Jeanie knew that meant she hadn't a hope in hell of getting it.

'In the meantime we do use it quite a lot. Tim and I come

up here every lunchtime. It gives us privacy and peace; it's a bolt-hole away from the noise and frenetic rush of the sewing room, and isn't it a great place to hold a party like this?'

Jeanie whirled angrily away from her, swearing under her breath. She marched over to Flo, held out her empty glass and had it refilled. She'd been hopeful she'd get what she asked for and felt rebuffed. Patsy was totally selfish and determined to part with nothing for her brother.

She turned round to find Patsy behind her. 'Jeanie,' she said. 'There's another house in Forest Road just come empty. It's advertised for rent or sale. You'd find that more comfortable than this flat, I'm sure.'

'If we could afford it,' she snapped, without thinking. She'd intended to make a friend of Patsy. She was sure it would pay her to; Patsy had the power to give so much.

Patsy was filled with guilt that she'd refused Jeanie's request. She knew it was what Barney wanted. Hadn't he already asked for it? Yes, they were married and their need for a home was greater than hers.

Bill Bentley came behind her. 'You did the right thing,' he said. 'I couldn't help but hear. Beatrice has always favoured Barney, given him too much. I'm afraid he's come to expect it as his right.'

'Am I being greedy?' Patsy cringed. 'Barney's struggling while I keep everything for myself.'

'No you're not. Let me tell you a little story. Hubert wanted Barney to join him in the business; he meant to teach him all he could and hand it over to him when he was ready to retire. For you, he'd been saving for a long time so you could have a year at a commercial college and train to be a shorthand typist.'

'That was Mum's idea. She'd done office work and thought it a ladylike career.'

'But Barney never settled in the business. He took a dislike to the rag trade and walked out after a few short months. He then found himself several dead-end jobs which he thought he was going to love but soon found he hated.'

'I know all about that. Barney was in trouble all the time about not keeping a job.'

'Did you know that when Barney was about sixteen, he decided he wanted to go to sea?'

'Yes, I remember it well.' Patsy smiled. 'He was really keen on the idea. He read everything he could about it and never stopped talking about the sea.'

'Yes.' Bill nodded. 'Beatrice liked the idea of his being a seagoing officer and Hubert wanted to do his best for him. They thought it would give him a solid career and a decent standard of living.'

'We all thought Barney was going to be settled at last.'

'At that time, officer cadets in the merchant navy were indentured for four years and spent three and a half years of that period at sea. Their parents had to buy their uniforms and also pay over fifty pounds for their training, which was paid back to the cadet during his indenture as pocket money.

'Your father found it a struggle to collect the money together at that time because the depression was at its height. So he handed over the money he'd saved to send you to commercial college, because for Beatrice's sake he felt Barney must have his chance.'

'I didn't know about that,' Patsy said. 'Not about the money.'

'Barney stayed on the course for about nine months. When

he walked out of that, Hubert told me he was giving up on him. "The lad will never stick at anything," he said. "I'd be better off training Patsy up to take over from me when I finish." '

'Did he?' she marvelled. 'Did he say that?'

'Yes, and he was right about it. You've proved you can do it and you've earned the right to use this flat as you want to. If you'd not taken over, the business would have gone down the drain. I'm sure Barney wouldn't have done what you did.'

'He could have stayed to help me. I wanted him to at the time.'

'You're better doing it on your own, Patsy. He'd take all the kudos for your success and blame you when things went wrong.'

They were standing quite close to the table and Bill turned and loaded his plate up with more food. 'This is absolutely delicious. Where did you manage to get food like this?'

'Rupert ordered it for me and then was unable to come.'

'Oh! There's something else I want to say to you. I know it's none of my business but if your dad was here he wouldn't let you entertain that boyfriend of yours up here when the workshop is closed and there was nobody else around. So I'm speaking on his behalf. He'd want me to. I'm afraid you're going to get hurt.'

'I won't. You know me. I always do the right thing, don't I?'

'But do you trust Rupert Alderman to do the right thing?'

'Of course.' Patsy felt her cheeks burn. His hands were straying more frequently to more intimate places. Up till now, he'd always stopped when she'd asked him to, but the next time he came, his hands would go inside her underclothes again. He said it was because he loved her.

213

'I wouldn't be too sure of him,' Bill said. 'I feel you'd be safer with George Miller, the man who looks after me.'

Patsy was afraid he might be right. 'I don't understand why we don't have the same person from the agency when our workshops are only half a mile apart. You'd think it would make the job easier if we did.'

Bill sank down on the sofa and she perched on the arm beside him. 'Neither do I and that bothers me. I asked George if there was a reason and he told me Rupert was his boss and, like most of the staff, he'd only been recruited recently. It is Rupert's job to assess whether our workmanship is adequate and if so put us on their list, and George's to deliver the cut-out garments and collect the finished work. George says Rupert just never handed you on to him.'

Patsy smiled. 'I hope he's going to propose,' she said shyly. 'I wouldn't tell anybody else that, not until he does – but you're standing in for Dad, you said so.'

'I am, but I'd say that makes him more dangerous. To be in love, Patsy, is to be intoxicated. You look at Rupert Alderman but you don't see any faults. To you he seems perfect.'

Patsy said nothing. He was perfect; Rupert was a one-off.

'I'm not saying he isn't,' Bill went on, his voice gentle. 'I know very little about him, but you lose your defences when you're in love, you're in a vulnerable state. People who care about you feel helpless, they can only stand by and worry you may be hurt.'

'I won't be,' she said.

He pulled his bulk to his feet. 'No, of course not. I'm just an old man, what do I know? You may be on the brink of a long and happy marriage. I do hope so. I wish you both all the best life has to offer.'

Patsy got up too and kissed his cheek.

'Forgive me if I speak out of turn,' he said, taking a last petit four from the table. 'I have your best interests at heart.'

'I know, Bill, thank you. I'll bear what you say in mind.'

CHAPTER EIGHTEEN

J EANIE WENT BACK TO Chester on the bus, seething with resentment against Patsy. By the time she met Barney in the Boar's Head later in the evening, she'd worked herself up into a real paddy.

'Your sister wants to keep the flat for her own use. She's thinking of marrying that boyfriend and moving him in. It's not as though they haven't enough money to live anywhere they want to. We are the ones who are hard up and need a helping hand. D'you know what she suggested? There's an empty house in Forest Road which she thought might be more comfortable for us. She's no idea what it's like to live on pay. How does she think we'd be able to set up home in a place like that when we haven't even a stick of furniture?'

'I did tell you we hadn't a hope.'

That made Jeanie fly at him. 'Why do you give up at the first sign of opposition? You're a soldier now, where's your fight?'

Barney's face was carefully expressionless. 'What d'you want to drink?'

'You know I always have half of mild.'

She watched him get up and amble over to the bar. When he came back and pushed the drink in front of her, she said, 'Now you're my husband you've got to forget your family and think of me. You've got to make sure you get your share of

216

what's on offer. That's only fair. We'll starve in the gutter if you carry on like this. What sort of a man have I married?'

Barney edged his chair away from her. It was his way of showing his hurt.

'She's your younger sister, for God's sake. You shouldn't let her twist you round her little finger.'

Jeanie went back to Aunt Cissie's house feeling furious with Patsy. All her early resolve to make a friend of her melted in a sea of resentment. She was full of vengeance and wanted to get her own back on both Patsy and Beatrice. She thought she might be able to do that if she could find out about Barney's other family, the Tavenham-Strongs. There was some secret about them that the Rushtons were trying to keep quiet, and if they were also rich, perhaps they'd be prepared to help them get a home.

Her Aunt Cissie was just as curious as she was about Barney's background and was keen to help her. They both went to the reference library and Cissie explained to the librarian exactly what details she wanted to find out.

'Local military history?' The librarian pushed her heavy spectacles further up her nose. 'A local family called Tavenham-Strong? Yes, I have heard of them. Sit down, would you, and I'll bring you what I can find.'

Jeanie shepherded Cissie to a table and took out her notebook and pen. Most of the tables were empty but there was a student in the corner with books spread all round him. In the heavy silence, the librarian's rubber soles squeaked on the parquet floor. She brought them a pile of books and pamphlets. Jeanie opened the top one eagerly and set to work. Beside her she saw Cissie do the same.

Until now, Jeanie had had very little interest in military matters and it seemed that was true for Cissie too. It wasn't long before she whispered, 'This is tedious work. It makes my head spin.'

But Jeanie kept at it, searching for any mention of the name Tavenham-Strong and making notes of anything they found. She came across a photograph of Brigadier Edmund Tavenham-Strong taken in 1902 and brought it to Cissie's attention. Stern eyes stared straight out at them. He was tall, standing to attention with his shoulders well back, wearing his dress uniform with polished Sam Browne belt; he looked as though he expected instant obedience from all under his command. He was the picture of authority.

'Barney looks nothing like him,' Cissie said. 'There's no family resemblance there.'

'No,' Jeanie had to agree. 'Let's see if we can find out more.'

She kept Cissie at it, but after a couple of hours Jeanie, too, was fed up with the wisps of information they'd turned up. 'We need to come back tomorrow,' she said.

The next day Jeanie went alone and found she was better able to concentrate. She came across a biography of Brigadier Sebastian Tavenham-Strong who had fought very bravely with General Gordon in the Sudan. It gave her information and she was pleased to find Barney came from such an important family. She learned of the Tavenham-Strong estate outside Chester and their manor house called Aldford Hall.

Jeanie couldn't believe her luck. It was as she'd thought, the family were rich. It seemed quite unfair that Barney was not benefiting from this. 'I've been through Aldford on the bus,' Cissie said when she told her. 'I think I've seen Aldford Hall.'

The next day she took Jeanie to see it too. They sat one each side of the bus and kept a careful watch out of the windows as they didn't know on which side of the road they'd find it. Jeanie saw a large house of reasonably modern build standing importantly on rising ground. Its lawns ran down to the road.

'That must be it,' she said, but by the time Cissie turned, it was no longer to be seen. The bus swept on past large imposing iron gates with a lodge on one side.

'No, you're wrong. This is the hall here.'

Jeanie was in time to glimpse a magnificent eighteenth-century grey stone mansion some distance away through the trees. They got off at the next stop and walked back to see all they could of it.

'Such a posh house,' Cissie breathed.

'But I liked the other house too,' Jeanie said and they walked a little further back to see all they could of that too.

'I find this hard to believe.' Cissie pulled her to a halt. 'OK, Barney grew up in a smart semi but that's light years away from this.' Her middle-aged face under its no-nonsense iron-grey hair puckered in disbelief. 'Are you sure what he told you is true?'

'Ye-es,' Jeanie said. 'Well, I was, but . . . Barney said he saw that name on his birth certificate.'

'Have you seen it? Does his mother confirm it?'

'No, he says she won't talk about it, that it sends her over the edge.'

'It sounds like a figment of his imagination to me,' Aunt Cissie said. 'I don't believe it.' She was striding on again in her sensible lace-ups. Jeanie had trouble keeping up in her high heels. 'Do you believe him, Jeanie?'

'I did. Now, well, you've made me think. We need to find out more about this family.'

'You need to see that birth certificate before you go any further.' They returned to the bus stop. Cissie leaned up against the wall. 'I wonder how long we'll have to wait for a bus back.'

A few days later Tim was working in the office when the phone on Patsy's desk rang. He watched her pick it up and her face brightened up like the sky at sunrise.

'Lovely, I'm coming straight round to get it,' she sang out. She turned to him with shining eyes. 'Tim, that was Mr Spencer at the garage telling me my new car is ready for collection. Will you come with me to pick it up?'

'You bet,' he said, leaping to his feet and grabbing his coat. Patsy was giving little skips and jumps as they walked to the garage. When they turned the corner into Hoylake Road he could see a brand new shiny Morris Eight standing on the forecourt and knew it must be hers.

'Marvellous.' Tim wanted to stare at it. She almost pulled him into the tiny office to see Mr Spencer.

Patsy had given him a cheque two days ago, everything was ready for her. Mr Spencer pushed some forms in front of her to sign and gave her two sets of keys and some documents. Then he took her out to the forecourt and explained some details about the car. A few minutes later Patsy had the car bowling down the road into town.

Tim sniffed at the smell of new leather. 'Wow,' he said. 'This is wonderful. I'm green with envy, I wish I could drive.'

Patsy pulled into the park and drove as far as the pond. There she switched off the engine and stared straight ahead. 'I've been thinking, Tim,' she said. 'You've helped me make a lot of changes in the business and it's all going well. I know you've been dying to learn to drive for ages. I'm going to book a course of lessons for you from the man who taught me and the business will pay for them.'

Tim's eyes fastened on hers. 'Would you do that for me? Should you?' He felt filled with wonder.

'Why not?'

He laughed aloud and leaned across to kiss her cheek. 'Gosh, Patsy, I don't know what to say. I never dared hope it would be possible. It's awfully kind of you, but you pay me very well. Your dad did, but you've given me a rise since.'

She was laughing with a joy that almost equalled his. 'It's no good increasing your salary,' she giggled. 'You'll just spend the money on your mum, or on making a more comfortable home for her.'

'We moved house not so long ago,' he said. 'We need so much.'

'OK, let's call this a bonus. I'm going to lend you the old van to practise on and ask Bill Bentley if he'll help you. You deserve it, Tim. I couldn't have done all this without your help.'

'You've floored me, Patsy. I'm thrilled to bits. There's nothing I want more.'

'I know that.' She flashed him a smile as she turned the key in the ignition. 'You'll be more useful to the business too; every so often we need somebody to drive the van.'

'I don't know how to thank you.'

'Then don't try. I'm going to take you home now, Tim. Then I'm going to pick Mum up and take her for a run to West Kirby. She's dying for an outing in it and I've got to get the feel of this car. I think I'm going to love it once I get used to it.'

A few minutes later, Tim stood at the front door of his home feeling quite dazed. He'd told Patsy there was nothing he wanted more than to learn to drive, but it wasn't true. He wanted her love. This afternoon, it had almost seemed he had that too.

Beatrice was all excited and came running down the path when Patsy drew up outside the house. 'It's lovely. Nobody else in the road has a brand new car.'

Patsy leaned over to open the passenger door and her mother went on, 'It's so smart and smells like new shoes inside. If you can afford to buy this, it shows everybody you're making a huge success of Hubert's business.'

Patsy was excited too but she had to concentrate on what she was doing. They had both calmed down by the time she pulled up on the promenade. She switched off the engine and they sat looking across the boating lake to the Irish Sea.

Beatrice sighed with satisfaction. 'I'm so thrilled that we have a car again.'

'I'll not let Barney take this one,' Patsy said before she could stop herself.

She saw her mother's face cloud. 'He isn't like you, love. He can't help being the way he is. It's in his nature.'

Patsy had tried several times to get her mother to tell her more about Barney's father but without success. She'd grown more curious about why her mother was so uptight about her first marriage and thought it incomprehensible that she'd known nothing of it until recently. Now suddenly she had a natural opening.

'I'd like to understand why Barney's like he is,' Patsy said, 'and be more sympathetic, but it's hard when I know so little. I wish you'd tell me more about his father.'

Her mother was staring stiffly ahead and it took her a long time to begin. 'Rowley was always ill. He had strange moods.'

'How did you meet him?'

Beatrice sighed heavily. Patsy thought, as the silence length-ened, that she was never going to hear any more, but eventually her mother said in a voice scarcely above a whisper, 'I went to work for him. He was my boss.'

Patsy gasped, hadn't she said the same about Hubert? 'But I thought Rowley was an army officer?'

'That was during the war. The Kaiser's war, but we were married in nineteen twelve, and I met Rowley two years before that.'

'Oh! You were a secretary, weren't you?'

'At that time I'd just finished my training. I was a shorthand typist and not even a good one. It was my first job and I was sixteen years old. The Tavenham-Strongs owned a sweet factory.'

'Good Lord! A factory the size of ours or a bigger one?'

'A bigger one, much bigger. They specialised in soft crystallised fruits, but they made fruit sweets of several kinds. I saw them being sold in shops everywhere.'

'Wow, so they were rich?'

'Yes, his branch of the family had no shortage of money.'

'So what was their problem?'

'It was a family split in two parts.'

'Mum, our family is like that, always has been. I said that to you ages ago, but it doesn't make for problems, or it didn't until Barney . . .'

'Exactly. In character Barney seems to be the very opposite of you and Hubert. You can't understand him. It was the same with the Tavenham-Strongs. One half of the family was making a fortune in sweets and the others were all high-ranking officers in the army. There was a feud between them that boiled over every so often. They seemed to hate each other more with every passing year.'

Patsy frowned. 'I can see they might not get on.'

'My family thought I was doing very well for myself, getting a rich husband.'

'You were.'

'Rowley was thirty-one and I was head over heels in love with him. I thought he felt the same about me. He and his family planned an extravagant wedding and a honeymoon in Paris. He already had a house in Liverpool near his factory, and a wing in his family's fine mansion near Chester. I was looking forward to moving in with him. I thought we were going to live happily ever after.'

Patsy heard her voice change and guessed that she hadn't been happy. 'Tell me about him.'

'He was very introverted, all his family were. He didn't talk about himself and I knew very little. I found out I wasn't his first wife on the day we got married.' Her face was stiff and without expression. 'Nobody had so much as mentioned it, but I saw from our marriage certificate that he was described as a widower.'

'Mum!' Patsy was horrified and felt for her hand. 'I'd call that being secretive. That's a terrible way to find out.'

'It was, and of course I wanted to know all about his first wife and how and why she'd died.'

Patsy heard her voice quiver and saw she was gnawing at her lip.

'It wasn't easy to get anything out of him and that upset me more. I had to ask his father and other members of his family, but nobody ever wanted to divulge anything to me. I managed to find out that her name had been Elsa Palfry and her family had been wealthy, but I couldn't get anybody in the family to explain how she'd died.'

Patsy felt cold inside. This wasn't how she thought a

marriage should be. 'Go on,' she urged.

'The family kept two housemaids and I tried to get facts about the family from them, but neither had been employed by them when Elsa was alive. It was an old maiden aunt who told me Elsa had fallen downstairs in the dark one night, and it was the gardener's wife who told me that she was pregnant at the time and lost the baby as a result. She also injured her head and never recovered. It was awful . . .'

Patsy could see she was quite distressed. Reluctantly, she said, 'Perhaps we should go home.'

'Yes, yes,' Beatrice agreed. 'The thing was, if it had been a straightforward accident, why didn't they just say so? I thought they were trying to cover something up and that scared me.'

'Oh Mum!' Patsy put the car in gear and prepared to drive home. 'You have to believe it was an accident. To suspect anything else, well, that means you wouldn't be able to trust your own husband. It would ruin things for you.'

'It nearly did. But I loved him and he didn't seem close to anybody else. He needed me.'

Patsy felt quite sick. 'Mum, I never realised you'd had such a difficult life. I thought you'd married Dad and had had an ordinary, contented, humdrum life like everybody else.'

Beatrice had her handkerchief out and was dabbing at her eyes.

'Don't distress yourself, Mum. It's all behind you now.'

'I need to tell you, so you can understand.' Beatrice swallowed hard. 'Barney was not my first baby. Colin died when he was two years old.'

'Oh no!'

'His heart wasn't normal. And then I had two miscarriages. I began to think I'd never have a child to bring up.'

Patsy could feel a lump in her throat. 'You must have felt

terrible about all that. And I see now why Barney is so special to you.'

'Yes.'

'Mum, I'm so sorry. You had such a sad time I can quite understand why you don't want to talk about it.'

Her mother's chin was jutting with determination. 'There's one more thing you ought to know. Because of Colin and my miscarriages, I got to know the family doctor quite well. I asked him why Rowley was always ailing and why he so often needed time off work. He told me Rowley had had a complete breakdown after his first wife died.' Beatrice sniffed and blew her nose. 'It took me time to realise he was telling me that although Rowley complained of headaches, stomach aches and pains of every sort, his illnesses did not always have a physical cause. I knew Rowley was often anxious and depressed but it hadn't occurred to me up till then that his illness was in his mind.

'Dr Shaw went on to say that at least one member of the Tavenham-Strong family in each generation had suffered in this way. It shocked me because I'd never known anybody with this problem before. I found the doctor a great help and I discussed all manner of things with him after that. He helped me understand Rowley's mood swings and his panic attacks and that underneath he never felt safe. Rowley was a bag of nerves.'

Patsy thought about this for a moment. 'You're saying Barney is the same? He's the family member in the next generation who has inherited this problem?'

'Yes, he has different worries and behaves differently but yes, the underlying problem is the same. He can't help it, Patsy. You are much stronger. Try to be kind to him.'

'Kind to him?' Patsy was doing her best to damp down her

indignation. 'He's often very unkind to me. You knew he used to give me the odd punch when we were growing up.'

'I did my best to protect you.'

'Yes, if you turned on him he'd ignore me for a while, then it would all start over again. He ordered me about and tried to make me his dogsbody.'

'That's all in the past now.'

Patsy pulled up outside Fern Bank and Beatrice got out and opened the gates and the garage doors. Once she'd put the car away, Patsy hurried her mother indoors, raked up the embers of the fire and put more coal on. 'Would you like a cup of tea?'

'No, it's getting late for tea. I bought two nice pieces of cod,' she said. 'It's that for supper, with chips and peas.'

'I'll cook tonight.' Patsy felt sorry for her mother. She poured her a glass of sherry before going to the kitchen. All the time she cooked, her mind was on what her mother had told her. Having heard part of her story she was growing more and more curious about the rest.

By the time they'd eaten, Patsy thought her mother had recovered. She didn't want to upset her again and felt she shouldn't ask any more questions, but when she looked up she found her mother's gaze on her.

'The trouble with raking up the past,' she said, 'is that it stays to haunt you. I can't get Rowley out of my mind.'

'Oh Mum, I can't either. You had so many problems and it's not easy to understand why. Tell me more about the family.'

'The Tavenham-Strongs can trace their family tree back for generations. They're keen on family traditions and family names. Many are named Rowland or Charles. Many of them went to Rugby and then on to Sandhurst and rose to occupy the top ranks in the British Army. There was a general and a major general,' she gave a wan smile, 'and lots of colonels and majors.'

'Gosh, I don't know people like that.'

'I didn't either until I married. The military men held their heads high and were used to being obeyed.'

'But Rowley belonged to the sweet-making side of the family, didn't he?'

'Yes, and they were bullied by the other half who called them jelly babies. They were quite different, but there was lack of harmony there too, they were always bickering and squabbling amongst themselves. Apart from Rowley, I hadn't a friend among them.'

'You said you were worried about how his first wife died. Did you find out eventually that her death was an accident?'

Beatrice slowly shook her head. 'Legally it was. There was an inquest, and the verdict was accidental death but . . .' Patsy could see a tremor in her mother's hand as she went on, 'I think there was a cover-up, but I don't really know.'

Patsy stared at her in disbelief. 'You must have imagined that.'

'No, I don't think so. I've thought about it a good deal. No, Elsa wasn't popular in the family. I don't think I'm imagining anything. You see, it wasn't the only episode like that in the family history. Rowley's Aunt Jemima drowned in the canal, they said she slipped on the wet grass of the bank and fell in. Then there was an accident with firearms that led to the death of Brigadier James Tavenham-Strong in nineteen ten. According to Rowley, it was his cousin Edgar who fired the shot, but if it wasn't an accident, it was made to look like one.'

Patsy shivered. 'What are you saying, Mum? Surely you don't think the family killed off some of its members?'

'They wouldn't see it like that. They'd think it was more a

matter of easing them into the next world to prevent further pain all round. Nothing was ever said straight out. There were always rumours and counter-rumours and antipathy and aggression between the two sides of the family. They hated each other. Even now I'm not explaining it properly. You don't understand, but when things went badly wrong, I was devastated. His family blamed me. They said I should have known Rowley wasn't fit to return to the front and asked his doctor to help him. At the very least I should have warned them he wasn't thinking straight. They turned against me, and I had to get away from them all. I just packed up and ran.'

CHAPTER NINETEEN

B RITAIN WAS AT WAR and at first everybody expected to see immediate enemy action, but little seemed to change. There was one report of a ship being sunk by a U-boat. Ration books were issued, blackout was enforced, air-raid sirens were tested and the public advised to carry their gas masks at all times. Gradually barrage balloons appeared in the sky but for ordinary people life at work and at home went on as before.

Rupert was coming to see Patsy two or three times each week and although he did take her out, they were spending more time in the flat. She knew he was trying to persuade her to take their love-making a step further. 'If you really loved me you'd want to,' he told her.

Patsy had her mind set firmly on married bliss. 'I do want to,' she told him. She felt torn in two. When he held her tight and ran his fingers up and down the bare flesh on her back, she hungered for it and found it a struggle to say no to him. She longed to experience it and burned with curiosity to know what it would be like, but at the same time she was filled with fear.

All the teaching given to girls like her was that it should only happen within marriage. It was forbidden to everyone else. She knew the wrath of society came down on those who dared ignore this advice, but it was Madge's agony she couldn't forget and her advice that prevented her giving in to temptation.

One day, Patsy was sitting at the table in the flat with Tim, eating lunchtime sandwiches, when he put his teacup down carefully and looked up at her.

'Patsy,' he said, 'don't you think it's dangerous to have Rupert up here in the flat with you? I mean, when the sewing room is closed and there's nobody about?' He wouldn't look at her as he went on, 'You make no secret of being alone with him up here. Rupert comes marching through the sewing room with his bottle of drink and box of fancy food. Think of your reputation.'

Patsy felt guilt shaft though her. Hadn't Bill Bentley said exactly the same thing to her? She chose her words carefully. 'We are not doing anything wrong.'

'I'm sure you wouldn't mean to, Patsy, and I know it's none of my business what you do, but I worry. I don't want you to get hurt.'

Patsy was embarrassed and could see that he was too. 'Thank you, Tim,' she said. 'I'll make sure that I don't.'

It was Tim who broke the silence and changed the subject. His voice was gentle. 'Have you made up your mind which air-raid shelter to have at home?'

Patsy laughed. 'No, there's no decision on that. I suggested to Mum that we get an Anderson shelter and dig it in within easy reach of the back door, but she hated the idea. "It'll ruin my garden," she complained. "I'll not have that. And anyway, we might never need it. The Zeppelins couldn't come this far north in the last war." '

'I'm afraid all that has changed. German planes will have no trouble reaching Merseyside now.'

'I've told her that. What are you going to do?'

'It's difficult for us too. We step in straight from the street at the front and at the back there's a concrete yard. I thought of the Morrison shelter but our living room is so small we'd hardly be able to walk round it, never mind find room for armchairs. So under the stairs is the best we can do for ourselves but we are close enough to use the public shelter in the underground station at Hamilton Square.'

'There isn't a public shelter near us, but I can't see Mum using one anyway. I think the Morrison shelter would suit us best, but Mum doesn't like the idea of erecting a big metal structure in the dining room, which is the only possible place. "Where would we eat our meals?" she asks. So I'm doing nothing about it until she makes up her mind.'

Over the winter, new factories were built to make munitions, and many old businesses making products like cosmetics closed down. The civilian population was directed into war work and urged to put all their energy into the war effort. Shortages began to bite and the shops emptied of stock. It was not only food and clothing, the shortage of petrol meant Tim's driving lessons and practice sessions with Bill were curtailed.

'I'm afraid it's going to take you longer to get your licence,' Patsy sympathised. 'But at least you've made a start.'

Spring came and the news of the war was all bad. Everybody was afraid invasion was imminent. Supply ships were sunk in the Atlantic and there were daily battles for air supremacy over Kent.

Patsy was horrified when at mid-morning one day they had a power cut. Without electricity to power the sewing machines, her business came to a full stop. When she rang the electricity company, they said it was shortage of power to the national grid and it was likely to be the first cut of many. When she sent the girls home, it caused consternation all round because they needed their wages.

She and Tim ate their lunchtime sandwiches at their desks

and had only water to drink. 'We're doing vital war work,' Tim said, 'so we've got to have power.'

'I'm expecting Rupert to come this evening,' she said. 'He might be able to help.'

'He certainly won't want us to stop work,' Tim agreed.

'I'll see if I can have a word with him now,' she said, lifting the phone, but as she'd expected, he wasn't in his office.

Patsy sent Tim home early that afternoon as there was no sign that the power supply would come on again. She found it unsettling to have the whole building quiet on a weekday. It did nothing to calm her anxieties.

She felt stiff with worry by the time Rupert arrived. He came breezing into her office just after five, wearing a new Harris tweed jacket. She'd thought recently that war didn't seem to touch Rupert. He carried on as he always had and managed to find the luxuries he'd always enjoyed. He swept Patsy into his arms and she was able to relax at last.

'I thought we might go out for a meal tonight,' he said. 'I've booked a table at the Queen's Hotel for seven and I've brought a cake to have with our tea.'

'There's no tea to be had here,' she told him and explained why.

'I can solve that.' He smiled. 'We've been working on the problem of how to get round power cuts for some time. The government has made a few generators available for essential businesses. Yours is classed as an essential business and one will be supplied to you free of charge.' Patsy hugged him more tightly, that was music to her ears. 'I've even brought the forms for you to fill up.'

'Thank goodness for that,' she said. 'You're a miracle worker. How soon . . . ?'

'It won't take long. You sign your mother's name on the

form and we'll go out and post it at the main post office so it catches tonight's post.'

Rupert had it installed and working within ten days.

On 29 July 1940, in the early hours of the morning Patsy and her mother were woken up by the air-raid siren.

'What are we going to do?' Beatrice demanded. The blood-curdling sound of the siren had ceased but they were both listening intently.

'I'll make some tea.' Patsy got up to do it and her mother followed her downstairs. She was still wringing her hands when they heard a distant noise, a crump-crump as though bombs were dropping not far away and then the deafening boom of nearby ack-ack guns firing at the planes.

Patsy could see her mother was both horrified and frightened. They spent the rest of the night huddled together wrapped in blankets under the stairs.

'We'll have to get an air-raid shelter,' Beatrice wept. 'I don't feel safe here.'

They couldn't sleep even when the all-clear sounded and it was quiet again. Patsy insisted they go back to their beds and try to sleep and eventually she managed it. The next morning, she heard on the wireless as she ate a lonely breakfast that bombs had dropped harmlessly in fields between Thurstaston, Irby and Neston on the Wirral. She took her mother's breakfast up to her and told her to stay in bed and rest.

She found many of her workers were late arriving and once there they couldn't stop talking about the horror of the night.

'I've got to get an air-raid shelter,' she told Tim. 'Whatever was I thinking of, dragging my feet like this? Now the war seems to be getting under way, it's urgent.'

'One advantage of working with the Civil Defence,' Tim

said, 'I know how to go about getting a Morrison shelter delivered and I don't think it will take long.'

Six days later it was delivered. Arthur came and brought a friend to help him erect it in their dining room. It seemed an enormous thing and they had to move their dining table to their sitting room. Fortunately it was of a gate-legged design and could be folded back against the wall, or opened halfway to provide a table big enough to seat two.

'You could eat from this.' Arthur drummed his fingers on the thick metal top of the shelter. 'You could have a banquet in here. All you'd need is a tablecloth.'

'Two tablecloths,' Beatrice said. 'Or better still a sheet.'

He showed them how it worked. 'These sides slide back so you can get inside, then you slide them back to support the top. Should the ceiling fall in, you'd still be safe in this. All you need is a mattress underneath and you've got a bed. Room for two of you in here in total comfort, and you'll be as snug as a bug.'

'I'd be more comfortable in my own bed,' Beatrice said. 'If only Hitler would keep his planes at home.'

Arthur helped Patsy carry down the mattress from Barney's bed and get it inside the shelter. Beatrice collected together all their important documents and small valuables.

'We need to keep them near us,' she said grimly. 'In case the house is badly damaged.' Then she helped Patsy make up the bed with sheets and blankets. 'We might as well make ourselves as comfortable as we can.'

During the following days and nights the air-raid siren was silent though they heard of a plane dropping a bomb on Halewood cemetery, on the outskirts of Liverpool.

On 9 August 1940, the siren sounded just before midnight. Patsy was fast asleep in bed. It woke her up and she heard her mother shouting panic-stricken that they must get in the shelter. Feeling fuzzy, Patsy pulled on her dressing gown and slippers and ran down to the kitchen. Beatrice had decided they must take a flask of tea in the shelter with them in case they had to stay there for hours. Very soon they could hear the engines of enemy planes above them. The next moment a deafening explosion hurt their ears and they felt the building around them move. Patsy grabbed her mother and held on to her as though her life depended on it. Her heart was pounding fit to burst.

'God Almighty! What was that?' Beatrice's voice was a terrified whisper.

'A bomb, and it fell near us.' Patsy was aghast. 'Hurry, let's get into the shelter.' A nearby gun emplacement burst into a thundering retaliation of anti-aircraft fire.

She didn't know how long they kept their heads down and held each other close. When she realised the cacophony had subsided, she pushed her head clear of the blankets and listened. The night had gone quiet except for the distant sound of a police car.

'It's over,' she said. 'The planes have gone away.'

'Don't get up.' Her mother hung on to her pyjama jacket. 'The all-clear hasn't sounded yet. Let's have that tea. My mouth's as dry as the bottom of an ash can.'

Patsy found the torch and shone it at the clock her mother had brought in from the dining room mantelpiece, so they'd know the time. 'We've hardly been here an hour,' she said. It seemed like eternity.

Patsy shook up her pillows and poured the tea. The hot drink was comforting but she felt unaccountably hungry. 'Did you say you were going to keep a tin of biscuits here?' she asked.

'Yes, it's there with all the other things at the bottom of the bed.'

Patsy started to hunt for it and found it under a large well-worn manila envelope. She bit into a shortbread and asked, 'What is this?'

'Birth certificates and things like that.' Beatrice helped herself to a biscuit.

'The family secrets.' Patsy started to pull them out to read by the light of the torch.

'Not secrets any more.' Beatrice put out a hand to stop her. 'I must tell you more about Rowley's family one day.'

'You've said that before.'

'I know.' The all-clear sounded. 'Let's stay here and try and get some sleep before it goes again.'

Patsy tried to sleep, but the fearsome bombing raid had unsettled her. Her mother was restless too; she was tossing and turning. Finally, she said, 'Tell me about Barney's father now, Mum. We're never going to get to sleep after that.'

Beatrice rolled over on to her back and sighed to indicate reluctance, but eventually found the words. 'Rowley was very handsome and quite the man about town. He drove a huge American car – a sporty Chrysler roadster in black and yellow. He had very extravagant tastes and was used to having plenty of money. All the girls admired him, but he took up with me.'

'But you said his family was introverted, stiff and formal, and didn't take to you.'

'Yes, very much so. The Tavenham-Strongs had been landed gentry for generations.' There was a pause and she cleared her throat. 'Apart from their eldest son who was the heir and had to learn to run the estate, their other sons had traditionally made their careers in the army. But over the years the income from the land diminished and the cost of maintaining Aldford Hall, their grand house, increased. The officers began to find it difficult to manage on their salaries.

'Rowley's grandfather, Esmond Ewart Thomas, was a seventh son. He followed the usual path into the army but remained a second lieutenant without promotion for a decade. The family considered him to be the runt of the litter. He fell in love with a beautiful twenty-year-old heiress to a confectionery business called Dorothea Holt, and in eighteen sixty-eight he married her. But the Holts were in trade and the Tavenham-Strongs looked down on Dorothea for that. They considered her to be socially beneath them but when her father died, Esmond Ewart Thomas resigned his commission and took over the running of their factory. He made it grow and prosper.'

Patsy smiled. 'And that made the generals jealous?'

'According to Rowley, they were absolutely livid. The factory was in Liverpool and Dorothea also inherited a house in Princes Park near to it, as well as a small country house near Aldford Hall that they made their home.

'To start with, Esmond and Dorothea provided money for essential repairs, not only to the roof at Aldford Hall but to the dower house and other properties owned by the family. I gather that over the years they resented having to do this. The military gentlemen spent much of their time serving in the far-flung Empire and gave little thanks, while the ladies of the family continued to look down on Dorothea and belittle her family.

'So Dorothea and Esmond sold their small country house and used their profits to build an elegant new home for themselves in such a position that the ladies of Aldford Hall could not avoid seeing it every time they went into Chester. It's a large and very handsome house and they called it Aldford

Grange. The military gentlemen didn't like that either, because it meant the houses would be compared. Inevitably, they came to be called just the Hall and the Grange. Dorothea liked to spend part of the week in Liverpool with Esmond and they would travel back at weekends by train to spend time in their new house.

'By the time I married into them, the split between the two sides of the family had deepened. The military side had a very superior attitude and were disdainful, saying there were more important things in life than making money, as the sweet-makers did.'

'Dorothea and Esmond were Barney's grandparents?'

'That's right, the wealthy side of the family.'

'But you said when Rowley died you were poor and had to earn a living for yourself and Barney.'

'Yes, that's the thing about families. Everybody focuses on the differences but in many ways they were exactly the same. Even the confectionery-makers were snobs. They didn't take to me. I was just Beatrice Brown, a girl who'd worked in their factory. My father was a postman, and though my mother had been a shorthand typist too, she'd worked for the council and had had to give up her job when she married.

'We didn't have to buy a house when we were married. Rowley already owned a small house in Liverpool and also had a suite of rooms in the Grange which he'd furnished to his own taste. We travelled back and forth just like his parents, and his grandparents before him.

'We spent most of our time in Liverpool, although when I was having my first baby I found that hard going towards the end. And then I had Colin and he wasn't well; the smoky atmosphere of Liverpool was bad for him, he needed country air, so I felt I had to stay at the Grange. I was never accepted by the womenfolk of the family. They didn't include me in anything. I disliked my in-laws, all of them.'

'Couldn't you have found a cottage and lived by yourself?'

'Rowley said no, the family would frown on that. This was the way they lived so the senior members of the family could see what the younger ones were doing. It was a system of hierarchy, of control. Have you heard of Lieutenant General Sir Julian Philip Tavenham-Strong?'

'No.' Patsy yawned. 'Should I have?'

'No, you're too young, but almost everybody in England older than you will have done. He was head of the family.'

'Couldn't the other side just break away and have nothing to do with him?'

'They never did.' Patsy knew her mother was tiring. She was pausing often and it seemed to take her more effort to carry on. 'The confectionery side had little appetite for fighting, Dorothea's spirit had spent itself. I think Rowley, my husband, had been bullied since childhood.' Beatrice's voice trailed away.

A few moments later Patsy heard a gentle snore. She turned over and tried to settle down to sleep, but her mind still raced. Had Barney's father been talked into joining up? Or had he been caught up in the rush to volunteer, believing as most of them did, that it would be an adventure and a bit of fun?

The next morning, they heard on the eight o'clock news that a stick of high-explosive bombs had fallen in Prenton, the next Birkenhead suburb to their own. One bomb had fallen on the house of Mr Bunney, who owned Bunney's department store in Liverpool, and killed one of his servant girls.

Beatrice was shocked to the core. 'War seems suddenly very close.'

CHAPTER TWENTY

THE FOLLOWING EVENING, PATSY was closing up the workroom for the night when Rupert arrived carrying another picnic hamper. 'Shall I take it straight up?' he called.

'Yes.' Patsy ran after him. She'd been looking forward to him coming all day though she was beginning to feel guilty about spending time alone with him in the flat. She'd told her mother he'd be coming to see her tonight, that she'd be having dinner with him and that she'd be late home. She hoped Mum would infer that they'd be going out for a meal, and any time they spent in the workshop would be spent working.

At the bend in the stairs to the flat Rupert met Tim coming down and had to manoeuvre the hamper to let him pass. Rupert was the taller of the two and had the build of an athlete.

Tim waved a file at her, 'We left this up there at lunchtime,' he said. 'I'll be off home now. Goodnight.'

'Goodnight, Tim. See you tomorrow.' Up in the flat she found he'd tidied up a bit, though he hadn't looked pleased when she'd told him Rupert was coming.

Rupert's eyes were sparkling and as soon as they heard Tim slam the workshop door, he swept her into his arms to kiss her. 'I've been looking forward all day to this,' he said as they fell back on the sofa with their arms still entwined.

Patsy had never felt like this about a man before. Her face was now within six inches of Rupert's. He had strong handsome features. With her forefinger she traced the cleft in his chin, while his brown eyes smiled back into hers. 'I do love you, Patsy,' he murmured. 'I think of you all the time instead of concentrating on my work.'

She was head over heels in love with him and it was wonderful that he felt the same way about her. She ran her fingers through his mahogany-coloured hair, straightened out one of his curls and let it bounce back. That brought his lips down on hers again in a kiss that sent thrills down her spine.

Rupert moved back from her. 'I've brought some wine, let's have a glass.' He opened the hamper, it was equipped with all the glasses and plates they'd need. 'White wine,' he said as he poured it. 'Not as good as champagne but they say this sort isn't bad. I had it chilled. I think you'll like it.'

Patsy sipped it cautiously. She found it delicious.

'Are you hungry?'

'Starving.'

He began setting out the food. 'Do you like roast chicken?' In Patsy's family, that was considered a luxury too.

He smiled. 'It's only half one, with some salad. There's a sponge trifle with fresh cream and pineapple to follow. I thought this would be nicer than going out, especially as we have this very comfortable flat to ourselves.'

'It is.' Patsy felt he was opening up a whole new way of life to her and she found it exciting. She helped him set out the feast on the dining table.

He smiled fondly and arranged two chairs side by side. 'Have another glass of wine?'

Patsy pushed her glass forward. 'Thank you, this is a fantastic spread.' There were several different varieties of salad and freshly baked rolls and butter to go with it. 'Did you put all this together yourself?'

'No, there's a firm of caterers near the racecourse that does picnics. They provided the wicker hamper. I have to return it on the way home.'

'Glorious food,' she said when they'd eaten as much as they could.

'Let's go back to the sofa to finish the wine,' Rupert suggested, taking off his jacket and loosening his tie. 'It's more comfortable there.' He topped up her glass again.

Patsy expected his arms to go round her again and they did. It was what they both wanted. She loved to feel his firm body close against her own. When he pushed his hands under her jumper, fireworks exploded within her, making her catch her breath. He stroked her bare flesh gently so that she felt real desire. It was only when he tried to push his fingers under her bra that she pushed his hand away.

She was having to push his hands away more and more often. She'd explained why she didn't want him to do it but she sensed he was growing impatient with her.

'I can't help it,' he said. 'I love you so much I can't keep my hands off you.' He was reaching both arms round her to unfasten her bra.

'No,' she protested and jerked him away.

'If you really loved me you'd want us to be lovers,' he said, holding her shoulders at arm's length and gazing into her eyes.

'I do want us to be lovers as much as you do. That's the problem, isn't it?'

'I can't see any problem.'

Patsy pulled away from him. 'I'm not prepared to risk it.'

He drew away from her and his dark eyes stared imperiously into hers. 'You're not religious?'

'Not particularly but I go to church on Sunday mornings and take Mum.'

'Is she religious?'

'No, not really, it's just something we've always done, a family tradition, you might say. I think it calms her down, soothes her. It keeps us all from neurotic meltdown.'

'Then why not?' Rupert pressed. 'We've known each other for a long time now and it was love at first sight, wasn't it? Nobody could say we were rushing into it.'

He leaned over and felt for his jacket. 'Look, I've brought a condom.' He showed it to her. 'There's no need to worry about having a baby. You'll be perfectly safe with this. Making love is how we show our affection for each other. You'll come to no harm, I promise you.'

He came closer, wrapped his arms round her again and tried to kiss her.

'No, Rupert.' She had to fight to free herself from his arms.

'Come on, be a sport.'

'I don't want to.'

'There's absolutely no risk. You needn't be afraid.'

'I am afraid. I've told you why. After seeing what happened to Madge, I've decided nothing would persuade me.'

'You'll enjoy it, I know. Come on, Patsy, I've been very good to you. I sorted your business out for you, didn't I? You're making money now.'

Patsy froze. 'What has that to do with us becoming lovers?'

'You owe me, don't you?'

'Owe you? That's a step too far, Rupert.' She was getting angry. 'I'm very grateful for the help you gave me. You provided work for my sewing room when I needed it, but you can hardly expect me to return the favour by providing you with . . .'

His face flushed with anger. 'I don't expect you to provide me with anything! But no doubt you'll expect me to keep your sewing room busy. I could stop giving you work, you know.'

That took her breath away. Was Rupert threatening to ruin her business if she didn't sleep with him? She could feel a ball of fury building up inside her. 'That sounds like blackmail to me.'

'Now you're being silly. I just wanted to show you how much I love you, and I want you to show your love to me. You do say you love me.'

'Yes, you know I do.' She felt breathless, confused, upset that he could say such a thing.

'Then stop being such a tease.'

'I'm certainly not a tease.' This time she exploded with rage. 'I've been telling you for ages why I'm not going to put myself in that position.'

'Not this clearly, you haven't. I thought it was a delaying tactic, to build up my interest. Why else would you smarten up this place? You've made us a real love nest, with total privacy once the workers go home, and you were very keen to do it. It's the ideal place for us to show our love to each other. I thought that was what you wanted, a love nest. What is the point of it, if it isn't for that?'

'A love nest? For heaven's sake! If you really loved me,' she spat, 'you'd want to protect me from that. You'd wait until we were married.'

'Married?' he echoed, and something in his voice told her marriage had never been his plan. He was no longer smiling. His face was twisting with frustration and resentment. She felt as though he'd thrown a bucket of cold water over her. She'd been dreamily looking at engagement rings in jewellers' shop windows, and having visions of future married bliss.

'I didn't realise you were so naive.'

'What?' Just like Barney, he'd been thinking of sex. Patsy

felt stricken. There was no way now she was going to say she'd been thinking of marriage and seeing this flat as their first home. 'I think you'd better go,' she said quietly.

'I've given you a good time, haven't I?' Suddenly he was truculent. 'I've taken you to nice restaurants and theatres. What did you think I was getting out of it?'

'The same as I was. I thought we were looking for the same things,' she said. 'Please go. It's over. Don't come back.'

He stood staring down at her, breathing heavily. Then he picked up his jacket, put it on and made for the door.

'You're forgetting your picnic hamper,' she told him.

With a grunt of displeasure, he turned to retrieve it, pushed some of the food and crockery on the table into it, and rushed downstairs. When the door at the bottom slammed with cold finality, Patsy threw herself down on the sofa and wept for her lost dreams.

Rupert Alderman was not the sort of man she'd supposed him to be. But better she found out about her boyfriend this way than in the way Madge had.

By the next morning Patsy wasn't so sure. She felt as though the bottom had dropped out of her world, it seemed empty without Rupert. His handsome face came between her and everything else, she was afraid she'd made a big mistake. She loved him and had thought she'd spend the rest of her life with him. Should she ring him, say she was sorry and had changed her mind? Tell him she loved him and would do anything to keep him?

She hated being cut off from him, and on top of that she felt a fool because she'd made no secret of the fact that she was expecting him to propose. Hadn't she told Bill Bentley, Tim and Jeanie? Why had she opened her mouth so wide? Mum thoroughly approved of him and was already thinking ahead to the wedding, as she herself had been.

But no, Patsy hardened her heart, she wouldn't ring him. She mustn't forget that Rupert had threatened to stop bringing her work if she didn't sleep with him. It had sounded like blackmail at the time and he hadn't liked hearing her say that. But if that was his intention, it would ruin her business. Thinking of what she could do to prevent that gave her another sleepless night.

All the next day Patsy worried silently though she didn't really believe it was within Rupert's power to stop her supply of work. Hadn't Bill Bentley mentioned that he had a different agent? If the Ministry of Defence wanted uniforms sewn together, she thought she'd be able to get the work by a different route. All the same, it added to the upset she felt.

All the next day she said nothing, half expecting, half hoping that Rupert would ring and apologise and all would be back to normal. But he didn't and she realised she'd have to accept that he had no intention of resuming their relationship. It was definitely finished.

She was setting the table for supper that evening when Beatrice said, 'You've not seen much of Rupert this week. Is he busy or are you saving up to get married?'

'Neither.' Patsy crashed the forks down. 'It's off, all off. He's not been near since Monday.'

Her mother tried to soothe her. 'You've had a quarrel, but that doesn't mean he won't want to make it up.'

'We'll never make it up. It's over.' Patsy flounced into the kitchen.

'Oh. Well, never mind, there are plenty more fish in the sea, aren't there?'

Patsy wasn't sure about that but having spoken about it to

her mother, she told Bill and Tim at lunchtime the next day.

Tim was cautious. 'I had noticed he hadn't been round this week,' he said.

'Rupert was too posh and polished.' Bill bit into his cheese sandwich. 'I didn't much care for him. Not the sort to settle down, Patsy. I didn't trust him.'

'No, and I shouldn't have done. Bill, what is the name of the agent who supplies work to you?'

'George Miller. Rupert will still continue to look after you, won't he? I mean, that's a working relationship and it is war work you're doing.'

'He said not. Well, he threatened not.'

'Good Lord!' Bill was on his feet reaching for a piece of paper on the other side of the table. 'I'll write down George's name and telephone number for you. I'd get on to him, Patsy. Are you running out of work?'

'No, I've got three weeks to a month in hand.'

'George will take care of your needs. I told you a long time ago I thought you'd be better off with him, didn't I?'

As soon as she went back to her office, Patsy tried to ring George Miller. She knew it would settle her mind if she could ensure there would be no hold-up in getting more work.

'I'm sorry,' she was told. 'Mr Miller isn't in the office at the moment.'

Patsy wasn't surprised. She knew the agents spent a lot of time out with their clients. 'When is the best time for me to catch him?'

'Either early in the morning before he goes out, or late in the afternoon when he returns.'

Patsy rang again before she went home at five o'clock and was told he hadn't returned to the office. 'Could you leave a message on his desk asking him to ring me tomorrow morning?'

she asked and left her name and number. 'I'll be in the office shortly after eight o'clock.'

Patsy spent another anxious night but Mr Miller rang her the next morning. Patsy didn't find her problem easy to explain.

'So you think Rupert Alderman will no longer be dealing with your business?'

'That's right,' Patsy said. 'I don't want to run out of work and have the girls idle.'

'Of course not. Are you running out?'

Patsy had to admit she still had about three weeks' work in hand.

Mr Miller seemed at a loss. 'Mr Alderman hasn't mentioned anything about this to me. I'll need to have a word with him and take a look at your file. I'll ring you back when I have,' he told her.

Patsy felt at least she'd made contact. Hopefully, she wouldn't be left high and dry now. She slept better that night and the next morning he rang her again as he'd promised.

'Mr Alderman has handed your file over to me, so I shall be attending to the needs of your business in future. I'm a bit busy this week, Miss Rushton, and you seem to have work in hand for the moment, so can we leave it until I'm due to visit your area?'

He made an appointment to come and see her in a couple of weeks' time. 'I look forward to meeting you,' he said.

Patsy put the phone down with a sense of satisfaction. She'd managed it; Rupert might have broken her heart but her business was going to survive intact.

Later that afternoon, Tim was on the telephone ordering cleaning materials while Patsy was checking the sundries expenses account he'd worked on that morning, when she suddenly demanded, 'Gladys had to take one of the irons to be repaired, didn't she?'

'Yes.' Tim was surprised at her angry tone.

'There's no payment shown for that,' she snapped irritably. 'You've forgotten all about it.'

'No,' he said quietly, 'that came out of petty cash.'

She looked at him then and her lips trembled. 'Oh! I'm sorry, Tim. We must try and buy some new irons, they're all getting old. I'm cross and out of sorts. I'm sorry.'

'Don't worry. You're just not yourself.'

Patsy slammed the accounts ledger shut. 'I wish I hadn't told everybody I was expecting Rupert to propose,' she said heatedly. 'It lets everybody know I've been jilted.'

'It doesn't, you've changed your mind, that's all.'

'He must have thought I wasn't good enough for him. He was disappointed that I wasn't more fun. He's rejected me.'

'Patsy! You mustn't think like that, you're worth two of him. Rupert has let you down.'

She sat ruminating at her desk, her eyes bright with unshed tears. She told him then exactly what had led to their break-up.

'I'm glad you were strong enough not to be persuaded.' Tim was pleased she'd been able to tell him. 'Very glad, you should feel proud of yourself for standing up to him. Rupert was no gentleman to try that.'

'Very much like Barney.'

'You must forget him,' he urged. 'Put him behind you.'

She gave him a little smile then. 'He's taken himself off, hasn't he? He doesn't want me and that hurts.' She sighed. 'Everybody's saying there's plenty more fish in the sea, but . . .'

Tim wanted to tell her he'd loved her for years and was

glad Rupert was gone. The words were hovering on the tip of his tongue, but was she ready to turn to him or, in this frame of mind, turn to anyone else?

He said sadly, 'You don't want other fish, do you? You want him.'

Patsy pushed her hair back from her forehead in an impatient gesture. 'Life has fallen a little flat. Rupert's been taking me out and about for the past year and I'm missing that too. All I do now is sit at home with Mum.'

Tim felt relief run through him. 'I can help there.' He smiled. 'That's if you think coming to the pictures with me would be any improvement.' Her blue eyes were examining him as though for the first time. 'It's not an exciting change for you when we've been sitting here side by side all day,' he added.

'It would help, Tim. Thank you. I feel chained up, I'd like some entertainment, some sort of a social life again.'

'Do you fancy seeing *The Philadelphia Story* with Katharine Hepburn, Cary Grant and James Stewart? That's showing at the Ritz.'

'Yes, I would.'

'Great, then be my guest. What about tonight?'

'Yes, tonight would be lovely.' She was frowning. 'But only if you let me pay my own way.'

Tim swallowed hard, he'd always been afraid this would be a problem. Patsy was, after all, his employer.

As she'd arranged, Patsy collected him in her car. His mother was surprised when he told her he was taking his boss to the pictures. He saw their neighbours' curtains twitch when her new car drew up at his front door. Once they were bowling down the road, he could see that she'd changed her dress. This one was a deep blue and she was wearing lipstick which normally she didn't for work. She'd made herself really beautiful for him!

In the foyer of the Ritz, he asked, 'Where d'you want to sit?'

'I don't mind,' she said. 'It doesn't have to be the most expensive seats.' He felt her slide a coin discreetly into his hand.

When he took his mother, they usually sat in the one and nines, but the coin in his hand was half-a-crown. 'The best seats tonight,' he told her. 'This is a real treat for me.'

Patsy laughed and chatted as she did at work, she was good company. Tim was thrilled to be squiring her round and could hardly believe she was here at his side.

'I loved the film,' she said as they walked back to her car afterwards. 'A marvellous story, wasn't Cary Grant great?'

As she was driving him back, he remembered she was twenty years old now, and asked, 'Should I have taken you for a drink before we came home?' He knew that is what Rupert would have done.

He saw her smile in the semi-darkness. 'That's for people who need to get to know each other. We've passed that stage.'

She drew up in his road again. He was feeling for the door handle when she said, 'I'm very glad to have a friend like you, Tim, someone who'll take me round.'

'We could do it again?'

'Yes, I'd like that.' He wanted to kiss her but he hesitated too long. She said, 'Goodnight and thanks. See you tomorrow.'

Although he was later than usual going to bed, he couldn't get to sleep. He was reliving every moment of the evening.

A week later Tim suggested they go again to the cinema. They were both more relaxed this time and though the film wasn't as good, Patsy said she'd enjoyed it. An unexpected heat wave had blown up and he'd told her how he'd learned to swim in the Mersey while he was at school and how much he enjoyed the beaches all round them at this time of the year.

'I can't swim,' she said. 'I wish I could.'

Tim said eagerly, 'If you'd like to learn I could teach you.'

'Yes, but in the river? Mum says it isn't clean enough to swim in.'

He laughed. 'I couldn't afford a swimming pool when I was growing up but now there's that huge new open-air pool in New Brighton, we could go there if you like. Have you been there to sunbathe yet?'

She shook her head.

'I'm told it's one of the biggest and best in the country. Would you like to go on Saturday afternoon or on Sunday?'

'Saturday please. I usually take Mum out for a run in the car on Sundays.'

Tim bought himself a new pair of bathing trunks in the market. He didn't want her to think he looked scruffy.

'Wow,' she said as soon as they'd gone through the turnstiles. 'It's enormous, and just look at all those seats, it's like a grandstand.'

'They hold competitions here. The seats are for the audience.'

'And beauty contests, they're advertising the next one over there.'

He thought it rather daring of him to say, 'You'd win hands down if you entered for it.'

She smiled. 'That's kind of you, Tim, but you ought to see the competition before you decide things like that.'

He rushed to change and was back waiting for her outside the ladies changing rooms when she came out. She was small and dainty and he'd known she had a neat figure, but his first glimpse of her in a swimsuit made him gasp. She had a wonderful figure.

He led her to the steps into the pool and jumped in before turning round to help her. She came in gingerly. 'It looks lovely but it's cold.'

'It isn't when you get used to it. We'll start with breast stroke. You know how to move your arms?' He showed her.

'I'm a bit nervous of lying on the water and taking my feet off the bottom.' She pulled a face.

'No need to be. Just float, Patsy. I'll hold your chin up with one hand and put my other arm under your waist. You're quite safe like this. I won't let you go. Try to relax. You're as tense as a board.'

After a few minutes, she struggled to stand up again. 'I'm not very good at it, am I?'

'It'll come with practice,' he told her. 'Come on, let's try again. This time move your legs like a frog.'

Tim felt better that he'd found something he could teach her. Up till now, she'd seemed to lead and he'd had to follow, but he was almost scared to touch her. If she hadn't wanted Rupert to do that, would she allow him the privilege? But in the water he had to touch her if he was to teach her to swim. She was clinging to him and he wanted to support her. Eventually she went to splash around by herself in shallower water and Tim did a few lengths of the pool.

Later she bought him a bottle of lemonade and they sat in the sun to drink it. Tim thought he'd had a blissful afternoon. When she took him home, he asked if she'd like to do it again.

'Yes please, I would. I don't seem to have much talent for swimming but I'm not going to give up.'

'Good, then we'll come once a week while it's warm enough.'

'I've left it a bit late to start.' She smiled. 'The summer is nearly over.'

'Then we'll carry on next summer.'

'Yes.' It pleased Patsy to think Tim was a permanent fixture in her life. 'There's another thing,' she went on. 'This way of me paying my share by slipping you a couple of bob here and half-a-crown there won't do. It's embarrassing for both of us. In future, we'll have a box in the office. We'll call it the entertainment fund and you can draw on it to pay for both of us.'

'Heavens, Patsy! But then . . .'

'Don't say anything. If we are to be friends and go out together, and I want us to be, then we have to face the fact that I don't pay you enough for you to foot the bill every time we go out. It needs to happen, Tim. Anyway, I'd like you to take me to a restaurant from time to time. Now the war is on, they're only allowed to charge five shillings for a meal so it doesn't cost the earth to go to the most expensive places.'

'But I've never eaten in an expensive restaurant. I'm not as sophisticated as Rupert.' Tim sighed. 'I haven't had the time or money to go out and live it up. I know nothing about wine. I wouldn't know what to do.'

'You'll soon learn.' Patsy laughed. 'We'll try it and learn together.'

CHAPTER TWENTY-ONE

IN SEPTEMBER 1940, THE bombing started in earnest. Patsy found it terrifying to hear the planes overhead and think they'd come to drop bombs on them. The enemy wanted to render the port of Liverpool unusable so that essential foodstuffs and materials needed for the war effort could not be brought in. The docks stretched along both sides of the Mersey estuary for many miles, and in the moonlight the river acted as an unmistakable marker for the bombers.

Sometimes the siren went before their bedtime, but even if it didn't, if there was bright moonlight, Patsy and her mother found it better not to go upstairs to bed. They settled down for the night in the Morrison shelter, and were rarely able to sleep undisturbed until morning.

Barney had now moved to his new posting, a base of the Royal Army Service Corps on the outskirts of Liverpool. Jeanie had moved to Liverpool too and was lodging with her Aunt Lil in order to be near him. Occasionally they came to tea on Sunday afternoons.

Patsy knew Jeanie was cross with her because she'd refused to let her move into the flat and now she'd broken off with Rupert and no longer had plans to use it herself, it was on her conscience.

One Sunday morning, Beatrice and Patsy were making

scones because they were expecting Barney and Jeanie to come for tea, when Beatrice said, 'Perhaps you should let them use the flat now they're both living in Liverpool. What d'you think?'

Patsy frowned. 'His base is miles away, almost in Maghull. Barney can't live over the sewing room and get to work on time in the mornings.'

'There's a good train service.'

'Mum, a train was bombed on the track last week and that stopped the service to Southport for two days. He's got to cross the river and the blitz is playing havoc with public transport. We never know whether the buses are going to come or not.'

'I know, but mostly he'd get there and it gives Barney a base, a home of his own.'

'Mum, I'm not sure I trust Barney not to meddle in the sewing room.' She didn't want to tell her mother that she'd found money was missing the last time Barney had been there. 'I'm worried that I wouldn't be able to lock up the business securely, not away from anyone in the flat. I know Jeanie would be there alone most of the time but the same applies to her. Once we close for the night, they'd be able to look through all our figures, everything. I'd prefer to keep things the way they are.'

'Well, I'm not sure Barney would think that fair.'

'He wouldn't, and neither would Jeanie, but when Dad died, Barney wouldn't have anything to do with it. I pleaded with him to help run the business but he took off for the whole summer to sell ice cream.'

Patsy could see her mother wanted to indulge Barney as usual; she was screwing up her face. As she slid the tray of scones into the oven to cook alongside the tiny joint of pork, she said, 'Well, if you don't want Jeanie living there you'd better not tell them you've broken off with Rupert.'

'Jeanie is nearer to Barney's depot if she stays with her Aunt Lil.'

That afternoon, Patsy answered their knock on the front door. Almost the first thing Barney said was, 'How is Rupert? Are you engaged yet?'

Without thinking, Beatrice answered, 'Patsy has broken off with him. There won't be an engagement.'

'Oh!' Barney sneered. 'Going to confine your talents to business then, Patsy? I hope you aren't too disappointed.'

Jeanie was quick to pick up on Patsy's changed plans. 'Does that mean your plans for the flat have changed? If you're not going to move in, would it be all right if we did?'

'No, Jeanie, it wouldn't,' Patsy said. 'I'm sorry, but I need to think hard about a step like that. It could lead to security difficulties.'

'Please do think about it.' Jeanie's face was cold and, after that, Patsy thought she seemed more distant than ever. She smiled less and made no further effort to please.

Throughout September, the bombers flew regularly to Merseyside. Patsy thought that on some mornings Tim looked exhausted when he came to work after a busy night on Civil Defence duty. He told her fearsome stories of bomb damage, the homeless and the injured. Patsy felt she should volunteer to spend two or three nights a week on fire-watching duties too, but Beatrice was terrified of being left on her own in a raid, and pleaded with her not to do any such thing. Patsy felt she couldn't leave her.

They were spending more nights in the Morrison shelter than they did in their beds. They were both scared stiff when the bombs started to fall and spent hours holding on to each other for comfort.

In November, Liverpool had a terrible month but the

Birkenhead side of the river got off lightly. Everybody began to think about Christmas and hoped the Luftwaffe would give them a real break. They got no respite. In the weeks before Christmas the raids intensified and nobody got much sleep. There was heavy damage and mounting numbers of people were made homeless, injured and killed.

To get away from the bombing, Jeanie had returned to her Aunt Cissie's house in Chester. Her Aunt Lil had a job that kept her in Liverpool during the week but she joined them in Chester at the weekends. Jeanie was looking forward to Barney's next forty-eight-hour pass, which was to start on the evening of 2 December and, also, it was his birthday on 6 December. She planned to stay with Aunt Lil over that time. Barney would be free in the evening and she'd meet him and perhaps book a variety show at a theatre, or a dinner some-where. She'd see what was on when she got there.

Cissie baked him a birthday cake. It had to be sponge because dried fruit was hard to get and couldn't be decorated because icing sugar had disappeared from the shops. Jeanie had to look long and hard to find a birthday card, and finding him a gift was equally difficult.

The best she could think of was cigarettes, although she knew he could buy those in the NAAFI. She managed to get him forty from her friend Vince at the Eagle and Child pub where she used to work. She'd popped in for a drink and he'd kept her there until closing time. His dad had asked her if she wanted her job back.

All the time her curiosity about Barney's family was growing and she went in and out of the reference library to see if she could find out more details. She felt she was amply rewarded when she came across a thin book of nostalgic reminiscences written by one of his forebears and learned from editorial comment on its paper cover that there were two parts to this large family and that Barney's side owned a famous sweet factory in Liverpool, and they therefore had another source of income.

She hadn't time to read the book through, so she slipped it into her handbag when nobody was looking. Then she placed the other materials she'd requested back on the librarian's desk and strode out before it was missed.

'I felt it in my bones,' she said, showing it to Aunt Cissie as soon as she got home. 'They're rich, really rich. They have two family mansions, the Grange and the Hall that we went to see.'

'Yes, so it makes no sense that Barney hasn't got two pennies to rub together.' Cissie was indignant. 'He should be able to keep a wife in style.'

'This makes me more determined than ever. Surely a share of this fortune is Barney's birthright?'

Jeanie went to the shops to get something for their dinner and when she returned, Cissie said, 'You won't get much more information in this,' as she pushed the book away from her. 'It's all about the heroic military adventures of a Colonel Humphrey Tavenham-Strong in the Boer War. It's all ancient history.'

Jeanie sighed. 'How do I go about finding out more? Barney's father was in the last war. I think something happened to him then and I want to find out what it was. Do you know anybody we could ask?'

'Well, I've been thinking. There might be. There's a woman I used to work for, her name was Chloris King. Miss King, I called her, I used to clean for her three mornings a week. She was a journalist and there was an article she'd written in the *Gazette* last week, so I know she's still there. If we could look at back numbers of that newspaper we might come across more relevant stuff.'

'Cissie, that's a marvellous idea!'

Cissie was frowning. 'It's going back a few years since I worked for her. She may not even remember me. She may not want to help me.'

'Cissie, don't back out now. I want you to do this for me,' Jeanie urged. 'It could turn out to be very important for me and Barney.'

'OK, but only if you get hold of his birth certificate first. It would give us a reason to be delving into all this and without that nobody will believe you are related to them.'

Jeanie returned to Liverpool the day before Barney started his leave and it was their intention to spend it together at her Aunt Lil's house. She wanted to tell him all she'd found out about his rich relatives and the plans she and Aunt Cissie had discussed about how he might benefit from the relationship.

While she waited for a bus outside the station, she met a girl, also waiting, who used to work in the grocery shop where she'd once had a part-time job. The girl told her she'd seen a smashing cowboy film the night before called *Jesse James*, about an outlaw. Tyrone Power was the star and all the girls were swooning over him. It was in the new Technicolor and her enthusiasm made Jeanie keen to see it. That evening she persuaded her Aunt Lil to go to the pictures with her.

The air-raid siren sounded while the film was showing and a notice flashed on the screen advising those in the audience to go to a shelter, but by then they were all gripped by the story. On some occasions, the siren sounded and the enemy planes didn't come, so many people didn't move until they heard the guns start or the bombs drop.

Aunt Lil thought it would be a shame walk out halfway

through a good film, so they sat tight even though they did hear one loud explosion not very far away. The all-clear sounded and they relaxed back in their seats. When the film ended they walked home arm in arm, with Jeanie's mind still on Tyrone Power's skill in the saddle.

'The streets are busy tonight,' Lil said. 'And very noisy, there's ambulances screeching everywhere.'

The noise seemed to get louder and as they rounded a corner, Lil let out a wild scream and pulled to a halt.

'Oh my God!' Jeanie was shocked.

They could see that Lil's house had been damaged, as had six more surrounding it along the terrace. Bomb blast had blown some of the chimney pots off the roof, and in falling they'd dislodged some of the roof slates. All the windows in the front had been shattered, and in some houses, Lil's included, the front doors had been torn off too.

The Civil Defence workers were there in force, the ARP and even the WVS. They were told that nobody living in Lil's terrace had been hurt but their way was blocked when they tried to go inside.

'It's not safe,' they were told. 'The buildings will have to be checked over first and will probably need to be repaired.'

'What about my belongings?' Lil roared at them, as did some of the other residents. 'I want to go in and collect some things before everything is looted.'

They were allowed in at last, one at a time to pack a few things in bags and roll up the eiderdowns from their beds. Jeanie retrieved Barney's birthday cake and cigarettes. Like many who had neither family nor friends to take them in, the WVS directed them to an emergency rest centre where they had to spend the night.

* * *

At seven thirty on that same evening, 2 December, the first air-raid siren of the night wailed at half six, while Tim and his mother were eating their dinner.

'We've got to go.' Eileen Stansfield jerked to her feet and rushed to the bathroom.

Tim grabbed his uniform coat and tin hat, and stood ready to lock up their house. Hurriedly he took another slice of bread, piled on fried bacon and baked beans, and with another slice of bread pressed down hard on top, bit into his sandwich.

His mother was pulling on her hat and WVS coat. She snatched at the slice of bacon left on her plate. 'I'm ready,' she said. They set off at a jog, Tim still eating his sandwich.

'Slow down,' his mother panted, 'I can't keep this up.'

'Sorry,' he took her arm, 'I'd forgotten about your leg. You're walking so well nobody would know it had ever been broken.'

'It's my age and my build, love. You have to allow for that.' Eileen Stansfield was heading for the emergency canteen behind the market while Tim was going to the ARP post in St Lawrence's Church Hall, but for part of the way they followed the same route.

Tim thought in the blackout she needed somebody to hold on to, though tonight it didn't seem quite so pitch black because searchlights were criss-crossing the sky. There was a spat of deafening noise as the anti-aircraft guns on Bidston Hill opened fire, and they could hear the distant crump-crump of bombs already falling. In a short lull they heard the drone of engines overhead and that seemed even more frightening.

When their ways parted, his mother squeezed his arm. 'Best of luck,' she said.

Tim hurried on, thinking of Patsy. She'd said she was scared stiff when the bombs began falling and she thought him brave to volunteer to work as a warden, but nothing could be further from the truth. Everybody was afraid. He'd seen terror in almost everybody's eyes and knew most people made an effort to hide it and not give in to panic. He had to force himself to follow their example and keep his mind firmly on what must be done and get on with it.

St Lawrence's Church Hall had already been damaged in an earlier raid and all the windows had been boarded up. Before he could reach the door, it burst open and three wardens rushed out with spades over their shoulders.

'It's Market Street, Tim,' one of them called. 'A row of small shops has copped it. They say the owners are buried underneath.'

Tim snatched open the door. 'Reg,' he called. 'Shall I go with this team?' In the dim light from a storm lantern he could see tatters of blackout material flutter in the draught he was causing and a grizzled old man in his seventies sitting at a battered kitchen table, talking on the telephone. It was Reg's job to coordinate the wardens and the calls for assistance. He covered the mouthpiece with his hand and called back, 'Tim, yes, you go to Market Street with that rescue squad.'

Tim ran after the others and caught them up before they reached their destination. He could see a large gap in a terrace of small shops that was now reduced to a jumble of collapsed masonry, broken glass and torn roof timbers. A small crowd of neighbours had already gathered and were tearing at the rubble with their bare hands. The situation looked grim.

An agitated woman in apron and slippers shouted to them, 'My friend Elsie is trapped in her cellar. There are others too. It was a direct hit.'

Tim learned that Elsie and her husband were known to shelter in the cellar under the greengrocer's shop, a family with two children was under the hardware shop, and two elderly women who ran the sweet shop were under the third.

'Impossible to see where one shop finishes and the next begins,' murmured George, who was the rescue team leader. With the help of the neighbours he tried to work out where they could expect to find the victims. The bombs continued to fall and the guns bark as they set about getting them out.

It was back-breaking work. Many bricks were held in large blocks by their plaster, and these and the heavy timbers had to be lifted off and pitched aside. Tim had been provided with heavy gloves and felt he couldn't have managed without them. By nine o'clock the all-clear had sounded and they'd dug the family out from under the hardware shop. The mother and son were alive and virtually unhurt, but the daughter was badly injured and the father not breathing.

An ambulance had already been called and Tim and his colleagues turned immediately to burrow into the next cellar. They found the bodies of Elsie and her husband an hour later and went on to the third cellar where the elderly ladies were trapped. Miraculously they were alive but very shocked and frightened. The siren wailed once more as they were dispatched to hospital.

There was no mistaking what the shops had traded in. There were cabbage leaves and pieces of apple, together with sweets of every variety, scattered all around and being trampled into the rubble. The population was forbidden to take anything from bombed buildings, and there were notices everywhere telling people that the punishment for looting was death. But one neighbour had found a damaged carton of liquorice allsorts with the contents mostly unsoiled and was passing the box round, regardless of the warnings. Tim straightened his aching shoulders and took a handful. His energy was running out, he felt ready to drop with exhaustion. Another neighbour had made mugs of tea for them. When they set out to walk back to the ARP post, they could hear the throb of enemy engines above them once again and bombs began to fall.

'This time it looks like incendiaries,' a fellow rescue worker breathed. They could see them being dropped into fires that had been started earlier and there was no immediate explosion.

'Look,' Tim suddenly shouted and pointed. A partially inflated barrage balloon, already in flames, was falling out of the sky.

He heard a shocked whisper behind him, 'It's coming down in Price Street. Isn't there a garage about there?'

They all broke into a run, their exhaustion forgotten. It was indeed coming down on the garage and by the time they reached it, the buildings were blazing fiercely and men were trying to bat the flames out with spades and a hosepipe that trickled water.

'We've sent for the fire brigade,' an excited bystander shouted. 'But heaven knows when they'll come. There are fires everywhere tonight.'

'Stay well back,' George yelled to his team. 'Don't go any nearer, there'll be petrol stored here. Get everybody else well back before this place goes up. Tim, you start knocking on the doors of those houses over there and get the people out. Doug, you start on the other side of the road.'

Tim felt he was running about like a headless chicken, they all were. They got all but one couple well back before a series of explosions began to rip the night apart, hurting their ears and temporarily blinding them. With relief they saw the fire brigade arrive.

'Right,' George shouted to his team. 'Doug, you stay and

advise those whose homes have been damaged, everybody else back to the ARP post. You've done well, all of you.'

'Hope we aren't going to get many more like this,' a fellow rescue worker said. 'I'm half dead.'

'It's as much as I can do to put one foot in front of another,' sighed another. Tim agreed, he had no energy left.

Back at the post, they found the WVS had delivered some sandwiches and Reg was making hot tea to go with them.

He handed a mug to Tim and drew him aside. 'Bad news, mate, I'm sorry. The canteen at the back of the market was hit, your mother's been injured.'

'Oh my God!' Tim sat down with a jerk. 'Is she badly hurt?'

'She was taken to the General Hospital with several others. It was in the second air raid, but I don't know any details. Somebody telephoned and asked me to tell you.'

Tim was shocked. 'I'd better get to the hospital and find out.'

'Eat and drink first,' Reg advised. 'You look ready to collapse.'

Tim drank two mugs of tea and put his sandwich in his pocket. It was almost five in the morning and he felt too tired to eat. He set off to walk to the hospital but another bomb had fallen in the next street and casualties were being loaded into an ambulance. He asked for a lift.

The scene in casualty made his head reel. It was crowded and desperately busy. He couldn't see his mother anywhere. A staff nurse was helping a porter put a patient into a wheelchair, and when the porter left, Tim asked the nurse about his mother.

'Mrs Stansfield?' The nurse lifted weary eyes to meet his. 'Let me think, we've had so many new admissions. We have several patients waiting on trolleys in the corridor. Come this way.'

Tim saw her immediately. 'Yes, oh yes, here she is. Mum, how are you?' She opened bleary eyes and stared up at him for a few seconds. There was a large gauze pad strapped to her forehead. 'What happened to her?' he asked the nurse.

The nurse consulted the tag fastened on her wrist. 'Yes, Mrs Eileen Stansfield. We have no address for her, in fact no other details. Hello, Mrs Stansfield, how are you?'

His mother groaned and Tim saw her move.

'Are you in pain?'

Her lips moved to say something but Tim couldn't catch it. The nurse turned back to him. 'She's been seen by a doctor, but we're a bit worried about her. Come to the office and I'll tell you what he found.'

She walked at a pace he couldn't match. When he got to the office, she had a file open on the desk in front of her. 'Your mother was brought in from the canteen behind the market with several others, suffering we thought from bomb blast. She has cuts and grazes which have been dressed. She was unconscious for a while and seems to have difficulty speaking to us, but she said she'd hurt her shoulder, and also her arm and leg on the left side.'

'Mum fractured her left leg and only had the plaster off a week or so ago,' Tim tried to explain. 'I think it still troubles her.'

'She was treated in this hospital?'

'Yes.'

'Right, we'll get her old notes. They'll give us some medical history. She's had pain relief and been signed up for X-rays but it doesn't look as though they've been done yet. You're her next of kin?'

'Yes.'

'Then please fill in this form for me and either come back

or ring us after midday. The doctor will examine her again and we'll be able to tell you more. We may need to keep her in for a day or two, if we can find her a bed. You can stay and talk to her now. I'll come with you, I need to check her eyes.'

Tim followed her back to the corridor and watched her shine a torch into his mother's eyes. Mum hardly noticed. 'No change here,' the nurse said and left him.

The narrow passage was crowded with staff and patients trying to pass and there was nowhere for him to sit. His mother recognised him but could say little, she seemed only half conscious.

'You go back to sleep,' Tim told her and kissed her cheek. 'I'll come back to see you later in the day.'

He started walking in the direction of home, but a workman's bus came along and he hopped on that. He rested his head against the window feeling utterly exhausted, and as the bus went down Conway Street, he was appalled at the destruction that had occurred during the night. He got off at his usual stop, relieved he had only a short walk before he could shut his front door and fall into bed.

Tim turned the corner into Henry Street and stopped dead in his tracks. He tottered forward a few steps to hold on to a decapitated lamp post and stared round him in horror. His house and several near to it had collapsed and had become a pile of rubble. Civil Defence workers and their helpers were still at work on it.

Only one wall of his home still stood. The roof, ceilings and bedroom floors had fallen in. Two Victorian bedroom grates were high on the wall, and the wallpaper he'd so recently put up still looked fresh. He'd chosen green stripes for his bedroom and Mum had wanted pink cabbage roses. Of the bed he so badly needed there was no sign. His knees felt like rubber, while tears of desperation and exhaustion stung his eyes.

'Tim, thank goodness you're all right.' It was Mrs Cooper, whose house was on the opposite side of the road and just a little further along. He didn't feel all right, he couldn't speak.

'You've had a shock, come in and sit down.' She took his arm, led him indoors and pushed him towards a battered armchair. He fell into it.

'You've been lucky here.' He felt dazed.

'Yes, just the odd broken window, the blast went the other way, but Steve, our lodger, copped it last night. There was a fire in Brunswick Street and he went into a terrace of houses to rescue a child who was trapped, but they both died of smoke inhalation.'

Tim's head was spinning, sleep was suddenly miles away. 'Poor Steve, he was only seventeen, wasn't he?' A few moments later he felt a mug of hot tea being put into his hands. He sipped it slowly, wondering what on earth he could do now.

'Where's your mother? I've been watching for her but I haven't seen her.'

'Mum's in hospital.' He found the words to explain what had happened and how concerned he was.

'Tell Eileen I've found that pair of shoes she bought on Saturday. They were still in the box without a scratch on them. I'll help you search for anything else that's still usable. I wish I could offer you my spare room now Steve won't be using it, but I've already taken in Mrs Hall and her new baby from number twelve. Though I don't think she'll be staying all that long, she's talking of going to her sister's place in Cumbria. She wants to get right away from here, but there's the funeral and all that to see to first. I hear that school in Cole Street is now an emergency rest centre. They'll let you stay there for a day or two if you can't find anywhere better.'

'I know,' he said. 'I saw the notice at the ARP post.'

'So you'll go there?'

'No, I think I'll go to work.'

'Tim, you're in no state to work today.'

'I have friends there who might help me.' He sighed. Would Patsy think it enormous cheek if he asked to rent her flat? After all, she'd split with her boyfriend, so she wouldn't want it for herself. If not, perhaps Bill Bentley would take him in for a few days. Or he'd have to ask in the sewing room if anyone had a room they could spare.

CHAPTER TWENTY-TWO

PATSY WAS ONLY TOO aware that last night Merseyside had received a thorough pounding from the Luftwaffe. Mum had been panic-stricken and impossible to calm. Even when it went quiet between the raids she'd been too agitated to sleep or allow Patsy to do so. After breakfast and before coming to work, Patsy had packed her off to bed to get some rest.

As she'd cycled down to the sewing room she'd seen several buildings with their windows blown out, some with slates off and roof timbers sticking out like broken limbs. Firemen were still at work in the timber yard where the blackened wood showed there had been a big blaze.

With her heart in her mouth, she rounded the last corner, half afraid her property had been damaged. To find it still standing with all the windows intact filled her with relief. There was no electricity, but she switched over to the generator and blessed it: it was proving a real life-saver for her business.

She was worried because not all the girls had come to work and she kept telling herself she must expect some to be late after a night like they'd just had, but she was afraid they could have been injured or even worse. She couldn't settle at her desk until she knew they were all accounted for.

One by one they came, some with messages about others. Pauline had to go to her mother's house, it had been damaged and she needed help. Sally's husband had been hurt and was in hospital, she'd be in later. Jane's little girl was sick and she had to take her to her gran's house, but she'd be in later too.

Patsy was delighted to see Gladys come in, even though she came without Flo. Gladys said the girl was in such a state that she'd be no use to anybody this morning and she'd sent her back to bed. 'May Osborne ran down to our house to say she wouldn't be coming in this morning either.'

'She hasn't been hurt?'

'No, her family's OK too, but her windows have been blown in and the ceiling is down in her living room. I can't believe she lives only five doors away, I feel very lucky we've escaped that.'

'That leaves only Tim,' Patsy said anxiously. 'Normally he's never late.'

The telephone system wasn't working this morning so he couldn't ring her but she was beginning to fear for him. ARP wardens worked on through the raids instead of going to a shelter, and last night must have been a busy and dangerous one for him. On several mornings in the past month, she'd sent him up to the flat to catch a couple of hours' sleep on the sofa. He always insisted on working late on other days or taking work home to make up the time.

She went to the office but couldn't settle to do any work and kept getting up from her desk. She was at the window when at last she saw Tim coming slowly towards the building. His head was bent and he was dragging his feet, and he was still wearing his ARP warden's uniform. She felt as though a weight had lifted from her shoulders. She rushed down the stairs to meet him. 'Tim, you look all in. Are you all right?'

'No.' He slumped on to his desk chair. 'My mother's in

hospital and our home had a direct hit last night. We've lost just about everything.'

Patsy felt a ball of sympathy rise in her throat. 'I'm so sorry. That's awful and you've only just got the house straight. Thank goodness we have the flat, you must use it. You and your mother must move in.'

He looked up at her then; his eyes were over-bright but there was some semblance of a smile on his lips. 'I was wondering if I dared ask to rent it. Everybody's looking for somewhere to live after all these raids.'

'You don't have to ask,' Patsy told him. 'It's the least I can do for you. Your mother's been injured?'

'Yes,' and he started to tell her what had happened. It came out slowly, bit by bit. 'I was worried about finding somewhere to live, that they wouldn't let Mum out of hospital if the only place I could take her to was an emergency rest centre.'

'I'm afraid you'll need a few more things to be able to live in the flat, beds for instance. Come on up. I'll make you some tea and you can have a sleep on the sofa.'

'Forget the tea.' He really smiled then. 'I'm awash with that. Sleep is what I need, but wake me at twelve. I have a hundred things to do. I have no clothes apart from what I'm wearing and this uniform is covered with dust and dirt. I'm going to take it off before I spoil your clean loose covers.' He was unlacing his shoes. 'And I must see what I can salvage from our house.'

Up in the flat, Patsy went to a cupboard, took out the pillows and rugs she'd brought down last month and made a bed up on the sofa.

'I don't want to wake you at twelve. It's already half nine and you need more sleep than that, otherwise you won't be able to think straight.'

'Wake me, Patsy, you must. I have to ring the hospital to see how Mum is.'

Patsy left him to sleep but she couldn't settle to work. She decided to drive the van home to collect some of the clothes Barney had abandoned in the spring. Tim would find them useful now.

She passed the rest of the day in feverish activity. Between spells of doing her usual work, she drove Tim to the hospital to see his mother. They found she'd been moved up to Ward Four though she was still lying on her trolley. Patsy was shocked to find she looked really ill and was taking no interest in anything. It seemed too much effort for her to speak.

Tim was told that she didn't have a head injury as they'd first thought, and they'd be keeping her in for a few days.

'I'm worried about her,' he said. 'I can't believe the change in her. She's nothing like her normal self.'

Patsy drove him to the street where he'd lived and was appalled when she saw the state of his home. It was a complete write-off.

The neighbours had salvaged some of his belongings. Mrs Cooper had found some dishes and cooking utensils that were unbroken and had washed them, so Patsy took them back to the flat in her car. The Coopers had also propped up two brass bedsteads against their house; it was difficult to see how badly scratched they were as they were still coated with thick dust, but at least they were complete.

'I'll send Arthur down with the van,' Patsy told him. 'He'll help you load whatever is worth bringing.'

Once back at the sewing room, she had to reorganise the bedrooms in the flat. They were bare of furniture and had been repainted when the rest of the flat was done. She'd had new curtains made for them, and the stock she'd been sorting there had been moved downstairs and the rooms swept out.

The phones remained out of order so at the end of the afternoon she took Tim back to the hospital. The ward sister took them both into her office and told Tim that they thought his mother must have had a stroke on the night of the raid. She was very kind and explained that Mrs Stansfield had at first had less movement on the left side of her body but that seemed to be improving. They went in to see her and found she'd been given a proper bed but she seemed deeply asleep.

Patsy waited while Tim went back to ask the sister if his mother was able to speak and if she'd be able to make a full recovery. He said nothing on the way back to the office which made her think he hadn't been given too much hope. Her heart went out to him, he looked so sad. She wished there was more she could do to help him.

They tried the telephone once they were there, because Tim wanted to let his older sister Eileen know about their mother, but it was still out. Eileen was married with two children and living over a greengrocer's shop in Preston, which her husband managed, so he scribbled a quick note to her.

Patsy stuck a stamp on and said, 'We'll post it on the way home. I'm taking you with me because there's nothing for you to eat here.'

Tim was reluctant. 'I'm not hungry, but there's tea and biscuits if I am. I'll be all right.'

'You've got to eat. You've had nothing since that soup at lunchtime.'

'Your mother isn't expecting me. She won't like it.'

'She won't object, not after all you've gone through.'

'But I feel filthy, I'm exhausted and I won't be sociable.'

'You don't have to be. Come on, Tim, I insist. Go and

wash your hands and face to get rid of some of that dust. I'll run you back here when we've eaten.'

'You're doing an embarrassing amount for me. I'll be sitting my driving test next month. If only I'd passed it now I'd be a lot less trouble to you.'

'Tim, don't worry your head about that. You've been running round after me since I took over from Dad. I'm only too glad to give you a helping hand when you need it. We all are.'

An hour or so later, Tim was back in the flat and glad to be alone at last. The tears he'd held back all day streamed down his cheeks. Patsy had been an angel, she couldn't have done more for him and it made him so achingly grateful.

When she'd brought him back, a few minutes ago, she'd found the telephone in the living room was working again and had rung the hospital for him. His mother, she was told, was as comfortable as could be expected and there'd been little change in her condition. Tim was desperately worried and afraid it would take her a long time to recover.

He undressed and hung what had been Barney's best suit a few years ago over the back of a chair. Mrs Rushton had recognised it, of course, which had been embarrassing, but she'd been the perfect hostess and he'd wolfed down the stew and dumplings and the rhubarb crumble with custard and felt better for it. She'd even given him two slices of bread to bring back to toast for his breakfast, together with a sliver of margarine and a jar with an inch of marmalade at the bottom. She'd apologised for what would be a meagre meal and blamed scarcity and rationing.

He plumped up the pillows and was thankful to lie down. He'd nodded off in Patsy's car on the short drive back here and thought he'd go to sleep the minute he lay down, but now he couldn't. Last night's blitz had changed their lives for ever.

The following evening, Jeanie met Barney outside his barracks. 'Hello,' he said. 'I thought I was supposed to go straight to Lil's and have high tea with you there.'

'We're bombed out,' she told him and laid it on thick. 'We'll have to find a café, I'm hungry.'

Over the meal she moaned about her lot. 'The rest centre was a nightmare, I had to sleep on a wooden floor and the babies never stopped crying. And they expect us to get out of there as soon as we can.'

'You can go to your Aunt Cissie's. I could too, for my time off. Let's go straight away.'

'No, we need to see your mother first, don't we? I told you that I'd been to the reference library in Chester and what I'd found out about your father's family. Aunt Cissie thinks you should ask your mother for your birth certificate. We must have proof of who you are.'

Barney looked appalled. 'I told you I can't do that. Anything like that upsets Mum.'

'Barney, we need to know why it upsets her. I think you stand to gain much more from the Tavenham-Strongs than you do from the Rushtons. If we have proof you're related we can start asking searching questions. Without proof people could refuse to tell us.'

'I don't want to ask her.'

Jeanie could see his face working with anxiety. 'I've got to see it. Cissie's got to see it. We don't want to turn everything inside out and make a big fuss only to find you've got it all wrong, do we? We'd look complete fools. You've got to ask for it. It's for your own good.'

'It'll only cause trouble.'

'Why should it? She knows you've seen it, doesn't she?'

'Yes she knows that but she'll want to know why I want it.'

'You can tell her the army have asked to see it. That sounds logical. There's no reason why they shouldn't.'

'I can't ask her, Jeanie.'

'Well, I will then.'

'No, it would be worse coming from you.'

'Why don't we just take it then? You know where she keeps it.'

'Pinch it? No, I'm not well, Jeanie. It worries me, I haven't felt at all well this week.'

'In what way don't you feel well? What's the matter with you?' Jeanie wished he'd shut up about his health worries. He'd been perfectly all right until she asked him to get his birth certificate.

'I'm just not myself,' he said wearily.

'I'm the one that's lost half my belongings and have no roof over my head,' she said sharply.

'I don't want to stay at Mum's.'

Jeanie thought he was being pig-headed. 'I hate staying with your mother, absolutely hate it, but we've got to if we're going to make progress.'

'No, really, we need to get away from this bombing and have a bit of fun. I've got enough of the readies to take you to that boarding house in Southport. Let's do that.'

'Barney,' she spat out, 'you can't keep running away from what you don't like. I keep telling you we need a home of our own. I think it's awful that you let Patsy keep that flat empty when we are homeless.'

'You were closer to my barracks at your Aunt Lil's,' he said defensively. 'You agreed you were. That's why I haven't pressed for it.'

'Well, you'll have to press for it now and we've got to get your birth certificate. If we do those two things quickly, we could still spend a night in Southport. Come on, let's get the train and go over to Birkenhead.'

They walked up through the park and had reached the gate of Fern Bank when Patsy overtook them and ran her car into the garage. 'Hello,' she said, 'I didn't know you were coming tonight.'

'Your phone's been out,' Barney said. 'I did ring Mum from the station, she's expecting us.'

Patsy let them in with her key. 'We had a bad night here last night.'

'It was a bad night for me too,' Jeanie added, brimming with the bad news she had to tell.

Beatrice came out of the sitting room to kiss them. 'Barney, how are you?'

'Barney isn't well,' Jeanie told them. 'He's having headaches and palpitations and terrible attacks of not being able to get his breath.'

'It's stress,' he said. 'The bombing makes me worry about you all, especially Jeanie. I couldn't sleep last night. Sorry, Mum, we couldn't give you much notice of this visit.'

'That doesn't matter, but I don't know what I'm going to give you to eat.'

'Don't worry, we've eaten. I know rationing makes everything difficult so we went to a café first.'

'Then take your coats off and come to the fire. So you had a bad night too? We heard on the wireless this morning that it was Birkenhead that took the brunt of last night's raids.'

'We heard that too,' Jeanie said drily. 'I understand it was a quieter night than usual for Liverpool but for me it certainly wasn't. I'm now homeless and so is my Aunt Lil.'

Patsy's mouth dropped open. 'Homeless? I am sorry, Jeanie. That's dreadful!'

'You weren't hurt? What about your aunt?'

'Fortunately we'd gone to the pictures, but we had to sleep on the floor in an emergency rest centre last night, it was noisy and draughty.'

'Jeanie's looking for somewhere to stay,' Barney said.

'Jeanie, you can stay here,' Beatrice said. 'You know Barney's room is mostly empty these days. We had to use his mattress in the shelter but Patsy managed to get another.'

'What happened?' Patsy wanted to know.

Jeanie was not pleased at the way things were going. She tried to smile. 'It was bomb blast. The bomb fell in the next street,' she told her. 'The house is damaged and unsafe to live in, but it hasn't been demolished. There's a hole in the roof where the chimney stack was, and it's rained today so the furniture that wasn't blown to bits will be ruined.'

'I hope she was insured. Does she own the house?'

'No, it's rented, but it'll still be hers. She understands that because of the housing shortage, it may get priority emergency repairs, but who's to say how long that will take. In the meantime we're both homeless.'

'What is your aunt going to do?' Beatrice wanted to know.

'Well, it doesn't look as though she'll be able to find rooms or anything in Liverpool.'

'I'm surprised she hasn't gone to stay with one of her sisters to get away from the bombing. Isn't she frightened being on her own?'

'She's terrified but her job has kept her here. She thinks now she'll go to Rhyl and stay with my mother.'

'Much the best thing.' Beatrice sighed. 'What a good job, Barney, your barracks is on the outskirts of the city. It must be safer there. They're aiming for the docks, aren't they? Trying to put the port out of action and starve us all.'

Jeanie was losing patience. Barney was sitting beside her on the sofa; she rested a hand on his knee, willing him to ask for the flat. He'd agreed to do it on the way here, but now he was smiling at his mother who was engrossed in finding reasons why the Germans should bomb Merseyside. She could wait no longer.

She turned to Patsy with one of her fleeting smiles. 'What we'd really like,' she said, 'would be to rent your flat. Surely now I've been bombed out you'll let us use it.' But she could see from Patsy's face that she was about to refuse again. 'It doesn't seem reasonable to keep it empty,' she added. 'Not when Barney would feel more secure if we had a place of our own.'

'I'm sorry, Jeanie, it isn't empty.' Patsy looked guilty. 'Tim Stansfield is living there. His house has been flattened and his mother is in—'

'That's most unfair,' Jeanie spat. She felt engulfed by a sudden torrent of rage. 'Barney and I have never had a home of our own and have no other chance of getting one with so many houses being damaged. You knew we wanted it, we need it.' Her face twisted with anger and frustration. 'Surely he has a right to it? Surely family should come before an employee?' She dug her elbow viciously into Barney's ribs, hoping for his support. 'How long has Tim been living there?'

'He only moved in today,' Patsy admitted, her cheeks scarlet.

'Perhaps,' Beatrice said, 'you could tell him that Barney needs it.'

'The council will house him,' Barney said. 'It always has.'

'No, when they were pulling down Dock Cottages they were offered council accommodation in Bromborough, but both he and his mother had jobs in the north end and it would have been a long way to come.'

'For heaven's sake,' Jeanie exploded.

'That was before the war,' Patsy went on, 'so they were able to go for a privately rented house in Henry Street.'

'There's nothing available to rent now. We can't afford to be choosy.'

'Jeanie, as Mum has said,' Patsy said stiffly, 'you'll be very welcome to stay in Barney's old room.'

Jeanie's anger simmered all evening. She did her best to provide openings in the conversation for Barney to ask for his birth certificate, but he ignored them.

The siren wailed fearsomely at bedtime. 'Another raid,' Beatrice gasped. 'Where are you going to shelter?'

'The best thing for you tonight,' Patsy said, 'is to take some of the cushions off the sofa and make a bed under the stairs. You could bring the eiderdown and pillows off your bed.'

'It'll do for tonight, won't it, Barney?' Jeanie's face was pained. 'And we'll hope for a quiet night. But under the stairs isn't really a safe place. Despite your kind offer, that means I couldn't stay here for any length of time.'

'The flat would be more suitable for the long term,' Barney said as Jeanie had primed him. 'We'd have those big cellars to ourselves at night. If I was in barracks, I'd be able to relax knowing Jeanie was safe.'

Once Beatrice and Patsy were safely downstairs in the dining room, Jeanie insisted they seize the chance to look for Barney's birth certificate. 'If you're too scared to ask, we'll have to take it,' she told him. 'It's the only way.'

She'd already made him tell her exactly where he'd seen the large manila envelope, and now she made him keep watch in the darkness at the top of the stairs in case his mother returned. Everybody carried a small torch these days for the blackout and Jeanie used it to search the drawer Barney had indicated.

'Make sure you leave everything exactly as you find it,' he whispered hoarsely.

'I can't see it.'

She knew he was a bag of nerves by then, but she gave him the torch and they changed places.

'The envelope's not here, she must have moved it,' he said in his normal voice.

'Shush, we don't want them to hear us. We shouldn't be in your mum's bedroom.' Jeanie felt on pins too. 'Come here and let me have another go.' She had a quick look round in other drawers with no more success.

'Hurry up,' he urged. 'They'll wonder what we're doing. We should be settling down under the stairs by now.'

'You'll have to ask for it,' Jeanie said shortly as she crawled on to the cushions. 'There's no other way.'

He grunted and pulled the eiderdown over his head.

'You should be willing to help me,' she whispered. 'I've got to have somewhere to live.'

'Mother's said you can live here.'

'And sleep like this?'

'We could get you an Anderson shelter in the garden.'

'Nothing would make me come here to live with Patsy,' Jeanie retorted. 'You let her walk all over you and dictate everything, when you know I want a home of my own. We'll have to have another go at her before you go back.'

Chapter Twenty-Three

As Patsy and her mother settled down to spend the night in their Morrison shelter, Beatrice said, 'I'm so glad we decided on this instead of an Anderson shelter in the garden, it's freezing out there now.'

Patsy said nothing, she felt put out by her mother's support for Barney.

'Now Jeanie's been bombed out I think you must tell Tim he can't have the flat.'

'No,' Patsy said shortly. 'I need Tim to help me run the business. I want him to live where he's on hand. I don't want him travelling in for miles. I need him to be fresh, not exhausted.'

'But Barney isn't well. You heard him say he's worried about Jeanie when there's a raid. If they had the flat, at least they'd be together. They do need somewhere to live.'

'Barney is required to live in barracks, Mum. He could not sleep in the flat except when he has leave. It's Jeanie who wants the flat.'

'Well, I can see that, but if it stops Barney worrying, I think they should have it.'

'Well, I don't. I've told Tim he can have it and helped him move in. He needs a home if he's to bring his mother out of hospital and he's put heart and soul into our business. As far as I'm concerned, that's the way it's going to stay.'

'I wish you weren't so dogmatic. Barney isn't as strong as you.'

'Mum, Barney is selfish and self-obsessed. He'll take everything and do nothing, he won't even help himself. He makes a mess of things and walks away leaving other people to clear up. He's done that often enough.'

'I know, love, but I'm worried about his health. I've tried to explain how anxious he is, but you still don't understand.'

Patsy knew her mother was upset and wanted to soothe her. The night was still quiet outside but there'd be no chance of sleep until she calmed down.

'Mum, tell me more about his father.'

'Rowley fought in France for more than two years, he survived bitter fighting on the Somme for months on end. I really thought he must have nine lives.'

'But you said he wasn't a fighter.'

Beatrice took a deep breath. 'Rowley was sent to Rugby School like all his brothers and cousins. Like them he joined the School Cadet Corps and learned the rudimentary elements of military service, the duties and the drill. It was seen as a good grounding for a military career and those destined for the confectionery business felt they had to prove they could be as good at it as their cousins who were heading for Sandhurst. Like many of those not intending to pursue a military career, Rowley was persuaded to join the Special Reserve of Officers where he would be paid to undergo regular periods of training and attend camps, much like the Territorial Army of today.'

Patsy said, 'But didn't that mean . . . ?'

'Yes, it did.'

'So he wasn't pressurised by the other side of his family?'

'He got a lot of that too. But on the fourth of August nineteen fourteen, when England declared war on Germany, the Special Reserve Officers were called up, as they were considered to be already trained. My father told him he was a fool not to have foreseen that would happen.'

'He didn't want to go?'

'No, but he had to. Thousands of young men were rushing to volunteer. Everybody thought it would be over by Christmas. For once, the military side of the family congratulated him and told him he'd done the right thing. He was given a commission in the Royal Field Artillery and on the fifth of August he was posted to the Thirty-fourth Brigade. Two weeks later they were in France.'

'Gosh, he hardly had time to think.'

'My father thought that was just as well. As a second lieutenant, Rowley was in charge of two eighteen-pounder field guns; each gun was loaded on a limber and pulled by four horses. Rowley took his own horse to France and rode alongside his guns on the way to the front line at Ypres.

'Once there he found that his uncle, Lieutenant General Sir Julian Philip Tavenham-Strong, was assisting Field Marshall Sir George French, the Commander-in-Chief of the British Expeditionary Force in France. He knew he had several other relatives amongst the staff officers.

'The losses in trench warfare were soon horrendous and the gains minimal. Officers like Rowley in the lower ranks lived alongside their men in the trenches and many believed the war was being mishandled by their senior officers, because they were living in luxury accommodation some distance from the fighting and were shielded from the slaughter. Rowley and many others believed that ordering the men to go over the top to fight across no-man's-land to the enemy trenches was bad strategy. Particularly as everybody knew many thousands would be killed and many more die of the wounds they'd receive. For these reasons they resented and disliked the staff officers. Rowley was afraid many associated him with the high-ranking officers because of his name and his relationship to them.

'Rowley was engaged in fierce fighting in nineteen seventeen. His field guns had a range of almost eight thousand yards and were intended to be fired over the front line and on to a target behind. It was impossible for the gunners to see the target across such distances, so one of Rowley's jobs was to establish an observation post at a vantage point overlooking the battlefield. He was out riding his horse seeking a good vantage point one day when an enemy shell landed near him and he was buried with the earth it threw up.'

Patsy felt for her mother's hand. 'Buried alive, when he was out alone? That must have been terrifying. Was he able to burrow his way out?'

'He said he tried to, but he'd been knocked off his feet and found it difficult to move at all under the weight. He didn't know how deeply he'd been buried, or even which way he should burrow to reach the top. He was in the dark with a heavy weight on him and he couldn't breathe or hear anything.'

Patsy felt her stomach turn over. 'Mum! How dreadful! How did he get out?'

'Two of the signallers in his battery saw it happen and thought he might have survived. It killed his horse but they dug him out alive. He had a dislocated shoulder and a broken arm, and was deemed to be injured badly enough to be sent home for treatment.'

'I expect you were pleased to have him back and know he was safe.'

'I was delighted to have him back in Blighty. He was in hospital for a while but when he came home to me I found him changed. He didn't want to do anything. He'd sit for hours by himself staring into space and sometimes he'd wake up screaming in the middle of the night.'

'He was having nightmares?'

'Yes, about being buried alive, but Rowley was thought to be over his injuries and was sent back to France. That's when it all went horribly wrong. Rowley was a sensitive and gentle person and thoughtful of the men he commanded, nobody could understand how he came to do such a thing.'

'What did he do?' Patsy asked.

'He attacked his uncle, the lieutenant general. Hubert said it must have been shell shock. His years in the thick of the fighting had affected Rowley more than anybody realised at the time.

'I thought my life was falling apart. I'd been so proud of being his wife. His father was proud of his family name and considered Rowley had brought disgrace on us all. I was only a few months off giving birth and felt shamed, horrified and shocked. It was reported in the national newspapers as treasonable behaviour, and as you can imagine the story was in the papers for many weeks.

'I packed a couple of suitcases and took off. I grew to hate the name and didn't want Barney to bear it. I had no money and had to look for work to support my baby.'

'But Rowley had money and so had his family, didn't they want to help you?'

She shook her head. 'They blamed him. His family turned their backs on Rowley and me. They said he'd got what he deserved.'

Tears were flowing down her mother's cheeks. Patsy had a lump in her throat and could hardly speak. It took her a few moments to recover. Then, full of sympathy, she put an arm round Beatrice's shoulders and pulled her closer. 'But Mum, I still don't understand. Did he really hurt his uncle?'

Beatrice mopped at her eyes. 'He killed him! Everybody was reading about us in the papers, they turned to look at me in the street. I had to hide. I didn't want the neighbours to tell Barney. Patsy, you must promise never to tell him.'

'Of course I won't. But I still don't understand, what happened to—'

At that moment they heard the guns on Bidston Hill open up. It made Beatrice scream. They clung together and covered their heads with their pillows but that couldn't shut out the horrific explosions as bombs fell on the town.

An hour later, they were able to relax when they heard the all-clear blow. The stairs creaked as Barney and Jeanie went up to their bed.

The next morning Patsy got up before anyone else and went to work. George Miller had made an appointment to come to her office today and she would meet him for the first time.

She arrived before any of the staff and found a rather sleepy Tim having breakfast in the flat. She poured herself a cup of tea from the pot he'd made and sat down with him.

'You had a disturbed night,' she said. 'Did you go down to the cellar?'

'No, I slept soundly. I did hear the guns but they only half woke me. I stayed where I was on the sofa, so I've had a good night's rest. I'm a bit sleep-fuddled at the moment but that'll clear and I'll be all right today.'

Patsy laughed. 'I'm glad to hear that because you'll be busy again. Mum and I clung together in terror in our shelter.'

'Did any bombs drop?'

'Yes, but they were a mile or so away. Barney and Jeanie came to stay and had to huddle under the stairs. I heard them going up and down so they didn't have much sleep.'

'Bill Bentley rang last night to see how I was. He says he's got a spare single mattress and some bedding and he'll bring it down this morning.'

'Good, we'll get you straight. You must take Arthur and the van this morning, to get round all you have to do.'

'Patsy, I don't want to cause a lot of trouble and expense for you. I'll be able to manage though I'll need to take the day off.'

'Of course you will. Don't forget you'll have to go to the food office to apply for replacement ration books. Or do you still have them?'

'No, I don't think so. I don't know.'

'Well, let Arthur drive you to hospital to see your mother and ask her where they were kept.'

'Yes I must. Then I'll go down to Henry Street and see if they've been found. I can't sponge on you for food.'

'And see if there's anything else worth salvaging and bring it up. You'll need the van, Tim, take it and I'll ask Arthur to help you. We all need a helping hand when things go wrong.'

'I know and I'm very grateful.' He gave her a wry smile. 'Without you, I wouldn't know where to turn.'

Patsy was moved by his gratitude. 'What are friends for if they can't give a hand when you're in trouble? I'll tell Arthur you'll need an early start.'

She went down to the office to start work. She was expecting George Miller to come in at nine thirty.

Tim began to get ready. He went to the bathroom and eyed the old-fashioned geyser that provided hot water. He knew it hadn't been used for years, and wished he'd asked

Patsy to show him how it worked. Gritty dust from the bricks and plaster of bombed buildings was on his skin and in his hair, he needed a bath badly.

He decided not to try fiddling with the geyser. There was a small water heater over the kitchen sink so he filled the washing-up bowl several times and tipped that into the bath. By the time he'd added enough water to sit in, it was only just lukewarm. He had no shampoo so he washed his hair with toilet soap. That woke him up thoroughly. He had no tooth-brush and no razor either, only the small comb Patsy had given him from her handbag yesterday.

He dressed quickly in Barney's clothes and was about to go down and look for Arthur when he heard a brisk rapping on the door of the flat. Until yesterday, the key had always been left in the lock outside, which was the only way in, but Patsy had taken it out and given it to him. 'If it's to be your home you'll not want people walking in on you,' she'd said. Patsy was very thoughtful, though the rest of the staff didn't come unless they were asked.

Tim expected to find Arthur on the landing. It took him by surprise to find Barney and Jeanie there, each carrying a large cardboard box.

'Hello,' Barney said as they bulldozed their way past him. 'I gather you've spent the night here. Patsy told us she'd said you could.' They put their boxes on the kitchen table and started unpacking them. 'I hope you can find somewhere else to go now because Jeanie and I want to move in here. She was bombed out the other night.'

Tim could hardly get his breath. 'So was I. Patsy said it was all right for me to live here.'

'That was before she knew Jeanie had been bombed out.' Barney's voice was cold. 'I know it's hard for anybody when they lose their home, but it has to be family before an employee, doesn't it?'

Tim felt weak at the knees. The last thing he could cope with now was a confrontation with Barney and his wife. It would be a battle he couldn't win. He made himself say, 'Well, that's not what I understood. Perhaps we should ask Patsy to confirm things.'

'This flat belongs to the family,' Jeanie said firmly. 'It's not up to Patsy to decide who lives here. Barney needs it himself.' She went to the living room to look round. Tim's bedding was still on the sofa and there were clothes on a chair. 'Could you put your bits and pieces together and take them away?'

'I'm going down to talk to Patsy,' Tim said, heading for the stairs.

Barney followed him. 'She's busy, or I'd have done it myself on the way up. I think some important businessman arrived just before us.'

Tim guessed it would be George Miller, and knew how concerned Patsy had been about keeping the supply of work coming in. He didn't want to barge in with a domestic problem in the middle of that. At that moment, he saw Arthur coming upstairs.

'Sorry I've been rather a long time,' Arthur said. 'There was a job I had to finish off. Patsy says you've a busy day in front of you and I'm to drive you round.'

'Yes, thank you.' Tim looked at his watch, it was already after ten. He went to the kitchen and scooped up the keys to the flat where Patsy had left them. He didn't mean Barney to have them. On the way out, he picked up his coat.

'I'm ready, Arthur,' he said. 'I'd just like a quick word with Gladys before we go.'

They clattered down the stairs together. He wanted Gladys

to tell Patsy, when she was free, that her brother was trying to move into the flat. It was yet another worry, Tim was afraid he'd have to move out. The problem then was that he'd have nowhere to take his mother when she was discharged from hospital.

He must try and put that out of his mind and concentrate on essentials. 'Let's start by going to the hospital, Arthur. I'm worried about my mother.'

CHAPTER TWENTY-FOUR

Patsy spent most of the morning with George Miller. She'd shown him round her sewing rooms, introduced him to some of the staff and discussed the sort of work they did best. Bill Bentley had told her he was a pleasant and reasonable person and she was pleased to find she agreed. She was going to get along fine with him.

She was showing him out when Bill turned up in his van. He wound the window down and said, 'I've brought that mattress down you said you wanted, Patsy, and some bedding to go with it.'

'That's wonderful, Tim will be very grateful.'

'How is he?'

'Fraught,' Patsy said, and then she saw Gladys come out.

'Tim asked me to tell you that Barney is trying to push his way into the flat,' she said. 'He thinks he should have it, not Tim. I haven't seen him come out, so I think he must still be up there.'

'Oh no!' Patsy said. 'I was telling myself I'd had a good morning and now this! Come on, Bill, I want you to help me get him out of there. Can we carry up this mattress between the three of us?'

Bill was puffing by the time they'd manoeuvred the mattress up the last flight of narrow stairs but she was glad she had him with her for support. He flung the door open and together they heaved the mattress inside. Her brother and Jeanie were sitting one in each corner of the sofa in the living room, hands clenched and clearly spoiling for a fight. Tim's bedding had been tossed on the floor.

'Barney,' Patsy said, 'haven't you anything better to do on your leave but sit up here?'

He jerked to his feet and knocked an empty coffee cup and saucer off the sofa arm. 'We're going to move in,' he said. 'We need somewhere to live.'

'You won't like it if you do,' Patsy mocked. 'You'll find things a bit tight. Tim's already living here and we're about to put this bed up for his mother. She may be out of hospital this afternoon. How's your nursing, Jeanie? I don't know how much she'll be able to do for herself.'

'Where d'you want the bed made up?' Gladys asked.

'Tim brought two of his bedsteads here.' Patsy could see them propped against the living-room wall. 'It would have helped, Barney, if you'd erected them, he'll need one in each bedroom. We'll put the mattress in the smaller bedroom over there and keep the main room for Tim.'

'I want the keys to the flat,' Barney demanded, his face white and anxious. 'And I don't want other people here.'

'They're here already,' Patsy said shortly. 'Gladys, we might as well make the bed up for Mrs Stansfield now.'

'I'll fetch up the bedding you brought, Bill.'

Jeanie was on her feet. 'Barney, don't let your little sister boss you around.' Her voice was shrill. 'You tell everybody to get out. This is going to be our place.'

It was impasse; they stood staring at each other.

'Come on, both of you, see sense.' Bill nodded towards the door they'd left open.

'I'm afraid you'll have to go, Barney,' Patsy said. 'I need

this flat to house Tim in this emergency. I have to have someone to help me run this workshop.'

'It's not fair,' Jeanie spat. 'Barney is entitled to something, isn't he?'

'Barney refused to have anything to do with this place when Dad died. He would have sold the place off and pocketed the money, and that would have been the end of it.'

Barney was moving towards the door. Jeanie stood firm. 'Give me the key,' she demanded.

'I've given it to Tim,' Patsy said. 'I can't argue with you, Jeanie, I haven't time. Barney has to go back to his barracks but you are very welcome to stay with us at Fern Bank.'

Jeanie let out a scream of frustration and clattered downstairs after Barney.

She had to run to catch Barney up. 'Whatever made you give up?' she demanded furiously as she reached the ground floor.

'We were getting nowhere,' he grunted, stepping out fast.

'You said you'd help me, but you slunk away with your tail between your legs. That was cowardly.'

Jeanie told herself she should have expected this from Barney. Wasn't it what usually happened when things didn't go his way? He was totally gutless. She'd have to accept that Patsy had won and they were unlikely to be allowed to live in the flat after a showdown like that.

'Where are we going now?' she asked. His face was still ghostly white and sweat glistened across his forehead and also across his nose. 'Whatever is the matter with you, Barney?'

She had to ask twice before he grunted, 'Stress. I can't stand the stress and we're going to be late for lunch.'

'Are you hungry?'

'No, I have a headache, I want to lie down.'

So it seemed they were heading back to Fern Bank. It left Jeanie feeling edgy and itching for revenge and she thought the best way to get her own back on the Rushtons was to find out all she could about the Tavenham-Strongs. She was sure there was something about them that Beatrice wanted to keep hidden, something that worried her and she couldn't handle.

At Fern Bank Barney went upstairs to lie down and Jeanie spent a miserable few hours trying to get information out of Beatrice without asking direct questions which she might resent. It got her nowhere. Late in the afternoon, Jeanie asked her if she might ring her Aunt Cissie. Cissie was working as a school cleaner at this time of the day and could usually be contacted there. Jeanie found her familiar matter-of-fact voice a comfort.

'Your Aunt Lil's gone to Rhyl to stay with your mother.' Cissie had heard all about the bomb damage to her house. 'You'd better come here, Jeanie, if you can't find anybody to take you in on Merseyside.'

'Thanks,' she said. 'That's what I was ringing about, I'd much rather be with you than stay here. I'll see you tonight, but I'll be late because I want to stay with Barney until he goes back to barracks.'

But first she had to get his birth certificate from his mother; she didn't plan on returning to Chester without it. Barney was in the kitchen with Beatrice, she was preparing onion gravy to have with bangers and mash for their evening meal. Jeanie joined them. Barney was talking about two late roses that were still blooming in the garden, but she could see he was a bag of nerves. There was a tremor in his fingers.

'Barney,' she said, hoping she sounded innocent. 'You haven't forgotten, have you, to ask your mother for your birth certificate?'

The effect was electrifying, Beatrice whipped round from the stove. 'What?'

'Yes,' he stammered, unable to look at her. 'I need it.'

'The army needs it,' Jeanie corrected. 'The army has asked for it, haven't they, Barney?'

'What for?' Beatrice barked.

'We're all asked to produce them.'

'Employers often do ask to see birth certificates,' Jeanie added.

'In times of war like this, traditionally the army does not. Aren't there countless stories of boys of fifteen joining up?'

'That was the last war,' Jeanie said. 'They want to stop that happening this time.'

Beatrice's cheeks flamed. 'But why now, after all this time? You've been in the army for months.'

Jeanie had to stop herself answering for him. Instead she gave him a nudge.

'They've been asking for it for ages, but I kept forgetting to ask you.' Barney shot Jeanie a glance that was both hostile and desperate.

'Then I suppose you'll have to have it.' His mother didn't look happy. She turned back to the stove.

'Had we better find it now?' Jeanie was not going to let her shelve it after getting this far. 'You know what Barney's like, he'll forget about it again if you aren't careful.'

Beatrice's tongue clicked with irritation but she swept into the dining room and groped around inside the Morrison shelter. Jeanie could feel Barney's tension growing as she fished out a torn and shabby manila envelope and emptied the contents out on top.

Her fingers closed on a smaller envelope; reluctantly she held it out to him. 'Here you are then.' But immediately she withdrew her arm. 'It might be easier if you just say you can't find it.' Beatrice's pale eyes switched wildly from Jeanie to Barney and back again. 'Tell them it's been lost in the bombing or something.'

Jeanie couldn't stop herself. 'Why?'

'Barney knows why. They don't know you by this name. Darling, they'll start asking questions about it. A change of name like this makes you look like a criminal, and really none of it was your fault.'

The tears were rolling down Beatrice's face but Jeanie couldn't stop a broad smile spreading across hers. It seemed this wasn't a figment of Barney's imagination after all.

He took the envelope and, all thumbs, tried to prise the document out. Jeanie craned to look at it, and full of exultation read the name, Barnaby Rowland Arnold John Tavenham-Strong. His father's name was given as Rowland Charles Arnold George Tavenham-Strong. He'd told her the truth.

Jeanie's mind leapt forward. 'Did you change his name by deed poll?'

Beatrice stared silently back at her.

'So you didn't. You just changed it to suit the family.'

'So we'd all have the same name,' Beatrice admitted.

Jeanie felt her heart bounce. 'So legally I'm Mrs Tavenham-Strong?'

Grudgingly she said, 'Yes, I suppose you are.'

They all fell silent as they heard the garage door creak open and shut again as Patsy put her bike away. Jeanie held her breath until she came in through the back door.

Beatrice looked at her tearfully. 'Hello, Patsy. Is it that time already?'

Patsy paused on the step, looking from one to the other.

'What are you doing?' Then she noticed the birth certificate on the draining board and picked it up. 'Barney?'

Her mother dissolved into tears.

'For heaven's sake!' Patsy threw it back. 'You know this upsets Mum. Why can't you leave her alone?'

'I don't know why it should upset her,' Jeanie said. 'Barney had to ask for it, the army told him to bring it in months ago.' She picked it up and put it in her pocket.

For Jeanie, it was an uncomfortable evening. None of them was at ease; Barney and Beatrice were very much on edge and Patsy was not in a good mood. Jeanie decided she and Barney should leave soon after they'd finished eating. She was glad to get away and hung on to his arm as they walked through the park to the train station.

'What did you have to do that for?' Barney complained. 'You've stirred up real trouble for me today. First you upset Patsy and then Mum.'

'Don't blame me. I've been bombed out of my lodgings with Lil and you've done nothing to help me. I'm just trying to get a roof over my head. If Patsy hadn't dug her heels in and stopped us having that flat, we wouldn't be in this position. It's Patsy's fault. It's her you should blame.'

Barney was agitated. 'Where are you going now?'

'Back to Aunt Cissie's place.'

'But you'll come back for my birthday? It's the day after tomorrow.'

'No, Barney, you won't be free until evening.'

'Come and spend it with me, we'll go to the Adelphi for dinner.'

'No, it's hardly worth coming all this way for a few hours. The last thing I want is to end up in Liverpool at midnight with bombs falling all round me and have no bed.'

'Mum will give you a bed, you know that.'

'I'm not going there, especially not by myself. I'd rather sleep in a ditch. This is why we needed that flat.'

'But Jeanie, it won't be a birthday if I don't see you.'

'Of course it will. I've packed your present in your kitbag and, here, I'm still dragging round this birthday cake Aunt Cissie made for you.'

She showed it to him and knew he was disappointed.

'It doesn't look like a birthday cake,' he said.

'Cissie's done her best. She makes very good cakes. Nobody can get icing sugar now.'

His face was stiff and angry. 'Thank her for me. I am grateful.'

'Don't get the hump, Barney. Let's get off at Hamilton Square. I've got to change there anyway. We can have a drink at that big pub before you go back to barracks. We've got plenty of time for that.'

They found the bar so crowded there was nowhere to sit and, even worse, it was running out of drink. Barney managed to buy two halves of mild beer. He had not calmed down.

'But you knew I didn't want you to make all that fuss about my birth certificate,' he complained. 'How could Mum believe the army wanted it when you were pushing for it like that? I cringe every time I think of Mum's face. She knows you're up to something.'

'It had to be done if I'm to find out any more about the Tavenham-Strongs. There's a huge mystery about them. You should have helped instead of leaving it all to me.'

'Whatever it is, I don't want to know.'

'Then you should, it's your family, your own flesh and blood.'

'I feel all churned up inside and I've got a headache. I don't want you raking up this bad feeling in my family.'

'The Rushtons aren't your family, Barney. You're a Tavenham-Strong and you should know them. They are rich.'

'What difference is that likely to make to us?'

'Here we are with no home and hardly any money. We've got to look elsewhere if we're to have anything.' The wail of the air-raid siren killed the jollity in the pub and, moments later, the customers were crowding to the door.

'We can't stay here.' Barney drained his glass. 'I hate leaving you like this. Let's find somewhere else where we can have a drink.'

'Nobody will want to serve us now,' she said. 'I'll ring you at eight o'clock on your birthday.' They had agreed an arrangement by which Barney sat by the public phone in the mess at a set time, so that Jeanie could make contact. 'And I'll see you the next time you get time off.'

A warden appeared at the door and was hurrying everybody towards the deep shelter in the train station. Jeanie could see a bus waiting at the Chester stop at the Woodside terminus.

'I'm going. Goodbye, Barney,' she said and ran down to catch it.

Tim had been worried all day. He'd left Barney and Jeanie in the flat and they'd seemed determined to take it over and oust him. He'd hoped Patsy would be able to get them out and that he'd still have a home for his mother. That morning, he'd assured the Sister at the hospital that he had.

He and Arthur had spent ages raking over the ruins of his old home looking for anything salvageable. They'd found a few pieces of furniture: three dining chairs and a small table and also his mother's dressing table and a chest of drawers. In addition, they'd filled several boxes with oddments such as shoes, clothes, scrubbing brushes, dishes and even a brooch that Tim thought was gold. Everything he and his mum owned had been in the house. Much of what they'd found he had discarded; their clothes, rugs and curtains were not only torn but impregnated with thick grey dust.

Mrs Cooper had given him a bucket of water and some cloths and they'd washed the worst of the dirt and dust off the things he wanted to keep before loading them into the van. It was the middle of the afternoon when Tim got back to the workshop and he was almost dropping with exhaustion. The first thing he did was go up to the office to have a word with Patsy.

'It's all right,' she said. 'Barney's gone. I told Jeanie we were expecting your mother to come out of hospital soon and she'd have to nurse her. That saw them off.'

'Thank you, that's a great relief.' Tim saw Arthur and Gladys starting to carry his belongings up to the flat and went to help them. He filled the kitchen sink with hot water, and started washing everything that could be washed. Two minutes later Patsy came running up to see him with a bowl of the soup they had all had at lunchtime. She tipped it into a pan and set it on the stove to warm up. 'How's your mum? Did you go to see her?'

'Yes, she isn't herself, but they say she's doing all right. They asked me if I had a home to take her to, and when I said yes, they said she may be able to come out tomorrow. She'll be checked over by a doctor in the morning and I'm to ring up and find out what he decides.'

'Good, her bedroom is ready for her here.'

'She isn't all that well, I think she'll need a bit of looking after.'

'Don't worry, Flo can run up and down and see if there's anything she needs. She's a very willing girl.'

'I think it's a question of freeing up the beds for those who need them most. With these heavy air raids, the injured are pouring in. They tell me Mum needs peace and general nursing care. There isn't much specialised treatment to give her.'

Patsy knew Tim was worried about his mother. The next day, she drove him to the hospital to bring her home and Mrs Stansfield found it very difficult to get up the stairs to the flat. Tim had almost to lift her. She said she would like to lie down and no sooner had they got her tucked under the eiderdown on her bed than the air-raid siren wailed its warning.

'I'm afraid the shelter is in the cellar,' Patsy said. It was three flights of stairs down.

'Don't bother about me, Patsy,' she said. 'You and Tim go. I'll be all right here.'

'It's not safe here. We'll get your slippers on and help you down.'

'No, I can't be bothered. We've never had a bad raid in full daylight. Just leave me here.'

'Mum! What about tonight? You'll come down if there's a raid in the night?'

She sighed wearily. 'I'll see how I feel. For me it's hardly worth the trouble of struggling up and down those stairs.'

'Of course it is,' Tim retorted.

Patsy had made her a cup of tea and put it in her hand. 'I'm afraid this flat isn't all that suitable for you.'

Eileen Stansfield patted her hand. 'It's a lovely flat, Patsy, and I'm more than grateful for all you're doing for me and Tim. This bed is comfy, I shall be very happy here. You two go to the shelter and leave me.'

Patsy hesitated. 'Well, it's still quiet outside.'

'I knew she'd find the stairs difficult,' Tim said as they ran down to the office, 'but she's very frail – worse than I expected.'

Patsy shivered. 'She sounded almost as though life was too much trouble, as though she wants to give up.'

'No, no, it isn't that.' Tim was in denial. 'She's just tired and can't be bothered, and she's right about daylight raids, they've never given us much trouble.'

CHAPTER TWENTY-FIVE

BARNEY WAS SWEPT BACK to Hamilton Square Station by the rushing crowd. He was scared, everything was going wrong. He hated separating from Jeanie when they were on bad terms. He was afraid she'd go back to her mother in Rhyl and say it was too far to come next time he had a forty-eight-hour pass. This wasn't marriage. They ought to be together; Jeanie was right, they needed a home of their own.

He knew she was right, too, about his mother wanting to hide something in her past life. Any mention of his birth certificate frightened her. Her face had crumpled and she'd shot him such a look of recrimination when Jeanie had asked for it. But this wasn't his fault, he didn't understand what it was and he didn't want to. He wanted all that to be permanently buried.

Barney felt his leave had been a disaster. He'd had a real fight with Patsy and as usual he'd come off worse. On top of that, Jeanie had really upset his mother.

At least the trains to Liverpool were running. Sometimes even the underground stopped in a raid, and he had to get back to barracks before lights out or he'd be in trouble again.

He was back early for once and was glad to get to bed, but even there he couldn't relax. Other men kept coming in and talking between themselves. They all seemed to have had a great time on their leave. Jeanie hadn't been very friendly, she

307

had this bee in her bonnet about living in the flat. It wasn't all that good, but Jeanie had nowhere else now. As she said, really it was all Patsy's fault. Why did she have to be so difficult?

Barney slept eventually but the air-raid siren sounded at two in the morning. He would have stayed where he was if he'd been allowed to, because more than likely it was another false alarm, but the corporal came round and chased them all across the parade ground to the shelters where they had to sit on hard forms. He dozed there, they all did, leaning on one another, and there was another walk back to his cold bed at half three. They were all fast asleep when reveille sounded but they had to leap up and get going. Barney still felt half asleep. This business about the birth certificate had really knocked him for six.

He couldn't be bothered shaving this morning and anyway it was already too late. He trailed into breakfast after the others, but he couldn't get the awful sausages down. He hardly had time to drink his tea before he had to rush outside to the parade ground with the others. He felt light-headed and couldn't keep his mind on what he was supposed to be doing.

He was given the job of picking up a visiting brigadier and his wife from the colonel's quarters and driving them to Lime Street Station to catch the nine thirty-five train to London. Barney preferred longer journeys, but this taxi stuff was the sort of thing he usually did.

The colonel lived in a posh house and though his batman came out with the suitcases quite quickly, the brigadier and his lady kept him waiting. It gave Barney time to appreciate their higher standard of living. By the look of it, the colonel was provided with a spacious and very comfortable house, and senior officers had a taxi service laid on as and when they needed it.

He saw them coming at last and leapt out to salute and open the car door for them in the recommended manner. The lady was smartly dressed in fox furs and a big green hat with a feather in it. She passed in a cloud of perfume; that and the cold damp air woke him up.

'Don't go via Hatton Garden,' the brigadier ordered. 'I'm told that road is closed off because of a burst water main following last night's raid.'

'No, sir.' Barney usually did go via Hatton Garden. 'Which way shall I go?' He was asking himself, but he said it out aloud.

'This is my first visit to Liverpool.' The brigadier sounded irritable. 'Don't you carry a street map?'

'Yes, sir,' Barney said, but he felt quite strange, he couldn't think properly this morning. Not that it really mattered, he did know the way. He'd done this journey dozens of times, but there was a barrier across the street he was driving down and he was re-routed. It happened again in the next road and he felt he was losing his bearings. In Cheapside a building had collapsed and an ambulance was almost blocking the road. It began to rain heavily and it wasn't easy to see where he was going.

'I hope we aren't going to miss the train,' he heard the brigadier's wife say. Barney put his foot down to speed things along and the next minute he felt the car launch into space. It made him feel totally disorientated and he clung to the wheel for dear life. The noise of crashing metal was deafening though he heard the lady's scream above it. The jolt as the car landed pulled every muscle in his body.

The lady's ornate green hat flew over his head and landed on the dashboard in front of him. Its feather came loose and floated on to his knee. The car rocked on its wheels and for a moment he thought it was going to turn over, which made him cling more tightly to the wheel. His heart raced. He felt the car settle and the nose dig deeply into the earth.

When Barney dared to open his eyes he saw a policeman struggling towards him. He knew he'd done a terrible thing and was in big trouble.

Jeanie was more than glad to go back to Chester. It did not have any major industries and did not attract the attention of the Luftwaffe in the way Liverpool did. Cissie was in bed by the time she got there, but she'd expected that and her room was ready for her. After three disturbed nights, she slept for eighteen hours without waking up.

She got up in time for a late lunch. 'I've got Barney's birth certificate,' she told Cissie. 'You'll see it's as he said, his real name is Tavenham-Strong.' She spread it out in front of her. 'Will you ask your friend if we can look through the back numbers of the *Chester Gazette?*'

'She's hardly a friend.'

'We're bound to find a lot more about him in the papers.'

'All right, I'll try and ring Miss King now and see if we can go in.'

Rain was dancing down and it meant a trip to the nearest phone box two streets away. Jeanie sheltered her aunt's dumpy figure under a big umbrella and kept the phone box door open to listen but it seemed Miss King was out and they were advised to ring early tomorrow morning.

'Tomorrow we'll go into town anyway and ask for her,' Cissie decided. 'Phone calls like this are a waste of time and money.'

There was no problem the next morning. The office of the *Chester Gazette* smelled of ink and newsprint. Miss King did remember Cissie and seemed quite pleased to see her.

Jeanie had thought journalism a glamorous job and had expected Miss King to be a handsome commanding figure, but she was shorter than Cissie, gauntly thin, with a greying Eton crop and heavy glasses.

Cissie introduced her as Mrs Tavenham-Strong and asked if they might research back numbers of their newspaper.

'My husband would like to know something of his father's war record,' Jeanie told her and then put Barney's birth certificate into her hand. 'He was killed in the Great War.'

Miss King smiled. 'A well-respected local family,' she said and led the way down to the basement. It was a dark and airless place, and smelled of damp. Miss King switched on the lights, sat them down and brought great bales of old newspapers to the table in front of them.

'If you don't mind, I'll leave you to your search, Mrs Tavenham-Strong,' she said. 'I find it hard to breathe down here, I'm asthmatic.'

'Not at all, Miss King,' Jeanie said. 'You've been very helpful.' She listened to her footsteps mounting the stairs. 'Couldn't be better,' she whispered to Cissie. 'She probably thinks you're my daily cleaning woman.'

Cissie kicked her under the table before starting to divide the papers into two piles. Jeanie found the newspapers full of articles and facts about the war. She was both horrified and fascinated to find long lists of the names of those killed, printed inside a black border. Once she came across the name Tavenham-Strong on such a list, but his given names were Algernon Richard Charles. It wasn't what she was looking for.

From time to time, Cissie drew her attention to something she saw. 'Look at this advert for sweets.' She spread the paper in front of Jeanie; it covered half the page. ' "Try our delicious crystal fruit jellies, traditionally made by Tavenham-Strongs of

Liverpool."' They must have been in business in a big way. Their crystal fruits were in every sweet shop before the war.'

Cissie suddenly gripped her arm. 'Gosh, look at this.' She pushed another paper in front of Jeanie. The article was headed, 'Search for an heir.'

'We've struck gold,' Jeanie giggled, 'in more than one sense.'

The widow of the disgraced officer Lieutenant Rowland Tavenham-Strong is being sought. She is heiress to his considerable fortune but, according to the family, she left home suddenly and has not been seen since his court martial last year. She was expecting a child at the time, and they have no idea where she might have gone.

Lieutenant Tavenham-Strong's solicitors, Richmond Rayner and Sons of 36 Hamblin Street, Chester, has placed the following advertisement in several national newspapers on several dates.

Will Mrs Beatrice Rosanna Tavenham-Strong please contact the above firm where she will hear something to her advantage.

Jeanie read it through and gasped with astonishment. 'Isn't this exactly what I suspected?' she said.

'It is, but you always think there's money to be found under every stone.'

'Can Beatrice still claim this fortune? Surely now she'd settle some on Barney?'

'How would I know?' Cissie said, turning up the date of the newspaper: 'Eleventh of September, nineteen eighteen. That's how long ago? About twenty-two years? It's bound to be too late. The money will have gone to somebody else.'

'The fool,' Jeanie said. 'I just knew it. This makes me more determined than ever to get Barney his birthright. So his father was court-martialled. I want to know more about that.

Barney was born in nineteen seventeen, let's look through the papers for that year, they might have reported something about it.'

They turned page after page and found nothing. Jeanie knew Cissie was getting restive. Then she picked up a paper with banner headlines on the front page. It was dated 16 July 1917 and her eye was caught by a large headline: '*Disgrace for a proud family.*' The article beneath it continued on to page two. She read on avidly.

'This is it,' she breathed to Cissie. 'It's an article about his father. What he did.' Her amazement was growing. Jeanie read on with her mouth open.

'Here's another article about him,' Cissie whispered. 'This is an ongoing story about Rowley Tavenham-Strong. There's more the next day, and again the next.'

As she read, Jeanie could feel her heart pounding like a sledgehammer. 'I never imagined it was anything like this.' As soon as she finished one article, she passed it over to Cissie and reached for another.

'Coming here was a stroke of luck!'

'After what you've been through you're due for some luck.'

'This explains everything.' Jeanie laughed out loud. 'And isn't it exciting?' Jeanie's eye was caught by another screaming headline, 'A Family Feud Carried Too Far,' she read. 'Or Is This Treason?'

'Gosh,' Cissie said. 'Was Rowley accused of treason? That's really serious, isn't it?'

'Everything's here in black and white. The split between the two sides of the family and why there were two grand houses. We were right about the sweet factory too.'

Jeanie had to wait for Cissie to catch up with her and began reading again from the beginning. She was getting a clear

picture of what had happened to Barney's father and understood why Beatrice couldn't bring herself to talk about it.

'But what a fool she was to run off like that.'

'Here's some more,' Cissie said, folding the page back for
her. 'This is from a paper a week or two later.'

'It was a nine-day wonder,' Jeanie said, her astonishment
growing apace.

*Lieutenant Rowland Tavenham-Strong spent the last night of his
life writing his will. He said he left everything to his wife and
prayed and hoped she would use it to bring up their unborn child
without his help.*

'I know now how to get my own back on those two,' Jeanie
chortled. 'Barney knows nothing about this; it looks as though
Beatrice has kept everything to herself, hoping it will all
go away. I shall get them all together and confront them with
this story. It'll be one in the eye for the old bag, serve her right
for being so stuck-up. She behaves like lady muck and tries to
lord it over me. What a laugh! She'll collapse in a pool of
sweat when she hears me sounding off about this, I know
she will.'

'I thought it was Patsy who was getting up your nose.'

'She is, she's the complete despot. She won't like it either.'

Cissie laughed. 'This is a better story than we get at the
flicks,' she said. 'But will she believe you?'

'The mother knows it's true, that'll convince her kids, won't
it? But perhaps . . .'

Jeanie picked out the first of the papers with the banner
headlines, folded them quickly and slid them into her handbag.

'We can take some of these articles. They'll be proof enough
for anybody.'

Cissie gasped. 'We'd better get out of here before Miss King misses those pages.'

At that moment, Jeanie heard her steps coming down the stairs. She saw Cissie freeze but she kept on folding up the papers neatly.

'How are you getting on?' Miss King wanted to know.

'We've been lucky. I've got a whole notebook full of facts.' Jeanie patted the book she'd brought but never opened. 'But there's something I'd like to ask you. 'We've found this article about the Tavenham-Strongs searching for an heir.' She let her read it. 'They were searching for my mother-in-law. Well, I know where she is, so I can tell her to apply to these solicitors. But do you think it's too late for her to claim this money?'

'It was written twenty-odd years ago,' Cissie said.

Miss King sighed. 'I don't know much about legal matters. But certainly your mother-in-law could get in touch with them and see.'

A messenger came halfway down the stairs and called that the editor wanted a word with Miss King pronto. She turned away.

'Thank you so much,' Cissie said. 'We won't bother you any longer.'

'Yes,' Jeanie added. 'I can't thank you enough. You've been very kind. We've found out exactly what we wanted to know.'

Once Miss King reached the top of the stairs, Jeanie turned back to the article and tore out the whole page. Cissie folded the newspapers back in date order and, giggling, they scampered upstairs.

'It's like coming up from a coal mine,' Cissie said as they went out into the street; it was a bright and fresh day.

'A gold mine more like,' Jeanie chortled. 'This is going to stir things up at Fern Bank. I can't wait to see their faces. Barney's going to see that I'm right. Beatrice looks down her nose at me. I'm sure she thinks I'm not good enough for her precious son, that she's a cut above everybody else. This is really going to bring her down to size. We've really got something to celebrate, haven't we?'

They bought magazines and fish and chips on the way home, and spent a lazy afternoon. 'I'm quite sorry I agreed to go to start work at six o'clock tonight,' Jeanie said.

She was so full of joy at what she'd discovered and wanted to celebrate, but was soon engrossed in pulling pints at the Eagle and Child while the landlord's son and some of the customers flirted with her. By seven o'clock the premises were filling up, and by nine there was singing in the bar and a real buzz in the atmosphere. It proved a jolly evening and Jeanie thoroughly enjoyed it. It was only when she reached Aunt Cissie's house and was creeping upstairs to her bedroom that she remembered it was Barney's birthday.

Damn! She hung on to the banister in dismay. He'd be upset that she hadn't rung him, and would no doubt moan about it. Oh well, it was too late to do anything now. Luckily, she'd given him his presents already.

CHAPTER TWENTY-SIX

A WEEK LATER, JEANIE and Cissie were having their breakfast of toast and tea in the kitchen, when they heard the post fall through the letter box. Cissie went up the hall to see what had come and Jeanie was surprised when she put a letter down by her plate.

'It's from Barney,' she said as she tore it open. Normally he couldn't be bothered writing letters, and she was half expecting a tirade of complaint from him because she'd forgotten to ring him on his birthday. But there wasn't a word about that. He seemed to have forgotten all about it.

'Oh dear,' Jeanie said, 'he's had an accident and it seems quite serious. He's written off a staff car and put a brigadier in hospital with a broken leg, a dislocated arm and multiple lacerations.' She gave a little giggle. 'Even worse, the brigadier's wife has suffered a fractured skull and was unconscious for a time.'

'Trust Barney to get himself in a mess.' Cissie giggled too.

'"As far as I know,"' Jeanie read, '"she might still be unconscious. I clung to the steering wheel and I haven't been much hurt as a result, but my nerves are in shreds and I ache all over. I've been charged with driving without due care and attention, endangering the life of my passengers and writing off army property. I don't know what this entails, but the lads thought it a great joke and guffawed with laughter. Pity it wasn't the colonel you had in the back, they sniggered. It would have served him right, and go some way towards getting our own back. He comes down like a ton of bricks on us." '

They both choked with laughter. Jeanie had to mop her eyes before she could go on. ' "The corporal nearly split his sides and said I'll be court-martialled for it, but one of the squaddies said no, he was only teasing. I don't really know what's going to happen but I'm confined to barracks now, so for the time being I won't get any leave." '

'What a fool he is,' Cissie said but had another giggle. 'Surely he won't be court-martialled for an accident?'

Jeanie wasn't pleased. 'How can I have a showdown with his mother and sister if he isn't there to witness it? I was looking forward to getting my own back on Patsy. I'm jolly glad her fancy boyfriend rejected her.' Jeanie couldn't help but gloat. 'He found out what a selfish bitch she can be. I'll have to wait until Barney's allowed out again.'

'Perhaps they'll throw him out of the army.'

'No such luck. He'd earn much more in a munitions factory than he does now. Barney would love that to happen.'

'Honestly, Jeanie, where do you get them from? Barney hasn't got much go in him. He's dead from the neck up.'

'I'll get him moving. All he needs is a kick in the pants.'

'So what exactly are you going to do?'

Jeanie couldn't stop giggling. 'I'm going to take that old newspaper to Fern Bank and lay it out in front of that family and make sure Barney knows everything there is to know. He doesn't seem to accept that his father's side of the family owned and ran a big sweet factory. He needs to hear what his father actually did and how he met his end. That'll be a bit of a comedown but most of all each of them needs to read this bit.' Her finger found the place in the newspaper article and she read it out. ' "Lieutenant Rowland Tavenham-Strong spent the last night of his life writing his will. He said he left everything to his wife and prayed and hoped she would use it to bring up his unborn child without his help." '

Cissie got up to refill their teacups. 'Jeanie, I'd be careful if I were you. When people hurt you, it brings comfort to dream up ways to get even with them, but to actually do it – well, Beatrice won't welcome you to Sunday tea at her house again. You'll never be on good terms with your in-laws.'

'I don't want to go to her house, I hate going and she's never really welcomed me anyway. I want to see her knocked off that social pinnacle she thinks she occupies.'

'But what about Patsy? I thought you meant to make a friend of her?'

'That was a mistake. She doesn't like me either. I want to see her shocked to the core at what Beatrice has kept hidden from them all these years. Patsy is knocking herself out working, isn't she? If her mother had been sensible, she probably wouldn't have to.'

'Barney won't like it.'

'He doesn't know what side his bread is buttered. I want to hear him admit I was right to burrow into his family's secrets. He's bound to be pleased to hear how rich his real father was, isn't he?'

'Why? He isn't likely to get any of it, is he? All this is ancient history. All you'll do is point out to the family that Barney and his mother are very much alike. They both run away from anything they fear.'

'But perhaps it is possible to get Barney a share of that money. We could do what Miss King advised and ask that firm of solicitors.'

'You'd never dare.'

'I would, there could be money involved.'

'Well, you can count me out. I'm having nothing to do with that. Anyway, they'll probably charge you for their opinion.'

'I don't care. I've got a job. Having got this far, I've got to, haven't I?'

'I doubt it'll do you any good, but at least you're not a yellow-belly like Barney.'

'I'll go tomorrow.'

'Make an appointment first, Jeanie. They won't expect clients to march straight in on them. They won't take you seriously if you do.'

'Right, I will.'

'And I'd take your marriage and birth certificates to prove you are who you say you are.'

'Right. Anything else?'

Cissie sighed. 'I wish you the best of luck.'

Jeanie had had second thoughts long before she'd set up the appointment with Richmond Rayner and Sons, but after sounding off about it to Cissie, she felt she couldn't back down. She was feeling nervous when she walked to the telephone kiosk to make the call, but was glad to have the privacy. She was asked about the subject she wished to discuss and said it was an inheritance problem.

'We can offer you an appointment next Monday at eleven o'clock with our Mr Yardley,' she was told. Jeanie accepted.

It gave her several more days to grow more anxious. Cissie said she should look more like a member of the Tavenham-Strong family who might have expectations from a substantial will, so she bought herself a new silver-grey hat and a formal suit in the same colour.

She had never been in a solicitor's office before and the

handsome old building and the traditional formality did nothing for her nerves. The middle-aged receptionist wore a black suit and looked as though she was going to a funeral. When Jeanie was shown into Mr Yardley's office, he seemed relaxed and younger than she'd expected, though dressed in a pinstriped suit and waistcoat. He shook hands with her and asked how he could help her.

She had prepared what she was going to say. 'I'm sure you are familiar with the circumstances of the Tavenham-Strong family,' she began. 'I am here on behalf of my husband and mother-in-law.'

Mr Yardley was sitting up straighter and no longer seemed relaxed. Jeanie spread out the newspaper cutting about Lieutenant Tavenham-Strong writing his will on the night before he was due to be shot at dawn.

'I have brought proof of who I am and who my husband is.' She laid out the documents before him. 'My mother-in-law was married to Lieutenant Rowland Tavenham-Strong and my husband is his son. They received nothing from his will despite this.' She spread out the cutting that asked Beatrice to get in touch with them. 'She would like to know now what happened to that money and whether it would be possible for her to claim it.'

'Why did she not get in touch?' He tapped the cutting with his pencil.

'She said she knew nothing about it. She was grieving, of course, and had given birth to her son, my husband. It made her ill, mentally ill, she saw no newspapers.'

'I'm sorry to hear this, but the rest of the family must have known.'

'They didn't want to know Rowland. He'd brought disgrace on the family name. They cast him and his family off.'

'It's all a very long time ago. Let me see, yes, twenty-two years.' He got to his feet. 'Yes . . . Erm . . . Will you excuse me a moment? There's something I should perhaps check on.'

He gathered up what she'd brought and left the office. He was away for some time and the waiting put Jeanie very much on edge. When at last he returned, it was with a much older man who was introduced to her as Mr Rayner.

'I'm sure you know we act for the family,' he told her. 'You're asking about a will which we must have handled almost a quarter of a century ago.'

'We would like to know what happened to that money.' Jeanie was not going to give up after going through all this.

'Details of this will have been in the public domain since it was settled. In other words, anybody can acquaint themselves with the details of it, or any other will, by applying to Somerset House.'

'Where is that?' Jeanie asked.

'The Strand in London, but we will do that for you if you wish.'

'Yes,' Jeanie said. 'I'd be glad if you would.'

'Then the best thing would be for you to make another appointment with Mr Yardley, perhaps towards the end of next week. That will give him time to look into the matter.'

Jeanie stood up, knowing she had another week to wait and not at all sure that she'd get what she wanted. Perhaps they'd tell her who had received the money, but it didn't look as though Barney had any chance of claiming it now.

'I told you so,' Cissie said when she got home.

By the following week, Jeanie was reluctant to return to the solicitors' office, where she felt out of her depth, but nevertheless, she gritted her teeth and presented herself to Mr

Yardley at the time she'd been given. It was the only way she'd get a clear picture of the situation.

'I have to tell you,' Mr Yardley said, 'that Lieutenant Rowland Tavenham-Strong died intestate. In other words, he didn't leave a will.'

That surprised her, she felt as though the ground had been cut from beneath her feet.

'But the newspaper cutting . . .' Jeanie had brought all her documents again and was rifling through them to find it.

'Journalistic licence.'

'What's that?'

'I suspect the writer wanted to make a more interesting story of it. He wanted to give the article a bit of drama.'

'But . . .'

'That's not proof Lieutenant Tavenham-Strong made a will. None was presented to us. As I said, he died intestate.'

'That means Beatrice would never have received anything?'

'Yes she would. It means the wealth Lieutenant Tavenham-Strong left would be distributed according to certain strict rules.'

'So what are they?'

'He had a child, you say?'

'Yes, my husband.'

'After his wife had received certain effects, the remainder of the wealth would have been divided between his dependants. One half would have been put in trust for his child and the rest put into another trust and his wife would have shared in the income arising from that. She would not have been allowed to use the capital.'

Jeanie lost the thread of what he was saying. What registered was that Barney would have inherited real wealth. She could hardly get her breath.

'What happened in this case was that we were approached by other members of the family, the parents of Lieutenant Tavenham-Strong, in April nineteen nineteen, who requested us to act in the matter of obtaining probate for their son's will. They told us that he had a wife, and possibly a child but that the family had lost touch with her. She had disappeared from her home shortly after her husband's death. We did our best to find her. We wrote several times to the address of her parents, the only address the family could give us, but we received no reply. Then we placed the statutory advertisements for other claimants against this estate, in several newspapers, several times, but we had no response to them. Therefore we proceeded to obtain letters of administration and wound up the estate.'

'But isn't time allowed for people to send in their claims?'

'Yes, it's strictly laid down and was adhered to in this case. It's six months.'

'So there's nothing my husband can do about it now?'

'Nothing at all, I'm afraid. It took us until January nineteen twenty to wind this matter up, which was longer than usual.'

'And who did benefit from this estate? Can I ask that?'

'Yes, as I told you it's been in the public domain for many years. The beneficiaries from an intestate will are strictly laid down, as is everything else. His parents inherited the bulk of it and the rest was shared by his other relatives.'

Jeanie felt deflated as she went back to Cissie's house. She'd never stood a chance to get this money for Barney. She couldn't believe Beatrice could have been such a fool to let all that money go back to the family when she had a legal claim.

But what it did give her was a stick to beat her with when it came to the showdown and Jeanie was more determined than ever to have that. She was going to get her own back on Beatrice.

Barney pulled the blankets over his head and tried to shut out of his mind the sound of the brigadier's groans and his wife's screams. They kept going through him and nothing could wipe from his memory the sight of those mangled blood-splashed bodies. The car had been a tangled mass of metal stuck nose down in the mud, which was rapidly becoming waterlogged. He found it hard to believe it had happened to him; he'd prided himself on his driving skill.

He felt shamed and disgraced, but it wasn't only that. If they thought him incapable of driving, there was nothing else he wanted to do. Nothing else he could do. Everything seemed futile. He was near despair.

This evening, the corporal had spoken to Barney. He told him he'd received instructions to march him before the colonel immediately after parade tomorrow morning.

Waves of panic eddied through him at the thought. He couldn't sleep that night but dozed fitfully, waking up almost every hour. He was wide awake again at five thirty and could see it was getting light. He was cold and shivering with fear at the thought of facing a court-martial. He had to get out of here.

Silently he slid out of his bed and threw on his clothes. He crept out of the barrack room with his boots in his hand and didn't put them on until he'd streaked across the parade ground. In theory, it was impossible for anyone to get into the base or anyone to get out. There were sentries on the gates, it was a military establishment, but Barney had been there long enough to know how it could be done. He climbed the solid wooden gates near the garage through which he usually drove.

It was only when he was out in the street that he gave any thought as to where he could safely go. He couldn't go home to his mother because he'd given the Forest Road address when he'd joined up. He knew enough about what happened when soldiers went absent without leave; the military police would be sent round to arrest them and bring them back.

He could take the train to Chester and join Jeanie at her Aunt Cissie's house. But no, he could not, because though he'd been warned it was hopeless, he had applied for married quarters so Jeanie would have a home of her own, and he'd given her Chester address on the application form.

He meant to walk into the city centre but, feeling muddled and confused, he broke into a run. He ran on and on until he felt ready to drop. When he came to a bus stop he was panting and could go no further. A workman's bus came and he got on, although he didn't know where it was going. Suddenly the seat in front of him seemed a long way away and that scared him rigid. He held on to it and stared out of the window. He didn't know where he was or what was happening to him.

Then miraculously he recognised that he was in Lime Street in the centre of Liverpool and the bus was emptying. He trailed after the other passengers and saw that a small café was open and serving breakfast. He went in and sat in the far corner with his back to the window. He ordered tea and scrambled eggs on toast, but was dozing by the time the plate was slid in front of him.

He wasn't hungry and picked slowly at the food, trying to make up his mind what to do next. He could not stay out on the streets in public view wearing his uniform with its identifying insignia. If asked, people might remember and report seeing him.

He was beginning to feel he'd been there too long when two policemen came in. Fear made him shrink into his chair and half turn so they couldn't see his face. But they were not military police and they were taking no notice of him. He scrambled to his feet and rushed outside.

The panic and the cool morning air made him feel more awake. The shops were open now but there weren't many people about. He was walking quickly but had no idea where he was going, until he saw a small news cinema, advertising an hour-long programme.

A man was going inside; Barney followed him and found it warm and dark and almost empty. He was shown to a seat but when the usherette went away he moved to the back row so he could sit with his back against the wall. He felt safer now and this would give him time to think about what he should do.

The film was a noisy showing of battles and bomb damage, but it didn't keep him awake. The cinema had a much larger audience when he woke up and he felt he'd been there much longer than an hour. But the sleep had done him good, his brain was working again. He knew now he'd have to go to the workshop and ask Patsy to help him. There was nowhere else he could hide and no one else he could ask.

'I'm hoping we'll both be able to get some work done this morning,' Patsy said to Tim as she joined him in the office. 'It's stacking up because we've had so many other things to do recently.'

But at half past ten the air-raid warning wailed again. 'We don't often get a daytime raid,' Tim said. 'You go to the shelter, I'll stay here and try and get on with things. I can run down if things turn nasty.'

'It's such a waste of time if it's a false alarm.' Patsy listened. 'It's quiet enough. I'll go and see what the girls are doing.' She found the sewing machines whirring as busily as ever.

'I went down to the cellar,' Flo said, 'but nobody else did. I didn't want to stay by myself.'

'We're all ready to run down if the bombs start dropping,' Gladys told her.

'We can't work down there,' Vera Cliffe shouted.

'It's time for morning tea,' Mrs Dixon said. 'I can't make that down there either.'

Patsy laughed, and turned to go back to the office. It surprised her to see Barney coming through the front door and turning to close it carefully behind him.

'Hello,' she said. 'I didn't know you were due for more leave.'

'No.' It was a harsh whisper. He shook his head before running to the stairs and going up ahead of her. He was white-faced and agitated; by the time she reached the office door Patsy knew there was something terribly wrong. 'What's the matter, Barney?'

'I've got to stay in the flat now. I've had to run away.'

'Run away from what?' A cold feeling signalling trouble was settling in Patsy's stomach. 'You haven't run away from the army?'

'Yes, I had to.'

'You mean you've gone absent without leave?' His frightened eyes stared into hers. 'That'll land you in big trouble, it's not the same as leaving home.'

'I know that. You've got to help me.' He opened the office door and made to go in but saw Tim writing at his desk and slammed it shut again. 'I'll go straight up to the flat.'

He was already halfway up the stairs when she called, 'No,

don't go in now. Mrs Stansfield is in bed and trying to rest. She's quite poorly.'

'You've got to get her out,' he shouted at her. 'I couldn't stay in barracks. I've got to have somewhere else to live.'

'Barney, you can go home to Mum. She'll be glad to see you.'

'No, I gave the Forest Road address when I joined up. They'll come looking for me. You've got to help me. I've nobody else to turn to. You can't turn me away now. I need to hide.'

'Hush, Barney, they'll hear you in the sewing room. Come to the office and let's talk about it quietly.' She took his arm and tugged him inside. She could feel him pulling back when he saw Tim again.

She was trying to tell Tim that Barney had gone AWOL and at the same time tell Barney that Tim's mother was very ill and had nowhere else to go. 'What's happened to you?'

'It wasn't my fault. You've got to help me,' he was pleading.

Tim pulled a chair forward and pushed him towards it. 'Come on, sit down and tell us all about it.'

'I've had an accident.' He told them about the brigadier and his wife and the injuries they'd suffered as a result, and that he'd been charged with driving without due care and attention. 'It wasn't my fault. I drove into a bomb crater in the road.'

'You didn't see it?'

'No, it had only just happened, the police were there but they hadn't cordoned it off or closed the road. They were going to court-martial me.'

There was a sharp rat-a-tat on the door and Bill Bentley breezed in. 'Sorry,' he said, seeing Barney. 'I'm not intruding, am I?'

'No,' Patsy said. 'Come and listen to this. I think Barney is going to need all the help he can get.' She recounted his difficulties.

Bill looked thoughtful. 'If it was an accident, it doesn't sound serious enough for you to be court-martialled,' he said. 'Did they give you a date for it?'

'Not yet. I was to be marched before the colonel this morning. That's when I decided to get out in a hurry.'

Bill stroked his chin.

There was a long silence before Patsy said, 'Is that the full story, Barney?'

'Yes. The brigadier broke a leg and his wife has head injuries.'

'But if it's an accident, nothing more,' Bill said 'you might get off. I think to be court-martialled you would have had to commit a criminal offence.'

'Are you sure that's the truth, the whole truth and nothing else?' Patsy pressed. She knew Barney could be less than honest if it suited him.

'That's it, absolutely. It was an accident.'

'Then I think you might have got it wrong,' Bill said gently.

'But the corporal had been ordered to march me before the colonel.'

'Well you didn't expect the whole thing to be ignored, did you? Perhaps your colonel meant to give you a ticking off. What would they call it – a caution? I think you should go back before you're picked up.'

'I'm not doing that.' Barney was suddenly belligerent. 'You don't really know. I think you're wrong.'

'It's the best advice I can give you,' Bill said seriously. 'Go back and tell them the accident shook you up. You were not thinking straight; you panicked and ran away. And apologise.'

330

Barney shook his head. 'You've got to help me. I've got to stay in the flat now. You can't turn me out.'

'How can you live without a ration book and without money?' Patsy lost patience with him. 'Who is going to find you food and pay for it?'

'I'll work for you, Patsy, earn money for my keep.'

She gasped with exasperation. 'On past performance, Barney, how long could I expect you to keep that up? Give yourself up. It's the only sensible course.'

Barney sat motionless, his face paper-white, his fingers twitching.

'You can't hide here,' Patsy went on. 'Gossip is rife in the sewing room and everybody knows who you are. Many of the girls have been here for decades; they know you've joined the army. You've worn your uniform here. What will they think if they see you hanging about in civvies?'

'She's right,' Bill said.

'They wouldn't . . . tell anyone in authority.'

'They may not approve of what you're doing,' Bill said. 'Hardly likely to when their relatives are fighting. And if the military police come asking questions, any one of them could drop you in it without realising what they're doing.'

'Why don't you go to Chester and stay with Jeanie?' Patsy suggested.

'I can't, I applied for married quarters for her so she'd have somewhere to live. I gave her Chester address on the application form, so they could go looking for me there.'

'Jeanie will want to know.' Patsy sighed. 'She'll want to help you. Perhaps she knows of some lodgings where nobody knows you. Why don't you ring her now?'

'Cissie doesn't have a phone, or I would have done.'

Tim took a sheet of writing paper and an envelope from his

desk and passed them to him. 'You'll have to write to her then, and the sooner the better.'

'Yes,' but Barney looked at a loss.

'Here's my pen.' Patsy passed it over. 'But I want it back. Pull up your chair to my desk and do it now, so we can get it in the post.'

'I can't think. I'm too worried.'

'Just tell her to ring you urgently,' Patsy said. 'Give her this number.'

'It's lunchtime.' Tim got to his feet. 'I know that's why you've come, Bill. I'll go down and get the soup before Mrs Dixon brings it up. If you really don't mean to go back, Barney, the fewer people who see you here, the better.'

Tim took two bowls of soup up to the flat and had his lunch with his mother. Patsy and Bill shared their sandwiches with Barney and ate their lunch in the office.

Barney was tearful. 'I'm not well,' he complained. 'I've got a raging headache and feel sick with worry. And on top of that I feel absolutely exhausted.'

'When you've eaten,' Patsy said, 'I'll lend you a sleeping bag and you can have a sleep. We'll put our heads together and see if we can come up with any answers, but we still think your best plan is to go back voluntarily.'

'No, Patsy, I've told you, I can't do that. Don't nag me.' He lurched to her desk and picked up the phone.

'Who are you ringing?'

'Mum. She'll help me even if you won't.'

'Don't, Barney, it'll worry her if she knows what you've done.'

But it was already too late. Patsy knew he'd got through and was unloading his troubles on her. 'I wish I could come home to you, Mum, but I can't. Yes, you come down here. Of course I want to see you.'

Patsy indicated to him that she wanted to speak to her mother. She said when he handed her the phone, 'Mum, can you bring some food down for Barney? Something we can cook for his dinner?'

When the lunch hour was over and Tim came back to his desk, Patsy told him, 'We're no further on. Barney will have to go up to the flat if he wants to sleep.'

'I've settled Mum down for the afternoon,' Tim said, 'and closed her bedroom door.'

'Just creep in and lie down on the sofa,' Patsy told Barney.

When he'd gone, Bill frowned. 'I think Barney needs medical help and I don't know how we can provide that. He isn't acting rationally, is he?'

'A mental breakdown?' Patsy was alarmed. 'I don't know much about that sort of thing but Mum has been saying it's in his family.'

Bill sighed. 'I'm not sure I know much about it either.'

'He used to be bombastic, full of his own importance and throw his weight around. Now look at him. Mum said army life wouldn't suit him.'

'What we have to decide,' Bill said, 'is what we are going to do about him. We have three choices. We could ring up his barracks and let them know he's here. Or we could wash our hands of the whole affair and let him find his own solution. The third alternative is to do as he asks and help him to hide.'

'We might have to hide him for a very long time,' Tim said. 'Until the war's over.'

Patsy pushed her hair off her face. 'What would you do, Bill?'

'I'd let them know at his barracks. Let them come and arrest him. I was in the last war and I don't think he's likely to be court-martialled. It's all in his mind.'

'He'd see that as betrayal.' Patsy was frowning.

'The worst option as far as he's concerned,' Bill said, 'would be to opt out and do nothing. He'd be on the run and have little help. He might manage it, but knowing Barney . . .'

'It would prolong his agony,' Tim said. 'But it would also do that if we helped him to hide.'

Patsy was biting her lip. 'I wish I could make up my mind. If he moved into the flat with you and your mother, it would make life hell for you all.'

'Yes,' Tim said. 'He hates me.'

After a short silence, Bill said, 'I could give him a bed for a night or two, but I don't want him with me for ever. I couldn't stand it.'

'Thank you, I'd consider that a great favour.'

'Your dad would want me to help. He always saw Barney as a problem.'

Patsy heard footsteps on the stairs. 'Oh goodness, this will be Mum.' She got up to open the door.

'Patsy, where is Barney? Such a rush to get down here, you might have come to collect me.'

'Sorry, Mum, he's asleep on the sofa upstairs. Have you brought him some food?'

'I've brought some of his favourite biscuits.' She put the packet on the desk. Tim gave her his chair and went out to find another.

'He needs something for dinner, meat, eggs, that sort of thing.'

'You know I can't. Stuff like that is on ration. The simplest way is for you to bring him home for his dinner. Shall I go up and see him?'

'No point in waking him up, Mum, he said he was exhausted. We're trying to decide what we should do about him.'

For Beatrice's benefit Bill outlined the discussion they'd had so far. He looked from Patsy to Beatrice. 'You know my opinion, we should try once more to persuade him to return, and if he refuses, we should let them know he's here.'

Beatrice was aghast. 'No,' she stormed. 'No, he'd never forgive us. I can't agree to that.'

There was a long silence.

'I'm afraid this is up to you,' Bill said. 'I'll support you whatever you decide, he's your family.'

'Then of course we must help him,' Beatrice said. 'He's probably going through hell because of this. Worry isn't good for him.'

'Patsy, what do you say?' Bill asked.

'I don't feel I have much choice. He'd say blood is thicker than water. It's what Mum wants.'

Bill straightened up in his chair. 'He has to have an income if he's to survive. I could employ him in my business and pay him a wage.'

'Thank you, Bill,' Beatrice said. 'We'll both be grateful.'

'Though there could be people working for me who know who he is.'

'I might be able to find lodgings for him,' Tim said, and told them about Mrs Cooper. 'She was a neighbour of mine and a real motherly sort of person. But he'll have to have a ration book first. It wouldn't be fair to ask her to feed him without that.'

'You do realise,' Bill said, 'that if we help him hide from the military authorities, we'll all be breaking the law?'

'Nonsense,' Beatrice said. 'They can't expect a mother not to help her son.'

'In these circumstances, you'll find they do. But I have

noticed that relatives harbouring AWOL personnel are usually treated leniently if they are discovered.'

'You'll have to pay Mrs Cooper's fine if that happens,' Tim said. 'Oh Lord, what a mess this is.'

CHAPTER TWENTY-SEVEN

PATSY HAD A BAD night and for once it was due to domestic problems and not an air raid. She'd barely sat down at her desk the next morning when Jeanie rang up. 'What's the urgency?' she wanted to know. 'Is Barney there?'

'No, but he needs to see you. Can you come today?'

'What on earth for? I've got a job, I work in the evenings. I thought Barney was confined to barracks.'

Patsy brought her up to date with his problems. She knew from Jeanie's little squeals of shock and surprise that she was anxious for him. She went on, 'A family friend, Bill Bentley, has given him a bed for a couple of nights, but if he's going to survive away from the army, he'll have to have a ration book. Come and talk to him, he needs your help.'

'This is scary,' Jeanie said. 'I'll come now. Heaven help us.'

'We'll give you a bed in Forest Road,' Patsy said. 'I don't know whether Bill will be—'

'I'd prefer to come back here and work,' she said shortly. 'Should I come to your workshop?'

'Yes, I'll get Barney to come here.'

'I'll see you around late morning then.'

Patsy was cross to find Bill had gone to work and Barney was still in bed. 'Get yourself down here,' she told him. 'Jeanie is coming to see you.'

He turned up looking half asleep and hangdog miserable. It only added to her stress to have him in the office watching her and Tim trying to work.

'I need civilian clothes.' Barney paced restlessly to the window. 'I stand out in this uniform and I'll have been missed by now. They'll be looking for me.'

Tim glanced up from his ledgers. 'Patsy gave me your cast-off clothes because I lost all mine in a raid, but I've sorted out an outfit or two for you. They're on the sofa upstairs if you want to change.'

'Of course I want to change,' he snapped, his tone prickly.

'You must take your uniform away with you,' Patsy said firmly. 'We want no incriminating evidence left here.'

Jeanie wasn't all that surprised. Running away was what Barney did when he came face to face with something he couldn't cope with, but she wasn't pleased. She knew he'd be boiling over with anxiety about everything, from the hazard of seeing a fly in the kitchen to where he'd be able to find a clean pair of socks.

'Trust Barney to go AWOL,' Cissie said. 'I've told you, the man's a fool.'

Jeanie was beginning to agree. She was living on the regular allowance the army was sending her from his wages. Her first concern was that it could stop if Barney was not there earning the money.

There were two reasons why she'd chosen to return to work at the Eagle and Child. The first was, as always, that she wanted to have more money to spend, but also she found Vince Mayle, the owner's son, attractive. He'd made advances towards her, but at the time she'd been too enamoured with Barney to take up with him. Recently Barney had not come up to her expectations, and to have a little fun with Vince had seemed a good idea.

Patsy had sounded worried on the phone and had spoken of getting another ration book as a major problem. That had set Jeanie's mind working in a new direction: if Patsy was prepared to pay for a ration book for Barney, she might be able to bamboozle a little commission out of it for herself.

When she reached the workshop, Jeanie ran up to the office. As soon as she opened the door she could feel the stress in the atmosphere. Tim was uncomfortable, Patsy was frowning and Barney was a nervous wreck with his head in his hands.

They all started recounting the full story of what Barney had done. Jeanie had had time to think about this on the bus and as she'd known about his accident, she found things were pretty much as she'd supposed. They wanted her to persuade Barney to return to barracks, but she knew that would be impossible. He didn't have it in him to face that.

'Please help me, Jeanie,' he said tearfully. She moved her chair closer to his and took his hand in hers to show sympathy, but really to go AWOL was the most stupid thing he'd ever done. Now he had the military police chasing him. That was something else he wouldn't be able to stand up to.

When they started to talk about Barney's desperate need for a ration book, Jeanie had her ideas all worked out. She said, 'I think I might be able to help there. Working in a pub, I see things going on, you know.' She had their full attention now.

'Could you get one?' Patsy asked.

'I've been in Liverpool recently so I'm not sure. But in Chester, things might have changed, I might not be able to.'

'But you will try, won't you?' Barney pleaded. 'The rest of us have no idea how to go about it.'

'I'll do my best, of course, but it won't be easy.' She wanted to lay that on thick. 'It'll cost money too.'

'How much?' Patsy asked.

'I don't know until I start asking round, do I? It could be exorbitant, perhaps as much as a hundred pounds.'

'In that case, Barney, you might have to manage without,' Tim told him with a hollow laugh.

Jeanie saw him wince. She knew Vince would be glad to take what he could get and that he'd consider twenty pounds a good price.

'I'll do my best,' she assured them. 'I'll go back this evening to work in that pub, and if I can get you a ration book I'll bring it to you, but it'll take a day or two.'

They all seemed grateful and with that organised, Jeanie wanted to get away. 'Come on, Barney,' she said. 'I'll buy you lunch in some quiet café so you don't eat up other people's rations.'

'Lunch is the easiest meal to find for him,' Tim told her. 'We all have soup from the canteen.'

'Then,' Jeanie said sweetly, 'you can keep the soup for his evening meal.'

She soon wished she'd left Barney where he was. On every corner he saw people out to get him and in the café he was afraid every customers was waiting to jump on him. He hadn't bothered to shave and he looked an untidy mess.

'Going AWOL doesn't suit you, Barney,' she told him. 'You're a bag of nerves and absolutely no fun.'

Patsy was glad to see Barney leave the workshop. 'We'll be able to have a quiet lunch on our own, Tim,' she said. 'Then we need to get down to work this afternoon. It's pay day.'

'Sorry,' he said, pushing his hair away from his face in a weary gesture. 'I'll have to see to Mum.'

'Oh dear, of course you will. I'm not thinking straight any more. Is she well enough to get her dressing gown on and come to the table? We could all eat together.'

He smiled. 'It might cheer her up. Not that she has a dressing gown, the bomb got that, but she has a coat.'

'You go up and see, Tim. I'll go down and fetch three bowls of soup.'

Patsy took the tray up to the flat but Tim was shaking his head. 'Mum doesn't seem at all well,' he said. 'She was better earlier on. Come and talk to her, I'd like to know what you think.'

Patsy followed him to the bedroom. Mrs Stansfield had pushed some of her pillows away and was lying flat.

'You're very kind, Patsy,' her voice was a soft whisper, 'but I'm not hungry. I'll have a little sleep. Perhaps I'll feel better after that.'

'Are you in pain?'

'No, just weary – very tired.'

'Then we'll leave you to sleep and come back in an hour or so to see how you are. We can warm your soup up for you later.'

She pulled Tim into the living room and closed the door. 'We might as well eat up here.' She set out their soup bowls on the table.

'I'm worried about Mum,' Tim said.

'So am I. She wasn't like this yesterday, though she wasn't good then. She refuses to go down to the cellar when there's a raid, but I don't think I could get her up and down the stairs anyway.'

'Do you go down?' Patsy asked.

'No, I stay with her.'

'Tim!' But it's what she'd have expected of him. 'You're taking terrible risks.'

An hour later, Tim was engrossed in working out the wages for the week. He would have to get the money from the bank and pay the fifty-five employees before closing time today.

'I'll go up and see how your mother is,' Patsy said. 'You carry on here.'

She knocked before she opened the bedroom door and thought at first Mrs Stansfield was asleep, but her eyes opened.

'Hello,' Patsy said. 'Do you feel better now? Shall I warm up that soup for you?'

Mrs Stansfield looked ill and much older than she used to, but she tried to smile. 'No thanks.'

'You're not hungry yet?'

She shook her head and closed her eyes. 'Just want to sleep.'

Patsy ran back to the office. 'I'm really worried about your mum,' she said. 'She's slept pretty much all the time since we brought her here from hospital.'

'I know, and she's hardly eaten anything. I even have to press her to drink. I was hoping she'd pick up after a good rest.'

'We could ask the doctor to come and see her. Go up and see if you think we should.'

Ten minutes later, Tim returned to say wearily, 'Mum says don't bother the doctor, she's all right. But she isn't, and I think we should.'

'I'll ring him,' Patsy said. Then she rang her own mother, too, and asked her to come to the office to sign the cheque Tim would make out for the wages. Usually, they took the cheque to her on the way to the bank, but time was going on and the girls would want their money before home time.

Then she started to help with the task, by writing the name of each employee and the amount they had earned on a little envelope. Beatrice arrived, and Patsy asked her to sit with Tim's mother and try and get her to drink some tea.

Patsy drove Tim to the bank to collect the cash, always a job they did together. So was the chore of checking the amount put into each packet and taking the packets to the sewing rooms and getting each member of staff to sign for it. Patsy always found it draining because they had to be very careful to get their figures right, but today they'd been working against the clock as well. It was quarter to five when they finished and Tim was able to lock the ledgers in his desk.

'I'm whacked,' Patsy said. 'You've done well, kept your wits about you despite the pressure.'

'I mustn't let it ruffle me or I make mistakes and get the figures wrong.' He smiled. 'But I'm shattered now.'

'Let's go up to the flat, see how your mother is, and have a cup of tea.'

Beatrice set the kettle to boil and told Tim she was still waiting for the doctor to come. 'There's no change in your mother, she's dozed on and off all the time.'

When the sewing room emptied at five o'clock, they heard the usual commotion of happy shouting and slamming of doors. Patsy was thinking of taking Beatrice home when Flo came running up with the doctor.

'We'll wait to hear what he says,' Patsy whispered to Tim as he took him in to see his mother. Ten minutes later, the doctor came out, wished them good evening and clattered down the stairs.

'I'm not much the wiser.' Tim pushed at his unruly hair. 'I'm to let her sleep if that's what she wants, but I'm to make sure she drinks, water, tea, anything. I'm not to try to take her down to the shelter if there's a raid because rest is what she really needs. The doctor said he'd come back tomorrow to see how she is.'

'Then there's nothing more we can do.' Patsy stood up. 'We'll go home. Have you got enough to eat here?'

'Yes, Gladys took our ration books and registered us with her butcher. She brought me half a pound of mince, as she thought that would be easy for Mum to eat. Mrs Dixon turned it into a stew and provided just about everything else we'll need.'

'See you tomorrow then,' Patsy said.

'The girls are very good to him,' her mother said as they went out to the car. 'I went to the market this morning and managed to get some liver. I'm afraid it's pig's liver which isn't the best, but liver is good for you.'

They were cooking the liver and onions for their dinner and the savoury scents were filling the kitchen when the phone rang.

It was Bill Bentley. 'I intended to take Barney out for a meal at the Central Hotel tonight, but he won't come. I think he's scared of going out in case he's seen and recognised. Would you have anything at all we could eat for dinner? I'm not very well organised about food. All I have apart from bread and potatoes is one egg.'

'Tell Barney from me he's a damn nuisance,' she said.

'Sorry to bother you, Patsy, anything will do – another egg to put with this one, or some cheese.'

'It's not your fault, Bill. I'll have a look round here and bring a meal up to you. I won't be long.'

Her mother was mashing furiously at the potatoes when she told her. 'We've nothing else.' Beatrice was cross. 'What could I possibly spare for Bill Bentley?'

'He's keeping Barney safe for you, isn't he? Shall I take our dinner to them? Drain the cabbage, Mum.' Patsy got out a large wooden tray. 'Have you any old towels to wrap the pans in to keep them warm? I can put them in the car boot.'

'But what about us? You've been working all day, you've got to eat.'

'I'll see if I can get fish and chips on the way back.'

'I can't see why Bill Bentley can't do that,' she exploded.

'I'm sure he would if he'd thought of it. Mum, he's doing a lot for Barney, don't be hard on him.'

Patsy had to queue outside the chip shop, and when her turn came they had no more fish left, but she did manage to get two fishcakes with her chips. She was starving by the time she returned home; her mother wanted to put them in the oven to keep warm, together with some plates so they could eat at the dining-room table. Patsy felt exhausted and insisted they sit by the fire and eat them straight from the paper. She felt able to relax for the first time that day and was having a cup of tea afterwards when the phone rang again.

'Whatever will Bill want now?' Beatrice asked angrily.

But it was Tim on the phone. She could hear the panic in his voice. 'I need you to help, Patsy. Can you come back?'

'Now?'

'Yes, straight away. It's Mum. I don't know what to do.'

Patsy felt his sense of urgency. 'I'll be as quick as I can.' She was pulling on her coat and kicking off her slippers simultaneously.

'You're not going out again?' her mother demanded. 'You're rushing round far too much. This isn't good for you. You ought to slow down.'

'I'll be all right, Mum,' she said as she went out. 'I think Mrs Stansfield has taken a turn for the worse.'

Patsy raced up the workshop stairs and found the front door of the flat standing open for her. Tim was in the bedroom, he was sitting by the bed holding his mother's hand. As soon as he saw her, he stood slowly and pulled the sheet over her face.

It took Patsy's breath away when she realised what had happened.

'Tim! When . . . ?' She could see tears on his cheeks. 'Come and sit down.' She led him to the living-room sofa.

'Oh God!' He collapsed back. 'I'm not sure when.'

Patsy threw herself down beside him and put her arms round him in a hug.

He swallowed hard. 'I thought she was sleeping and I decided a bath would make me feel better. When I'd had it, I looked in on her again and realised she wasn't breathing. She died alone, Patsy. I wasn't with her and I should have been.'

He wept on her shoulder in a storm of tears and grief. Patsy held him close and patted his back, wishing she knew how to comfort him. She was in tears herself but knew the tears were for Tim rather than for his mother.

She could feel him quietening and relaxing against her. He lifted his head. 'Thank you,' he murmured and kissed her cheek. He stayed close, his tearful eyes looking into hers; then he gently kissed her lips. Patsy felt an unexpected frisson of attraction shoot through her.

He pulled himself away from her, mopping hard at his eyes with a damp handkerchief. 'Thank you for coming so quickly, and for everything else.'

Patsy asked shakily, 'Should we ring the doctor to let him know what has happened?'

'I already have,' he said. 'His wife said he was out on a

case, but she'd send him as soon as he came back.' He gave Patsy a wry smile. 'I'll wash my face and try and pull myself together before he gets here.'

'I'll make some tea.' Patsy's head was spinning. She could think of nothing else that might help. While she waited for the kettle to boil, she saw through the kitchen window the dimmed lights of a car approaching. When it pulled up in front of the building, she knew it was the doctor and ran down to let him in.

Tim, looking pale but composed, was standing at the door of the flat when she brought the doctor up and he led him into the bedroom. Patsy poured herself a cup of tea and collapsed on the sofa to wait. She was shocked by what had happened tonight but felt it had opened her eyes to what she felt for Tim. At last the bedroom door opened again and they came out.

'Come to the surgery tomorrow to collect the death certificate,' the doctor told Tim as he shook his hand. 'As I said, your mother was already disabled by the stroke and the injuries she received in that raid.' He looked at Patsy. 'Mrs Stansfield had another major stroke.' Then his feet were echoing on the bare stairs as he went down.

Patsy poured another cup of tea and put it into Tim's hand. 'I'm so sorry,' she said. 'You were such a help to me when Dad died. I know only too well what it's like to lose a parent, but I don't know how to comfort you.'

'But you have comforted me,' he told her. 'I don't know what I'd have done without you. You've been an enormous help letting me use this flat and suggesting I get the doctor and everything. I wish I hadn't broken down and wept on your shoulder. I can still see a wet patch on your blouse.'

'It doesn't matter.'

'It does. I'm sorry you saw me in tears. I don't want you to think of me as a crybaby. I like to think I'm strong and have a stiff upper lip.'

'You were showing natural feelings, Tim. Your mum died suddenly, it was shock and grief and loss and love that you were showing. It's better not to bottle up that sort of anguish.'

'D'you think so? I like to think I'm strong and manly.'

'You are, Tim. You were emotionally distraught at that moment. Anyone would be. It's not surprising you showed your feelings.'

The phone rang. Tim answered it but handed it to her. 'It's your mother,' he whispered.

She took the handset, unable to drag her eyes away from Tim. 'Hello, Mum.'

'Patsy, please come home immediately.'

She could hear the panic in her mother's voice. 'Has something happened?'

'Yes, the military police have been here looking for Barney. Four of them. I don't think they should call on widows at this time of night. They were enough to frighten the life out of anyone. They insisted on walking all round the house and moving things round in Barney's room. They even had the things out from under the stairs.'

'What did you tell them about Barney?'

'They fired questions at me. When had I last seen him? Had I spoken to him on the phone recently? That sort of thing. I refused to tell them anything. I told them I'd complain about them calling late at night. I was in bed, I had to answer the door in my dressing gown. I didn't want to let them in, but they pushed into the hall. Always when I need your help, Patsy, you aren't here.'

She felt full of guilt. 'I'm sorry, Mum. Truly sorry.'

'Do you know what time it is? It's gone eleven and high

time you were home with me.' She sounded angry. 'We should both be in bed.'

'Sorry,' she repeated.

'You can't work night and day, you know. You'll make yourself ill if you carry on like this. And you shouldn't be alone there with that lad at this hour.'

'I'll come home now.'

'How is his mother?'

'It's bad news, Mum. I'm afraid she's died.'

CHAPTER TWENTY-EIGHT

PATSY DROVE HOME FEELING edgy about the speed at which problems were unfolding in her life. The air-raid siren sounded before she got there, so instead of going to bed she lay down beside her mother on the mattress in the shelter.

Mum was full of worries about Barney and they were both full of trepidation for the future. It was only when Beatrice fell asleep that Patsy was able to settle down and think of how much harder it must be for Tim at this moment.

She couldn't believe she'd been so blind about her feelings for him. Putting her arms round him and trying to comfort him had changed everything for her within moments. Why had she wasted so much time longing for Rupert Alderman when right at hand she'd had Tim? She'd been dazzled by Rupert's good looks, his fine car and his fancy lifestyle. Tim had none of those things but he was worth two of Rupert. She could trust him; rely on him to always do the best for her. Why had it taken her so long to realise what he meant to her?

She had been close to Tim for so long. They talked about every aspect of the work and the staff and had been the best of friends. For years they'd offered each other support and a safe haven from the daily ups and downs of life. They were very much at ease together yet she'd never really considered what she felt for him. She'd talked of friendship but now she knew it was much more than that. Why hadn't she seen that she was in love with him.

When her father had died and she'd really needed help, it had been Tim who had responded to her need. When she'd sought help with the business, Tim had been there behind her, helping her take the risks she had. He'd been her security, always supportive and sympathetic. Earlier tonight, when she'd tried to do the same for him, she'd seen for the first time that she was totally attached to him, and yes, she felt love for him. She wanted to feel his arms round her and his lips on hers. Thinking of Tim lulled her to sleep.

In the morning she was up bright and early. She couldn't wait to get back to the workshop to see him again, but she had to remind herself that his mother had died last night. The last thing he'd want was a lot of rejoicing this morning. She had felt low for a long time after her father died. But she wanted to be with him, to help him where she could.

In the office, Tim was very pale but composed. He set about contacting an undertaker who came that afternoon to lay out his mother and put her to lie in her coffin. It was made of strong cardboard and was the only type available. Beatrice gave her a white silk nightdress for Mrs Stansfield to be buried in and Patsy and the girls brought flowers to put in her room.

It was another busy day interspersed with the wail of sirens that brought their hearts into their mouths, though no bombs dropped nearby. Due to the casualties from the heavy bombing, Tim was told he'd have to wait eight days before he could bury his mother.

Last month, he'd been given a date for his driving test; it was now imminent.

'You could ask if you could postpone it for a week or so,'

Patsy suggested. 'You'll find it hard to concentrate on driving just now.'

Tim sighed and pushed himself back from his desk. 'I need to be able to drive,' he said. 'I can't keep relying on you for that. I've got to be able to do it myself.'

'Bill says you're well up to standard,' Patsy told him. 'He thinks you'll pass.' Bill had been taking him out to practise his driving. 'But my nerves would be in rags if I were going through what you are.'

Tim's face was determined. 'I'm going to try.'

Jeanie was glad to return to work at the Eagle and Child. She slid back into the routine she enjoyed and felt life was normal again.

Vince Mayle had a collection of ration books, clothing coupons, petrol coupons, sweet coupons and points, just as she'd known he had. A few months ago, he'd helped a friend with a robbery from a food office and the spoils had been shared. They were both selling off the ration documents on the black market when and where they could.

Jeanie persuaded him to give her a ration book and some clothing coupons in return for favours and without any cash changing hands. She thought she was on to a good thing because she'd fully intended to have a fling with Vince. It was why she'd returned to the pub to ask his father for her job back. She reckoned he was a lot more fun than her husband had been recently.

Barney rang her up every day to inquire about the progress she was making towards getting him a ration book and pleaded with her to return to Birkenhead. But she was enjoying herself so much with Vince she was in no hurry and she had the perfect excuse that she had to wait to get a ration book.

However, Jeanie didn't want him to be picked up by the military before she got her hands on Patsy's cash, so when she had two nights off from her pub job, she told Barney she would be bringing his ration book the next day.

On the last evening she worked, it was two in the morning when she crept up Aunt Cissie's stairs, and so it was late when she got up the following morning. She was eager to be on her way. She'd told Barney she'd be there early in the afternoon and he promised to ask Bill's permission to leave early and meet her there. It seemed Bill expected Barney to put in a full day's work.

Jeanie packed her overnight case, and took not only the ration book but the pages she'd torn from the 1917 newspapers in the *Chester Gazette* office. She was looking forward to this showdown with Beatrice.

It was two o'clock when she climbed the workshop stairs. She found Patsy and Tim working quietly in the office and both greeted her warmly.

'Come and have a seat. I hear from Barney that you've got him a ration book.' Jeanie could see Patsy was quite excited.

'And a sheet of clothing coupons,' she said with a smile, taking them from her bag and pushing them across the desk.

Tim got to his feet. 'How much did you have to pay for them?'

She tried to look innocent as she met his gaze. 'They asked sixty pounds but I got them for fifty-five. I argued them down.'

'I'll get the tea,' Tim said and went out. Patsy was examining the ration documents.

'They are genuine,' Jeanie hurried to assure her. 'They were stolen before they could be issued.' She saw Patsy recoil from that fact and vowed she'd be more careful in future about what she told her.

'Thank you for getting them and putting the money up.' Patsy took a chequebook from her desk drawer and made it out. 'I'll have to get Mum here to sign this for you.'

Jeanie listened to the phone conversation. She was pleased Beatrice was asked to join them. She wanted the family all together before she started. 'Does your mother run the business?' she asked. She'd never been sure about that.

'No, but I have to be over twenty-one before I can be held legally responsible for a business transaction. Mum has to sign the cheques.'

Tim returned with three cups of tea. 'I can give Barney Mrs Cooper's address now,' he said. 'I have spoken to her and she's expecting Barney any day. I've told her he's moving here to work for Bill, but I wasn't sure when he'd come. She'll provide a safe lodging for him but we couldn't move him in without a ration book.'

Jeanie listened to what was said, but she'd heard all this before. 'When will Barney be here?'

'Any minute now,' Patsy said. 'Bill Bentley is bringing him. He's coming to take Tim for his driving test.'

Moments later they heard them clattering upstairs. Barney crossed the office with two strides to kiss Jeanie's cheek and hold her hand. 'It's lovely to see you, it seems ages, and thank you for all you've done for me.'

'You'll have to fill in your name and address on all these documents before you give them to your new landlady,' Jeanie explained. 'Are you going to give your real name?'

'That wouldn't be safe.' He frowned. 'I don't want to be picked up because I have to register to get my rations.'

'So what are you going to call yourself?' Tim was filling in Mrs Cooper's address in block capitals.

'Tavenham-Strong,' Jeanie suggested.

'That's a name that draws attention to itself,' Patsy objected. 'Something more ordinary would be better.'

They agreed on Barnaby Charles Strong. Tim wrote that in block capitals on all his documents for him and passed them over. 'Give these to Mrs Cooper,' he told him. 'She'll do the rest.'

'We'd better be on our way, Tim,' Bill said. 'We don't want to be late for your test.'

'I'll keep my fingers crossed for you,' Patsy said, and watched Tim get up, his chin jutting with determination. Jeanie wished him luck.

No sooner had they gone than Beatrice arrived with a covered basket. She nodded towards Jeanie but kissed Barney and made a fuss of him.

'Darling, I've brought you a helping of beef stew with a potato and a bit of cabbage for your dinner. There's an old steamer in the cupboard here that I left behind, you can warm it up in that. And to finish off, I've made you a little trifle. You've always loved my trifles.'

'Thank you, Mum, but what about Jeanie? She'll need to eat too.'

'Oh dear, I'd forgotten you'd be here.' She surveyed Jeanie sourly.

'Mum,' Patsy said, 'I thought we'd agreed Jeanie would come home to eat and spend the night with us.'

'And leave Barney here by himself? You won't like that, will you, darling?'

'I want to stay with Jeanie,' he mumbled.

'Barney doesn't like anything we do for him,' Patsy said wearily. 'Doesn't like what other people do for him either. Come on, Mum, sign this cheque for Jeanie. It's what we said we'd do.'

Jeanie thought her mother-in-law was about to refuse. She looked daggers at her. 'That's a lot of money,' she said.

'It's what I had to pay out,' Jeanie told her frostily, 'and I had to work hard to get it.' She slipped the cheque into her handbag. So far so good, but her heart was pounding, the scene for her showdown had set itself with no effort on her part. She was itching to do it now, pay Beatrice back for her latest kick. It was time to put what she'd planned in action.

'There's something else I've brought for you all.' Jeanie brought out the pages of the 1917 newspapers from her bag with a flourish and opened them out carefully on Tim's desk. Then she handed one article to each of the Rushtons.

'What's this?' Beatrice asked suspiciously. 'I can't read it without my glasses.'

Barney gave a shocked gasp.

'I went to the offices of the *Chester Gazette* to get these,' Jeanie said. 'It's something you, Patsy and Barney could have done for yourselves. As for you, Beatrice, I feel despair. How stupid can you get?'

'Hold on, Jeanie,' Barney protested.

She ignored him and continued to stare at his mother. 'You've survived for years with thrift and hard work on a small income, congratulating yourself that you've got the energy to keep your tablecloths starched and cut flowers for your table. But you threw away a fortune because you were too scared to claim what was rightfully yours. I pity you.'

Jeanie tapped the newspaper pages she'd given Beatrice.

'You've kept Barney quaking in his shoes while you've talked vaguely about a dark family secret. But you kept all the details hidden from him and presumably from Patsy too and pretended to be too nervous to bring the whole thing out in the open so they can understand. And it all happened twenty-three years ago and should have been long since forgotten.'

Barney was shaking, Patsy looked horrified.

'Jeanie,' Beatrice said. 'Say no more, you don't understand.'

'It's you that doesn't understand,' Jeanie jeered. 'Look at them, Beatrice, they haven't a clue what I'm talking about. You strut about and claim status from the family you married into, and look down your nose at me and my family. But you can't tell them Rowland Tavenham-Strong was a murderer. You're ashamed of that, aren't you, Beatrice?' Jeanie felt she'd got the Rushtons where she wanted them at last; all three were curling up in horror. 'That has to be hidden because how could you feel superior if everybody knew he'd been shot for what he did?'

'Stop it, Jeanie,' Barney pleaded. 'We don't want to know.'

Jeanie saw Patsy lick her lips and knew she hadn't known about this. 'You ought to know, so I'm going to tell you what your mother should have explained years ago. Lieutenant Rowland Tavenham-Strong was fighting with the British Expeditionary Force. It was commanded by Sir George French but Rowland's uncle was his chief of staff, Lieutenant General Sir Julian Philip Tavenham-Strong. When orders were issued for another offensive, Rowland went to divisional headquarters and shot three senior members of staff, one of whom was related to him.'

Patsy's mouth was hanging open; Barney looked dazed.

'Go on, read all about it,' Jeanie sneered, waving towards the cuttings.

'Your husband was found guilty of murdering his uncle. He was court-martialled, cashiered and sentenced to death by firing squad.'

Tears were rolling down Beatrice's face. 'Stop, please stop,' she moaned.

'I've brought proof because you, Beatrice, might deny it was true, and then Barney and Patsy wouldn't believe me. It was, I'm told, reported in all the national newspapers at the time. In other words, it was a sensation that gripped the nation. Right, so you don't want to see the proof? Let me read some snippets out to you.

' "Is this a family feud carried too far? Is this murder or treason? Had it anything to do with espionage? It was certainly a disgrace for a proud family. The top brass shot by one of their own side." '

Jeanie picked up another of her newspaper cuttings and read on.

While a ferocious battle was raging, in this war to end all wars, a British serving officer, Lieutenant Rowland Charles Arnold George Tavenham-Strong, entered staff headquarters in northern France and shot dead his own uncle, Lieutenant General Sir Julian Philip Tavenham-Strong, and seriously injured Brigadier George Madison and Captain Terence Holt, and caused minor injuries to others on the staff of the British Expeditionary Force under the command of Sir George French.

In his defence, Lieutenant Rowland Tavenham-Strong said he felt strongly that it was not just bad strategy on the part of the top brass to ask the men to go over the top, but an entirely wrong strategy. They knew how many men would be killed and how many more would die of the wounds they'd receive, and how little ground would be gained as a result. It was causing an unnecessary death toll among serving soldiers and he felt it had to be stopped.

Jeanie looked up from the paper. 'He didn't seem to realise

that to kill a superior officer while the war was raging would help the enemy. And there's one last article on a subject you ought to know about, Beatrice. It says your husband wrote his last will and testament as he was about to die – during his last night while he waited for that fateful dawn to break. It says that he left all his worldly goods to be shared between you and Barney. Quite romantic, isn't it?' Jeanie was gloating. At last she had Beatrice at her mercy. 'For heaven's sake, you knew he was rich. You were his wife. You must have known he'd leave you well provided for.'

Beatrice moistened her lips. 'His family said—'

'You were scared of them,' Jeanie said contemptuously.

Beatrice could not stem her tears. 'They were saying that Rowley knew little about running a sweet factory and even less about winning a war. They thought the military strategy was well worked out.'

Jeanie taunted Barney. 'Your mother knew this all the time. She knew she had a legal right to this money and the family wouldn't have let her or you starve, but she ran away and hid from them.'

'Mum?' he asked. 'Is this true about the money?'

Beatrice mopped at her eyes. 'I'm sorry,' she sobbed.

Jeanie crowed. 'Your mother was so cowardly she hid from the Tavenham-Strongs. She was so scared she couldn't even do things that were to her own advantage. She wouldn't contact their solicitors to get an income for life. She says you're nervous and sensitive, Barney, and you inherited that from your father, but it's from her you get it. Your dad at least found the guts to shoot the uncle he disagreed with. She ran away just like you do, with her tail between her legs.'

'Jeanie, you've got to stop,' Barney pleaded. He looked shattered.

'You've gone too far,' Patsy said. 'You're upsetting Barney as well as Mum. You're no longer welcome here. I think you'd better go.'

'Your mother couldn't stand the disgrace of being married to a soldier who was shot at dawn for treason,' Jeanie taunted. 'Not when every other soldier was fighting for his country.'

'Jeanie, get out. Now, this minute.' Patsy got to her feet, her face working with anger. 'And don't come back.' She went to her mother and took her hand. 'Take no notice of her, Mum.'

In the dead silence that followed, Jeanie slowly and deliberately collected the documents she'd brought and packed them in her bag and clipped it shut. 'Nothing would drag me back. I shall be very happy if I never set eyes on any of you again.'

Her footsteps were clattering on the stairs when Barney let out a scream and ran after her.

After taking Bill back to his workshop, Tim drove the van into the yard, closed his eyes and sat back in the seat. He was exhausted, absolutely dog tired, but underneath he felt quietly satisfied that he'd passed his driving test. He'd wanted this for years, longed for it. He'd imagined he'd feel gloriously triumphant at this moment, joyously happy that at last he'd achieved it, but with his mother's body still lying upstairs in the bedroom awaiting burial, he didn't. He'd felt totally numb the last few days and at least that was easing. He felt undyingly grateful to Patsy for making it possible.

He gathered his strength to go up to the office and had got as far as opening the front door when Jeanie raced through it. Her face was like thunder; she ignored him. Tim had only just got inside when Barney came hurtling after her. 'Get out of the way,' he grated, and rushed out in her wake.

As Tim was climbing the stairs to the office, he saw Patsy bringing her mother down, holding on to her arm. Mrs Rushton seemed very upset.

'Has something happened?' he began. He hardly needed to ask, it obviously had.

Patsy's worried eyes sought his. 'Have you passed?' she asked softly. Tim nodded. 'That's one good thing. Congratulations.'

'Can I do anything to help?'

'Yes, run me and Mum home, would you?'

They helped Beatrice into the passenger seat, and when he went round the back to help Patsy into the body of the van, she whispered, 'We've had a terrible row with Jeanie and Barney. I'm afraid it's finished me for the rest of the afternoon. I'll have to stay with Mum. She's in a bit of a state too after that. I'll see you tomorrow.'

The journey passed in complete silence apart from an occasional sniff and a nose-blowing from Beatrice whose face was blotchy with weeping.

Tim felt washed up too, and after driving back he went straight up to the flat to lie down on the sofa.

The girls woke him up when they switched off their machines and started banging and chattering to each other before going home. He lay still, until all grew quiet again, then he went downstairs to lock up for the night.

Tim was hungry. He'd been too tense to eat much at lunchtime, so he went to the kitchen to see what he could find. There were two dinners; he put the stew and potatoes in the pantry and ate the scouse because it could all be warmed up in one pan. He finished off with a beautifully decorated trifle and blessed Patsy or Gladys or Mrs Dixon or whoever had been kind enough to make these meals for him.

He felt better when he'd eaten and went to the bedroom to see his mother. He folded back the sheet from her face and was pleased to see she looked rested and younger than she had for years. He held her cold hand and said his goodbyes to her. Up till now, he'd hardly had time to realise she'd gone for good. All his life they'd lived together and since his father had died she'd devoted herself to him. He could hardly imagine life without her.

Barney was distraught as he chased after Jeanie. He caught her up as she headed down the road to the train station. 'Jeanie, where are you going?' He caught at her arm and swung her round.

She shook him off. 'Back to Chester.'

'Don't leave me.'

'How can I stay with you now? You heard what Patsy said, she told me to get out and never come back.'

'That's not what I want.'

'Patsy didn't like me telling you about your father. She wants you to see things her way. She has the power now.'

'Why did you have to upset her and Mum?'

'They've both hated me from the moment they saw me,' she flared. 'I wanted to get my own back.'

'Don't go. Don't leave me.'

'We have nowhere to stay. You wouldn't do anything to get that flat so you'd better go home to your family.'

'You know I can't go to Fern Bank. I'll be picked up. The military police have already been round to check if I was there.'

'Doesn't that mean it's safe now?'

'No, they could come back. Let's take the train to Southport and stay at that hotel where we were going to spend our honeymoon. Let's give ourselves a good time for once.'

'Well.' Jeanie paused. 'I've got two nights off from my job. I won't want to stay longer than that, but I'll come if you're paying.'

She knew the moment the words were out of her mouth that he had no money. His face crumbled.

'Patsy gave you a cheque for fifty-five pounds. Couldn't we use that?'

'No, I want to buy some new clothes. You go back to Patsy. She'll look after you.'

'No, she doesn't want to help me. If she'd let us move into the flat maybe all this wouldn't have happened. I'll come to Cissie's place with you.'

'Don't bother, Barney,' Jeanie said scornfully.

Barney stood stock still. 'What's the matter? Don't you love me any more?' he called after her.

'No, I've had more than enough of you and your family. You're a pain in the neck. Get lost.'

Barney shivered as he watched Jeanie stride into the train station. He felt bereft, what on earth was he going to do now? His head was reeling, he could think of only one thing: Jeanie didn't want him.

He walked aimlessly, hardly caring where he went, but keeping his face half-hidden. It started to rain and when he saw a small café he went inside and ordered tea and cakes.

'Sorry, cakes have finished. Only toasted tea cakes left.'

'I'll have those then, with butter and strawberry jam.'

'No jam,' the girl said, 'and it's margarine. There's a war on.'

'I had noticed,' he told her. 'I'll just have a pot of tea.' He sat over it for a long time, grieving for Jeanie and brooding about what he should do now.

Patsy had driven Jeanie to do this, she'd been spiteful towards her. It was all Patsy's fault. She'd given herself the job of running the business while his back had been turned. It was a job that should by rights have been his. If Hubert had been more patient with him, tried to teach him as he'd taught Patsy, he'd have learned to do it. He'd been driven into this hole.

He hated working for Bill Bentley, he was a slave driver, and who was this Mrs Cooper? She was a friend of Tim Stansfield and probably that meant her house would be a slum. He drew the ration book from his picket and studied the address. But where else could he go? Life was pure hell.

CHAPTER TWENTY-NINE

THE NEXT MORNING PATSY was early getting to work, although she'd been very late settling down in the Morrison shelter. They'd had a heavy raid in the night that had kept them awake for several hours, thinking their last moments had come. She found Tim was already at work in the office when she arrived.

'Hello, how are you?' she asked.

He gave her a wry smile. 'I'm OK, up and going again.'

'Tim, you are so resilient, you put me to shame. I feel as though I've been put through the mangle.'

'I find it helps to keep working. It doesn't give me time to think.'

'You need time to grieve.'

'I'm doing that.' He couldn't look at her.

'And time to rest. When things like this happen to you, it's very wearing. And I'm distracted by Barney and his problems and by Mum, I'm afraid I've not been much help to you.' It wasn't the time to tell Tim she loved him. His mind was weighed down with other things.

'You have, Patsy. It's been hard for both of us recently,' he said. 'Until the funeral is over, I feel as though I'm marking time. I'm in limbo. I can't move on.'

On the morning that Tim's mother would be laid to rest, Patsy got up early and dressed herself in the suit she'd worn for her father's funeral. She drove her car to the workshop so she could use it to take Tim to church for the eleven o'clock service.

He was wearing one of Barney's old suits, which was a rather flamboyant blue. It didn't look a good fit, although Gladys had turned up the trouser legs and the jacket cuffs for him yesterday.

'Mum won't mind,' he said. 'She'll know I've done my best.'

The undertakers were round shortly after nine o'clock to carry Eileen Stansfield's body down the stairs and take her to the church. Patsy asked Gladys to clean out the room and make up a bed for Tim, and she arrived with Flo straight away to do it. The undertakers had taken the flowers to church so Patsy carried out the vases they'd been in to wash them out.

'We'll see to all this,' Gladys said. 'You've got more important things to do, I'm sure. Flo, help me lift this mattress to the other bedroom.'

Patsy could see Flo was horrified. 'Tim isn't going to sleep on that, is he? His mother died on it.'

'He's applied for and received a docket to allow him to buy a new mattress,' Patsy told her, 'but he tried two shops and both were waiting for mattresses to come in. He isn't finding the sofa all that comfortable to sleep on, so that is the only alternative.'

'It's clean,' Gladys said briskly. 'Come on, there's nothing the matter with it. He won't even see it when we get the clean sheets on.'

Flo pulled a face. 'It would give me the heebie-jeebies.'

'Tim isn't a nervous kitten like you.'

It was a wet morning, Tim looked cold and sad. He had no coat or mackintosh.

'You'll have to have a coat,' Gladys said. 'It'll be raw in that cemetery. I'll have a word with Arthur.'

Half an hour later Arthur brought up a gaberdine and trilby. 'Patsy gave them to me when her father died,' he said. 'It looks as though your need is greater than mine right now, but I'll have them back when you've finished with them.'

Arthur had asked if he could have time off to come too, and Bill walked down so he could come with them to save his petrol ration.

'Barney hasn't come to work this morning,' he told Patsy as they went out to her car. 'Or he hadn't arrived by the time I left.'

Patsy frowned. 'Trust Barney to mess things up when we've all done our best to help him, but there's nothing we can do about him now.'

There were more people in the church than Tim had expected. Several of their old neighbours were there, as well as some of the staff from the canteen where Mrs Stansfield had been doing voluntary work on the night it was bombed. Mrs Cooper came and Tim introduced her to Patsy.

'Thank you for offering my brother lodgings,' Patsy said.

Without being asked directly, Mrs Cooper assured Patsy that Barney had arrived last night and was settling in. He'd gone off to work this morning. Patsy wondered where he was now. Perhaps he was on his way to work.

All her concern was for Tim, he looked pale and composed but the service seemed over very quickly and as they left, the mourners for the next funeral were collecting outside. The number killed in air raids was keeping undertakers and churches busy.

By twenty to twelve, they were all heading back to where Patsy had parked her car and feeling rather flat. Last week

Patsy had suggested to Tim that they lay on some refreshments in the flat, but he'd said, 'There's nothing we can get that isn't either rationed or in short supply.' Now she wished she'd insisted.

Bill seemed to agree with her. 'We can't just go back to work,' he said. 'How about having a drink at the pub?'

'Good idea,' Tim said. 'It'll give Mrs Dixon time to get the soup organised and we can go back and have that.'

Bill insisted that Patsy have a glass of sherry and also on paying for them all. It bothered her when they began to talk of day-to-day happenings and didn't mention Mrs Stansfield. But Tim had kept a stiff upper lip throughout the morning and seemed content with that.

When Patsy returned to the workshop, Flo told her that her mother had rung and would like her to return the call. She lifted the phone immediately and found Beatrice was quite excited.

'Barney's come home,' she said, 'and I've been out and used all our meat ration to buy a small joint of lamb. We'll have a good dinner to welcome him home. I'm sure he'll be better with us.'

'Mum!' Patsy let fly. 'He was the one who said he couldn't risk staying with us. He should be at work now. Put him on, I want to speak to him. What does he think he's playing at?'

'Don't be cross with him, Patsy, he isn't well. He says he doesn't like the lodgings Tim found for him.'

'Put him on. I want to speak to him.'

'He's sleeping. He said he didn't sleep at all last night, the bed was awful.'

Patsy breathed fire for what seemed an age before she heard Barney mutter a reluctant and sleepy, 'Hello.'

'Barney, this won't do,' she shouted. 'You aren't even

trying. You said you wanted us to hide you and a lot of people have bent over backwards to help.'

'I'm not well, Patsy. I think I'll be better off at home with Mum. She'll look after me.'

'Get back to work. Bill is here, I'll tell him to expect you for the afternoon shift and you're to go back to your lodgings this evening for your dinner. Mrs Cooper has the ration book we went to a lot of trouble and expense to get for you. You can't eat our rations. I'm not having this, do you hear?'

'Yes,' he mumbled. 'Listen to me, Patsy. I can't—'

'Either you keep to the arrangements we've made or I'll ring your barracks and let your colonel know where you are.'

He let out a little scream. 'No, you can't do that. Please.'

'Then get back to Bill's workshop now.' She slammed the phone down and strode up to the flat. Tim had got the soup on the table and they were waiting for her before they began.

She was fuming. 'Barney's gone home to Mum and she's preparing a big welcome home dinner. I told him to get back up to your place, Bill, and get to work.'

He asked, 'Shall I let you know if he turns up?'

'No, I don't want to know.'

'Calm down, Patsy,' Bill said. 'You didn't think he'd stick it for long, did you?'

'I expected him to last longer than this.'

'No point in worrying about Barney,' Tim said. 'We've done exactly what he asked of us. If he's changed his mind, there's nothing more we can do about it.'

By the time Bill left, Patsy felt better and had accepted that Tim was right. 'I'm going to put Barney out of my mind and do some work,' she said.

'Tomorrow will be pay day again.' Tim sighed. 'I want to

get more of the work done today. We don't want another last-minute rush like last week, do we?'

But Patsy was unable to settle and Tim seemed no better. He was up and down to the file cabinet and to the window. He went down to the sewing room to check something with Arthur. Patsy could see he was still raw and smarting from his mother's death. He was finding it impossible to put that out of his mind.

She wanted to tell Tim she loved him but the time seemed wrong, they both had too much on their minds. But she knew if she brought that out in the open and told him she loved him, it would soothe her and it might help Tim. So the next time he slumped back on his chair she got up and put her hands on his shoulders.

'You're feeling restless, Tim,' she said. 'You could leave all that until tomorrow. It's turned out bright this afternoon, why don't you go out for an hour or so, ride round on your bike or something?'

'I had to dump what was left of my bike. It was in smithereens.'

'Sorry, I forgot. A walk then, a breath of fresh air would make you feel better.'

'Perhaps later. You're being very kind, Patsy. I'm all right.'

'I know what you're going through. I've been in your position and I sympathise. I'm fond of you, Tim, and I know you aren't all right. You're upset and grieving, aren't you?' She paused, that wasn't exactly what she'd meant to say.

Tim got slowly to his feet. He was looking at her steadily with such a blaze of love, of adoration even, on his face, that she knew he loved her. He put his arms round her, and bent to give her a lover's kiss that lasted a long time.

'I was trying to tell you that I love you,' she whispered.

'I know.' His arms tightened round her. 'I didn't dare hope you would. I want to spend the rest of my life with you.'

Patsy felt on top of the world, she couldn't stop smiling. 'What more could I want?'

'Your mother will think of a few things,' he said quietly. 'She won't approve.'

'My father would. He liked you.'

'Yes, but not necessarily as a son-in-law.'

'I love you,' Patsy said. 'That's all that matters. You're what I want.'

'I've loved you since you used to come here on Saturday afternoons when your dad was teaching you how to run the business. I've thought about you all these years, fantasised about you, but I didn't dare tell you. I want us to be married though I've nothing but love to offer you. Will you—'

The phone rang, intruding on what Patsy saw as a magic moment. It went on ringing, forcing them apart. Reluctantly she picked it up before somebody came running in to answer it.

'Patsy,' it was Beatrice, she sounded agitated, 'what did you say to Barney? He went rushing straight out and I haven't seen him since.'

'He agreed to work for Bill. I told him to go back and do just that.'

'I'm frightened, Patsy. Barney isn't well enough to work. You should have let him stay here where I could look after him.'

'Mum, he said he didn't want to stay at home. He's afraid the military police will come back and pick him up.'

'But that was before Jeanie left him. He's a broken man and it's all her fault. Will he be home for his dinner?'

'I told him to go to the lodgings we found for him. Mrs

371

Cooper was going to provide his dinner. You shouldn't have encouraged him to do otherwise.'

'But now I don't know whether to roast this joint or leave it.'

'Mum, there's something else I should tell you.' Patsy wanted her to know that things had changed between her and Tim.

'What do you think I should do – about the joint?'

'I don't know. Cook it, I suppose, you and I have to eat.'

'You won't be late home tonight?'

'Don't worry if I am a little, Mum. I'll be back in plenty of time for dinner.' Patsy put the phone down and pulled a wry face. She'd felt very happy, now she was exasperated. 'What I really want to do is to stay with you, but Mum is so agitated and upset, she needs me.'

'You have to think of your family.'

'Let's go out for an hour or so,' she said. 'We need a little time to ourselves. I want to get away from all these problems.'

'I wouldn't argue with that, let's switch off. We could take the train to New Brighton and have a walk along the prom,' Tim suggested.

She smiled. 'We'll walk upriver, not towards Harrison Drive.' She hadn't been to that part of the prom since the night she'd gone looking for her father.

The rain had stopped but it was a very cold day. She pulled on her heavy tweed coat and wrapped up in the hat, scarf and gloves that Mum had knitted for her. There was no heating in the train. They sat shoulder to shoulder; Tim held her hand in his and drew it into the pocket of the gaberdine that had belonged to her father. It relaxed her and she felt the tension leave him too.

The promenade was deserted, there were angry white-tipped

waves racing towards them under a charcoal sky and the wind had the edge of their sharpest cutting-out scissors. They walked upriver as far as Vale Park and sat on a damp bench to survey the soggy grass and dead leaves. The bandstand looked forlorn and abandoned and the café was closed.

Tim put his arm round her shoulders and pulled her close. 'I can't believe you want to marry me,' he told her. 'I couldn't let myself even hope for it. I'll be so proud to have you as my wife. That is what we agreed, isn't it?'

She laughed. 'It's what we meant to do, even if we didn't quite get round to it. Tim, you've been wonderful for me, always ready to help.' She kissed him. 'I couldn't have managed without you.'

It was too cold to sit even with their arms round each other. They stayed only for ten minutes and had to jog back to the station to get warm again.

Barney was tramping round Birkenhead Park in a state of distress. Today, the lakes seemed to consist of black ink and the paths were in a lethal state of slippery mud. The trees dripped with moisture and the icy drizzle started again. He'd crossed the Chinese bridge several times already on his circuits but this time he stayed because the roof seemed to offer some shelter. He was scared stiff.

Two mallard ducks swam past beneath him. 'I don't belong,' he told them, speaking aloud. 'I'm on my own, a lost soul. Patsy has turned everybody against me. Nobody wants me now.'

Barney knew something terrible was happening to him but he couldn't explain it to anybody. Jeanie might have understood but Patsy had hated her and driven her away. She'd even turned Mum against him. He didn't feel safe anywhere.

'I'm scared,' he said aloud but the ducks had gone. Even they wanted nothing to do with him. 'I want to sleep but I can't. I've hardly slept for the past four nights. I lie on my bed and smoke. I can't eat and what Patsy is doing to me is driving me out of my mind.'

These days he was always fighting to appear normal. It was Patsy's fault he'd had that terrible accident, though everybody was blaming him. If only Patsy had let him and Jeanie live in the flat, things would have been different.

Night was drawing in early on this dark midwinter afternoon. Was that a soldier he could see creeping up on him? Yes, and there were more of them trying to hide in the bushes. There was one behind that tree trunk and he was pointing a machine gun at him. Barney let out a little cry and tried to run away, but he was stiff with cold and was slithering in the mud.

He reached a firmer path and shivered. He felt desperate now because he could see that Patsy had called out the military police to catch him.

Yes, he was in big trouble now, he could fight off Patsy but he couldn't fight a whole army like this. Being on the run was ghastly. He urgently needed to find somewhere safe to hide. He couldn't spend the night out in the open in this weather.

CHAPTER THIRTY

TIM AND PATSY JOGGED the fifty yards from the train station to the workshop. It was just on five o'clock and already dark. The workforce came streaming out to meet them with a chorus of 'goodnights'.

'You are clever,' Tim said as they went to the office, 'to know we'd feel better after a break like that. It's really raw outside now.'

'Don't do any more work tonight,' she said as he sat down at his desk.

'Are you going home now?'

She could see he wanted her to stay and there was nothing she wanted more. Reluctantly she said, 'Mum was agitated earlier. I'll have to go, Tim.'

'You told her you might be a little late,' he pleaded. 'I'll make a cup of tea. Have that with me first.'

'I'd love to, but it's the day for George Miller's monthly delivery and collection in this district. He'll ring up early tomorrow morning asking how much finished work we have for him to collect. I'll just find my notebook,' she rummaged in her desk drawer, 'and I'll spend ten minutes going round the stockrooms and then I'll be off.'

She turned to kiss him, his arms tightened round her for a moment. 'I do love you,' he said. 'It's a great comfort knowing you feel the same. I mustn't begrudge the time you spend with your mother when Barney's such a problem.' He began to tidy his desk and lock the file cupboards. 'I do hope he settles down with Mrs Cooper.'

Patsy nodded. 'So do I. I'll see you in the morning, Tim. Goodnight.'

She intended to start her check in the most distant place, the two small stockrooms they had in the next-door building. She still felt all of a-tingle from Tim's hugs and kisses, and to think of the improvements and growth they had achieved in the business made her very happy. What a fool she'd been not to see what Tim meant to her.

She ran down the main staircase, flicking on the light switches as she came to them. At the bottom she turned right to pass the canteen kitchen and a sudden increase in the darkness gave her the feeling that the light in there had been switched off only seconds before.

'Is that you, Arthur?' She paused at the door, thinking perhaps he hadn't yet gone home, but all was dark and silent. She felt inside for the light switch and as the kitchen flooded with light, she was shocked to see Barney crouching down half hidden by the large table and the many chairs.

Fear throbbed through her. 'Barney? What are you doing here?' He straightened up and advanced towards her. 'Won't Mrs Cookson be expecting you back?'

There was menace in every bone of his body as he crept closer. His eyes were full of hate and she felt trapped in his gaze, like a rabbit caught in the headlights of a car. She tried to still her shaking hands.

'What's the matter?' she asked, trying to keep her voice normal. She was horrified. Barney had suddenly gone berserk.

'You know what you've done,' he snarled. 'You've taken

everything that was mine. You've turned everybody against me. You're going to pay for this.'

She was already backing away before she saw Mrs Dixon's meat cleaver clutched in his hand. Terror shot through her, she felt vomit rising in her throat. 'I've always tried to help you,' she gasped.

'You've pretended to.'

Patsy's knees felt as though they no longer belonged to her but she knew she had to stay in control.

'Why don't we go upstairs and sit down where we can talk?' She wanted to get back to Tim, she needed his help. 'You can tell us how we can help.' She knew the moment the words were out of her mouth that she'd made a mistake.

'Us,' he repeated. 'I know you've got that lad up there, I saw you come in as thick as thieves. He could do with a good thrashing. I expect he's put you up to this.'

Patsy saw light flash on steel as he raised his arm. She came to life and leapt for the doorway but she was too late. She let out a piercing scream as she felt the blade bite into the flesh of her arm. She kept on screaming as he came at her again and put up her hands to keep him away.

Tim was just leaving the office to go up to the flat when he thought he heard voices. He paused hopefully, wondering if Bill had come down to keep him company. Patsy's scream of terror made him spin round and dive down the main stairs two at a time.

As soon as he reached the ground floor, he knew she was in the canteen kitchen. Her scuffles and screams were turning his blood to water. He shot inside and saw that a man had her pinned against the wall and was waving a cleaver at her.

'What are you doing?' Tim yelled. 'Stop that, d'you hear?'

Patsy screamed again and he realised the man had a cleaver in one hand and a carving knife in the other.

He looked round wildly and saw the heavy iron saucepan on the stove, grabbed it and brought it down as hard as he could on the back of the man's head. As he slid to the floor, the cleaver skidded away from him. It was only then that Tim recognised the man he'd hit – Barney. He hoped he hadn't killed him.

He dropped the saucepan with a clatter and put his arms round Patsy. She'd have slid to the floor too if he hadn't held her up. He was shocked to see the gash in the sleeve of her coat. She was bleeding from a cut in her upper arm and her thick tweed coat was soaking it up like blotting paper. Her hands were bleeding too. He could feel a ball of panic rising in his throat. He must get help for her.

But Barney's eyes dazed eyes were staring up at him. Slowly he pulled himself up on all fours and groped for the cleaver. Tim leapt to kick it out of his reach then followed it, picked it up and threw it into the sink.

He turned back to Patsy, and half dragged her to the bottom of the stairs. He had to get her away from Barney. Miraculously, she seemed to find her feet and he was able to get her up to the office. He sat her on a chair but she was slumping against the arm and sliding down. He laid her flat on the floor where she couldn't fall and hurt herself more.

As he grabbed for the telephone, he saw the blood his fingers were leaving on it. It was everywhere, on the front of his suit and his hands felt sticky with it.

The operator answered immediately. 'Please put me through to nine nine nine, it's urgent. My girlfriend has been hurt. I want an ambulance and the police.'

He was kept talking, giving the address and describing

378

exactly where he was. He itched to put the phone down and go to Patsy but he stayed to answer questions about her condition. He didn't know how badly she was hurt, she could be bleeding to death for all he knew.

When he could put the phone down, he crouched beside her, and tried to gather her in his arms. 'Patsy, talk to me. How are you?'

He thought she said, 'Don't worry,' but her voice was just a puff of air.

There was no lock on the office door and he was afraid Barney would follow them up and hack at them again with that cleaver. He pulled the phone handset down on the floor beside him and asked for Bill Bentley's number. He was only half a mile up the road and goodness knows how long it would take for that ambulance to come from town.

CHAPTER THIRTY-ONE

TIM WAITED IMPATIENTLY FOR Bill to pick up the phone. When he did he could hardly get the words out. 'Bill, I need you urgently. Barney's come to our office and stabbed Patsy.'

'What? Is she badly hurt? Shall I call an ambulance?'

'I've done that, called the police too. I bashed Barney on the head, but I didn't hit him hard enough. I'm afraid he'll come up and have another go.'

'I'm on my way.'

Tim pulled Patsy closer and cradled her head against his leg. Her eyes were flickering open. 'Tim?' She moved and he saw her wince with pain.

'Yes, don't worry, love. You're safe with me now.'

He did his best to sound soothing, though that wasn't how he felt. He kept on talking to her, though he wasn't sure he was making sense. There was blood on her cheek; he spat on his handkerchief and wiped it off. 'At least he didn't nick your face.'

It was a huge relief to hear the front door crash open. He waited, holding his breath and, yes, the heavy footsteps were coming upstairs. At the same time he could hear the distant wail of an ambulance siren.

Bill burst in on him. 'Oh my God! Is she badly hurt?'

'She's still bleeding but the ambulance is comig. What about Barney?'

'He's at the bottom of the stairs and bleeding too. He seems confused. I'll go down and bring the ambulance men straight up here.'

Tim felt he could breathe again. 'The waiting's over, Patsy,' he soothed.

He watched the ambulance men remove Patsy's coat and her jacket. A thick pad was applied to her arm before he could take in the size of the cut under all that blood. They were getting ready to carry her down between them in a fireman's lift when the phone rang again. Tim felt his way towards it.

Beatrice's voice demanded, 'I want to speak to Patsy. Is she still there?'

'I'm afraid . . .' He cast round wildly, wondering what he should tell her. 'Patsy's had an accident.' He could hear her asking impatiently what sort of accident and was she badly hurt. The ambulance men were disappearing with Patsy.

With Beatrice's voice sounding like a wasp in his ear, he said, hoping he sounded coherent, 'She's being taken care of. I called an ambulance for her and she's on her way to hospital. I want to go with her so I'll hand you over to Bill Bentley to explain what's happened.' He pushed the receiver in Bill's hand and rushed after her.

He saw several policemen at the foot of the stairs and their concern seemed to be for Barney who was lying at their feet in a pool of blood. Both the ambulance men were now attending to him.

'Where's Patsy? I thought you were going to take her to hospital?' Tim asked. One of the policemen led him outside where he found Patsy was being put in the back of a police car.

'We are going to run her to the hospital,' the police officer said. 'And you want to go with her, right?'

'Yes, but I thought she'd be going in the ambulance. Why are you taking us?'

'The ambulance will be needed for the other patient. It seems his need for medical attention is greater.'

'Barney was all right when I left him fifteen minutes or so ago. Why is he bleeding?'

'We don't know yet. The ambulance men are trying to find out.'

Tim clambered on to the back seat of the police car and put his arm round Patsy.

An hour or so later, Tim took Patsy home by taxi, wrapped in her blood-soaked coat. Her hands were both swathed in thick bandages. 'I haven't thanked you,' she said, 'for rescuing me from Barney.'

'Thank goodness I was there.'

'I was absolutely terrified,' she said.

'It frightened the life out of me when I saw Barney slashing at you and there seemed to be blood everywhere. It must have hurt having all those stitches in and you had lots of scratches and grazes too. Are you in pain now?'

'I'm a bit sore, but I've had painkillers. I'm all right.'

When the taxi pulled in at the gate to Fern Bank, they saw Bill's car parked there. 'He must have come to explain things to Mum,' Patsy said. 'Thank goodness she's had someone with her.'

Tim would have gone back to the workshop, but she said, 'I want you to come in too. She'll be out of her mind about Barney.'

He had long wanted to be invited to Patsy's home. He'd been curious about it, tried to imagine her there and been jealous when Rupert had meals there. He'd never thought his chance to see it would be in circumstances like this.

'Feel in my coat pocket for the key, Tim.'

He'd barely got the door open when Beatrice shot out of the front room with Bill behind her. Her face was ravaged by anxiety and tears.

'Patsy, what a mess you're in. All that blood on your best coat. Do take it off.'

Tim slid it off her shoulders.

'Just look at your grey suit!' Beatrice helped her out of the jacket. 'My goodness, this is ruined too.' Her blouse sleeve had been rolled up above the thick bandage and was covered with blood too. 'You'll have nothing left to wear.'

Patsy said, 'I'm cold now.'

Tim led her into the sitting room and settled her into an armchair by the fire. 'I need a cardigan,' she said to her mother. 'The thick fawn one you knitted for me is on the chair in my bedroom.'

'What a terrible thing to happen,' Beatrice went on, wringing her hands. 'I can't believe it.'

'Shall we ask Tim to run up and get my cardigan?'

'It's not like Barney to do things like this.'

'Don't fret, Mrs Rushton, come and sit down.' Bill eased her into the armchair on the other side of the fire.

'Will you get it for me, Tim? I sleep in the small front bedroom, second door on the left off the landing.'

He crept up the carpeted stairs and could hardly believe he'd been allowed to come up here alone. He'd never been in such a smart house before and held his breath as he pushed open her bedroom door. It was all very neat and tidy, with a snow-white candlewick bedspread covering a narrow bed. On the chair was a cardigan he'd seen her wear to work; he snatched it up and sped down again to help Patsy put it on.

'Are you warmer? How are you feeling now?' Beatrice was still fussing.

'I'm all right, Mum. There's nothing to worry about.'

Tim was embarrassed to find his stomach rumbling audibly. He was hungry and very conscious of the delicious scent of roasting dinner coming from the kitchen. The dining table in the window alcove was set for three. It looked as though Bill had been invited to eat with them. He'd have to leave before they started. He turned his back on the table and sat down next to Bill on the sofa.

'Patsy's left arm needed twelve stitches and she's had several more in the palms of her hands,' he told them. 'She put them up to defend herself. She tried to hold Barney off.'

'Patsy, love!' Beatrice gasped. 'Whatever did you say to make him do that?'

'I'm sure it wasn't anything she said, Mrs Rushton.' Tim was indignant.

'Of course not,' Bill agreed.

'But Barney, poor darling.' Beatrice dissolved into the tears which had never seemed far away. 'He wouldn't want to harm Patsy. He loves his sister.'

'Don't upset yourself again, Mrs Rushton.' Bill got to his feet. 'Let me pour you a little more sherry. I explained, didn't I, that Barney hasn't seemed himself.'

'Mum, you kept telling me how easily he was upset. How nervous and unstable he was.'

'I'm sure Barney didn't realise what he was doing,' Bill went on. 'I've been spending more time with him recently and thinking about him. After what's happened today, I'm sure he must be ill – mentally ill.'

Beatrice shot an angry look at Tim and Bill. 'But you called the police. You knew he didn't want that. Where is he now?'

'The ambulance took him to the hospital,' Tim said. 'I had to hit him or he'd have had another lunge at Patsy.'

'Hit him?'

'Yes, I had to stop him knifing Patsy.'

'But I want to know how he is. Didn't you ask while you were at the hospital?'

'Yes.' Tim didn't want to tell her he'd been told Barney's condition was critical. He was afraid it would upset her more. 'The police are trying to get to the bottom of what happened. While I waited for Patsy's cuts to be stitched, they took a statement from me. It could be a criminal case.'

'You mean you've hurt him so badly?' She was distraught and in floods of tears again. 'They're going to charge you with criminal assault?'

That took Tim's breath away. 'I don't know. Surely not. No, I don't think it was about what I did.'

'Then what? I don't understand.' Beatrice was losing patience. 'What will happen to Barney when he's better? Will he be handed over to the military police?'

'If he is, Mrs Rushton, that's the best thing for him. After what he's done to Patsy, he has to be stopped. He's dangerous and could attack others. The constable told me that they had informed the military police of his whereabouts but because of his condition he'll be kept where he is until he's stabilised.'

'But poor Barney, in the hands of . . .'

'He needs treatment, Mrs Rushton,' Bill said seriously. 'If he gets that he'll get better. He couldn't survive on the run, that was too much for him.'

After a long pause, Patsy said, 'You must have known, Mum, that he wouldn't be able to stand it.'

She nodded. 'I was afraid . . .'

'Mum, the dinner smells lovely. It wouldn't do to let it burn.'

'Oh dear!' Beatrice mopped at her eyes and got un-steadily to her feet. 'What am I thinking of? It'll be done to a frazzle. Patsy, will you see to the cabbage? I'm afraid that'll be overcooked too.' Patsy stood up to do what she was asked.

'I'll see to it,' Tim said. 'You can't manage pan lids with your hands bandaged like that.'

Beatrice shook her head. 'Patsy, I'm sorry. Are you in pain?'

'I'll be fine in a day or two, Mum. Shall we ask Tim and Bill to stay and eat with us? You did say you had a small joint. I'm sure they must be hungry by now.'

'Yes, dear, I'm not myself tonight. I bought roast pork for Barney. It's one of his favourites, but as he's not here . . .' She smiled weakly at Bill. 'Yes, of course you must both stay. You've been very kind. We'll have to eat in here, I'm afraid, our air-raid shelter is in our dining room. Such a nuisance, when we need the space. It looks as though the raids have finished, doesn't it? Bill, would you pull the table out a little? We need to set another place.'

Patsy took Tim to the kitchen where under her instruction he drained and chopped the cabbage and made gravy. Bill came to help and she got him to carve the joint. They dished up together, setting the meal out on four plates, and Bill cut her meat up for her. 'You'll not find it easy to do this with those bandages on,' he said.

'Oh Patsy, we have guests. You should have used the vegetable dishes. I did put them to warm.'

'Sorry, we're all tired tonight, Mum. Let's just eat.'

Tim helped carry the plates to the table; it was set

immaculately, with a starched white cloth and napkins and an early daffodil in a silver holder.

They had apple pie for afters but Beatrice was upset because she hadn't made the custard to go with it.

'It's beautiful apple pie,' Bill told her. 'The best I've tasted in years. Lovely on its own.'

Beatrice was alternating between episodes of being a good hostess and fussing because their new car had been left at the workshop.

'I made sure it was locked up before I came,' Bill assured her. 'And I locked the yard gate too. It'll be safe enough there.'

'I'll drive it up tomorrow,' Tim promised.

Tim and Bill were standing up, about to take their leave, when there was a knock at the door. Tim was nearest the door and went to see who it was. His heart sank when he saw the police constable who had taken down his statement about what had happened to Barney.

He took him into the sitting room and announced, 'This is Constable Langham.'

He asked who Bill was and then said, 'Mr Bentley, I understand you were at the workshop when this happened. I have to ask you to come to the police station at ten o'clock tomorrow to tell us what you know of these events.'

'Oh. Yes, yes of course.' Bill sat down.

Tim thought they all looked as though they were expecting bad news. The constable was twisting his helmet in his hands and it took him some time to get anything out. 'I'm sorry to have to tell you that your son Barnaby Rushton died at seven thirty tonight. It proved impossible to stop his bleeding.'

It was as though they were set in stone, nobody moved a muscle. Tim's mouth went dry. Finally he broke the silence.

'But why was he bleeding? I mean, where from? Was it his

head?' He closed his eyes, dreading to have that confirmed. It would mean he'd killed him with the saucepan.

'No. He had a knife wound in his chest. It went in between his ribs and though it missed his heart it damaged major blood vessels.'

Tim felt he could breathe again. But Patsy gasped, 'Who knifed him? There was nobody else there.'

Beatrice let out a scream. 'Murder? Is it murder?'

'We don't think so, Mrs Rushton. We think the knife was in his hand. But we don't know whether he fell on it, or whether the wound was self-inflicted.'

'Oh my God!' Beatrice was overcome, her whole body shook. 'My poor Barney.'

Patsy put her arms round her mother and pulled her close in a hug. Beatrice wept noisily on her shoulder while the constable went on to tell them there would be an autopsy and later on an inquest to inquire into the circumstances of his death.

When he went, Beatrice struggled free of Patsy's arms. 'I've always been afraid for Barney, he was so like his father. I knew he was following in his footsteps. I knew he'd turn against someone in his family. I was afraid it might be me.'

Chapter Thirty-Two

T IM WAS VERY GLAD to accept Bill's offer of a lift back to the workshop. It was a pitch-black night and had gone midnight when they left. Tim sprawled back in the worn seat of the van as Bill pulled away, peering anxiously into the blackout.

'It's not easy to see anything with these dipped headlights,' Tim said.

'No. Beatrice is in a bad way, isn't she?'

'It's hardly surprising, especially given the manner of Barney's death.'

'That shocked me to the core too,' Bill said. 'I know Beatrice is highly strung but do you think she really meant it when she said she was afraid Barney would kill her?'

'I asked Patsy that, and she said they were always expecting him to do something terrible, so yes, perhaps she was. Barney has given them terrible problems all his life.'

'It's a bad business all round.'

'I'm glad we were there to help Patsy,' Tim said. 'Fortunately, she understands her mother. Ringing the doctor and asking for his advice when she became hysterical was the right thing to do.' The doctor had prescribed a sedative for her and Bill had driven down to collect it. 'We'd never have got her settled for the night otherwise.'

Tim had had to help Patsy get her upstairs, undressed and into bed and then persuade her to swallow the pills.

'What a day it's been,' Bill said, 'and it's been worse for you, seeing that it's also the day you laid your mother to rest.'

'It's been a terrible day for all of us. Except that . . .' Tim remembered that Patsy had told him for the first time that she loved him, so it wasn't all bad.

'Patsy must have been in pain but she managed to cope marvellously with her mother. When we were leaving, I reminded her to take a couple more painkillers before she went to sleep.'

Tim sighed. 'Patsy's very thoughtful for others and very patient with her mother,' he said. 'She gives her a lot of time and attention.' Tonight's events had made it clear to him that Beatrice would need Patsy with her over the coming months and that she would feel it was her duty to stay. Beatrice wouldn't like him marrying Patsy and taking her away. He couldn't see they'd be able to do that any time soon.

'Poor old Beatrice, she did go to pieces. But she's a good cook,' Bill said. 'That was the best dinner I've had in a long time. A good-looking woman too.'

'They're both going to need a lot of help over the coming weeks,' Tim said.

'I wish there was something I could do to help.'

'Bill, there is,' Tim hurried to point out. 'Beatrice is bound to feel her loss, she was devoted to Barney. She needs something else to fill her life. Patsy takes her out for a little run in the car on Sunday afternoons. You could do that for her and perhaps take her out for a walk or something one night in the week. Beatrice would like that.' Tim smiled in the darkness. 'Patsy and I . . . Well, we'd like to have more time to ourselves.'

'I'll try,' Bill said as he dropped him off.

* * *

Patsy expected the following days to be dark and difficult but now she and Tim had an understanding and were able to discuss what they felt for each other, they were not. Having Tim behind her telling her how much he loved and needed her brought a glow to the daily routine.

She found it almost impossible to do anything over the next few days because to bend or stretch her hands was painful. The doctor called on Beatrice several times and kept her sedated for a day or two. He re-dressed Patsy's wounds on the third day, and without the heavy bandages she found it easier to use her hands. The stitches were taken out ten days later and though her hands were still sore, she was gradually able to return to normal.

Beatrice did not improve. She spent much of her time in tears and couldn't stop talking about her son. There were a hundred things the family had to attend to as a result of Barney's death but Tim helped Patsy deal with everything. He escorted her and Beatrice to the inquest, which found Barney to have committed suicide while being of unsound mind.

Patsy felt she ought to keep in touch with Jeanie to let her know what was happening, though any mention of her name upset Beatrice, who couldn't forgive her for raking up Rowley's troubles and blamed Barney's unsound mind on that. Patsy sent Jeanie a telegram and asked her to phone. When she did Patsy told her about the funeral arrangements and Jeanie said she'd come, but on the day she didn't turn up. Beatrice wanted the funeral to be as quiet as possible. Only Bill and Tim joined them.

Everyone else had Christmas on their minds. They hoped it would provide a break from the air raids, which if anything seemed even heavier and more frequent, until miraculously on

23 December it all went quiet. Patsy invited Tim and Bill to have their Christmas dinner at Fern Bank. On the 24th Bill managed to buy a duck, which he presented to Beatrice. Poultry was unrationed but very scarce and expensive, and it proved to be a great treat. Patsy had to prepare it, as her mother wasn't yet up to cooking for visitors. It stayed quiet after Christmas too and people began to hope that bombing raids were a thing of the past.

Patsy began to worry about her mother. Bill Bentley was as good as his word and often took Beatrice out for little trips in his car suggesting local places of interest she might like to visit, and Patsy invited both Bill and Tim to a hotpot supper once a week.

After one of these visits they were washing up together in the kitchen when Beatrice said, 'That young man is very attentive to you.'

'Yes, I told you, we want to get married.'

'Oh no, Patsy, he's a nice enough lad but he grew up in Dock Cottages.'

Patsy laughed. 'Does it matter where he grew up? I love him and after all he's done for us, he's proved himself, hasn't he?'

'You're still very young and marriage is an important step.'

'You didn't think I was too young to marry Rupert. Tim is twice the man he was.'

'I'm not sure that Tim is suitable. He's got absolutely nothing to bring to this marriage. You will have to provide a home for him, his living, everything, and it's all come from your father. I can't let you marry without giving it more thought than this.'

'We've both thought a lot about it, Mum. I'll be twenty-one at the end of May and I've made up my mind to marry Tim.'

'You are so determined – too impulsive. You make up your mind in an instant.'

'I've had to be in order to run this business. I know he's right for me. He loves me and he's reliable, isn't he?'

'He may well be, but why rush into it like this? We'll need time to arrange a wedding and there's a war on. A wedding cake needs a couple of months to mature.'

'Mum, wedding cakes have to be cardboard cutouts these days. They're placed over something simple like a Victoria sandwich cake for the sake of the photographs.'

'Oh dear, I hope you aren't making a mistake.'

'I know I'm not, Mum.'

'Well, at least you won't have to worry about finding a house. You and Tim can take over the back bedroom, there's even a double bed there ready. Tim is very lucky that we can provide everything.'

Patsy gasped. It had always been her intention to move into the flat with Tim. They'd talked over every aspect of that, they'd made lists of all they'd need and other lists of what they'd like to have when it was possible. But she didn't dare tell her mother that. Not yet. She'd have to break it to her gently.

Patsy knew Tim was as keen as she was to have a home of their own once they were married. At work the next morning, she said to him, 'I was hoping Mum would be happy to let us do that now Bill is providing a bit of social life for her, but she doesn't want to let me go.'

'Perhaps she needs more to fill her days,' Tim said. 'She doesn't have many friends or go out much by herself, does she?'

'She goes to see Madge and baby Katrina quite often, and she has a cup of tea with the neighbours occasionally.' Tim's expression was telling her that wasn't much. 'She goes to the shops and the housework keeps her busy.'

'Would she like a part-time job with us?'

'I doubt it. With the garden, she feels she has more than enough to do. Next door to us they have a woman coming in to help three mornings a week and I think she'd like that too.'

Tim was frowning. 'She needs more time to get over Barney, Patsy. She's not ready to move on yet.'

When Bill came down at lunchtime to have a bowl of soup with them, he said much the same thing. 'She doesn't want to live on her own and she isn't ready to accept me or anyone else instead of you.'

'There must be something else we can do,' Patsy said. 'I'll encourage her to go on having us all round for a hotpot supper on Thursday evenings, and she says she enjoys going out with you on Sundays, but it's not enough. Bill, I hardly like to ask this, but could you invite her out earlier in the week as well? Take her to the pictures or something?'

'I'd be glad to, Patsy, but I'm afraid it's too soon for her. I did tentatively suggest taking her to see George Formby in a variety show in Liverpool, but she considers herself to be in mourning and didn't think that would be seemly. She isn't over Barney's death yet. I don't want to rush things.'

'No, I do understand.' Patsy sighed. 'I know what she's like.'

Gladys told her that she'd been given two rabbits by a neighbour and she wanted to sell one of them. Rabbit meat was much prized because it was unrationed. Patsy jumped at the opportunity and so the following Sunday she was able to invite both Tim and Bill to Sunday lunch at Fern Bank.

Patsy took her mother to an early church service on Sunday morning and then Beatrice made a rabbit pie. When he came,

Bill was in a jolly mood and recounted anecdotes about the goings-on in his sewing room that made them all laugh.

At half past two, Patsy waved her mother and Bill off on a trip to visit Hill Bark, a local mansion, knowing that Beatrice wouldn't miss her for the rest of the day.

Petrol was rationed, and although they were allowed a little extra to cover their business needs, Patsy and Tim decided to take the train to West Kirby and walk round the retaining wall of the boating lake. It was a blustery March day with the wind straight off the Irish Sea and they received a real buffeting from it. After that they went back to the flat and put together a salad for their evening meal.

To have a quiet evening on the sofa with Tim was Patsy's idea of the perfect way to finish the weekend. To feel his lips on hers and his arms round her made her feel safe. He had already told her he would not rush her into deeper love-making, and he was happy to wait until they were married for that. Patsy had promised they'd be wed as soon after her birthday as could be managed, though now it looked as though Beatrice would not be happy with that, and Patsy didn't want to upset her mother.

Since the heavy raids before Christmas, Birkenhead had been enjoying something of a lull. The air-raid siren still regularly wailed its ominous warning but the residents had come to expect that no bombs were likely to fall. They told each other that the worst of the bombing was over. Only eight people had been killed and fifteen seriously injured in the month of January, and nobody at all was hurt in February. That was not the case in Liverpool but the raids were lighter there too.

So when the siren sounded at some time after nine o'clock that night, it no longer frightened Patsy. Tim would see her home about ten. Even when they heard the throb of enemy planes overhead, she said, 'They're heading for Liverpool,' and stayed on the sofa in Tim's arms.

There was a sudden loud explosion, so close it hurt their ears and made their building shake. Tim pulled her to her feet and together they fled down to the cellars.

There was little comfort down there. Benches were provided for the staff to use during a daylight raid and Mrs Dixon had brought Tim an old deckchair and a blanket which he'd used once or twice at night. Now he wrapped the blanket round them both and they huddled together on a bench. It was one of the heaviest raids they'd ever had and it seemed to go on for hours.

At midnight everything went quiet. Patsy waited for a few minutes for the all-clear to sound, but when it didn't, she said, 'I think I'd better go home. I'm worried about Mum, she'll be terrified on her own and our house could have been damaged.'

'I'll drive you,' Tim said.

They went outside where searchlights were criss-crossing the heavens, trying to pick out enemy aircraft. In addition they could see a brilliant orange glow in the sky and clouds of whirling black smoke rising higher and higher. The night was filled with the clanging of fire engines and shrilling of ambulances and police cars.

'The docks are on fire,' Tim said. 'Can you smell it?'

Patsy shuddered. 'I can even hear it crackle.'

The next moment the anti-aircraft guns on nearby Bidston Hill opened up and Patsy covered her ears with her hands. Even so she felt deafened when another series of bombs exploded. Tim pulled at her arm. 'We can't go yet,' he said. 'It would be dangerous to try. Did you see those sticks of incendiaries being dropped into the fire?'

Patsy shuddered. 'No,' she said but she'd seen enough.

Another wave of bombers was coming in. Back in the cellar, Patsy buried her face in Tim's shoulder and was glad to have his arms round her again.

The next lull came at half past two. Patsy shot upstairs to the office. She was worried about her mother and wanted reassurance that she was all right. As she'd half expected, the telephone was dead, the lines were down, so that was no help.

She went down to the kitchen where Tim was boiling the kettle on the gas for a cup of tea. 'I know you want to go home,' he said, 'but we can drink this while we wait for the all-clear.' He was setting out two mugs when another almighty explosion shook the building again. Patsy felt the floor move beneath her feet. It was followed by an ear-splitting series of bangs and crashes, then by a prolonged sound of splintering glass. In the seconds before the lights went out, Patsy saw Tim turn off the gas and come towards her. The cups slid off the table and crashed to the floor.

'Downstairs,' he said calmly and, with one arm round her, led her through the pitch darkness and falling dust to the top of the cellar steps. 'Hold the rail. Have you got it?'

'I'm fine,' she said, though her mouth was dry and her heart was pounding. She felt anything but fine but Tim was setting a standard she was striving to reach. 'I'm worried about the building. Was that a direct hit?'

'No, but it was near.'

'It sounded as though half of it had collapsed.' The cacophony outside told them the blitz was still at its height.

'We'll stay here in the cellar.' Tim sounded unruffled. 'We couldn't see anything if we went to look. We'll have to wait until daylight to see the extent of the damage.'

They sat down on the bench again and Patsy pulled the

blanket over her head. Tim put both arms round her and pulled her close. 'This is the only safe place at the moment.'

It lasted another half hour and then all went quiet. Shortly afterwards the all-clear sounded. Tim stood up, 'Come on, I'll drive you home.'

At the top of the stairs, their feet crunched on broken glass.

'The front windows have been blown in.' Patsy was horrified.

'If that's all it is, we'll have got off lightly.' Tim took her arm and steered her towards the yard where the van was parked. 'I need to go to the ARP post to see what materials are available to make the windows weather-proof and secure against theft. There'll be a huge demand for that after tonight. They'll also have the forms to fill in for emergency reglazing.'

As they drove along Forest Road, Tim said, 'Bill's car is parked outside your house, so your mother hasn't been on her own after all.'

'Thank goodness, and it doesn't look as though the house is damaged. Mum should be all right.'

'You worry too much. I'll just drop you, Patsy. I want to get back to the workshop as soon as possible.'

'Try and get some sleep,' she said. 'I'll see you later.'

Patsy was desperate for sleep too, she felt shattered. She put her key in the lock and pushed the door open.

'Mum? Bill? Where are you?' There was a strict wartime rule that the door had to be closed before any light was switched on. She kicked it shut and felt for the switch but there was no electricity here either.

'We're here, Patsy,' her mother answered, and came out of the dining room shading the flickering candle flame with her hand. 'Thank goodness you're all right, we've been worried about you. What a night!'

'The windows have been blown out at the workshop,' Patsy told her, 'and I don't know what else, we'll have to wait for daylight to find out.'

'Sorry to hear that.' Bill came out of the dining room, pulling on his jacket. 'It's such a problem getting anything fixed.'

'Tim has worked with the Civil Defence team so he knows what must be done. He's seeing to it now,' Patsy said. 'Thank you for staying with Mum, I was worried about her being alone in that raid.'

'Bill was on the way home when the air-raid warning sounded,' Beatrice said, 'and he turned back. That was kind of him, wasn't it?'

'Very kind.' Patsy smiled. Her mother was seeing Bill in a different light.

'I need to get back to my place now to see if there's any damage there,' Bill said. 'So I'll be on my way. Try and get some sleep, Beatrice. You too, Patsy, you'll have plenty of clearing up to do tomorrow.'

When he'd gone, Beatrice said, 'I'll make us a cup of tea. You go up and get undressed and I'll bring yours up. I'll be glad to get in my own bed, that mattress on the floor is very hard.'

'I've been sitting on a bench all night,' Patsy said before heading for the stairs. 'I'd have been glad of a mattress on the floor.'

She reflected that with a Morrison shelter like theirs, lying down inside it was almost the only possible position. The roof was just about high enough to allow sitting up, but with one's legs stuck straight out in front, it wouldn't be comfortable for long. It would have been impossible for Mum to maintain a formal front while she and Bill were lying side by side on a mattress. Perhaps some good did come from these raids after all. Bill had kept her mother's fear at bay, and provided what Mum always sought from her.

CHAPTER THIRTY-THREE

PATSY WOKE UP ABOUT half nine to full daylight and the sound of dishes clattering in the kitchen down below. She pulled on her clothes and ran downstairs.

She felt half-asleep but her mother looked fresh and alert. 'Lucky we have gas,' she said. 'The electricity is still off.'

Patsy had a hurried breakfast of tea and toast and set off to the workshop on her bike. There were holes and debris all over the roads and she had to be careful to steer clear. The atmosphere was still smoke-laden, there were not many people about and the amount of damage to the buildings shocked her.

It made her fearful for the workshop, but her first sight of it from the front was reassuring. It looked undamaged and once inside she could hear the usual busy whirring of sewing machines. Patsy knew there was damage but she breathed a sigh of relief. She'd insisted that every machine was covered before its operator left for the night and the same with the garments they were working on. So at least their work was dust-free and clean this morning, and thanks to the generator they still had power, so work could go on.

The sewing stopped as soon as they saw her and the girls were all trying to tell her at once. 'Mrs Dixon and her husband were killed last night. Their house got a direct hit.'

'Oh no! That's terrible!' Patsy closed her eyes in horror. 'Has everybody else come in?'

'No,' they chorused. 'Maud Hughes and Marion Davies have been hurt. Maud will probably be back next week but Marion's ceiling collapsed on her and she has head injuries, she's in hospital and will be off for some time.'

'Oh my goodness!'

'Jenny Lomax asked me to tell you that she's gone to Liverpool because her parents' home has been badly damaged and they need help.'

Patsy swallowed hard. 'The bombing came very close to hitting us last night.'

Vera Cliffe's harsh voice shouted, 'Too damn close. That glue factory also got a direct hit last night and it's only some thirty yards behind here.'

She went on to say that the six-foot brick wall round their yard had protected the windows on the ground floor but the blast had shattered all their upstairs windows at the back, including that of the office and the kitchen window of the flat.

Patsy ran up to the office to see the damage for herself. She found the window had already been boarded up and Gladys and Flo were sweeping and dusting.

'Good job you criss-crossed the windows with that sticky paper,' Flo told her. 'That and the blackout curtains stopped the glass splintering and flying everywhere so it won't be too big a job here.'

'I don't know about that, just look at the dust,' Gladys said. 'It's been shaken out of every nook and cranny. Have you heard about Mrs Dixon?'

'Yes, I'm gutted,' Patsy said. 'Thanks for getting on with things, Gladys. Where is Tim?'

'He and Arthur are nailing up boards on the windows in the flat. They've done them all on this floor.'

Patsy went up and found they'd almost finished the kitchen window. 'The last one.' Tim blew out his cheeks and sagged with exhaustion. Both men were covered with dust and wood shavings.

'You look as though you need a rest,' Patsy said. 'I don't suppose you've had breakfast.'

'No, I didn't want to stop until the place was secure,' Tim said.

The kitchen was covered with dust too but they still had water, so she put the kettle on to make them some tea. There were a couple of rashers of bacon in the larder and she made them each a bacon sandwich.

'Marvellous,' Tim said, biting into his. 'I haven't eaten since last night and it was only salad then.'

'You're giving me Tim's ration,' Arthur told her. 'But I'm ravenous too.'

'We've all got to eat,' Patsy said, thinking of lunch. 'Poor Mrs Dixon, how on earth are we going to manage without her?'

'I've been thinking about it.' Tim sighed heavily. 'Why don't you ask your mother to step in and give us a hand? She likes to cook, doesn't she? I'm sure she'd want to help you through this crisis.'

'Yes.' Patsy backed into the living room and saw for the first time that the bomb had shaken down a fall of soot from the chimney. The grate was full and it had spilled out all over the new hearth rug; there was also a light dusting round the rest of the room.

She was appalled at the mess. 'Have you seen the living room, Tim?' she called. He came to look. 'If nothing else, Mum could help me clean this up. I'll go home and ask her, we'll all need hot soup at lunchtime.'

'It's Monday morning, and Gladys said the butcher hasn't delivered.'

'I'd better check first to see if there's anything in the kitchen to make soup from.'

'I passed the butcher's shop,' Arthur pursed his lips, 'the front has been blown in. I doubt he's going to deliver anything this morning.'

Patsy saw Tim yawn. 'You haven't been to bed all night. You must go now,' she told him. 'You're almost asleep on your feet.'

'I'm going. I've got to lie down or I'll drop, but don't let me sleep all day. I want to be up by two o'clock at the latest.'

Patsy nodded. 'How about you, Arthur? I don't suppose you've had much sleep either.'

'Not a lot.'

'Do what you can today and go home early. Tell the girls to do the same.'

Patsy drove the van up to Forest Road to see her mother.

'Of course I'll help you,' she said. 'This is an emergency. What do you want me to do?'

Patsy told her about Mrs Dixon. 'I need you to make soup for fifty to sixty people, two fish kettles full. The girls have had a terrible night but they've come to work. They'll need something hot in their stomachs at midday.'

'I can do that. What sort of soup?'

'That's another problem. I'm afraid there's not a lot to make it from,' Patsy told her. 'There's a sack of potatoes and a few onions and other vegetables, but no meat bones or anything like that.'

'Vegetable soup then,' Beatrice said. 'Just as well as it cooks more quickly, there isn't much time left before lunch. Can we detour to that greengrocer's shop on Hoylake Road? It's not much out of our way.'

Inside the shop, Beatrice's eye was caught by a whole crate of leeks. 'Leek and potato soup, Patsy. Will that do? Have you got milk I can use?'

'There's dried milk and bits of rice and barley and lentils, that sort of thing.'

'That'll do fine.'

By getting Flo to help clean the leeks and peel the potatoes, Beatrice managed to get the soup ready to serve by lunchtime.

The girls couldn't stop praising her, saying her soup was delicious. Beatrice was beaming with pleasure. Patsy thought she'd enjoyed the challenge and the fact that she'd performed well had given her confidence.

She seemed quite pleased when Patsy asked if she'd carry on doing the job for the time being.

The following days were hectic. The staff helped to clean up the mess while she and Tim reorganised the things that had to change. Everybody was given time off to attend Mrs Dixon's funeral.

Patsy began to think her mother had more energy. On the following Monday morning, she looked across the office to Tim. 'Mum seems suddenly much less clingy,' she said.

'I think this job is going to suit her. I've been trying to persuade her to do it permanently.'

'She's said nothing to me about that. Has she agreed?'

'Not yet but I believe she will.'

'So you don't think I need to worry about her.'

'I'm hoping you won't,' Tim said. 'This job could be her salvation. If she works with us five days a week, you'll remain close because you'll see a lot of each other.'

'And if she finds it too much to work all day, she could go home once the lunchtime dishes are cleared away, and we could get somebody else to make the afternoon tea. That would give her time to do her gardening and housework or whatever else she wants.'

Tim smiled. 'A whole new way of life for her and she's got a new man in it.'

Patsy laughed. 'We don't really know how far that will go – unless Bill has said something to you.'

'No, he hasn't, but for one reason or another there's more spring in your mother's step and she isn't clinging on to you.'

'I'm just pleased to see her happy. We're still having the odd air-raid warning to disturb our nights but nothing like that night and with the business on an even keel again, I think you and I should start thinking of ourselves.'

Tim smiled. 'So do I. Let's go ahead with our wedding plans, get things organised and set the date.' He was beaming at her. 'You know it can't come quickly enough for me.'

Patsy was thrilled. 'What about the end of May, the Saturday after my twenty-first birthday? That was always the day we were aiming for.'

'Excellent, but that's only just over a month off. Can we be ready in that time?'

'With a war on, we can't have all the traditional pomp and splendour of a normal wedding. For a start, a wedding cake is out of the question and so are lots of other things.'

'We'll still need to allow three weeks to have the banns called in church.'

Patsy felt excitement fizzing inside her. 'Come on then, let's walk up to St James's and see the vicar now. We need a definite date before we do anything else.'

They walked up past the two tower blocks of flats that had

replaced Dock Cottages where Tim had been brought up, and were shown into the vicar's study. They had both known him since childhood. He congratulated Tim and told Patsy he was pleased to see her so happy, but when they asked him to marry them on the last Saturday in May, he said, 'I'm very sorry, I can't. I'm fully booked up that day, the Bishop is coming. I could fit you in on the day before or on the following Saturday. Is that any help to you?'

Patsy thought Tim was on the point of suggesting the following Saturday but she said quickly, 'Friday has certain advantages. We could trust the girls to work on their own for half a day, couldn't we? If the ceremony was late in the afternoon, it would give us a two-day honeymoon.'

The vicar smiled. 'Right, would Friday afternoon at four o'clock suit you?'

'Yes.' Tim beamed at him. 'Our business is considered to be priority war work, you see, and we're always being pressed to increase production. Our private life has to be fitted round it.'

'My wife will be pleased that you want to be married,' he said. The vicar's wife was also the organist and had taught both Patsy and Tim at Sunday school. 'She'll want to provide the music for your wedding. Think about what you want and let her know, won't you?'

Patsy was thrilled and almost danced her way back to the workshop hanging on Tim's arm. They went straight to the canteen to tell Beatrice. The morning tea break was due and she was busy setting out the cups.

'What? Getting married? Patsy, you've always been impulsive. You are sure? You've even fixed the date?'

'On my twenty-first birthday, Mum.'

Her mother swept her into her arms and kissed her, she

even hugged Tim. She was pleased – more pleased than Patsy had dared hope. She'd never seen her so excited, and as the girls came drifting in for their tea, she was laughing and telling them the news. They began firing questions at Patsy.

'What sort of a wedding will you have?'

'Where will it be held?'

'Are you going to have a white wedding, Patsy?'

She pulled a face. 'I don't know. I haven't decided yet. There's not much in the shops, is there?'

'We can make something for you,' Gladys said. 'We're all dressmakers here.'

Patsy thought of her ruined winter coat and best suit. 'I don't have many clothing coupons.'

'You can apply for extra coupons for your wedding,' Flo told her.

'I'll do that for us both tomorrow,' Tim said. 'And I haven't used the clothing coupons I was given when I was bombed out. You can have those, Patsy.'

She laughed. 'You need a new suit, you desperately need a new suit.'

'I know a girl who wore her mother's wedding dress when she got married,' Flo went on. 'Have you kept your wedding dress, Mrs Rushton?'

Beatrice nodded. 'I have, yes.'

'Mum, I didn't know that! Could I borrow it?'

'If you want to, but goodness knows what it'll be like. I haven't looked at it over the last twenty-odd years and you're not my build. It'll look old-fashioned.'

'Patsy, haven't you always dreamed of walking up the aisle in a white gown with a flowing veil and a long train?'

She smiled. 'Perhaps when I was fourteen.'

'Get your mother's wedding dress out and try it on,' Gladys

advised. 'There's no point in keeping it wrapped up in tissue paper.'

It seemed a good idea and that afternoon, Patsy could hardly wait to get home. Her mother looked drained, and her enthusiasm was sapped. 'You aren't going to like my dress. I don't think it'll be any good to you.'

'Show it to me, Mum. I can't decide until I see it.'

'It isn't white.'

'Oh!' Patsy had understood that it was. 'What colour is it?'

'Come and see. It's the dress I wore when I married your father, my second marriage.' Reluctantly her mother led the way upstairs to her bedroom.

There was a large dusty cardboard box on the bed. It took Beatrice a long time to get it open and part the yellowing tissue paper. Patsy's first glance was of shimmering gold. 'Mum, the material is absolutely beautiful. Is it what they call cloth of gold?'

'It's gold silk.' Beatrice picked it up and held it against her. 'Part of it has a satin finish and part is dull gold. The skirt is quite intricate, and has both sorts in it.'

Patsy spread it out. 'I love the skirt, but I'm not so sure about the bodice.'

It was cut straight without darts and fell to below the natural waistline and had a low neckline and long straight sleeves.

'It's too big for you,' Beatrice said doubtfully. 'I knew it would be.'

'You're a bigger build,' Patsy said. 'But Gladys can make it fit. Would you let her try?'

'Of course, if you like it.'

'I've never seen such beautiful material.' Patsy stroked it. 'It wouldn't be possible to buy this today.' She lifted it against her. The gold silk ran through her fingers like liquid. 'And I like the thought of wearing the same dress as you did when you married Dad.'

'You should be wearing white.'

'I was thinking of a new suit. Nobody in their right mind would spend clothing coupons on a dress they'll wear only once. Did you have a headdress?

'A hat.' Beatrice took down a hat box from the top of the wardrobe.

Patsy laughed when she saw what was inside. 'I can't wear that, it looks positively Edwardian.'

It was an enormous confection of flowers, fruit and ribbons. 'It was very fashionable in nineteen eighteen,' her mother told her. 'The colours haven't faded. It looks as fresh today as it was when I wore it.'

'I'll have to think of something else,' Patsy said.

'Perhaps Gladys could make some ornament for your hair from these flowers? Why don't you ask her?'

For Beatrice the days seemed to be flying past now she had so much more to fill them. Plans for the wedding were gathering speed. They talked of little else in the workshop.

Today, Patsy brought Tim into the canteen at lunchtime when the staff were eating and announced, 'We want to invite you all to our wedding. Everybody working here is invited, you've all proved to be good friends to me and Tim.'

The girls cheered, stamped and whistled as they shouted their thanks.

'On the day, it'll be work as usual until three o'clock,' Patsy went on, 'because we've got to keep up the war effort, but that will give us an hour to get ready and walk up to St James's.'

Tim put in, 'Patsy and I will walk up too unless it's raining – we're lucky the church is so near. Oh, and Arthur has been kind enough to consent to being my best man.'

'After that,' Patsy said, 'we'll all come back and have a celebratory tea here in the canteen with cakes and whatever else we can get.'

'We'll all bring something to help out,' Arthur said. 'My wife makes very good cake.'

'We will,' Gladys agreed. 'We'll all try to bring something.'

Back at home that evening, Beatrice said to her daughter, 'You told me it was going to be a quiet wedding. You can hardly call it that when you've just invited all the staff.'

'I know, but Tim said we have to ask everybody. If we leave some of them out they'll feel slighted.'

'They probably would, but what about our special friends like Madge and Bill? Tea in the canteen isn't that much of a celebration. I'd like to put on a special dinner as well that evening.'

'That's a lovely idea, Mum.' Patsy kissed her.

'And what about Tim's friends? I should be inviting them, shouldn't I?'

When Patsy asked him, Tim said, 'Most of my friends are serving in the forces, and I lost touch with others when we were all moved from Dock Cottages. There's Mrs Cookson and some of our old neighbours, I shall tell them and if they want to come to the church and afterwards to the canteen that should be enough. And the same for a few of my mates from the ARP – I don't know them that well.'

Patsy had asked Madge and Katrina to be her bridesmaids. 'I'm not sure about Katrina.' Madge smiled at her fondly. 'She's not old enough to understand what we want her to do. She's quite likely to go down on all fours as we go up the aisle, or throw her skirts over her head.'

'But you?'

411

'Patsy, I'd love to. I'll get my mother to look after Katrina on that day. What do you want me to wear?'

Madge remembered that she still had a dress length of cream satin she'd intended to have made into a dance dress in her college days. Patsy offered to have it made up in her sewing room.

'Thank you,' Madge said. 'I'll look for a pattern that will take me to parties or dances afterwards. If I ever get any invitations like that again.'

Patsy had intended to have only one bridesmaid, but the next day Flo came to the office. 'Please,' she said to Patsy, 'will you let me be your bridesmaid? I've got a lovely frock I could wear. My sister was a bridesmaid last year and she'll let me borrow her dress. It's a very pretty blue, I know you'll like it. Please, Patsy, I'll be over the moon if you'll let me.'

Patsy hadn't the heart to refuse her. She laughed. 'I'll have two bridesmaids then. This is turning out to be quite a big wedding after all.'

'Thank you, thank you.' Flo swept round her desk to give her a hug.

When she'd gone back to the sewing room, Patsy said to Tim, 'The only thing left to decide is where we'll go for our two-day honeymoon.'

'Where would you like to go?'

'We have so little time I don't want to spend much of it travelling.'

'Then let's go back to the flat when we leave your mother's after this dinner she's giving for us. We could get up the next morning and go to West Kirby or Southport for one night.'

'Southport is more of a treat but if the railway line is bombed we might have trouble getting back.'

'West Kirby it is then. I'll book a nice hotel.'

* * *

Beatrice looked over the food she'd hoarded since before the war started, and planned a large contribution for the party in the canteen. In addition she would make a birthday cake and a wedding cake, though she had no dried fruit and little was available. She really regretted using up what she'd kept last Christmas.

She found last year's cake frills and birthday cake candles in a kitchen drawer. They'd all been used before but once the candles were lit nobody would know the difference. It would make it more of an occasion for Patsy.

She spent an afternoon looking through her wardrobe, trying to decide what she would wear. So many of her outfits were sombre black and she couldn't wear black for Patsy's wedding. She sank down on her bed, deep in thought.

Loss, and mourning for those she'd loved, had played too large a part in her life. She'd never been able to put Rowley's ghost behind her and enjoy life with Hubert. She'd leaned on him, taken his love and support and given little in return, and when she'd lost him, she'd transferred all her needs to Patsy and pressurised her, a young girl in her teens. Patsy had coped magnificently, but it had taken her forthcoming marriage to show Beatrice that what her daughter really wanted was a life of her own.

Beatrice still felt raw after losing Barney but she mustn't mourn him in the same way and let what had happened to him ruin the rest of her life and Patsy's too. Despite their wealth and power, the Tavenham-Strongs had been a tragic family and she'd let them influence her more than she should. The time had come when she must put them behind her once and for all and live in the present.

At the back of her wardrobe she found a pale blue georgette

floral dress and a summery hat to go with it. They looked a bit dated, and must be ten to twelve years old, but she wasn't going to worry about that. She would give her clothing coupons to Patsy. She needed them more because Barney had ruined so many of her winter clothes.

As the days went on, Patsy and Tim made their final preparations. After being bombed out, Tim had applied for dockets to allow him to buy more furniture, but he'd been unable to find a shop with mattresses in stock. He used the dockets now to buy a double bed with the bedding they'd need for it.

'The girls have got wedding fever.' Tim laughed. They had seen many of them in church to hear their banns called. 'They can talk of nothing else.'

One morning Gladys told her she'd finished altering her wedding dress, but she'd like her to try it on to make sure it fitted. Patsy took her up to the flat and when it was lifted out of the carrier bag, she couldn't help but gasp. 'It's gorgeous.'

'Come on, put it on. I've darted the bodice and made it fit to your natural waist,' Gladys told her. 'And I had to lift it on the shoulders to make it fit across your back, which has made the neckline higher. I can cut it deeper if you don't like that.'

'I do, I thought the original neckline was a bit low for me.'

'Good, and of course it's shorter because I've reduced the length of the bodice. If it's too short there's a bit of a hem I could let down. What d'you think?'

Patsy went to look in the wardrobe mirror. 'No,' she said. 'It is just about to my ankles but any longer and it would trail the pavements when I walk to church. It feels light and comfortable. I think it's absolutely perfect. Thank you, Gladys, you've done marvels.'

'Hang on, you haven't seen the hat. What d'you think?'

'Oh, how small it is now.'

'I don't know much about altering hats, I just took the scissors to the brim and cut it down by half and then bound the edge with the length of gold silk I cut off the bodice. I took off all the fruit and most of the flowers and finished it off with another band of gold silk round the crown.'

'Gladys, you are clever.'

'I've had the brim weighted down with books because originally it went up on one side. I've also fixed a couple of the flowers to a headband with the last of the gold silk and a bit of veiling. You can wear whichever suits you best.'

During the week before the wedding, Patsy could see her mother was working hard to get everything organised, she was going round like a whirlwind with her lists and seemed to be enjoying it.

She had arranged for Madge to come round on the evening before the wedding to make the bouquet for the bride and buttonholes for the other main guests.

Patsy was polishing up the black patent sandals she intended to wear when she heard the bell ring and rushed to the front door. It took her a moment to recognise that it was Sheila who had come with Madge and Katrina.

'I've not seen you in your Wren uniform before.' She laughed and threw her arms round Sheila in a welcoming hug. 'You look so sophisticated.'

'I managed to wangle a forty-eight-hour pass,' she chortled. 'So I've come up from Portsmouth to see you married.'

'I'm thrilled that you have. If only I'd known you were coming, I'd have asked you to be a bridesmaid too. I don't suppose you have a posh dress that would do? It's not too late.'

Sheila giggled. 'I think it is, I've brought nothing but my uniform.'

'Madge, you must certainly bring Sheila with you when you come up for dinner tomorrow night,' Beatrice said, turning to Sheila. 'It's to be a celebration for family and friends, and you were Patsy's best friend all through her school years. Come on in.'

'Sheila's going to be a bride herself soon,' Madge told them as she lifted Katrina and an armful of flowers wrapped in newspaper from the pushchair.

Sheila held out her hand and a large diamond flashed before Patsy's eyes. 'In September. My fiancé is a naval officer.'

'That's marvellous, I wish you all the luck in the world,' Patsy said. 'I feel everything's happening all at once and my feet aren't touching the ground.'

'Hello, Granma.' Katrina tugged at Beatrice's skirt. She swung the child up in her arms.

'Aren't you absolutely gorgeous?' Katrina was a very pretty toddler with pale blond hair.

'How are you keeping, Madge?' Patsy asked.

'I've been feeling a bit down since my Great-Aunt Grace died, although she told me I mustn't, that everybody has to go at some time. It was traumatic looking after her and watching her fade before my eyes, but your wedding has cheered me up and given me something else to think about. Also, she's left me her house and a little money and once Katrina's in school, I intend to go back to college and have another go at training to be a teacher. Beatrice, I need to make a start on these bouquets. I've brought some flowers and stuff from home but I'd like to see what's in your garden.'

Sheila pulled another bag of things from Katrina's pushchair. 'Madge failed to buy any cellophane or suitable paper to use in your bouquet, but we came across some large paper doilies in Mum's kitchen drawer, which she thinks will work.'

Patsy was unpacking the buttonholes Madge had already made for the men. 'These look great,' she said. 'It's still possible to get silver paper then? Though it isn't really silver paper, it's not so shiny.'

Sheila laughed. 'That came from cigarette packets, Madge asked me to collect it. There's no shortage of smokers in the mess.'

'Cigarette packets?'

'Don't worry, it doesn't smell of tobacco any more. Oh, and we've brought up our wedding presents tonight.' She presented Patsy with two parcels.

'Thank you, you're very kind. I'm going to open yours now, I can't wait.'

'It's a glass dish I found in an antique shop, I thought it was pretty.'

'It's beautiful, Sheila, I love it – a bowl to put fruit in. I'll leave Madge's present until she's finished doing the flowers.' Patsy was in no doubt that it was a table lamp. 'Tim and I have been very lucky.'

They went out to the kitchen to find Madge fashioning a generous bouquet from cream roses, gypsophila and maiden fern. 'It looks absolutely professional,' Patsy breathed. 'I'm thrilled with it.'

Madge was now making a large ornate buttonhole for Beatrice.

'You could make a career as a florist,' Patsy said. 'It gives me a warm feeling to think all the flowers have come from our own garden.'

Beatrice brought out her sherry bottle and insisted they all raise a glass to Patsy and Tim before they went.

'See you in church,' Sheila and Madge chorused as they settled Katrina in her pushchair and set off for home.

When the big day came, Patsy had to get out the car to transport Beatrice's wedding outfit and all the flowers and food she'd prepared to the workshop. The girls arrived, many with their best outfits over their arms and all with a covered plate of delicacies for the afternoon tea party.

The whole place simmered with excitement from early morning. For lunch Beatrice prepared a special soup. Their butcher had donated two ox tails to add to their vegetables.

Patsy tried to work because the sewing machines were whirring as busily as ever, but she couldn't concentrate. Tim had to work because George Miller arrived with another consignment of garments to be sewn up and his van had to be loaded with the work they'd done.

Early in the afternoon Tim appeared in the office already washed and changed. 'Your mum said I must get ready early and leave the bathroom and the flat free for you.'

'You look very handsome,' Patsy told him. He was wearing the new grey lounge suit she'd helped him choose. 'It's utility, but I'm surprised how good it looks on you.' His face lit up and her heart filled with love for him.

On the dot of three o'clock, work stopped and Beatrice and Patsy went up to the flat to change. She'd hung her gold dress on a hanger in the wardrobe. Everything was ready and waiting for her.

'You've made up your mind to wear the hat Gladys made for you?'

'Yes, it goes with the dress, Mum. It's nearer to what you wore – a modern take on it.'

'I'm flattered you want to be like me.' She was biting her lip.

'Of course I do.' Patsy threw her arms round her in a hug. 'I'm afraid you'll feel I'm deserting you.'

'It's only right you should. You're right about Tim and I want you to have a happy life.'

'I want you to be happy too.'

'I'm happier now I'm doing something to help win the war. And I'll be happier still when it's over.'

'Won't we all?'

'You look radiant and very bridal. Let me spray some scent on you then we'll both smell glamorous. Are we ready?'

Patsy found Tim, George Miller and Bill Bentley waiting for her in the office. Bill had agreed to give her away and was wearing full morning suit with a top hat.

'Does this look all right?' he asked her. 'Not over the top?'

'No, you look magnificent.'

'I smell of mothballs, I should have hung it outside yesterday. This outfit belonged to my great-uncle. I've never worn it before. I've never been invited to give a bride away or to anything else where I could wear it.'

'I'll see you in church,' Tim whispered as his lips brushed her cheek in a gentle kiss. 'You look lovely.'

He called to the staff that it was time to go, settled Beatrice's hand on his arm and they set out to lead the way to St James's Church, with the girls strung out behind.

'We'll give them five minutes' start, so they have time to settle in their seats before you arrive,' Bill said.

'Thank you for standing in for my dad.'

'I'm proud to have you on my arm, Patsy, proud to do anything for Hubert and you. You've made me feel like part of your family.'

Many people turned to watch them walk by, many called greetings and good wishes. Patsy knew almost all of them, she felt surrounded by friends. A crowd had gathered outside the church and Madge and Flo, her bridesmaids, were waiting for her on the steps, one in cream and one in pale blue. Both wore some of the silk flowers from Beatrice's hat, woven with gold satin and fixed to a headband. Patsy heard murmurs of admiration for the bridal party's smart turnout. They fell in behind when Bill led Patsy into the church porch.

Once there she could hear the organ playing softly. 'Give yourself a moment,' Bill whispered, putting a comforting hand over hers. She knew she was shaking. 'No need to be nervous.'

'I'm not,' she said. She was quite sure she was doing the right thing, but her mind was a riot of emotions, she felt excited and thrilled and happy about it, but at the same time a little anxious, even fearful, that all might not go as they'd planned.

She heard the music fade, there was a moment's silence, then the organ broke into a more tuneful piece and Bill was urging her forward down the aisle.

It was a huge church but she came every Sunday so its soaring roof timbers were familiar to her, although today it felt very different. She'd never seen so large a congregation. People were turning to look at her, people she knew well. It awed her to think they were all here to see her and Tim married and it drove home to her the importance of the step she was taking.

She could see Tim and Arthur waiting at the front of the church. When she was about halfway down the aisle, Tim turned to smile at her, his face lighting up with love and tender encouragement. She smiled back, feeling heartened and quite sure now that all would be well.

The beautiful service started and Patsy could think of nothing else. Tim was here beside her. The vicar was asking him, 'Wilt thou love her, comfort her, honour and keep her in sickness and in health, and forsaking all others, keep thee only unto her, so long as ye both shall live?'

'I will,' Tim was holding firm to her right hand and he made his responses clearly and sincerely. She could see love for her in every line of his face and body. She felt elated and knew they would both keep the promises they were making.

It seemed no time at all before the organ burst forth triumphantly and thundered out its final cadences. She held on to Tim's arm as they left the church and led the procession through the streets back to the workshop.

'I feel I've been given everything I could possibly ask for,' Patsy whispered.